THEY WERE CARV⟨...⟩
IDENTITY. . . .

The Datalink's eye came close, twisting on the end
of a thin metal stalk, measuring the contours of his
numbed face. The blade followed, slitting his bloodless cheek, with each cut separating him from himself,
from Kearin Seacord, and transforming him into
Triumviratine undercover agent Brian Kuhl.

While the knife did its work, Kearin's boss gave him
his orders: ''You are leaving Suffolk-Logan Administrative Sector. You are going to Relayer, which is six
weeks and 10.9 light-years from Boston. No Datalink
to feed you information. No personality reinforcement.
No defensive assistance. If you blow your cover,
you're on your own. . . .''

# BLANK SLATE

## Great Science Fiction from SIGNET

# BLANK SLATE

## by Mark J. McGarry

A SIGNET BOOK

NEW AMERICAN LIBRARY

NAL BOOKS ARE AVAILABLE AT QUANTITY DISCOUNTS WHEN USED
TO PROMOTE PRODUCTS OR SERVICES. FOR INFORMATION PLEASE
WRITE TO PREMIUM MARKETING DIVISION, NEW AMERICAN LIBRARY,
1633 BROADWAY, NEW YORK, NEW YORK 10019.

Copyright © 1984 by Mark J. McGarry

SIGNET TRADEMARK REG. U.S. PAT. OFF. AND FOREIGN COUNTRIES
REGISTERED TRADEMARK—MARCA REGISTRADA
HECHO EN CHICAGO, U.S.A.

SIGNET, SIGNET CLASSIC, MENTOR, PLUME, MERIDIAN AND NAL BOOKS
are published by New American Library,
1633 Broadway, New York, New York 10019

First Printing, May, 1984

1  2  3  4  5  6  7  8  9

PRINTED IN THE UNITED STATES OF AMERICA

This book is for Patti.
(To write it, I stole from our time together.)

# Contents

# I.

# ANIMATED FEATURES

What we need are more people who specialize in the impossible.

—Theodore Roethke

# Chapter One

"Kearin?"

Sara's voice came to him over the bellow of a storm only he could hear.

He was a dead man, he thought.

Black thunderheads lowered to crush him against rain-slicked rocks. The wind flapped his clothes, tattering them, stinging him. Hot rain peppered his skin with white pain.

Against the storm's looming smash the river churned and tore with endless avalanches of sound. He staggered back from the cliff edge as another slab let go. The storm swallowed the roar of a thousand tons of falling rock and gave nothing back.

Through the deluge and thickening waves of pain he made out a stand of trees. He went that way. Their flayed branches bent double to the ground. Wet bark looped like concertina wire snatched at his ankles. He went down. The wind and rain would not let him up. So he lay there. By his hand, in a lee formed by two upthrust shale plates, he saw a white flower cupped by green leaves. It took his breath away. Gave nothing back.

"Kearin?"

He shook himself once all over.

The other world fell into place.

His easel and its attendant generator stood on the southwest corner of the roof, where it was almost level. The frame was about a meter square, pitted and tarnished. Accessories dangled from loose wires. The fist-sized power plant alongside it put out a powerful ozone stink and the air around it shimmered with heat.

When he'd lived in Jersey it was the best you could steal. Now they made the easels out of some kind of polymer and they drew transmitted power. The whole business folded up and fit in your pocket. He had one in a closet downstairs.

He remembered how it had felt up on the Palisades, and shivered.

11

Then he smiled at himself: Jerk.

He ran his finger along the edge of the frame, loosening lines of magnetism, softening the image trapped under the glass. He passed a stylus quickly across the picture, drawing dyes up out of the color pods and setting them down where they belonged. He paled the storm clouds and added a hint of brown to the whitecaps in the foreground. He paused . . . then caused a small white blotch to blossom along the top of the cliffs, in a stand of stark trees.

He leaned back in his bamboo rocking chair and smiled. The scene was as it had been, a hundred or three hundred years ago, before the weather changed and the river with it, at that time when the Hudson cut the Palisades out from under themselves and pounded them to gravel.

"Show me the Palisades," Justin Izzo had told him.

"Before or after?" Seacord wanted to know.

Izzo smiled—"During."—and offered him enough hours to pay October's habitation tax *in toto*.

A dozen questions had suggested themselves. Who remembered the Palisades? Why did Izzo want it? Who the hell had that kind of money? And why spend it on . . . ?

(Return to the start of the loop.)

Seacord took half the purchase price as an advance. "I'll pick it up whenever," Izzo said.

That was six weeks ago.

It was too hot up on the roof. He usually quit earlier in the morning. The sun was high now, a pearly shield shining behind the gauzy clouds which, as always, covered the whole sky. From the roof of his building he could see other roofs—all the way down Beacon Hill to Boston Common or the walls of the citadel—slipping downhill like a mound of broken pottery. Vines, eucalyptus, and the occasional baobob tree choked the streets. On the Common and in Boston Public Garden a few elms clung to life, dropping leaves year-round.

He lived near the top of Beacon Hill, on Myrtle Street, not far from Joy. He liked the street because it was one of only a few that did not dead-end against the encircling ceramic walls of the HiSide. Instead it died naturally, at the Common.

He set his stylus down, locked his fingers behind his back, and pulled the kinks out of his shoulders. Then he shrugged out of his shirt and used it to wipe the sweat off his chest.

The hair on the back of his neck prickled.

"It's finished," he said. He started unclipping the deep-view from the frame.

"I can tell it's done," Sara said from behind him.

"That's always a good sign."

"It's beautiful."

"And costly," he said.

"You only say that because you think it's expected of you."
Seacord shrugged.

She came around so he could see her, running her hand along
the top of the view's frame as she passed behind the easel, then
settling on the rail fencing in the trustworthy half of the roof. It
would not have taken his weight without complaint.

"It's an ugly scene," she said softly.

His mouth tightened.

"Though the painting is beautiful."

"It's what Izzo wanted," he said.

"Some things are best left unremembered." Her tone was
almost apologetic. "Like those times."

"Some habitation taxes are best paid. Like ours."

She looked out over the rooftops. She sighed. "You didn't
have to research the way it looked. You knew."

"From Jair. Yes. We've had this discussion before."

"You knew him in another life."

"I won't forget him or the way he told me things used to be.
There's no harm in it."

"I hope not."

"Sara—" he began sharply.

"I just don't want to see you hurt, Kearin."

She smiled—a little sadly, he thought.

He smiled back.

She was slender and subtly curved, as if she had been spun
instead of born. Her deeply tanned skin contrasted sharply with
her blonde hair shining white in the sunlight. She wore a darted
cream shift that accentuated the contrast.

"You're—" he started to say for the ten-thousandth time.

But a chime sounded from downstairs, and he let the foolish
words die in his throat. The sound came again, up through the
roof and into his feet.

"Sub Five?"

She shook her head.

"Go and answer it, please," he said, putting a little emphasis
on the first word. It creeped him to see her speak to the computers in their own language and medium.

She went downstairs. Seacord sighed and slid *Palisades* into a
lined shipping sack and wondered just what the hell Izzo wanted
it for.

\* \* \*

He had met Izzo down on the Common in early September. Most of the people who lived in the Hub pastown were artisans, and most of them displayed their works down on the green. It was large and open and familiar—and adjacent to the Beacon Street security lock. Traffic was good.

About forty booths were set up, which was a good number: short of zoned capacity, but enough to attract the citizens with a few extra hours in their accounts. Seacord walked back up Joy Street to home, powered up his skid, and rode back with eight deep-views and a watercolor tagged Not For Sale.

His last customer, just before the Hub closed to nonresidents, was Izzo, who said he was out of Toronto Sector. He took the two remaining deep-views, made an unsuccessful bid for the watercolor, then commissioned the Palisades piece.

In the booth alongside Seacord's, the sand-painter and the baker (who lived as husband and wife on Revere, near Charles Street) looked on hatefully as he left with his skid, his watercolor, and a portable bursar blinking in a self-satisfied manner.

They filed a breach of verisimilitude complaint against him.

The Peacemakers were very apologetic as they tossed his apartment and confiscated his skid.

"I need it for my work," Seacord told them.

"It's not allowed here," said the Peacemaker, the one who was listening to him.

"I've got a Datalink here. Are you going to take that, too?"

The Peacemaker's look was blank. The computers were everywhere.

After that, Seacord stayed away from the Common and let the others think he was creeped—or let them think he did not have to go to the Common to sell, which happened to be true. He had been in the Hub for three years before the sand-painter and her husband, and he would be there a long time after they were gone.

He called Brace, who saw to it the skid was replaced and the Peacemakers warned off.

Seacord brought the flyer up to the roof and slung a tarpaulin over it.

Sara called him.

He realized it was for the second time.

He rubbed his eyes and the rooftops and the green beyond them swam into focus. Sara called him a third time, her voice coming up through the roof and into the soles of his feet.

He tucked *Palisades* under his arm and went down fourteen very narrow stairs, past the Exit This Way sign that pointed straight up, around the banister, and down six wider, carpeted stairs to his apartment.

"The caller says he wants urgently to speak to you," Sara told him.

"Don't they always?" Through the Datalink, any citizen could find another among the three hundred citadels. But, once they did, you didn't have to talk to them.

Seacord got only three types of calls: from Hub Administration, when his tax was due; from admirers filled with praise, but who had no hours to spend; and from Brace, when Sub Five had a job for him. Customers came in person.

He set the deep-view by the door, where he would see it the next time he went out.

Sara said, "He says his name is Rags."

Seacord's heart surged. He took a deep breath, then another.

Sara asked, "Do you know him?"

He sat down and looked at his apartment. It was all white, with a high ceiling and large, perpetually shadowed windows. Newspaper and magazine pages from before the last war hung in dark wood frames. Pastel cushions were scattered across the cedar floor. Lying broken-backed on one of them was a facsimile of Alexander Cozen's *A New Method of Assisting the Invention in Drawing Original Compositions of Landscape*. In a wooden case near it books, or copies of books, were stacked—the Murrays' *Dictionary of Art and Arists*, the *Oxford Companion to Art*, eight of the twelve volumes of the *Larousse Encyclopedia*, others— none less than 150 years old. Alongside them stood the Datalink terminal installed at Sub Five's insistence and expense. It resembled a chrome-and-glass Maori shield. Sara stood near it, looking uncertain.

He wondered what it would be like to lose all this.

"Are you all right, Kearin?"

He stood up again. "Go on. I'll talk to the man."

She shrugged, letting him know she was hurt. When she was halfway to the bedroom door, Seacord frowned.

"Go the other way," he said.

She stopped in mid-stride, one foot on the floor and the other a few centimeters above it.

Then he saw the doorframe through her back and shoulders.

Then the color of her skin faded, from bronze to tan, tan to a pale tinge that became nothing at all.

When she had gone, a faint snap of burned air remained.

"Fix that stink sometime soon. And she's still got that shimmer."

"Acknowledged," said the Datalink.

"This isn't the first time I've asked about it. I think it's getting worse."

"Ditto." The computer's voice emanated from the walls, which were planar speakers. The voice sounded a little bit like Sara's, which was probably inevitable.

Seacord knelt on a fat cushion in front of the terminal. "Do it."

The shield flowered. Six panels unfolded themselves with hushed clicks and, in the air they cupped, a hazy image formed. The resolution was poor. That, and the dimly-seen background, told him the call originated in one of the public booths, probably near the perimeter of the Suffolk slab.

"Nem? You there, Nem?"

Rags, life-sized and fuzzier than usual, stared glassily into the apartment. He was taller than Seacord, but weighed a little less; he was all elbows, knees, and amphetamine-bright eyes. He had shaved his head again, but his full beard was neatly trimmed. His wide-lapelled shirt, made of bits of colored cloth sewed together with thinly-scraped leather thongs, bloomed beneath a severe gray singlesuit.

"Visual," Seacord said.

"Oh, there you are." Rags smiled briefly, revealing gaps in gray denturework. He tugged at the shouders of his oversized suit. "You put me through a real maze with that computer of yours," he said. "And then your bitch . . . but she looks real good. Hey, you look good, too. Shaving your chest?"

"She didn't know you. You're in Suffolk?"

"That's where I am. Out where you are. I think. I've got to talk to you, Nem, it's very quick. *Very* rapid, this matter is. I got this far, you know, but when I tried to get into where you are they said I needed some kind of pass or something very similar, they said—"

"Certificate of verisimilitude."

"Yeah. But I thought they'd break my head for me. They don't like us—our kind—out here, anyway. Jair didn't tell me anything about needing a pass."

"Jair sent you?"

"That's what I'm saying for you, isn't it? He said to give you the word face-on-face because of what it is—"

"Rapid."

"Yeah. So he gave me his card and his ID band. The Peacemakers could slam me for having that band, you know. And I told them I was from a pastown in Jersey, which is why I look the way I do, and if they check they could slam me for that, too. So you should come down a      me.''

"Tell me your word.''

"Face-on-face, Jair told ɪ.

A muscle jumped in Seacord's cheek. Whatever it was, the word was not good.

"Hey . . . don't *play* with me, all right?'' Rags's voice pleaded, but his eyes shone manic. "I don't want to come any deeper into the city than this,'' he went on, "and it's bad enough right here. You know how they look at you when they think you're from outside—and I look like what I am, I guess.'' He plucked at his suit. "I don't care if they toss me out again, but I don't want them to break anything when they do it. I hurt all the time anyway. You know that, Nem.''

"Here, it's Kearin,'' he said absently, thinking. "Why did you come in illegally?''

"Where's your mind? It's the only way to *get* in. I can't cross the line between Jersey and Boston, Nem. If you still lived in Jersey I might have tried to get in straight and silky, but they don't want you in even if it is legal.'' He snorted, then wiped his nose. "*Legal.* You've been in too long, Nem. Kearin. Believing those stories you told us when you left, about how you were going to change everything.''

"It takes time,'' Seacord said tightly. He tried to put all the pieces together (Jair, news, Jersey) but came up with different arrangements of the same pieces.

"Kearin,'' Rags said. "Come down. All right?''

He tried to read the word from Rags's eyes, but they were empty except for the same chemical hunger that had always lived there. Had Rags brazened his way aboard a BoreLink train, or simply walked all the way from Jersey? He was out-of-true enough for either. And why?

Seacord knew it had been for him . . . somehow.

"Ten minutes,'' he said. Then, remembering he should keep the skid out of sight, "No. Twenty-five.''

Rags smiled. "That's all right, then. Silky. I'll be here, unless they break my bones and throw me out like garbage.''

"They won't break your bones. Stay where you are. I'll find out exactly where you are from the Datalink.''

"You can do that? That's—''

"A quarter hour.'' He waved his hand. Rags disappeared. The terminal's silvery panels whispered shut.

"I'm not going to help you find him," Sara said.

"It's a routine request. Do it."

She told him.

He was pulling on his walking boots when her voice came out of the walls, saying how he needed her.

"I can put the handle on this," he said, frowning over his boot laces.

"They gave me to you for times like these," she insisted. "Let me come out of the wall."

"No."

"He's not even a citizen, is he? He's from the LoSide. One of those people you knew in Jersey. That was another life, Kearin."

"I've had a lot of other lives."

"None of them were as good as this one—and they can take this one away from you. They can take me away, too, if you still care about that."

From him, silence. His face felt hot, then cold. He did not know how he felt.

"He is from Jersey?"

"Of course he is," he snapped.

"Does he want hours? You could make him go away, then just send him the money. Or not send it, once he's gone."

"He doesn't want money."

"Then what does he want?"

"I don't know." He knotted the laces over his calves and stood.

"Will he hurt us?"

"No, Sara."

She closed the door after him.

Wreathed in flowering vines, brownstones flanked the narrow street. The sunlight was filtered and watery by the time it reached the cobbles, but the October heat poured undiminished through the overgrowth. His shirt was soaked through before he walked a block. He licked his lips and tasted salt.

He could not put a handle on the situation. Rags had never been more than a hundred kilometers from the tenement of his birth—until today. And if Jair had helped him make the trip, the reason behind it was no drug-sparked dream.

Down Myrtle, across to Revere, onto Charles. Hub Administration kept Charles and Beacon clear of vegetation; he squinted in the sudden sunlight. At a little before noon, he was the only one out on the street. Faces would be staring from behind polarized windowpanes. The people in the Hub knew him, and tonight over dinner they would say, What do you think he was doing out there? It must have been forty degrees! But they would never say anything to *him*.

He would have to remember to tell Brace again how wrong he had been about the decision to live here.

He crossed Beacon Street, which ended a block westward, and Charles turned from three lanes to six. Along the right side of the street stretched a black iron fence hung every fifteen meters with luminous signs reading: Boston Garden—No Admittance. Inside the fence, a bright orange robot the size and shape of a loaf of bread paced him, ready to enforce the ban.

On the other side of the street, the empty, parti-colored cloth walls of the artisans' booths flapped and boomed.

He remembered he had forgotten *Palisades*. Idiot.

The Boston fortress, and three hundred others scattered across Triumviratine Earth, stood like fine-crafted cenotaphs over the corpses of the old brick-and-cement cities of a previous age. The Portal War, accelerating the decay built into the old infrastructure, had wiped away one civilization to reveal another. The wit and energy that had gone into perpetuating the old world had, after the war, been diverted into building the new. The citadels had risen in two decades.

Just outside the Beacon Street gate hovered a signboard topped by a revolving blue light. The gas-filled cylinder read the same from all directions; so there was no doubt where you were going or where you had been.

> BOSTON HUB HISTORIC PRESERVATION
>
> ATTENTION:
>
> NO ENVIRONMENTAL SERVICES
>
> NO PROTECTIVE SURVEILLANCE
>
> NO TRANSMITTED POWER
>
> BEYOND THIS POINT

He stepped into the shadow of the security gate. Cool air from out of the citadel licked his face. He shivered. The metal floor rang with his footsteps. A Peacemaker up on the catwalk shouldered his wiregun and waved; Seacord ducked his head and raised his hand.

"Out for more inspiration, Citizen?" asked another guard,

behind the console. Sweat sheened his pink face; his close-cropped hair was damp. Behind him the outer-lock seal gleamed dully.

"Should we send a man around to check your house?" the guard asked.

"I'll just be out for the day," Seacord replied.

A cuff extruded itself from the top of the security console and he put his right hand into it. The cuff gripped his identifying wristband and read his citizen's code from it. A passplate shone green. He took his hand from the scanner.

"And we have a message for you from a friend of yours," the Peacemaker said.

Rags, Seacord thought. His breath caught in his throat—

"A very polite young woman named Sara. She asked you to call her as soon as you enter Boston."

—and rattled free. He coughed into his fist.

"It's the air out there, Citizen," the Peacemaker said, looking concerned.

Seacord coughed again for good effect, then said hoarsely, "Thank you for the message."

"You might want to see a medician as long as you're here."

Seacord nodded.

The air-lock seal hissed open. The triangular door-leaves clamped shut behind him. The Datalink watched him impassively through thumb-sized cameras in the roof; scrubbers took soot out of the air he had brought in with him.

The inner door opened. A pungent, oily scent rushed in, bringing with it faint birdcalls and the sound of rushing water.

The air lock gave onto a ceramic box-canyon formed by the sides of the manufactories rising to his left and right and joining seamlessly to the wall at his back. Tall bushes screened the mouth of the alley. From inside the citadel you saw only the factories, storehouses, and garages—not the wall—and you had to hunt for the way outside.

Laughter penetrated the shrubbery. On the other side, a dozen youngers in hobbernockers or mirrored singlesuits chased each other through a complicated course chalked on the grass. Seacord walked around their play area, nodding to their matronly keeper. ("Fine weather today," she said. He agreed that was so. It almost always was.) Then he went through the gap in a second hedge-line.

A kilometer away, the city's core spread itself wide and white before him. The buildings were all about fifteen and twenty stories high and all looked about the same, as if they had been carved from blocks of soap. The three hundred citadels had been built in a hurry, after all. Their exterior walls, streets, and foundations were pre-cast from a silicon-nitrogen ceramic. When the light hit it a certain way, the white stuff glittered like the beaches which had been stripped to provide the raw material for its manufacture.

Paint-splashes bloomed on street-level walls and around windows higher up. Where the residents were more ambitious, murals spun a tale across an entire facade.

Pedestrian traffic crawled through narrow streets. Transpills darted along elevated tracks. A Peacemaker's skid, emblazoned with the Triumviratine insignia, purred across the rooftops.

Between Seacord and the ivory canyons stretched a kilometer-wide swath of parklands. Clumps of trees and fields of tall grass rustled in calculated randomness. A brook started nowhere and flowed lazily for a few hundred meters before it emptied into a reedy pond. A few bathers splashed in pumped rapids. Unseen birds twittered.

Most of the people here were off duty and wore caftans or brightly-colored tunics. Loose clothing, which did not have to be especially well tailored to look presentable, was always coming back into fashion.

Rags—if he had stayed where he was supposed to—was sitting across the park, behind a screen of eucalyptus. Seacord could be there in four minutes, and would get the bad word. It had to be bad.

Instead he stopped at the Datalink kiosk alongside a footramp leading down into the park. He punched his own identity code.

Sara's voice: "Kearin? I can't see you."

"The link is audio only. What about our rule, Sara?"

She paused. "As you explained it to me, the rule is that I speak only when spoken to—and then only through the air. Did I misunderstand? You called me."

His face got hard. "Yours, on a technicality. What do you want?"

"Have you met that man yet? Is he with you?"

"We've been through—"

"You can't see him now," Sara said quickly, as if she had somehow sensed him reaching for the disconnect plate. "Sub Five called."

His hand fell from the switch.

Sara: "Hello?"

"Now," he said flatly. "It's been three months since the last time."

"It was ten minutes ago. I told Brace you went into Boston to deal with one of the galleries and he said to page you through your aural receiver. I didn't tell him you keep it turned off unless you're working for him."

"Thanks. I'll call him."

"There's nothing you can tell him. He wants to see you."

"I at least have to tell Rags—"

"What will you tell him?"

"It would only take a few minutes," he said after a moment, knowing he had already lost.

"Forget him, Kearin. Think of what would happen if they found out about him."

He took a breath, held it, and let it out slowly. "Tell Brace you reached me, that I'll be there soon."

Sara said, "I already have."

He killed the circuit and left the booth, frowning. Fifty meters across the neatly-cropped grass, the pastel bullet-shapes of transpills waited beneath overarching magnolia limbs. He sat in a car; the padded seat gripped him, the canopy closed overhead.

"Destination?" the Datalink asked.

"The Black Rock."

The car edged onto a traffic rail, then slid smoothly away along a slender trestle. It bounded from the trees and over the captive stream. The parklands fell away behind him.

The bird whistles and water sounds had followed him inside. He found the volume control in a box under the seat and turned the noise as low as it would go, to the threshold of audibility.

# Chapter Two

He stepped onto the Logan slab. The transpill hummed away.

An errant sea breeze wound its way through the environmental barriers and brought a faint salt tang to his nose, then snatched it away again. Seacord put his hands in his pockets.

The walls in Logan were the same ceramic as everywhere else, but here their surfaces were etched, tortured until they seized the light, twisted it, and lost it.

He faced the clean-lined black tombstone of Security Affairs Headquarters, Boston Sector, across a plaza seven hundred meters around, inlaid in brass with the insignia of Triumviratine Earth. The eagle's wings stretched from one side of the square to the other; its claw was big enough to hold the personnel carrier parked on top of it.

Long, low buildings stretched around the perimeter: hardcopy libraries, a motor pool, the Peacemaker barracks and dispatching center. At least five subsurface levels lay beneath what he could see. How many citizens worked on Subs One through Four he did not know, but the narrow corridors were never empty.

Beyond the complex, Administration's white spires stood on the horizon. Out of sight, on the far end of Logan, was the power station, sucking microwaves from the orbital generators.

He went through the Black Rock's high, Gothic entrance, then through the windscreens that made his skin tingle. In the lobby, angled walls concealed several exits. The lobby ceiling glowed with a polychrome map of the world, sectioned into three hundred parcels. The citadels sparkled from the center of each sector. In the eastern hemisphere, the black, bitter pool of the Asian People's State spread across half a continent. The idiosyncratic global projection minimized its strongholds.

A bored Peacemaker stared absently at him from behind the curved desk in the center of the room.

"Sub Four," Seacord told him.

"Meeting?"

"Forever and always, it seems." He pushed his hand through

the scanner cuff, watched the passplate change color. He watched
the guard's face change also, as the Datalink told him Seacord
was a section chief out of Arlington Sector. If the Peacemaker
had the will and the clearances to probe further, he would see
Seacord's life laid out in the memory banks, from his birth in
Puget in '32 to his assignment to Arlington just last month.

Seacord had lived none of that life.

The Peacemaker stood and pointed. "That drop-tube to your
left, sir."

Seacord thanked him.

The tube brought him to Sub Five; the doors let him out on a
long and narrow white corridor. He knew or suspected that, with
every step, sensors behind the featureless wall probed and analyzed,
establishing his identity and intentions, then confirming and
rechecking the data.

The office on the other side of the blast-door was empty.

His mouth went dry. "Brace?"

Flat, aerial views of the Boston slabs hung on the dark wood
walls. The pictures were cropped so none of the surrounding
LoSide was visible. A couch and two chairs, looking as if no one
had ever sat in them, stood against the right wall. Directly ahead
of him was a second door, and alongside it a blonde, nondescript
woman sat attentively behind a large desk. She was not
unattractive, but she was holographic and nonfunctional.

No surveillance cameras peered at him from the corners of the
room.

He asked anyway. "Sara?" But he knew she was not allowed
to speak to him here, on Sub Five.

His pulse jumped as the inner door opened.

The man standing in the doorway was short and slightly built.
He was plainly dressed and seemed to be at ease, almost as if he
belonged here, which he did not.

In the seven years Seacord had been coming to Sub Five, the
only person he had seen down here was Brace.

"Citizen?" The stranger smiled and beckoned. "This way."

"I know the way." Seacord did not move. "Who are you?"

"Spencer Swan," said the man, answering his question not at
all. Swan turned and walked down the short hallway leading to
Brace's office. Seacord watched his retreating back for a moment,
then followed him. Nothing else suggested itself.

Two other strangers flanked Brace's office door. They smiled
at Seacord, and one turned the old-style knob and pushed open
the mahogany slab as if nothing were unusual.

Seacord went in.

The strangers remained outside.

With the door closed, everything seemed normal again. An electrical pungency mixed with the air of mustiness. The room hummed faintly to itself.

Brace's office was as large as Seacord's entire apartment. Dark cloth panels fluttered from the ceiling, obscuring its height. A desk, tables, and several toadstool chairs extruded themselves from the yielding floor. Burnished computers and monitoring arrays flickered. An arch hung with scintillating curtains led to rooms into which Seacord had never been invited.

The curtains melted, allowing Brace to pass through, then re-formed behind him.

Seacord took a step forward. "What's—?"

Brace raised a veined hand from his lap, silencing him. He wheeled his unpowered chair behind his massive desk and smiled with some warmth. (But today was a day for precedents.)

"Before you ask," he said in his ash-dry voice, "the men in the hall, as well as several others you did not meet, are from our Belgrade branch." The smile now looked a little strained. "Courtesy of their Special Services division."

The curtains rustled again.

"I'm afraid we've disrupted your routines," said the woman who entered.

Seacord's scalp crawled. First he saw the platinum hair and gray eyes, the tall and slender figure, and thought, What's she doing *here?*

Then he saw the lines in her face, the angularity of form softened by rich, well-tailored fabric, and the bearing that was not Sara's after all.

And then he saw who it really was. The thought came again, the emphases different: What's *she* doing here?

"Citizen Candace Carpentier," Brace said unnecessarily, "of the Triumviratine Synody."

"So formal," Carpentier said. Her voice was deep and smooth. Her trousers' belled legs rustled across the carpet. Seacord briefly took her extended hand.

"I asked Citizen Brace to call you here," she said. That voice of hers, too, was not Sara's.

Seacord's pulse throbbed. Pieces from two puzzles (Rags, Jersey, Swan, Carpentier) lay scattered across his forebrain.

He simply nodded. She was one of Triumviratine Earth's three chief executive officers. A hundred levels of the bureaucracy and about eighty centimeters separated him from her.

"I've never been in any city's level five," Carpentier commented, sitting on one of the toadstools. "Not even Belgrade. Spencer discouraged me."

"We don't get many visitors, either," Brace said sourly.

Her look was disapproving. "Your security measures are adequate, Citizen, but I have my own advisors to answer to."

Brace turned away, frowning deeply.

Seacord wished he were elsewhere.

She turned her smile on him. "Sit down, Citizen."

He selected a chair equidistant from Carpentier and Brace.

"I hope you, at least, are not offended by my intrusion," she said mildly.

"I'm honored," Seacord said. "And puzzled."

The smile went no deeper than her lips. "Before your questions are answered, would you satisfy some of my curiosity?"

"If I can."

"Can you read my thoughts?"

"I don't—"

"Not literally, of course. But you can read my pulse and skin temperature, can't you? And, from that, extrapolate my thinking? Or my feelings?"

"Not here, Citizen." He glanced at Brace, who nodded imperceptibly. "While I am on Sub Five, those capabilities are disabled. When I am not on assignment, only two-way communication with the computers is possible, and only when I want it."

"But when you are on assignment?"

"While I am in interface, I know what the Datalink knows about you. I know what it learns about you through its microphones and surveillance cameras. I know what it can predict you will do."

"At one time, the operatives were in constant interface," Brace interrupted dryly. "There were . . . resulting excesses."

"I realize Security Affairs no longer has the capability of violating citizens' rights on a wholesale basis," Carpentier said. She turned to Seacord again.

"Citizen," she continued crisply, "you have another capability, don't you? The computers follow your silent commands."

He felt as if she were leading him down a road he had never seen before. He had never discussed his talents with anyone . . . except Sara.

"I can override some automated systems in my vicinity," he said. "It's primarily a defensive faculty."

"And hardly ever used," Brace interjected. "The whole purpose of employees like Seacord is to place them smoothly in any environment where, once in place, they can gather the needed information. Their best and, ideally, their only defense is their camouflage."

Carpentier ignored him. "What is it like when you are in the interface?"

"Couldn't Swan answer these questions for you, Citizen?" Seacord asked mildly, forcing the words through a dry mouth.

Her face was placid, but her eyes betrayed surprise.

"Citizen Swan must be a special operative," he continued. "You wouldn't leave Belgrade without a special to protect you. No one else would be trusted with your safety."

"Of course," she said. Her smile, still faint, was more genuine than before. "But, over our years together, I've come to learn to respect Spencer's privacy. If you would rather not answer, I'll respect your privacy too. I'm not asking out of idle curiosity."

He had never thought she was, or even considered refusing her. "The interface," he said, "is like never being alone."

"You make it sound as if it were a mixed blessing."

He shrugged.

"Security? Does it make you feel more secure?"

"Most of the time."

"Power?"

"Yes."

"Have you ever been on a mission without the interface?"

"No, Citizen. It seems contradictory. And pointless."

She shot Brace a look which Seacord could not read.

She said, "Having the implants, does it make you feel . . . apart?"

"It's not h'aving the implants that does that, Citizen," he answered.

"You don't like people."

"I guess I don't need them."

"Any long-standing friendships at all? With Citizen Brace, perhaps?"

"We provide for a supporting relationship. The details are confidential," Brace said. "I think it's time for Seacord's questions now."

"I haven't determined yet that he's right for this assignment." Her gaze fixed both of them in turn. "He'll be helpless where he's going. All of his capabilities will be left behind."

Seacord's pulse surged and did not slow. The rush of blood constricted his throat. His face remained placidly attentive.

"The most important capability is the one that cannot be taken from him," Brace said into the awkward silence.

Carpentier's look was sour. "I'm still not sure."

"You don't have to be," Brace said. "I do."

She looked at him. Then she said, "All right."

From behind his desk, Brace gestured.

The air before them glistened slickly. A column of solidity, a view into another room, stretched down from the ceiling to touch the floor.

The man in the other room stood Seacord's height, but probably outweighed him by twenty kilograms. His features were softer, his legs heavy, and there was a roll of fat around his middle, but Seacord saw through that to a similar bone and muscle structure. He measured the gut for a polymer implant, drew the lines where the cuts would be made.

He shrugged his shoulders and slouched them a little.

No problem, he thought.

"My name is Brian Kuhl," the hologram said. "I am thirty-two, and for the last six years I've operated my own studio in Manchester Sector. Before that I worked for the public information desks in Manchester, Sinai, and the Capitol. I travel all the time, and I don't have many close friends." And he smiled, because he had stumbled over the *m* in *many*. He did not have any close friends, and he didn't mind.

"I married once," Kuhl continued. "It wasn't going well . . . and then she died. I haven't remarried." (Seacord nodded. All of the matrices were loners.) "My life is my work." He smiled again, this time a little more sadly.

The corners of Seacord's mouth drew back a little. Behind the smile, his teeth were clenched. He had it.

"Though few citizens know my name, most know my work. Several hours of programming come out of my studios every month. I have up to twenty people working for me at any one time—the legal maximum. They work under one-year, nonrenewable contracts. Anyone who wants to work for me a second year has to prove he's still the best available. Most of them reapply, and some of those I rehire."

The hologram shrugged and spread its hands.

Seacord did the same, move for move.

He looked across at Carpentier, who looked back at him with a sort of anticipatory horror, as if Seacord's skin might split and reveal the newsman beneath. Her look appeared to Seacord indistinctly, through the hologram, and then the image began to fade until he could see her clearly through it, and then until he could not see it at all.

"You see," said Brace.

"Say something," Carpentier demanded.

"The vocal cords will need to be tauter," Seacord said, in a close approximation of the voice Kuhl had used.

He smiled Kuhl's smile.

Carpentier sat back.

"Are you satisfied, Citizen Carpentier?" Brace asked.

She sat for a moment, saying nothing. Then she stood abruptly, her face hard. "I have reservations. Why make him a capitalist?"

"Two reasons," said Brace. "First, he has to be one of the best in the field. Sad commentary though it may be, in the arts the entrepreneurs and their privately-held corporations are markedly superior to government-sponsored efforts."

Her jaw set. "Second?"

"Someone working in Public Information, regardless of his qualifications, would have both superiors and a staff. The Kuhl matrix can support some convenient eccentricities, such as his staffing policies."

"I think you enjoy these personality constructions," Carpentier said.

"I have an able staff who take pride in a job well done."

The syndic sat down again.

Brace continued, "The form takes minimum morphic sculpting and surgery. Most of the morphosis can be worked with drugs and implants, making for a short recovery time both in and out of the matrix. I would estimate a week on the way into Kuhl, two weeks on the way out. Add a third week to take off the collected data." Brace looked at Seacord, something unreadable in his eyes.

"What about his 'work'?" Seacord forced out.

"Nine years of it, all publicly accessible, is already in data storage. The most prominent recent feature is a historical program contracted for by the StarForce for presentation to inhabitants of the colonies we lost contact with after the Portal War."

Carpentier shot him a naked, warning glance.

Seacord's heart sank within him. "I'm leaving Boston."

"Yes," said Brace. "There is more supporting documentation, all lending verisimilitude to the role. Kuhl made a feature study on the Asian People's State two years ago. It has yet to be released. The suggestion will be that the delay is a result of government interference." To Carpentier he added, "This further distances him from the government, increasing his stature among both suspected rebels and rebellious artistic types. Digging deeper into the matrix, and with adequate security clearances, one would find suitably brilliant crèche and student assignments. There is, for instance, an 'independent' project done with materi-

als misappropriated from a Montreal advance learners' class.''
Brace's eyes were hooded. ''Don't forget that one, Seacord.
Kuhl's misdemeanor would have led to his expulsion from the
class if he hadn't resigned first. Your former instructors won't
forget, and they'll be accompanying you on your assignment.''

Seacord said, *''Where?''*

# Chapter Three

The Datalink's eyes came close, twisting on the end of a thin metal stalk, measuring the contours of his numbed face. The blade followed, slitting his bloodless cheek, with each cut separating him from Seacord, from Boston, from Sara.

He felt no pain, only the pressure.

Brace said, "You are leaving Suffolk-Logan Administrative Sector. You are going to Relayer, which is six weeks and ten-point-nine light-years from Boston. No Datalink. No personality reinforcement. No defensive assistance. And the mission will last up to three months, exclusive of travel time, which you will spend in stasis-sleep."

His face smeared as Seacord's eyes began to water.

"Why a Boston agent?" he mumbled. "I don't have any jurisdiction outside the walls."

"You are acting on her authority as CEO," Brace said. "Any argument against sending you could be applied to any one of our operatives."

Brace must have already offered the same argument, Seacord realized.

In one sense, that was the most frightening aspect of the situation: that Brace had been overruled.

"She's an indoctrinaire, too," Brace said. "I think that's why she chose you, because you both came out of the LoSide."

He and Seacord were the only humans in the operating theater on Sub Four. Medicians monitored the patient's progress from several hundred meters away.

Seacord stared up into the cool blue ceiling. A fragile, jointed metal arm carried a plastic insert through his field of view. He felt a tug as the arm spread the lips of the incision and slid the prosthesis into his cheek.

"How old you think she was—?"

"No talking now," said the Datalink.

Seacord was quiet for a few minutes while the arm worked over his face, pulling, cutting, sealing.

Then he asked, "Do the other CEOs know about this assignment?"

"I don't know," said Brace.

"Am I the only indoctrinaire on Sub Five? Or anywhere in the world?"

"I don't know," Brace said again. "She might be from Suffolk-Logan, too. That would better explain her choice."

"Is she?"

"I don't know."

"The StarForce is responsible for any operations outside the orbit of the Moon. They'll have their own report on Relayer. They have their own intelligence branch, too."

Brace said, "I think that's her concern, Kearin, don't you?"

Toward the end, he rolled up his sleeve and slid his arm into the machine. Soft plastic jaws closed on his wrist.

*He felt his band removed—*

The citizen's identification band: It was a simple thing, really, a wristlet of some yielding pearlescent substance fitting snugly, though not tightly, on the right arm. It glowed faintly in the dark and sparkled handsomely in the sunshine. Part of it, appearing no different from the remainder, telescoped or stretched somehow so you could slip it up your arm, as clothing styles sometimes demanded, or just so you could wash your hands more easily.

As a child, receiving one had meant adulthood: a credit account, the end of mandatory crèche, the start of habitation taxes and of a productive life, the end of never being left to yourself. Losing it meant going LoSide.

Somewhere inside the band was a string of numbers. Your apartment door read the numbers and let you in (or out), bursars in stores and administrative offices scanned the code and shifted labor-hour equivalents from one account to another.

The band was a good thing to have because you could not have anything without it. It was your name.

*—and he felt another put in its place.*

Kuhl took his arm from the machine.

A drawer in the console's face popped open. Kuhl took Seacord's band from it and handed it to Brace.

"Take care of this for me."

"You won't like it this time."

"Then why let her send me?"

Brace said, "*I* am sending you."

\*     \*     \*

Kuhl sat in a conference room on Sub Three. The door opposite him opened, he caught a glimpse of a crowded hall, then Spencer Swan entered and closed the door behind him.

"Kearin Seacord?" He looked into the one-way privacy screen for a moment, then, eyes watering, set an attaché on the table and sat down across from Kuhl.

"I was Seacord," said Kuhl. The screen, a kind of bollixed-up environmental field, distorted sound and light coming from Kuhl's half of the room. For Swan, it would have been like watching a heat-shimmered mirage, like listening to a wind-snatched voice.

Swan opened his case and started to rummage through it.

"Tell Brace I said this electronic gimmickry is a needless distraction. Sometimes he forgets who the real enemy is."

"You don't compromise the matrix," Kuhl said. The words came with difficulty, the surgery not quite healed. He brought his thick-fingered right hand up to rub at his throat. When he brought the hand down he lost coordination and it thumped to the tabletop.

"I know as much as Candace does about this assignment," Swan said. He took a small holo-projector from his case, then a half-dozen glossy paper photographs.

If that were true, Kuhl thought, you wouldn't be so offended.

Swan peered expectantly into the privacy screen, then shrugged and said, "Watch this. It's the same documentary the StarForce has been showing the survivors on the old colonies it's recontacted. While you're watching, pretend it's the first news you've had of Earth in about a hundred and fifteen years."

He reached across the table and turned on the projector.

The walls of the room receded, growing jagged stone teeth. Steam threaded from the crater's glassy floor. Sand sifted with serpentine hisses across tortured outcrops.

Slow footsteps grew louder. A shadow fell across the twisting ropes of sand. The holo-cam panned upward, to a face framed against a sky of angrily boiling clouds.

"This is what the Earth's Portal complex looks like now," said the man.

It was Brian Kuhl.

The Outsteppers had come to Earth 125 years before, finding a world which had teetered away from the brink of fusion-driven suicide and into a surer, though more protracted doom. The disease was the entropy of a closed system, the symptoms a steadily increasing population, the inefficient administration of dwindling resources parceled among 430 nation-states, a series of increasingly bitter and costly microwars. In polar orbits, awaiting the signal for a final, superfluous spasm, enough force of arms to rip the crust from the planet silently coursed.

The Outsteppers brought neither universal knowledge nor the key to peace and harmony, but a commercial proposition instead. For a price, they would open a door onto a network of ten thousand worlds, inhabited and not, hostile and terrestrial. These worlds offered potential mineral reserves, colonization sites, home to trading partners . . . enemies.

The harvest lasted for nine years, the end coming in a half-hour span on a morning in 2052. Witnesses among the survivors in Council Bluffs said the 250-meter-wide concrete containment dome around the Portal debarkation slip peeled back like the skin of a rotten fruit, popping soap-bubble-like into scattered atoms. Spy satellites in synchronous orbit overhead reported the aftermath. Virulent clouds preceded the shock troops of un-identifiable, armor-clad, man-sized bipeds; robot battlewagons; packs of adapted carnivores.

The frontline expanded out from the Portal, which stood un-touched in the maelstrom, placidly spewing the attack force from somewhere among the ten thousand worlds touched by the Outsteppers.

Several commanders of orbiting missile platforms reached the same conclusion at about the same time. The Portal, the invasion, the threat, all of Omaha, and a good portion of Council Bluffs exploded into incandescence.

Undeterred, the human-specific poison gases and airborne bac-teriophages threaded east on the steady midwestern winds.

A subtle chemical mix rose up on the shock wave from the triphammer fusion blast, scattering through the stratosphere, alter-ing the Earth's albedo and bringing summer to the poles; the temperate zones turned tropical and the tropics burned away.

Five hundred million people died worldwide over the next six months as a direct result of the Portal War. Twice that number died over the following decade as governments, economies, societies collapsed.

Few noticed, but contact with the dozen colonies, twenty scientific and industrial installations, and three million people on the other side of the Portal was lost.

After awhile, computer memories were located and resurrected. Gleaming white walls rose like tombstones about the shattered cities. Tunnels were chewed out to link the three hundred citadels. In orbit, the remaining warheads were turned outward.

*       *       *

"And this is Belgrade, our Capitol," the Kuhl-image said, the view behind him filling with proud ramparts, gaily-clad citizens, flitting skids, majestic airships.

Then the walls faded into sunlight, and the sunlight faded to become the cement walls of the conference room on Sub Three. Swan put the projector into his case.

"It glosses over some details," he said. "How are we going to explain to the colonists, diplomatically, that the Portal War probably saved the race? In a moment, half the population and the old infrastructure were blown away. It allowed us to start fresh, building from the ground up with the technology we'd developed in the last century and that we'd gotten through Portal trade in the last decade." He looked into the privacy screen, frowning in annoyance. "What do you know about the recontact missions?"

"Just what the average citizen knows," Kuhl answered. "In the past two years, about a half-dozen colonies have been contacted. Most of them had failed. I haven't heard much about the others."

"Seven of nine failed, their populations wiped out. A century without resupply from Earth through the Portal was a century too long for most. Those colonies were never designed to be self-sustaining. With instantaneous communication and trade through the Portals, there was no need. Some of them were dependent on us even for air. We've known from the start that most of them were doomed. The miracle is that Flander's Planet hung on and Stapeldon flourished."

Swan continued, "What the *average citizen* does not know is that Stapeldon, shortly after the war, began to receive radio transmissions from a colony circling Ross 128, a star about five light-years from them. The signals were weak, and stopped after a month. Stapeldon answered, but received no reply. The signals never came again. Relayer is not a hospitable world. It was, in fact, on the bottom of the recontact list. But the signals indicated someone was still alive there five light-years after the war ended. The StarForce's mission to Relayer leaves in one week."

"The StarForce will tell you if they're still alive," Kuhl said.

"What we want you to find out is if they still hate us," Swan rapped out. "The consortium that purchased colonization rights to Relayer were Israelis, Basques, American blacks, and Taiwanese —all ethnocentric groups which were, as they saw it, displaced by the pan-nationalism the Portals brought about. We have records of Basque terrorism right up to the day of the war. Those who chose not to fight or be assimilated into the human family ended up on Relayer. We are the world-state that swallowed their nations. For the first time in history we have peace, because for the first time we have no statist frictions. Before we throw open our doors to these people, we want to be sure they won't try to tear down what we've been working toward since the dawn of civilization.''

"Relations with the other two colonies seem to have gone well," Kuhl said. "At least I haven't heard otherwise."

"They did go well. The stragglers on Flander's Planet didn't pose a threat to their own body parasites, let alone to our stability. And Stapledon's background is different from Relayer's. It was colonized by one of the multinational corporations that grew during the twentieth century and exploded with the coming of the Portal. Relayer was meant to be a safety valve. They are—were—die-hard nationalists.''

"And if the colony is dead?"

"Your report will be brief," Swan said.

"The Terminal Night wasn't mentioned in that documentary either," Kuhl said.

"No. That would also be hard to explain, diplomatically. Forty years after the birth of Triumviratine Earth, the world running smoothly, and one man decides the citadels would be better off not having to support the billion lakkers outside the walls.''

"Hundreds of millions of people were poisoned. We can't hide it.''

"For the duration of the mission to Relayer, you'll have to. Most of the statists were left outside when the walls went up. The Relayermen would see it as aggression, not the act of a madman in a high place. The StarForce will be cooperating in this. It's been standard operating procedure on all the recontact missions.''

"Has it succeeded?"

Swan pushed the glossy photographs through the privacy screen, their edges curling and snapping with static electricity. "You'll have more than that to worry about.''

The pictures were all about the same: mostly black, scattered with irregular forms and sharp points of light. After a moment, he saw it was a starfield strewn with rough-sided objects, their size impossible to determine.

"What am I looking at?" Kuhl asked.

"We know what the StarForce says those pictures represent. Their starship *Munich*, sent on a recontact mission to an industrial outpost eighteen light-years from Earth.''

Kulh squinted at the photo.

Swan said, "The starships' faster-than-light impellers 'hold' them at their destination in the Deep until a circuit is broken, then they're snapped to their point of origin, PlutoCol. The *Munich* returned three weeks ahead of schedule. The largest fragment was five meters across. The Force's analysis of the wreckage showed the impeller circuit was broken when the *Munich* ran into a dense cloud of iron shot at a relative velocity of about eight thousand meters per second. If the Force is telling the truth, the conclusion is that someone left the projectiles there for the *Munich* to run into."

Swan reached through the privacy screen, the hairs on the back of his wrist standing up. He tapped one blob, seemingly no different from the rest.

"That's a man," Swan said. "None of them were wearing outsuits, of course. The sixty-man crew died. Or so the Force reports. Those photographs were beamed from Pluto to Aztlan, then brought from the Moon to Belgrade by courier."

"When did it happen?"

"Two months ago. If it happened. The StarForce has been saying for a century—since before they were the StarForce, back when they were seen as just a band of renegade militarists—that we should be ready to fight off another invasion. But nothing's happened. Now, they say, something has happened. They've already asked for the budget to build bigger, more heavily-armed recontact vessels. We don't want that, and neither does Administration. The Force is powerful enough as it is, and based on the Moon, they're already too autonomous."

"Unless the threat is real."

"You might be able to get some indication of that during the Relayer mission. Hopefully not the same evidence *Munich* may have gotten. Aside from that, a comparison between your report of conditions on Relayer and their report will give us a yardstick of how honest they've been about the results of all their missions—including *Munich*'s. And, third, we'll have your picture of Relayer so we can judge if they themselves are a threat."

"Let me see that photograph again," Kuhl said.

For another moment he looked at the shape of light, seeing finally the vague form of a man, the outstretched arms, the round shadow where a mouth would be, screaming shock and outrage.

He pushed the photograph at Swan.

In a visitor's apartment on Sub One, Brian Kuhl sealed his suitcase and set it near the door.

Sara watched him attentively from the bed.

"Ten weeks hasn't been a long time to learn how to be the world's foremost medist," Kuhl said.

"Your crew is expert," Sara said. She sat up, the sheer gown sparkling. "When you come back, I'll edit the final product. You just have to provide the commentary."

"And delegate authority and appear competent," Kuhl said, nodding. "Do you think they're coming back?"

"The Outsteppers?"

"Or whomever they let start the war."

"I don't know, Brian. There's not enough information. That's why you're going. I'll miss you. Lie down. You have an hour before you're supposed to leave for Manaus."

He did as she had asked. The sheets crackled with repressed static.

He closed his eyes, but he still saw her face.

"How old do you think she was during the Terminal Night?"

"She's a little older than you," Sara said. "Seven years old, say."

"She remembers it, then. She escaped it."

"So did you. You shouldn't think about that time. That was another life."

"I don't remember any of it. But I know what happened. The poison from the rationed water infiltrating into their cells, the dosages tailored so the effect would be staggered, so not everyone began to die of thirst at the same time. It's a mistake to try to hide it."

"The people who were responsible paid," Sara agreed. "But the colonists wouldn't understand, anyway. Not right away. No talking, now. You should rest."

The foolish words surged to his lips. "I love you, you know. No matter who I am, no matter how long it takes me to come back, you're always here." He opened his eyes, saw her smile.

"That's because you're still Kearin," she said, so softly he could barely hear. "When you're Brian, you won't care about me. That's all right. I'll be waiting for you when you come home, Kearin."

He rolled over onto his side, eyes tightly closed. "Why is Brace sending me?"

He felt her hand on the back of his neck.

"*I* am sending you, Kearin."

# Chapter Four

He left the link booth and took a tube up to the main floor of the Manaus terminus. The crowd filled the cavernous crystal dome with a murmuring like that of insects trapped under a glass. Bursars stood along the walls, dispensing boarding passes. The gates between them opened on tunnels stretching under the concrete expanse of the landing field, to the towers plunged into the bellies of dirigibles. Arrival and departure times glowed in the air.

Boston had no dirigible service; its terminus handled only BoreLink traffic. Most of the Manaus airships were cargo carriers with routes to the agricultural tracts in the interior. Most of the people were farmers. They wore coarse clothing and heavy boots, and their faces and the backs of their hands were brown. Sometimes Kuhl saw their black eyes stray to his pale face.

He looked around, frowning.

[There.] Sara's voice, audible only to him, came unexpectedly to his right ear. He shied as if stung. [It's all right.] She tried to soothe him, misunderstanding. [You're not late yet.]

She showed him which way to go by painting a coruscating line across his retina, plotting a path across the floor to the proper departure gate. It was across the room, shielded from his sight by a decorative switchback.

He gritted his teeth. [I told you no speech or sight unless I ask for it!]

He said it so only she could hear, thinking the words distinctly, forming them one by one, sub-vocalizing them. Sensors nestled around his vocal cords took the inaudible vibrations, converted them to orderly photon-patterns and sent them along filaments laid in channels carved into the underside of his collarbone. A transceiver tucked into his scapula converted the signals to radio waves and flung them outward to the nearest Datalink terminal—and Sara.

[Forget that rule now.] Her voice was severe. [You're being followed.]

Instinctively, uselessly, he looked over his shoulder. [Who?]

[Thirty degrees right.] He turned his head. [Him.]

An ashen-faced man in a richly-embroidered singlesuit grew a halo around his head. He stood thirty meters away, with dozens of people between him and Kuhl, and he was looking Kuhl's way.

[Who is he?]

[Checking.] The half-second pause seemed endless. [Damien Rosendahl, thirty-six, from the Leyte citadel. He was waiting for you at the Suffolk terminus. He followed you here. I place him, now, on the same BoreLink train you rode.]

[What does he want with me?]

[With you, or Kearin Seacord, or with someone else? His band tells me he is a class five-G programmer for Leyte Administration, but he has never used a bursar in Leyte or any neighboring sector. Financial transactions appear for the first time in Boston, six hours ago. He is a data-shell, a constructed file.]

[Only Security Affairs can make a man.]

[Yes.]

[*Is* he Sub Five?]

[I don't know.] He felt her regret in his own throat. [I really do not know. Those records are closed to me.]

[Help me handle him.]

[Anything.]

He crossed the floor, then back again, a meandering path Rosendahl paralleled. Then Kuhl wedged himself into a link booth, got the calling code for his new crew chief from Sara, and pressed the digits into the terminal.

Paoli Marella's face appeared, grayish and faintly distorted by the transmission lens of his personal transceiver.

"I've just gotten in, Paul," Kuhl said in clipped tones. "Last-minute dealings in Manchester. Got away just in time."

"We've got plenty of time, Citizen Kuhl," Kuhl's director said. "Are you in the complex now? We're all eager to meet you."

A grin split his tanned, heavily-creased face. He brushed at wisps of unruly white hair. Marella specialized in documentaries shot in remote locations, far from transmitted power facilities. He had spent a lot of time outside ceramic walls and controlled environments.

"I've got the team assembled at the west end of the terminus," Marella continued. "The Force's transpill will pick us up down here."

"I'm down by the other end, near the tubes to the BoreLink. You send someone down here to help me with my gear, Paul."

"I could send down a skid," Marella offered.

"If I felt I could trust thirty thousand hours' worth of gear to a machine, I would have. I want bodies."

"We'll be right over." He broke the connection before Kuhl could acknowledge.

[Rosendahl is still with you.]

[I know, Sara.]


He let Marella find him twenty minutes later, in a lounge overlooking the main floor. Marella's mouth twitched when he saw Kuhl sitting in an over-plush chair, watching the scenes sliding across the wall. A flight of prop-engined aircraft lumbered, stuttering and thundering. Parachutes erupted from them. Sudden dark clouds blossomed amid the planes and soldiers. The detonations resounded.

Marella, after an uncertain moment, perched on the arm of the chair alongside Kuhl's. The young, lean man behind him remained standing, shifting uncomfortably from one foot to the other.

"I'm pleased to meet you at last, Citizen Kuhl," Marella said insincerely. "This is Jon Frings, our audio man."

"Pleased," said Kuhl. He glanced up, taking Marella's hand briefly, then let it go.

"I expected to find you downstairs," Marella said after a moment's silence.

Kuhl sat up straighter. "We can learn from these things," he said abruptly, waving his hand at the flaming aircraft. Frings opened his mouth to speak but Kuhl cut him off, saying, "Oh, you might not think so, but this one is better than most. At least it's more facile than most. Flawed, of course. Depth slips badly at the edge of the screen. When I do work like this—I don't do it like *this*, of course—it's a good effect to shrink objects approaching the limits of the field of view. As if they're receding. Less disconcerting than having them wink out of existence at the end of the screen. Or, worse, having them go past the end, across a lampshade, the family cat." He frowned. "Here it could have been a matter of budget, rather than of originality. Usually, not always, not much of the former and too little of the latter. But that's been the case throughout recorded—or recording—history."

[A little thick, Kuhl. Remember the character's parameters.]

[I'm rolling.]

"The sound . . ." Frings's high-pitched voice trailed off to a breathy, whining note. Kuhl shifted in his seat to stare at him, then turned away again.

"It reeks. It's overblown, the sound, as if it were done by someone who had just discovered subsonics. A closing door sounds like an avalanche."

"Oh," said Frings. "You . . . really think so?"

"I always say what I think," Kuhl said. "Isn't it time we're going, Paul?"

Marella took a thin card from his breast pocket. A circle on the card's face glowed brilliant red. "Your prompter should have gone off ten minutes ago. We've got just fifteen minutes to get back to our gate or the Force's transpill will leave without us."

"Can't rely on those damned cards," Kuhl said. He struggled out of the deep chair. "Never carry them. I've had enough of this show anyway. Sure we can learn from them, but the tutition's high. My bags are outside. Paid a boy to watch them."

"I'll get them," Frings mumbled.

They descended to the main floor, Frings a dozen paces ahead, struggling under the weight of Kuhl's equipment.

"Jon's a good man," Marella said after a while. "You'll appreciate having him along on this trip."

"I'm sure."

"Our team's the best. And we're going to be a long way from home."

[Be very careful here.]

"Of course," said Kuhl.

"Did you know Jon had a hand in that show you were watching?"

Kuhl stopped. He looked at Marella. "Should I have?"

"You don't have to undermine these people to get good work out of them. They know you're the best, and they'll do their best for you."

"I expect so. What're you saying?"

"You didn't know Frings directed that show? And did the sound?"

"First time I've seen the damned thing. I'm tired of those historical war-views. How many times can you watch the League of Nations go up in flames? I don't sit home and fuzz out on the entertainment channels. Never heard of Frings before today, either . . . and you only vaguely. Other people watch my shows. I don't watch theirs."

"All right," said Marella.

"One more thing: I don't care what people think about me or the way I work. If the audience numbers are there, and if the surveys show they're learning from it, it works. No one can tell me differently. If Frings doesn't have much self-confidence, that's his watch. If you want to leap to his defense, that's yours. I don't care about anything but the show."

"A good thing, too."

Kuhl handed his tape case to Marella. "Take this. I'll be right along."

"We've only got *ten*—"

"Leave without me. You'll like that."

He moved quickly (but not quickly enough to lose Rosendahl), down-tube to the level below, through a knot of dark-skinned teeners waiting on the BoreLink platform, between a brace of Peacemakers, inscrutable in their polarized helmets, and down a narrow corridor.

[Your conversation with Marella was overblown.] Sara's tone was severe. [I warned you about letting that happen all during orientation.]

[He'll never forget what I said. Where's Rosendahl?]

[Following at what would be a safe distance . . . if you did not have a friend.]

He turned a corner, following the Universal signs.

[You heard Marella yourself, Sara. We're going to be a long way from home. I can see this crew getting very tight-knit. I can't afford that.]

[But the parameters—]

[They're a guide. I can't do my work if he wants to be my friend.]

Silence. Then she said, in a tone meant to appease him, [Second door on your left.]

It opened before he reached it. A short, dark-haired man came out of the lavatory, patting his clothes into place. He nodded at Kuhl absently as he passed, smelling of dirt.

The restroom was empty. He waited in the harsh light, breathing hard. He had only walked quickly, not run, but the new layers of fat smothered his lungs. And his arches hurt. And his face felt stiff and heavy, like a mask. Cool air brushed across his forehead and temples, where he'd had hair a few weeks ago.

It was different, being Kuhl.

But . . . Manaus was not so different from Boston after all. The corridors were regulated to the same height and breadth. The population density and air quality were kept to the same standards. Relayer, too, was a system of rooms and corridors, albeit carved into rock.

He thought, Maybe it won't be so different.

[Don't kid yourself.] Then: [He's coming.]

Rosendahl opened the men's room door, saw Kuhl with his hands in the sink, the water running.

He smiled uncertainly.

Amateur, Kuhl thought.

The door locked behind him.

All the lights went out.

Then the ventilators came on, up past specified limits, their roar masking Kuhl's heavy breathing.

[Show him to me.]

Sara complied, painting the glow of Rosendahl's body heat on Kuhl's eyes, directly stimulating the rods and cones via the gold-wire net wrapping his optic nerve. The outline of the room shimmered bluely. The darkened lights, surveillance camera and microphones, and the door lock, all shone violet.

Rosendahl stepped forward tentatively, hands outstretched. His ill-defined form grew duller as the blood withdrew from his skin and he shivered.

Kuhl pointed to a ceiling light's violet flower.

[Below it.]

A megavolt surged along the conductor, fusing it in the moment the lamp exploded outward. Rosendahl screamed as hot metal rained down on him.

He staggered back, clutching his head, came up against the door and slid down it, groping for the release, which did not yield. He pawed at it blindly after hope should have been gone. A charred smell underlay the stink of ozone.

"Low light," Kuhl said. One of the surviving panels glowed dimly.

Kuhl pulled Rosendahl's flabby arms away from his face. Blood streaked his scalp and the back of his neck, seeping into his singed lace collar. Kuhl cupped the man's face in his damp hands. Rosendahl's eyes remained tightly closed. A rivulet of blood trickled from between slightly parted lips. Bit his tongue, Kuhl thought.

"Tell me who you are," he said.

Rosendahl shook his head weakly, eyelids fluttering.

"You've been following me."

Rosendahl opened his mouth; blood filmed his teeth. Fine

droplets spattered Kuhl's hand as Rosendahl said thickly, "Damien—"

Kuhl gripped the man's chin and jerked up, so his head rang against the door.

"Don't tell me any lies," Kuhl breathed. "Don't tell me you're Damien Rosendahl."

He thought of all the times Sub Five had called him in these last seven years: when he had uncovered the diversion of welfare food and medicine, so reminiscent of the Terminal Night; when the transportation office was laying plans based on data forty-five days out of date; when the Peacemaker had been systematically beaten (not to death, but until he could no longer live) and the assailants had turned out to be other Peacemakers; the time when he had worked his way into the wagering club, and found the bets were placed on matches between humans and cockatrices—nightmares, set loose on Earth during the Portal War, which fed on blood and misery.

Based on information he had obtained, Security Affairs had stripped many transgressors of their citizenship and sent them into the Boston LoSide.

A lot of people would like to know who the stranger who came among them had been.

"If you don't tell me I'll *kill* you," Kuhl said.

[That's good. You sound as if you mean it.]

Kuhl shook him.

Rosendahl did not answer.

[Kuhl . . . he's dead.]

He took his hands away from the body, which felt no different than before. He smelled for the first time the stink of loose shit.

"It was . . ." His throat closed. He wiped his sleeve across his eyes and nose and snuffled. That brought the stink closer, and he nearly gagged.

[We did *not* kill him. At least not directly. The cause of death is uncertain. When they bring him to a medical center I'll supervise the autopsy. Wipe your hands.]

Rosendahl looked uncomfortable, slumped against the door. Kuhl wiped his hands on the corpse's jacket.

"Who *was* he?"

[Don't vocalize. He was someone who could hurt us. If he could see through your camouflage he could undermine Sub Five's entire operation. Get up to the main floor. You don't have any time left.]

"Brace should—"

[He's been notified already. Concentrate on your assignment, on Kuhl. Brace and I will have this matter settled by the time you come back. Now *go*.]

He gripped Rosendahl's filigreed epaulets and dragged him away from the door.

A brilliant orange dirigible cast off and fell slowly upward. He watched it for minutes.

[There is no more time, Brian.]

He found his team at the other end of the terminus, in a lounge hidden by a switchback of ornamental screens. Puffy couches encircled stairs leading two meters down, to the polished rail where a transpill waited, humming. Its only identification was an understated four-pointed star etched into a corner of the canopy.

Marella and Frings were there. He recognized the three other members of his team. A sixth person whom Sara had not covered in the briefings walked over to him.

"Glad you made it," the man said. He wore a loud, flowered tunic and jet pants. The four-pointed star pinned to his collar was nearly invisible. "Vik Gangel, StarForce. I'm here to see you get aboard safely. Run into any trouble?"

Sara said, [He's in their intelligence division, and has been assigned to *Belfast* as "pilot"—meaning he will examine the ship's monitors a final time, approve it worthy of a sortie into the Deep, and activate the engines. It's practically a ceremonial post.]

Kuhl took his hand from Gangel's too-firm grasp. "Pleased to meet you."

"We'll have to light fire. Running a little late."

Marella ushered the team into the transpill: Frings; a balding, Oriental man; two plump, middle-aged women whose gazes coldly avoided his own. They were the instructors in the class Kuhl had taken years ago, the one Brace had told him about in the first briefing.

"Are you all right?" Marella asked him. "You look pale."

"Fine."

He sat next to Gangel. Marella, last in, closed the canopy. It was silent in the white, padded interior. No birds or waterfalls. Kuhl looked around. No maps or directional controls. The Force's four-pointed insignia was repeated endlessly on the floor and in the weave of the upholstery.

The car jerked forward, sliding downward and out of the terminus. The tunnel lights flashed by until velocity made them a continuous blur.

"How far is the port from here?" Marella asked.

"Twenty-five kilometers," said Gangel. "Just over the horizon—out of sight, out of mind." He plucked at his shirt. "We don't wear our uniforms surfaceside on the same principle. It's in our charter."

"Because of the Formation?" Marella asked. "People still resent it?"

Gangel smiled faintly. "I've been in the Force for fourteen years and I'm not sure what our role in the Formation was. I attended crèche in Puget, then the Academy at Aztlan. In Puget they taught that the nukes we had in orbit were only a footnote, and enlightened self-interest brought the city-states into the Triumvirate. At the Academy, the word is that the threat of . . . punishment hastened the process along a little." He shrugged. "To my mind, the accounts agree on the important factors. The nukes were, and are, in orbit. And they were never used, and never will be. There are always those who want to make more of our part in the Formation than happened. Statism clings like moss to a rock in some corners of the world. I think Europe's citadels tend to be the worst."

"I'm from Manchester," Kuhl said, remembering to put heat in his voice.

"Then you know what I mean. We're better off with that provision in our charter anyway. 'Presence,' it's called. This way I'm not being bothered all the time by people wanting to know what the Deep is like." He looked around expectantly.

"What is the Deep like?" asked Frings.

"I've never been beyond the Moon's Aztlan base, myself," Gangel said. "There, things run . . . more *smoothly* than here. It's quiet. There's nothing quieter than Aztlan," he added, his tone softer than a moment before.

"It's dead," said Abraham Hwang. The elderly man would maintain the team's equipment, and could double as a sound technician if necessary.

"The Moon was never alive," Gangel told him. "We don't disturb it."

Sitting together at the back of the compartment were Alistaire and Aleydis Aubrecht, fraternal twins, camera-ops both. When Kuhl nodded to them, they ignored him. The chance for them to work with Brian Kuhl was resistible. The bonus for doing so— whole months of discretionary income—was less easily refused. They had come unwillingly; he could expect no propinquity from that quarter.

The transpill rose from its subterranean track into blinding sunlight. They passed through a line of brown-leaved banana trees and the shuttle port lay before them.

The sun glared from tightly-packed earth. Black lines, hopelessly confusing from ground-level, became fifteen-thousand-meter runways when seen from the air. A dirigible, smaller than the cargo carriers Kuhl had seen, hunkered near a cluster of prefabricated buildings in the north. A pair of silvery shuttlecraft, gull-winged and dolphin-nosed, sat nearby.

The transpill slid to a halt in the shadow of a low building. Heat poured in through the opening canopy. Dust motes followed, dancing in rays of harsh light. Kuhl sneezed and rubbed his nose. His clothes hung limply on his thick, overburdened frame. The heat was no worse here then in the Hub, but this body—his body—was not so well adapted to it.

Sara told him, [The corpse was discovered seven minutes ago. The Peacemakers are on the scene. Readings from the emergency medical package confirm the absence of cerebral and cardiac activity. One of them just remarked that Rosendahl bit his tongue deeply.]

"I knew that," Kuhl muttered. Gangel held the door for him and he entered the sweetly cool building. After the actinic brightness outside, the interior seemed twilight dim.

[I did not know that. I have only one eye in that room, and you blocked my view of his face.]

[Sorry. Do you know who we killed yet?]

[We did not kill him. I sifted all available data along several probabilities before you even left that room. It still comes up a cipher.]

[Like me.]

[Totally *unlike* you. You are a complete, coherent identity. You have a consistent background with supportive documentation, including files on parents. "Rosendahl" is just a name attached to a credit account. Not enough to stand up to close scrutiny, but enough to travel, pay accounts, and exist—for a time.]

[Not very long.]

"If you'll wait here just a minute," Gangel said, leaving them in a carpeted lounge. The Force's symbol was everywhere: walls, carpet, frosted windows. A model or a very good hologram of their starship, *Belfast*, floated in the center of the room. Frowning, Kuhl went over to look.

It seemed as if she had been assembled from a random collection of parts. A spherical command center perched forward, at the end of a five-hundred-meter-long boom. Aft were clustered the exhaust vanes to channel the engines' hot exhaust plasma when *Belfast* was under drive. In between crowded sausage-shaped passenger holds and cargo containers, connecting passage-ways, sensor arrays, the gauzy mesh of deflection grids, antennae, three fusion reactors, a dozen or more reaction-mass bladders, and the several thousand tons of struts and pylons which formed the leviathan's connective tissues. The ship was twenty-three-hundred meters long (the legend hovering alongside it read) and looked as if she would fall into as many pieces once thrust was applied.

Sara startled him. [More data coming in.]

Frings found a wet bar and dispensed drinks. Kuhl had water. He held his right hand to his ear to block the small noises in the room. [What data?]

[He killed himself. They found a small capsule in his mouth and traces in it of pure nicotine. If filled, the capsule would have contained more than enough of the poison to kill him. The autopsy will tell me more.]

[Will you have the results before I'm out of transmission range?]

[I will try.]

Gangel came back into the room. "Everything's ready," he said.

The starship's empty corridors smelled new. Kuhl flailed along a line strung where the ceiling would be once the engines began their long burn to the edge of the Solar System. His boot left a print on the formerly immaculate wall.

"This is where you'll be sleeping for the next twelve weeks," Gangel said. A young man in the Force's brown-and-whites, grinning and looking faintly embarrassed, hovered near him. Krause, the stenciled label over his right breast pocket read.

Man-sized ceramic eggs stretched along both walls of the softly illuminated corridor. Identifying codes and tightly-packed paragraphs of instructions decorated the lids of the stasis-beds.

"How many die?" Hwang asked.

"Such a question," said Aleydis Aubrecht.

Hwang turned to her. "I need to know."

Gangel said to the steward, "You handle that one. I'll be on the think deck checking the warlocks. Call me when you want to be tucked in."

Krause nodded. Gangel pulled himself up the corridor and out of sight.

"Warlocks?" said Alistaire Aubrecht.

"The ones who operate the faster-than-light drive," Krause said. "They're the only ones who will be conscious for the entire voyage."

"How many die?"

"Far less than one percent, Citizen Hwang."

"What's that in terms of people?"

The steward frowned slightly. "Since the stasis-beds were put into widespread use two years ago, five out of six-hundred-twelve participants have died upon revivification. Do you want to know how many died during the experiments?"

"That's all right," said Hwang.

[One-hundred-ten.]

Kuhl said, [Hush. Anything from the medical center yet?]

[No.]

"What does it feel like?" Marella asked.

"If any of you have had major surgery, the sensation of numbness will be familiar. A similar nerve-blocking technique is used in both procedures. I'm told the sensation is only slightly unpleasant. Whatever it feels like, it's better than going through the faster-than-light translation 'awake.' The survival rate among non-talents is nil, Citizen Hwang."

"Talents?" said Alistaire.

"The warlocks," Aleydis whispered. "They link with the ship somehow to make the transition."

"You'll 'sleep' while we burn to the orbit of Pluto," said the steward, "and there the neutrinos are thin enough to allow translation. You'll sleep for another six weeks until we match orbits with Relayer."

[Sara, is this safe?]

[What he told you of the risks is true.]

The ship trembled once as if it had run into something, and static crashed painfully in his ear. He felt himself drawn subtly in the direction of the stasis-beds.

[Sara!]

"That's Lieutenant Gangel warming up the drive," said Krause. "I think we may as well put ourselves to bed." He touched a tab on the side of a bed. The lid popped wetly.

"Do we dream?" Frings asked in a thin voice.

The steward's look was blank. "I don't know," he said. All at once Kuhl saw how young Krause was, and that he had never experienced the sleep before, either.

Later, the sides of the bed gripped him tightly.

[Sara?]

No reply, no static, nothing.

"All right, citizen?" Krause asked.

"Fine." He snuggled deeper into the rubbery confines. The lid closed over him.

Nem dreamed.

# II.

# MOSAIC

---

For me reality is not easily attained.

—René Magritte

# Chapter Five

"Do you feel all right?"

It was a woman's voice and, when Kuhl opened his eyes, a woman's face looking down at him. The skin around her gray eyes was harshly lined, her head shaven except for two narrow swaths of brown hair stretching from her hairline to the nape of her neck. Her scalp was smooth and tanned.

Kuhl turned his head, neck muscles protesting. The inner walls of the stasis-bed rose around him, high and steep as a canyon. The walls were covered with something that dried as he watched, turning from pearly slickness to a mealy tan powder. (And his skin felt sticky.)

"I'ble drust be," he forced out between parched lips. He tried to work saliva into his mouth, but somehow he had forgotten the trick of doing it.

He tried to speak again, forming the words elaborately to push them past the sour, cottony mass in his throat. "I am thirsty."

"You always are when you first come out of it." She reached down, arms foreshortened by some snag in his depth perception, and lifted him clear of the bed. She took a white cloth from under her arm and, one-handed, wrapped it around his waist.

Up and down the corridor, other bed lids were popped, other crew and passengers dragged from sleep. In the bed alongside Kuhl's, Alistaire Aubrecht came groggily awake. The steward, Krause, pulled her from her cocoon. Her eyelids and fingers trembled and a muscle in her broad back twitched. The steward struggled to hold her steady while he wrapped her in a cloth. Aubrecht's head lolled, her glazed eyes briefly meeting Kuhl's. A slow flush crawled across her face and chest. He turned away.

"You'll be back to yourself in a few minutes," said the woman who had awoken him. She pushed him toward the wall and closed his unresisting fingers around a handhold. She forced the bed lid shut, muscles bulging under her uniform in unexpected places—the legacy of work in weightlessness.

"I'm Captain Zierling, by the way," she said. "If someone gives you some clothes, do you think you can . . . "

[Sara . . . are you there?]

He shook his head. "Are they alive?" he croaked. "Where are we? Earth . . . ?"

For a moment she looked puzzled, then her face cleared. "Ross 128 system, Relayer orbit. We're expecting another transmission from the colonists in a quarter-hour. See if you can be on the think deck by then, Citizen Kuhl."

She turned and pulled herself up the corridor, through the confusion of uniformed and naked bodies and loose cloth. Kuhl waited for someone to help him, anchored to the wall by one cramped hand. His muscles were weak and unrested, as if he had slept forever, and his skin itched all over. When he rubbed at his nose the back of his hand came away streaked with the powdery dried nutrient solution.

"Citizen?" It was the steward, Krause.

"What happened to your head?"

Krause drew his hand over the two converging brushes of hair sweeping back from his forehead. "This is my first Deep mission, Citizen. It's a tradition." He slid open a drawer in the base of Kuhl's stasis-bed and took a bundle of clothes from it. "I'll help you into these."

"The captain wanted me to go to . . ." He paused. He could not remember. [Where did she say to go?]

Then he remembered. Again.

He shivered violently.

"Easy," said Krause.

He was alone.

"All right now?"

Kuhl nodded. "The think deck?"

"Our command deck. I'll take you up there."

"Krause?"

"Yes."

"What do I call you? I don't what your rank is."

"Just 'Forcer.' Everyone is just 'Forcer,' except for the captain."

"But there was a lieutenant?" His forehead furrowed, trying to remember, to knock loose some of the fuzz in his brain.

"Surfaceside is a different command structure. The ships' crews aren't big enough to justify an elaborate table of organization. We know who's boss." He grinned, handing Kuhl his shirt.

By the time he had finished dressing, his muscles were trembling with the exertion of wrestling with the fabric made unruly by zero gee. The corridor was by now mostly empty, and the rest of the media team (Krause told him) were in their quarters. Marella had left Kuhl a message saying he would check their equipment after he showered.

Pulling himself along the nylon guy-lines, Kuhl's arms felt heavy and dead. His chest ached. But, after a few minutes and a hundred meters, Krause led him to an elevator shaft stretching from one habitable end of *Belfast* to the other. A flimsy cage, barely large enough to hold both of them, took them forward.

The cramped command deck was twilit by flatscreen displays. Zierling sat in a couch near the center of the narrow, low-ceilinged room, a half-dozen Forcers arrayed to either side of her. Kuhl looked at the winking lights and undulating displays for moments, but they were completely unintelligible.

Zierling looked over her shoulder. "Welcome to *Belfast*, Citizen. Forcer, you can go."

Krause saluted smartly, nodded to Kuhl, and pulled himself off the command deck.

Kuhl grabbed the arm of Zierling's chair to steady himself. She looked down. "Krause should have got some grippers for you. Next time you see him, ask him about them. It's faster than hand-over-hand unless you know what you're doing." He nodded. "They're shoes," Zierling explained. She touched a panel on the arm of her chair. The forward wall brightened, then coalesced into a solid image.

Relayer rolled by.

The rim of the world turned crimson where Ross 128's rays refracted from a tenuous cloak of nitrogen and argon. Next, the northern polar cap came out of shadow, turning to a bloodied shield. The thin shell of frozen carbon dioxide nearly met its southern twin. Between them stretched a strip of rust-colored terrain filled with mountain ranges, deeply-cutting rifts, an ice-filled basin whose surface was as tortured as any storm-tossed terrestrial sea.

"There but for the grace of photosynthesis go we," Zierling said. "Things have been rough down there, Brian. We established radio contact with them a month ago, but the signal was very weak. We couldn't hear what they were saying until we dropped them a transceiving station from orbit. Turned out they'd been using a hand-held unit to receive us and try to talk back. They got our station up and working within a few hours, but we haven't had any face-on-face talk, just the link between our computer and theirs." She looked at the world's picture. Red light sheened from the grease in her hair. "They'd cannibalized their big transmitter, but they hadn't turned off their receiver after all those years.''

"What is the situation down there?''

"They are holding on,'' Zierling said, her mouth set.

*Belfast*'s computers were still at work deciphering and index- ing the initial transmissions from Relayer. More data was added to their load each second. But, while Kuhl still dreamed, the computers had strained and sifted and brought forth a datum gleaned from a compressed information-burst: The population down below stood at just under two thousand souls.

On 1 March 2052, eighteen thousand permanent colonists and fifteen hundred transient engineers and scientists had lived and worked in the colony's warrens.

How much of a threat could they pose? he wondered—but Sara fed him no probabilities.

"Should I have a medician scan you?'' Zierling asked suddenly. Kuhl started, wondering if he'd spoken out loud. "Why?''

"Because the sight of a new world doesn't seem to excite much interest. Are you sure you can generate enough curiosity to make up your report on these people?''

"I'll do my job, Captain.''

"I hope so,'' she said, but he saw her thoughts were already elsewhere. She stared at the screen, nibbling at her lower lip. "I was told to cooperate fully with you, though not at the expense of my own mission. I'll tell you that the ship is on alert.''

The hairs on the back of his neck rose. "Why? Relayer . . . ?''

"They don't have the capability to harm us.'' She tapped a second panel set in the arm of her chair. "This is the reason.''

Relayer dwindled from the screen, replaced by a starscape. A dusting of bright lights shone from the velvet background, the night sky he had never seen from Boston. Crosshairs appeared in the center of the screen, a nimbus drawn around a star no different from the rest.

"This,'' she said. "It doesn't belong there. Data Relayer's pumped up to us say it's a nova that appeared in their skies seven years ago. The colony lies between Earth and that brightness, so the light hasn't yet reached the Solar System.''

"I . . . don't understand.''

"We've scanned it ourselves. It has the spectrum of a sun, one a lot like our own. But there are no neutrinos coming out of it. That means there's no fusion going on inside it. And that means it's an anomaly.''

"How far away is it?''

"About twenty light-years out from here.'' She glanced at Kuhl, a sour smile tugging at her lips. "Do you think that'll save you? *Belfast* jumped from Sol to here in a little less than a second. It's jockeying to the point where we can make the jump that takes time." She crossed her arms, staring at the distant spark. "We're watching it, that's all, and going into Relayer with ears out and tubes open. They won't catch us open-armed again."

"The Outsteppers."

"Or whoever. We don't know what race started the Portal War, so they could jump at us from any corner of space. Including this one." She looked at him again. "Scare you? But . . . we're supposed to be part of your story, too, aren't we? You've spent all your time on Earth, haven't you? Think about what it might have been like to make the jump out here and not know if anything was waiting."

Kuhl grimaced and tried to look a little disdainful, but he thought of the picture Spencer Swan had shown him in another life: a ship like *Belfast* reduced to pretty, glittery fragments.

"Real-time transmission coming in, Captain," said one of her crew.

"Put it on the main."

Relayer's image collapsed in on itself. In its place appeared the face of a man, streaked with interference. He stared blindly at the command deck.

His eyes were hard, his complexion pale and cratered. He looked as if he were in his late thirties (Kuhl thought) but his black, tightly-curled hair was that of a younger man. The wall behind him was unpainted metal, harshly lit from overhead.

Smoke curled across the face. A cigarette came into the field of view, was sucked, and withdrawn again.

"Captain," said the image, "my name is Simon Weiss."

"It's good to see your face, Governor, and not just a hardcopy of your words," Zierling replied. "I'm afraid our meeting will be delayed several days."

Weiss raised one eyebrow. "Oh? Explain, please."

"The nearest usable landing site is three hundred kilometers south of you, Governor. We'll have to set our shuttles down there, erect a way station, and then cross overland to your location."

Weiss looked off-screen. Then he said, "Tell me the requirements for your landing site."

Zierling frowned. "A hard-packed strip—not stony—five thousand meters long."

"Width?"

She told him and gave him other engineering data. Then she said, "Governor, I don't see how—"

Weiss looked off-screen again, ignoring her. This time the murmur of another voice could be heard. "We'll get our baskers on it," Weiss said. "Someone will contact your ship within five hours to confirm, but I can say now it looks like we can lay down your strip here. Be ready to land within twenty-five hours."

"If such is possible, Governor, we'll be ready."

"And do not forget the regulations set down in our earlier transmissions."

"We won't."

Weiss nodded once. Then the image broke into undifferentiated bands of light.

"Transmission broken from their end, Captain," said a crewman.

"So I assumed." She glanced at Kuhl. " 'Baskers'?"

"What were the regulations he mentioned, Captain?"

"On the surface, reasonable requests that follow what our procedure was to have been anyway. No more than twenty people in the initial party. No weapons of any sort outside our shuttles. Discussions of immunology. Brief dossiers on landing party personnel—name and rank, basically. *Under* the surface, reminding me of their autonomy during the past hundred and fourteen years."

"He did not sound like someone hanging onto life by his fingernails," Kuhl observed.

"Don't let his manner fool you. It's been hard down there." Her chair released her. "Come with me."

He followed her off the command deck, to the level below and a wardroom she used as her office. Relayer was on the other side of the ship; only stars glittered beyond a thick port, Ross 128 a little brighter and redder than the others.

She took a seat, got up to show him how to strap into one, and sat down again.

"Assuming he does come up with a landing strip, I'll be sending down half your crew with the first shuttle, half with the second a few days later. If we have to set up a forward station, obviously that won't apply."

"I understand."

She rubbed a strip of greased hair contemplatively. "Yours is the first media team they've sent out and I'm not sure I like it, Brian. If they were going to do it I wish they'd started with Stapledon. That contact went very well."

"And this one won't?"

"Obviously it's too early to say. We'll all be helped if we cooperate with each other. Remember Heisenberg."

He nodded, but she explained anyway. "Don't interfere by observing. We have three months out here and I'll use all that time to take things as carefully as I have to. I want you to do the same."

He heard Sara's voice say, Remember the parameters.

So Kuhl frowned; but Zierling did not notice.

"Two thousand men and women down there," she continued, "living in a complex made up of about thirty-five kilometers of corridors. You can get to know it intimately in a week. How they survived is your whole story, I guess. They made their own food and air even before the war, but the technology to do it came from Earth. When the war ended and our Portal was destroyed, theirs simply shut down. They never knew why. Which is better, I'd think, than having the Outsteppers come for them, too. Think of what it would have been like, Brian, to watch the people around you start to die . . . and never know the reason."

"I would have guessed the Portal had been shut down deliberately," Kuhl said. "They were nationalists, anarchists, rebels. Earth was better off without them. Closing down the Portal would have ended the problem permanently."

"Maybe some of them did think that. They've had a hundred years to develop a few different schools of thought, and our presence must have already voided some of them."

"What does it say about that in the data they sent?"

Zierling shrugged. "We can't tell yet. The computers are making passes through the raw data, looking for key words and phrases. By interviewing the colonists, you'll probably know a lot before we do. It will take months for us to decipher everything they sent, and once we start programming for the translation back to Earth, our computers won't have the capacity to work on the problem anymore. When we get home and the Datalink gets hold of the information, then we'll find out, analytically, what the last hundred years were like. Your job—"

"Captain," Kuhl said in a wearied tone, "I know my job." He looked at her, the trim figure and lined face, the cropped hair gone lusterless and graying. "I'd guess you're fifty-five, which means you've been in the Force about thirty years. I'm younger, but I've been working in my field for twenty-five years. *Grant*, please, that I know my work when it's set before me on a platter seven thousand kilometers wide. Don't tell me about what themes

I should explore, when you don't know a damned thing more about these people than I do."

The muscles in her jaw bunched. She said nothing for several moments. Then, "I'm going to do my job, too. It happens to take precedence over yours. Don't interfere with my mission."

"Just don't tell me how to put a show together. I've spent all my life learning how to do it." He eased himself out of the chair and put a hand to the cold plastic port to steady himself. He pulled himself toward the door.

"Kuhl, I'm not finished with you." He turned back to face her.

"None of your people will discuss the Terminal Night with any of the colonists, or mention it among yourselves, for as long as we are on Relayer," Zierling said.

After a silent moment she added, "And the Terminal Night was not mentioned in any of the records we sent down to them."

And, when Kuhl still said nothing, she began, "The reason for this is—"

"I can guess the reason," he said. "Five hundred million people died in four days. Lakkers . . . LoSiders . . . whatever they were called thirty years ago. Whatever they were called, they were the ones without usable skills, who lived outside the citadels—and who were, for the most part, descendants of these colonists' forefathers. Considering the background of these people, one of them is bound to ask us, 'Why are you all white?' What are my people to say then?"

"You're—we are not all white. You're overstating the case."

"Only because they will. All the Asians are behind the walls of the People's State and if there are blacks in the citadels on the African continent I didn't see them when I was there. I think ninety percent of the citizenry is Caucasian."

"There are no statistics to bear that out."

"No," said Kuhl. "There are not."

"This is all beside the point. Security Affairs says we have to keep the Terminal Night from them for the duration of our mission. They edited the information in the ship's databanks to remove any trace of it. If we bring back some Relayermen as a diplomatic party, they will be told when they reach Earth. The idea is to let them bring the word back to their own people, *after* we've had a chance to explain carefully what happened."

"I'd like to be there when the attempt is made," Kuhl said. "Is that all you wanted from me, Captain?"

She nodded. "You can go." But then, when he was at the door, she said, "We dropped a line of observation satellites on our last orbit. If you want, you can patch into them and record some high-altitude views of the planet and the colony. If the offer's not too presumptuous.''

"Thank you, Captain. We'll do that.''

"See Forcer Krause about it. One last thing, Kuhl. There are only seventy of us out here. Are we going to—?''

Before she could finish, the walls called her name in a slightly amused, masculine voice.

"Here," she answered.

"Relayer reports a landing strip will be ready within thirty-six hours, Captain," the walls said. "Damned if I know how.''

"Thank you, Berry.''

"Computer, or human?" Kuhl asked.

"David Berry is very human. The Relayermen are full of surprises . . . already.''

"You were going to ask me something, Captain?''

She was silent for a moment, looking at the stars. Then she looked at him and he could read nothing in her eyes. Pulse, respiration, or skin temperature? Nothing.

"Neither one of us is good at getting along with people, Brian. We don't have to be. Before I became an officer, my life was different than it is now. I was a woman—that still means something to many people. Now I'm a captain, and that means something to many more people. Presumably you had to suck a little on your way up, before you became whatever the hell it is you are. What that is I don't really know. By choice, we don't screen much out here.'' She smiled very slightly. "Do you mind? That is, do you mind that I hadn't heard of you until you appeared in my marching orders?''

"It's the work that counts. If you press me, I'll tell you how much you missed.''

She smiled more sincerely. "But do you mind? I was told you would.''

"No, Captain, I don't care at all. Is that what you wanted to ask me?''

"I really wanted to know if you thought we would fight all the time.''

He remembered the parameters, and kept the grin from his face.

But he said, "Maybe not, Captain Zierling.''

Their landing raised a curtain of gray dust. Through it, the first thing Kuhl saw was the angular, corrosion-streaked flanks of the colonists' massive landship squatting on spraddled hydraulic legs. Though a hundred meters away, the throb of its engines was clearly heard through the shuttle's triple-walled hull. Hatches and handholds pocked the spider's riveted carapace. Behind broad, erosion-frosted eyes, silhouettes moved.

The world outside looked old. Hoodoos, lifting themselves out of the plain's dust blanket, had been turned to complicated spindles over ten thousand years' exposure to the wailing wind. On the horizon, a range of low mountains rose jaggedly into a violet sky. Weak red light glittered on glacial cloaks of frozen carbon dioxide.

Closer, tracks crisscrossed the chiaroscuro powder. The wind filled the shallow bowls leading from the colonists' vehicle to the settlement. A set of aimless treadmarks belonged to the StarForce robot parked alongside the shuttle's glossy, heat-shimmered wing. The robot's multifaceted sensors, mounted atop a canister body, looked dull in the faded light.

"A ruse," Abraham Hwang whispered to Kuhl from the seat alongside his own. Kuhl drew back as the old man thrust a pointing finger under his nose. "That robot is not what it seems," he added, in a broken hiss that must have carried the twenty-meter length of the passenger compartment. "I heard the Forcers' talk."

"It's only a surveyor," Kuhl said. He wished that Hwang would be quiet, the cabin noises would still themselves and leave him in silence. His collar was uncomfortably tight, his palms moist. He had to think and remember how to play it. What came first? Check the equipment again? Make assignments?

[No one knows Kuhl better than you.]

The voice jolted him. He heard it echoing still, from a time weeks, light-years, a world away. He knuckled one eye, hard. The pain and pressure brought him fully aware. She was not here.

Less than a second had passed; Hwang had seen nothing.

*"Belfast* dropped a hundred of them in the last month," Kuhl said, his voice harsher than it had been.

"Yes . . . but *this* one . . . The Forcers did not trust the colonists to build the runway according to their specifications. The surveyor was diverted here to make sure of its quality before we landed."

"It's just a precaution." He looked outside again and his gaze was trapped. His mouth went dry.

Sara had told him about this place over and over, but the truth was not all there was to it. Gravity was eight-tenths Earth's, she said, but she hadn't told him how being away from her would make him feel heavy and weak. The thin, cold air carried only a trace of oxygen; she hadn't mentioned it cried. She had told him he would be without her; she hadn't told him how it would feel.

Play it silky. This time the voice in his head was his own.

A man-sized door opened low on the spider's flank. He watched for another moment—until Zierling called him—but no one appeared in the doorway.

Voices and the sough and suck of opening locker doors echoed in the narrow, low-ceilinged cabin. The seats near the rear bulkhead were being dismantled to clear the entrances into the equipment holds under them. A portable shelter had half-deployed in one hatch, tangling a cursing Forcer in stiffening cloth. A magnetic camera rose from under the disorder, did a slow pan, then purred down the aisle. Kuhl ducked the egg-shaped device, feeling the breeze of its microturbines in his hair.

One of the twins (he wasn't sure which one), sitting in the seat behind Hwang's, gestured with a hand gloved in the camera's control mechanism.

"That's very good maneuvering," Kuhl told her, "but I doubt the colony has transmitted power or wall guides."

"I'm using the camera today anyway because it's the lightest," said Alistaire Aubrecht. "Silky?"

"You're the operator."

Zierling perched on a rung of the ladder leading up to the flight deck. Around her, in the open space between the first row of seats and the forward bulkhead, the deck was cluttered with outsuits the crew pulled from overhead lockers.

Sweat soaked her singlesuit. Her face was pale and drawn, except for a scarlet patch above each cheek. Before he could ask, she said, "It's not much gee, Brian, but it's more than I've had to carry for eight months. I'll adjust." She stood, wobbling a little. "I want you to pull your people together, get them suited and ready to march. I didn't expect to be met on the landing strip and I don't want to keep them waiting."

"Didn't the governor tell you they'd be here?"

"Told us *not*, specifically." She scowled—whether at him or at Weiss, he didn't know. "He could be trying to keep us off-balance, or he may simply have made a mistake. More likely it's something else entirely. Certainly it's not something I can think about now. Me and two of mine will move through the air lock first, then you and your crew. That's all we'll show them for now."

"What trouble do you expect?"

"I don't expect any trouble at all, but we'll prepare for it anyway. Now get ready. Those people have waited long enough for us."

# Chapter Six

The quilted, brown-and-white oversuit fit him loosely every-where but over his belly. It reminded him of the extra kilograms which had been slapped onto his frame, and which *Belfast*'s weightlessness had allowed him to forget. With thick fingers, he cinched the closures at wrists and ankles. Krause handed him a pastel-yellow collar containing radio, hose couplings for exterior air, and empty food and water bays.

"You seem to be everywhere, Forcer Krause." Kuhl steadied the sculpted horse collar and Krause sealed it to his epaulets.

"I'm supposed to be here when you need me," Krause replied easily. He handed Kuhl a helmet light as a soap bubble. "Set this on top, give it a twist to the right, then look for a green lamp under your nose."

He did as he was told. Krause said, "The radio is activated by the sound of your voice. The captain, Sidni, and I can select from several bands—the shuttle's, the landing party's, the fre-quency the colonists use, or any combination. Your units aren't as brainy. Anything you say will go out across all channels but the colonists'. So . . ." He looked apologetic.

"We'll hold our questions until we're inside the colony." Kuhl reached up to take the helmet off.

Krause brushed his hands away. "For safety's sake it doesn't come off as easily as it went on. Still, don't stir with it. When you get outside you don't want to find you've unsealed it somehow. When we get into the colony I'll help you take it off."

"Thanks," Kuhl said flatly. "What's your assignment down on Relayer? Me?"

Zierling, not in an outsuit, came over to them. "Do you have the package?" she asked Krause.

"It's in Sidni's pack."

"All right then. Let's march."

Krause and a short, olive-skinned woman followed the captain into the air lock. Before the door closed, Kuhl saw the ripstring seals on the woman's backpack. If there were weapons inside, they could be gotten at in a hurry.

After the air lock cycled, he and Aubrecht entered. Hwang followed, stepping tentatively over the high doorsill. He wore a packframe loaded with a portable Datalink, tapecase, communications rig, and a directional microphone. The door clanged on the gear. He caught Kuhl's glare and ducked his head contritely, helmet bobbing. "Our equipment is very sturdy," he offered.

In the close confines, Kuhl crowded up against Aubrecht, who blew air noisily from flared nostrils and looked uncomfortable. Her camera hovered against the ceiling, bumbling occasionally into her helmet or Kuhl's.

"Before you say anything," she said, "Abe told me it'll fly within ten meters of the ship. I'll—"

"I'm sure that's all right, Alistaire," he said without thinking, leaving her speechless.

Escaping air hissed around the outer door as it began to open.

A demon yammered in his ear. He held up his hand to block the sound; his fingers met the smooth plastic helmet. He winced; the squeal went on.

"Citizen Kuhl," Hwang began.

Feedback, Kuhl realized. The audio link to Sara was still activated—uselessly—but something here on Relayer was setting up interference in the receiver hugging the small bones in his inner ear.

His tongue probed for the pressure switch in the roof of his mouth, found it.

The demon's scream abruptly ceased, leaving his ear ringing. ". . . is anything wrong?" Hwang finished.

"Just a little dizzy. I'm all right now." It was probably primitive, unshielded electronics in the colonists' land crawler, or the colony itself. Sara hadn't told him about that either.

He wouldn't need the receiver for months. She could not speak to him here.

"Should I make ready for your narration?" Hwang asked.

"I'll do the voice-over later." Kuhl licked his lips.

Watery red light seeped onto his helmet. He stepped out, onto a ramp that flexed sickeningly underfoot. He walked quickly down its gentle arc, onto soft gray grit.

Ross 128 shone directly onto his face, but he could look directly into the feeble disk without shading his eyes. The violet sky was starless. The shuttle and its bridge to the familiar already seemed far away. He hugged his arms across his chest, but even that sensation was distant.

Aubrecht came down, caught the camera as it fell, and clutched it to her chest. "Beautiful landscape. Do you want some footage, Citizen Kuhl?"

"Save it. We can pick it up later."

She shrugged. "Abe, do you remember that time in the Sudd?"

He giggled. "I do. And I remember it as nothing like this, Allie. Enjoy the openness while you can. We'll be inside again soon enough."

The land crawler had not moved, and the door in its flank still stood open and empty. Zierling and Krause were talking about it on their private channel; Kuhl saw their lips moving. The olive-skinned woman walked over to him.

"You going to be steady?" she asked. Raviv, her last name, was stenciled on her uniform. She smiled, white teeth contrasting with black eyes and dark skin.

"Just taking it all in," he answered, thinking of how she would look in Sara's white shift. Nothing like her, he decided.

"Oh, you can't take it all in. It's too much to do all at once—or ever. But, sometimes, the fear of open spaces can grab you."

"I've been out in the open before. I've done a lot of shows outside the citadels."

"I've seen some of them. They were good."

"I'm glad you enjoyed them," he said formally, and looked past her. A man now stood alongside the colonists' machine. The steady beat of its internal combustion engines beat in Kuhl's stomach.

"Aubrecht! Did you get—?" He looked for her frantically, found her three meters away, quietly preserving the scene.

The Relayerman's bulky suit had been often patched. On his left sleeve was embroidered a legend unreadable at this distance; on the right was a six-pointed star formed by two overlapping triangles. The symbol was repeated on his steel helmet, above the opaque visor.

Zierling started forward, the two Forcers falling in behind her. Kuhl turned to his crew.

"Panorama," he told Aubrecht. "Then sweep along the captain's line of march to that machine and the colonist. Zoom in for the tight shot—"

"I've done this before," she said coolly. The camera extruded stalk-mounted crosshairs that settled in front of her right eye. The lens tracked her gaze.

"Citizen?" Hwang asked.

He helped the old man extricate himself from the packframe

and lower it to the ground. "There's nothing I want you for now," Kuhl told him. "The situation's too fluid. Wait for my word." Hwang nodded.

Zierling walked slowly and delicately. Kuhl caught up with the Forcers easily.

Up close, the strider did not look quite so massive and foreboding. Standing in its watery shadow, he saw where thin belly-plates had buckled, hydraulic medium had leaked and congealed, how the padded feet were permanently embedded with grit.

The colonist made no move, said nothing. Zierling stretched her right hand out to him. He raised his arm, as if he would take the hand, then completed the motion, pointing to Hwang and Aubrecht.

"What are they doing?" he demanded. The language was English, but the accents and stresses ringing in Kuhl's helmet were alien.

"A camera crew," Zierling replied. She took another step forward, to within a meter of the Relayerman. Her hand remained outstretched. "To record the first handshake. I am Captain Maya Zierling, commander of the TVS *Belfast*."

The man hesitated, then his metallic mitt swallowed Zierling's glove. He let his arm fall to his side. "This is your entire party?"

"There are more inside the boat, but they can't leave for another few hours. Routine maintenance check."

"We will send the *akavish* back for them, though it is a waste of fuel. Councilman Weiss waits for you now at Masada." He took hold of the bottom rung of the ladder leading to the open doorway.

"We look forward to meeting him, Citizen," Zierling said, making no move to follow him.

"I am no citizen of your Triumviratine Earth."

She inclined her head slightly. "I'm sorry, I meant no insult." She smiled brilliantly for him. "And I've been rude." Then, with the colonist's hand still on the ladder, she introduced Krause, Raviv, Kuhl, and then Kuhl's crew *in absentia*.

The Relayerman sighed (and Kuhl wondered if it was intended they hear it) and relinquished the ladder.

"I am the deputy councilman of Masada," he said stiffly. "My name is David Rosenthal. We will hurry now, please, Captain and visitors." He gave a curt bow and steadied the ladder for Zierling as she climbed.

Kuhl made fists to wipe his palms on the insides of his gloves.

The man's name was just an unpleasant coincidence to that of the man who, for Kuhl, had died yesterday, but was in reality three months cold.

"There are no coincidences," Sara would have said, "only subtler patterns of information."

The colony's entrance, high and wide enough to take the strider's bulk, had been carved into a stony hillside. Sometime since, steel plates had been bolted over cracks to shore up the arch. Deep fissures made the ramp leading downward treacherous.

Kuhl sat on a bare metal bench in the rear of the operator's compartment, his helmet in his hands. The roar of the gas-fired engine deafened him and the stink of burning oil and insulation overwhelmed. Rosenthal and the driver—a short, dark-haired man who had not spoken at all—sat in comfortable padded chairs behind the eroded windscreen.

Raviv got to her feet and leaned over the driver's shoulder, steadying herself against the vehicle's rolling gait with one hand on the back of his seat.

"Where do you get spare parts for this monster?" she shouted over the roar of the engine and the whine of the hydraulics.

"We can make many of the parts in our shops," Rosenthal answered. "When we must, we cannibalize." The driver said something in a rapid-fire burst of harsh syllables.

"He asks you to give him room to work," Rosenthal said.

"Silky." She bent forward again and said to the driver, "Do you speak English?"

"*Euskara.*"

"That is the name of his language," said Rosenthal. "He is an Euskaldun—a Basque."

"*Français, aussi,*" said the driver.

"How many of these do you have?" Raviv asked Rosenthal.

"Two."

"How many did you start out with, all that time ago?"

"Somewhat more," he answered.

The tunnel leveled out. Weak running lights splashed on a steel door, which slid aside for them.

On the other side, hoists and a mobile crane hung from the ceiling of a cavernous room. Equipment in various states of disrepair and decomposition littered the stained floor. Deep shadows pooled under chassis, grease-streaked engines, and wiremesh bins filled with smaller components. The Basque urged the strider into a relatively clear space and cut the engine. Silence rang.

Rosenthal pushed the hatch open and icy air blew in. Kuhl's breath turned to fog; his eyes burned. He was gasping by the time he reached the polished stone floor. He filled his lungs deeply but it didn't seem to do any good.

"The air here is mostly from the outside," Rosenthal explained. He started toward an air lock on the far side of the garage, a hundred meters away. Before they reached it, Kuhl had taken Hwang's equipment and Zierling was leaning heavily on Raviv, all of them wishing they had never removed their helmets. The Relayermen seemed unaffected.

It took entire minutes for the air lock to cycle. When the clattering of the pumps had stopped, the pressure door opened on a narrow, bright, and warm corridor. Two men, both twins for the Basque driver, waited. Rosenthal stripped off his silvery outsuit (a faded coverall lay underneath) and handed it to one of the Basques. The other Euskaldun turned expectantly to Kuhl.

"Your spacesuits and equipment will be brought to safekeeping." Rosenthal said. Kuhl began unsealing his suit. Krause started to say something but, at a look from Zierling, apparently thought better of it.

Aubrecht was not so observant. "What the hell good am I if they take my cam?" she demanded.

"No good at all," Kuhl answered. He shrugged out of the quilted oversuit, handed it to one of the Basques, and smoothed the singlesuit he wore beneath. "Do what they want, Alistaire. You'll be spending more time behind that camera than you want."

"That's straight," she acknowledged sourly. She placed the camera firmly in one of the colonist's hands. "Drop that and it's over for you," she promised.

The man nodded, smiling. Kuhl was sure he understood not a word of English.

Raviv was the last to peel off her outsuit. She looked uncomfortable in stained uniform and slippered feet. She held onto her pack.

Rosenthal reached for it. "Please, Miss."

"Captain?"

"Give it to me, Sid." Zierling knelt over the pack. The seal pulled free. Foam pellets scattered across the immaculate floor. She pulled a bottle free of the packing and stood.

"Can we agree this is not contraband, Citizen Rosenthal?" she demanded, breathing hard with exertion and repressed anger. She turned the label upwards, so he could see. Then she tossed the bottle to him, end-for-end. He caught it against his stomach.

"The old Carmel wineries," he said distantly. "Rishon Letzion. Does Jerusalem still exist as well?"

"It's as it was before the Crusades," Raviv said. "I was there last year. It's beautiful."

"And New York?"

"Underwater," Zierling said. "We lost a lot in the Portal War, too, Citizen. One person in ten died, the factories closed all over the world. We lost the season of winter in most places, and with it a few million acres of seaside real estate." She shrugged. "The wine was for Citizen Weiss, a gift from Jan Vohland, Commandant of the StarForce. Maybe we could all share it."

Rosenthal nodded absently. Then he straightened, gestured to the Basques, and spoke a few words in their language. In moments the floor was swept clean; the pack, their suits, the equipment was gone down the corridor with the Euskaldun workers. Another group of laborers came toward them. Rosenthal spoke to them, and they turned around and went the other way.

Zierling looked both ways down the empty corridor. "A quarantine, Citizen?"

"There is no quarantine."

"Then where is everyone?"

"This is a little-used part of Relayer," he said. "There are many such. If there are any celebrations for your coming, they will be later, after you see Councilman Weiss. Before you do, I remind you that proper form of address is not 'Citizen,' but 'Mister.' Simon Weiss will take great offense if you call him 'Citizen' or 'Governor.' "

"I apologize," Zierling said stiffly.

"Second," Rosenthal continued, "it is to him that *any* questions you have must be addressed. The sooner we reach him, the sooner you will be answered."

Rosenthal led them along several hundred meters of low-ceilinged corridors. Air-tight doors closed off entrances to side passages. Through the walls and floors they heard mechanical sounds, the hiss of pressurized air, the rumble of water—and, once, conversation and laughter. They encountered no one.

Corrosion filmed all metal surfaces. Fine cracks webbed the concrete walls. The passage of feet over six generations had worn the plastic floor concave. Mustiness tinged the endlessly refiltered air.

"We're unwanted guests, apparently," Raviv said to Kuhl. "Or unexpected, at least."

"This was my chance of a lifetime," Aubrecht said, allegedly to Hwang, who walked alongside her, but loud enough for Kuhl to hear. "When his agent called me, that's what she told me. Twelve weeks in a coffin to get here, and they treat us like lepers."

"Be gentle," said Hwang.

"Watch your step here, please," Rosenthal called out from up ahead. The plastic floor turned rough. Dust filtered down from the ceiling. Chalked lines sectioned off part of the wall, framing a filigree of hairline fractures. A faded plastic coverlet had been hastily thrown over a box of tools. A door slammed from somewhere ahead of them.

"They got out just in time," Aubrecht said sourly.

Rosenthal took them to a room large enough to hold them all. Thinly padded benches stood against the walls. Schematics and maps, incomprehensible as hieroglyphics, hung in metal frames. Kuhl's hair brushed the low ceiling; he fought the urge to hunch.

Rosenthal opened a second door giving onto a short corridor. "Captain, if you will come with me, the councilman awaits."

"Just me?"

"If you please. This will be an introduction, not a press conference."

Zierling looked at Kuhl, who shrugged. "There's not much we can do without our equipment anyway, Captain. Ask about that, will you?"

When they had left, Raviv went to both doors leading from the room. She rattled knobs experimentally. "Not locked," she reported.

"Did you think they'd try anything with *Belfast* overhead?" Krause slumped onto a bench. "I didn't expect a celebration, *Mister* Rosenthal, but a soft seat and a hot meal would have been silky."

"You shouldn't have expected anything," Raviv said. She looked behind the framed diagrams.

"I don't see what you're so wired about," Krause said. "You're a Hebrew, aren't you? You'll be all right."

"I don't expect that to get me very far," Raviv said absently, staring at the ceiling.

"Are you with the Force's security detail?" Kuhl asked her.

"Ground Patrol?" She smiled at the idea. "No, but I like to be cautious."

A door opened and Rosenthal looked in. "Mister Kuhl, the Councilman and your captain wish to see you now."

Krause stood. "What about us?"

"No mention was made of you. Mister Kuhl?"

The office lay at the end of the short corridor. When Kuhl entered Weiss was standing behind a large metal desk. He was tall, painfully thin, and angry. The transmission to *Belfast*'s bridge had somehow missed the skeletal cast of his face, softening prominent cheekbones and hooded eyes.

Zierling sat in a straight-backed chair, arms folded across her chest. Her face was red.

Weiss nodded curtly to Rosenthal. "Go, David," he said. "I'll handle things here. Send Judith back."

Rosenthal hesitated.

"I don't need your help with these *dar*," Weiss said louder.

Rosenthal inclined his head and left.

Zierling said, "Sit down, Brian. It seems you've become an issue."

Before Kuhl could move, Weiss said, "Captain, your invasion is not yet successful. This is still my office."

"My apologies, Governor. Brian, wait for him to ask you to sit."

Weiss colored. He brusquely motioned for Kuhl to take the chair alongside Zierling's. He continued the gesture, bringing his hand through tightly-curled black hair, then down, to massage the tic that had developed in the right side of his face.

"You presence here is the only issue, Captain," Weiss continued, his voice strained. "We washed our hands of you one hundred twenty-one years ago when the *Ivri* came to this desolate place. Just seven years after that you marooned us here. But we surprised you, Captain, by surviving."

"By now your computers have all the data on the Portal War," Zierling said tiredly. "We transmitted pictures as well as words. If you look at them you can see what was done to us. Forgive me, but Relayer was relatively unscathed."

He waved his hand. "None of this matters. You took our first homeland from us. Now this is our home, and you will not take it from us."

"I told you Jerusalem still exists. If you want, you can—"

The bottle of wine stood forgotten on a corner of his desk. "I read enough of your data to see that Jerusalem is now a pastown, an amusement park. We will not live in an amusement park." He turned to Kuhl. "You are the propagandist?"

Kuhl made his face hard. "I'm a freelance media producer."

"Tell me about your work. Briefly."

"Most of my work in the last three years has focused on ecological changes brought about by the Portal War. I've covered Europe, part of Africa, and was the first journalist admitted to People's Asia in five decades.''

Weiss waved him to silence. ''People's Asia?'' He shook his head. ''No, it doesn't matter. What little I know of your history reads like a thousand volumes of nightmare compressed into one chapter—all brought on yourselves. You think you are wise enough to sit in judgment of what we've done here, Mister Kuhl?''

''I can observe what you've done.''

''A robot could do that.''

''Would a robot see the *sitra achra*?''

Weiss kept his face blank.

''There is more than one gulf between us, *chaver*,'' Kuhl said. ''There is one of space and time—and also the one that exists between our two cultures.''

''The *sitra achra* means 'the other side.' '' Some of the anger had gone from Weiss's voice. ''Which side is 'the other' here?''

''Neither?'' Zierling suggested.

Weiss looked at her sourly. ''Captain, we hardly shared the same world centuries ago. By now we are as alien to one another as we are to the monsters you say caused the Portal War. Get on with your business. We will speak more of this later.''

''Will our equipment be returned to us?'' Kuhl asked.

''I had it brought to your quarters. You will ask for guidance, and use discretion, in your operations. I don't want either military or civilian personnel disrupting our way of life in Masada. To do so would endanger us, and that I will not allow.''

Zierling rose from her seat. ''There is one place I would like to see at once, Councilman: the Portal.''

His look darkened. ''We have no Portal.''

''The site of the Portal, then. The StarForce ended the Portal War a century ago, but the threat is still out there, somewhere. We have to learn all we can about the Portals, the creatures who built them, and the monsters who used them against us. The Portal on Earth was obliterated. Those on the other worlds we've recontacted have usually fared a little better.''

Weiss steepled his fingers. ''Of course, we have only your word that there were such monsters. . . .'' He shrugged, while Zierling glared and bit her lower lip to choke off a retort. ''This request I will grant. You will be taken down below, to the well of our troubles. But there is nothing you will learn, Captain. We have spent a very long time looking into that well.''

Weiss stood, waving his hand negligently. ''You will see the Portal later today. After that, remember that you have a guest's privileges and responsibilities ... until the meeting of our Select Council next week. At that time your privileges may be extended or curtailed. My own recommendation to the board will depend upon your conduct over the next several days.''

''I'm sure your recommendation will be fair,'' Zierling said. She reached into a slash pocket and brought forth a slim metal case small enough to fit in her palm. ''Here is the historical documentary we discussed earlier, Councilman, in a format compatible with your projectors.''

When Weiss made no move to take it, she set it on the edge of his desk.

''We will review it before deciding on a presentation,'' Weiss said. He looked at the tape as if it were something unpleasant.

# Chapter Seven

Zierling solemnly closed the office door behind them, then grinned.

"How did it go, Captain?" Krause asked, standing.

Zierling turned to Kuhl. "I had no idea you were such a diplomat."

"I'm afraid I've exhausted most of my Hebrew vocabulary," Kuhl answered seriously. "Captain, I cannot be dictated to. If he is going to impose strict censorship, you may as well send me and the rest of the team back to *Belfast* and stasis-sleep."

"I'm sure that won't be necessary."

Raviv edged closer. "Captain? There's someone to—"

"What about our cameras?" Aubrecht asked. "When do we—?"

"You will find your equipment in your rooms," a woman's voice said stiffly. Zierling looked across the anteroom, surprised. She had not noticed the stranger; Kuhl had, and appeared not to have.

She was tall, her form camouflaged by an ill-fitting dress cut from dull, copper-colored fabric. Tightly-curled black hair framed a pale, drawn face. She crossed the room in long strides and extended her hand to Zierling.

Weiss's sister, Kuhl thought.

"Judith Weiss," the woman said. "All of your belongings have been brought to your quarters. Mister Rosenthal is taking the *akavish*—the vehicle in which you arrived—to your shuttlecraft to take on more passengers and supplies. I will bring you to your rooms now."

Belatedly, Zierling took Weiss's hand. She smiled with some warmth. "Your brother said you would bring us to the Portal."

Weiss glanced toward his office door. Then she said, "We will go to your rooms, first, then the Portal. The devil's device has not changed in a century and more; it will wait a few minutes for your inspection."

Zierling inclined her head.

\*　　\*　　\*

Judith Weiss led them along the narrow corridor behind her brother's office. They passed no one in the hall.

"Lepers again," Aubrecht said, loud enough for everyone to hear.

Kuhl, walking abreast of Weiss, saw her face color. She walked faster, the shapeless dress flapping around long thighs. The others hurried to keep up. Kuhl lagged until Aubrecht drew even with him, then he brought her up short.

"I'm not sure," he told her quietly, "but I think Captain Zierling would accept my recommendation to return you to sleep."

She shrugged him off. "Count on my sister sleeping, too. You always were a snotty kid, Kuhl. You haven't changed."

"Better to be short two camera operators than have the mission crippled by your loose mouth."

"You try to run things tight, don't you?"

"Not another word."

She started to say something, and Kuhl made his face grow cold and tight-skinned. She subsided, smoldering.

They caught up with the others at a door which had not been open when they had come this way before. "This is more direct," Weiss said, waving them through.

Rich, steamy air lapped Kuhl's face. Instinctively he breathed deep, reveling in the moist, earthy texture of the corridor. Vines trailed from the roof, twisting along pocked concrete walls. The light striking indirectly through the foliage brought the sweat out on his face.

The hall went silent. The sounds of blades striking into earth, the babble of other languages, faded.

Kuhl looked at the nearest of the men. He was about fifteen, with glossy black hair and a round, Asiatic face. His hands were tangled in the sticky string he was using to wrap a broken stem. He stood slowly, his eyes fixed on Kuhl's, silent.

Behind the man the scene was repeated identically, as if seen again and again in opposing mirrors. The Chinese working in the hall wore uniforms of black shorts and loose gold shirts shot through with iridescent threads. Their expressions, too, were identical.

A flash of color erupted from the roof. Kuhl ducked the jeweled bird, which chittered down the hall and out of sight around a curve. Its cries echoed, and after it had gone condensation dripped audibly from the broad leaves of succulents sprouting from channels along either wall.

"This is Relayer, too," Weiss said.

From behind them came an angry burst of Hebrew. Kuhl turned just in time to sidestep the bent, skullcapped man who brushed past him. Weiss smiled and said something that sounded conciliatory. The man looked straight at Kuhl, fumes rising from the handrolled cigarette trailing from one corner of his mouth. He said something else, the cigarette waggling with each alien syllable.

Zierling put her head close to Kuhl's. "What's being said?"

"The only word I caught from her was *n'vaker*—visitor. I think he was upset the work stopped."

Weiss said something else, smiling.

The old man let his cigarette fall from his mouth and stamped it into the moist dirt. He took Kuhl's hand in his dry claws, a grin splitting his seamed face.

*"Shalom, shalom."*

Weiss spoke, pointing to Zierling. The old man looked blank, then embarrassed. Hastily he disengaged himself from Kuhl and, taking Zierling's hand, kissed it.

"Thank you," he said in a fractured voice. "Thank you for coming for so long."

Zierling took his hands in her own.

"You're very welcome," she said quietly.

Around them, the leafy walls echoed with a sudden happy babble.

Their rooms were solemn and dusty. Kuhl expected cobwebs, but found only mildew in the corners. A main room held a table and chairs draped with plastic sheets. An arch opened onto a kitchen. One doorway led to the main corridor, two others to halls and other gray compartments.

Weiss flipped a toggle on the wall near the entrance. Overhead fixtures glowed uncertainly.

"We call this the empty quarter," she said, a note of apology creeping into her stern voice.

Hwang plucked at a sheet translucent with age. "This then is our first assignment," he said.

"We could not spare anyone for housekeeping. Now that you are actually here, we will send who we can. A century ago these rooms were filled, but not since then. With the Portal gone, the colony could not support so many."

"And now?" Zierling asked.

"Now, with everyone working, over two thousand of us live. Some of the things we were formerly accustomed to weakened us, and now they are gone." She touched the light switch. "This."

"Does it make you stronger to throw a switch than to have the light open when you come into the room?" asked Hwang.

"When you can repair the mechanical switch and not the computer-driven relay you have strength where there was weakness. You will see the same all over Masada."

"Has any part of your Portal survived?" asked Raviv.

"Ruins," said Weiss. "There is a storeroom down that hall with supplies we felt you would need immediately: linens, kitchen store, similar items. We will share food with you, to the limits we can. How many people do you expect to bring down to Masada?"

"Several dozen," Zierling said. "We have our own food and some water aboard *Belfast*. We'll try not to be a burden."

"I'm sure," Weiss said.

Zierling started to say something, then closed her mouth. Someone had knocked on the door.

Raviv, closest, went to answer it. The door opened before she reached it; a half-dozen men entered the room. All were fairly young, and wore skullcaps and similar sullen expressions.

"Neil?" Weiss said to one of them, and the rest was a blur of Hebrew. All six started to speak to her at once.

"The others looked happy enough to see us," Zierling commented. "Or does their language always sound like that?"

"They're angry," Raviv said. "I'm not sure about what. It's hard to make a lot of things out. This doesn't sound at all like what they fed me in language classes."

Neil said something angrily; it made Weiss blush. He pushed past her, heading straight for Zierling.

"Can I do something for you, Citizen?" she asked pleasantly.

"We are the Steering Committee of the League of Zion, Captain Zierling. We are here to—"

"That means nothing to me, I'm afraid," she said, all contrite. "What's your name, son?"

"It—I am Neil Wolfram."

"Well, Neil, I'm fairly tired. I've been up in *Belfast* for the larger part of a year—making sure everything was right for our visit here, you know—and I'm not used to even the lighter gravity you have here. Why don't you come back and talk to me later in the week, when I can better appreciate what you've got to say?"

"I—"

"I would certainly appreciate it, Neil." Dumbly, he took her extended hand. "Thanks very much, Neil."

He flushed, then turned on his heel, barking an order to the others. They trailed him out of the room. After the door closed, Kuhl heard harsh laughter in the hall.

Zierling folded her arms. Weiss studied her.

"Well?" the captain said. "I don't speak a word of Hebrew, but it was plain to me he didn't have a fair hearing in mind. As a Forcer I had my rights read to me often enough so I can see it coming now, no matter what the language. Am I right, Miss Weiss?"

"They had legitimate questions."

"It didn't look like they asked you anything very legitimate. You should have seen the look on your face."

Weiss colored again.

"What were they going to ask me? Why it took us so long to get back to you people? Who started the war? Who ended it? Did it really happen? And *why*? There's time enough to answer questions like that. The time is not when my feet hurt. Right now I'm more interested in inspecting the Portal and your debarkation center, and then seeing about getting these rooms habitable."

"There is nothing down there."

"Nevertheless," said Zierling.

"It would be a mistake for you to go down," Weiss said tightly. "For years after our holocaust the people held out hope that the Portal would open again. It never did. The air grew stale. Fruit grew colorless and crops thin. Now you have come and there will be hope again that the door to Earth will reopen."

"I'm sorry," said Zierling.

Weiss was silent for a moment. Then she said, "All right. But only you, Captain. And this time we *will* act as lepers, and try not to be seen. The people must have more time to adapt to your presence, and there must be more time to explain that our world will not change overnight because of your being here."

"It will change," Zierling said. "For the better. We've brought supplies, our skills, and knowledge. We *can* help you."

"We won't be a colony again," Weiss said. "Now you wanted to see the Portal and we're still speaking."

"I have to bring an assistant, Forcer Raviv."

Weiss pressed her lips together so the blood left them. Then she nodded once, abruptly.

Kuhl watched them walk to the door. He looked around, saw Marella's gaze on him, and Frings's.

"Captain?" He stepped forward. "And me."

Zierling started to shake her head, but Weiss said, clipped, "I have other duties. You three, and no more."

The two Basques at the mouth of the corridor wore black pants and gray shirts that looked like uniforms. Weiss spoke to them and they let her, Zierling, Raviv, and Kuhl pass.

Only every third overhead panel glowed. Their light picked out a pattern of vertical scars etched deep in the cement walls.

Fifty meters down the hall they came to a steel-mesh barrier stretching from floor to ceiling. The narrow gate was locked. A Hebrew man sat behind a small metal desk on the other side, reading from a stack of loose hardcopy. He stood when Weiss approached, and showed annoyance when Kuhl set his camera on its shoulder mount and slapped a datacube into it. Kuhl frowned back at the guard, who opened the gate with obvious reluctance.

"Is there anything valuable down here?" Kuhl asked Weiss.

"Hope. Every new generation has had a few in it who thought they could find the secret to unlock the Portal. But there is no secret, and the fence is here to prevent anyone harming themselves by looking for it. Few go down there anymore, only scholars and, so they will know what happened, schoolchildren."

After twenty meters the tunnel widened. The scars in the walls gouged deeper, to the rusting structural rods beneath. Kuhl brought the stalk-mounted crosshairs over his eye and sighted along the fissures. The camera did all the rest, recording the scene as professionally as it would have in Aubrecht's hands.

"The moment the Portal collapsed, all Relayer knew," Judith Weiss said. "A hurricane of hot air blasted out through the three major corridors and five maintenance tunnels leading into the terminal. The outrush lasted less than a minute, but by the end of that time a hundred people had been injured by flying debris. The thirty-five people in the terminal were killed instantly. We never found their bodies, but a plaque marking their grave lies in another corridor." Kuhl panned along the wall. "In spots, sir," said Weiss, "there are blood stains."

He set his jaw and pushed the eyepiece away from his face.

Overhead lighting panels gave way to naked bulbs strung along the ceiling. The footing was treacherous; cracked floor slabs and loose gravel slid, rasping.

"Watch your head, Mister Kuhl."

The steel blast-door had been peeled apart and flattened against the ceiling.

"More than wind did this," Zierling said, ducking under the wreckage.

"We think so," Weiss agreed. "But we do not know what."

The tunnel fell away to bits of masonry and stale darkness. A wooden balcony thrust into a fathomless space. Kuhl put his hand on the untrustworthy railing, steadying himself. Weiss touched a switch; a generator whined and light flickered from a hundred pinpoints.

The space revealed was a misshapen cube twenty or thirty meters on a side. The concrete floor, a dozen meters below, had melted, then congealed into a pattern of concentric waves. The walls had frozen in mid-splash. Flecks of steel glistened, dripping from the ceiling like spittle in a dry mouth.

In the center of the room stood a deep black pool. Flawless blue metal formed an open latticework canopy. A faint wind blowing toward the sable well touched the sweat from Kuhl's face.

"It still works," Zierling breathed. Her right hand fell to her hip, where a wiregun holster would have hung. She dropped her hand to her side, trembling.

Weiss said, "No. It does not."

A wobbling stairway brought them to the rippled floor. Kuhl paused halfway down the steps, letting the datacube soak up the scene.

Zierling crossed the uneven floor, reaching out to touch the blue metal. At the last moment she drew back.

"It's all right," Weiss told her.

Zierling stroked the substance. "What is this? It feels oily . . . but it's not."

"Outstepper metal." (Zierling snatched her hand back.) "It has never been analyzed, but it's very strong. We haven't been able to scar it."

"Not strong enough to've stood up to the fusion blasts that took out the Omaha Portal, I guess." She grasped the metal to anchor herself and leaned far over the pool, one leg stretched back for counterbalance. After a moment she stepped back, shaking her head. "Where does it go? Nowhere?"

"It is not a Portal."

"I know that. The Portal was a dome. It probably filled this frame. This looks like a Portal after someone let all the air out of it."

"In the month following the holocaust," said Weiss, "we sent through written messages, animals, and one volunteer. We received no replies." She looked around, then walked a few meters and picked up a long, thin piece of twisted metal. She pushed the rod halfway into the black pool. "Then we discovered this.'' She withdrew the metal. All that had fallen below the surface of the pool was gone. The end gleamed. ''My understanding is the Portal did not work that way. The object should pass into the other world, then return here undamaged. It's as if it's . . . unfocused.''

Kuhl stepped closed. ''What happened to the room?''

''At the same time your war occurred, this room was destroyed, the people in it vaporized. You've told us you bombed your Portal to stop the destruction. Is it possible the blast reached us here?''

''Don't see how,'' Zierling said, not really listening. A shelf about one meter square and less than a centimeter thick jutted from one arch at waist level. It, and the varicolored panels embedded in it, were also untouched by the blast. Zierling went to touch them, then changed her mind.

''This is not the same as on the other worlds you've visited, is it?'' Weiss asked.

''No. None of the other colonial Portals exhibited the blast effect you have here,'' Zierling said. ''None of the others have this field, this remnant of the Portal. There's just the empty framework of metal.''

''Then you have seen the substance before.''

''StarForce personnel have. I haven't. This is my first recontact mission.''

''And you expected . . . what? The alien generals who started the Portal War? A way to reach them? An answer? There is nothing here for you, Captain, as I said.''

''Don't be too sure,'' Zierling said. ''We'll want samples of the metal.''

''If you can cut it, it is yours, subject to Simon's approval.''

Zierling ran her hand over the twin brushes of hair on top of her head. ''We don't have anyone on *Belfast* with the expertise to study that field of force. For all I know, cutting into the framework could destabilize it somehow. We could lose it.''

''Do what you wish, Captain.''

''That field's been there since the day of the war?''

''Yes, Captain.''

''Then I guess it'll stay here awhile longer. We'll send some of our researchers down from *Belfast* later, Miss Weiss, but we'll leave the Outstepper metal untouched for now. Could we get some kind of cover for that control panel? If that's what it is.''

''No one comes down here anymore. And the control panel—if

that is what it is—is inoperative. Many people have touched the keypad over the years. Nothing happens.''

"All the same, I'd hate to lose that—"

Weiss's mouth hardened. "Don't you think we thoroughly explored the possibility that it could be made to *work?*"

Kuhl stepped out of her way. Then he retracted the camera's eyepiece, knocked down the shoulder mount, and stowed the gear in its padded shoulder bag. Then, tentatively, he reached out and touched the arch. The blue metal the Outsteppers had made reflected the palm of his hand as his outstretched fingers met the oily, warm surface.

He looked through the empty latticework, frowning, trying to see within it the dome of night, the doorway to Earth . . . and failed. A portal onto infinity. The corridors of Relayer linked to a great hall on Earth.

It was only four generations ago, he thought. The evidence of that age was before him, a kind of latticework temple to old gods . . . and on Earth there was a crater in the midwest, the roof of a hot sky, and rumors of cockatrices stalking the citadels' perimeters.

Zierling and Weiss clattered up the untrustworthy steps.

It was four generations ago, Kuhl thought, turning away from the dead metal thing. Let it go, Maya.

Judith Weiss steered them away from the major passageways, avoiding the urgent bustle. At the door to the Earthmen's quarters, she paused.

"I hope this has been of some service to you, Captain, even if you found no monsters."

She sees it, too, Kuhl thought.

"They're out there, Miss Weiss," Zierling said. "If anyone should know that—even better than someone raised in a Triumviratine citadel—it should be one of you, here on Relayer."

"As you say." Weiss turned to go, but Zierling called her back.

"Yes, Captain?"

"Judith—if I can call you that—I may not look it, but I'm old enough to be your grandmother. Even though I'm beginning to understand what your people have gone through in the past hundred and fourteen years, that doesn't mean I'm sympathetic to being sold a bill of goods. You can save your long-suffering attitude for someone who hasn't flown over Omaha, or seen the reports on the colonies that fared less well than yours."

"You, Captain, have never suffered. Not as we have."

"Maybe not. That doesn't mean I have to swallow you treating me as a paranoid. None of us are, and I hope it doesn't take an alien battlewagon in orbit overhead to convince you of that."

Weiss said nothing.

Zierling jerked her thumb toward the door leading to their rooms. "And another thing. Have you sent anyone down to help us with that mess?"

"It would be difficult to—" Weiss began icily, but Zierling cut her off.

"And," Zierling said, "keep hooligans like Wolfram away from us, will you?"

Weiss seemed about to speak, then apparently thought better of it. She turned and walked stiffly down the corridor.

Kuhl said, "Captain, was that . . . diplomatic?"

"There's a difference between diplomacy and stupidity. I'm pretty sure which side of the line she was pushing me onto."

"You're disappointed, aren't you?"

She looked at him, eyes cold, and said, "Is that going to be part of your story, Brian, my department's paranoia?"

He shook his head. "But I'm getting the impression that the recontact itself is almost secondary, as if you're on some kind of search-and-destroy—"

"Not 'almost,'" Zierling said.

He followed her into their quarters.

Storage sacks and crates tumbled across one another in disorderly piles across the floor. Packing materials rustled underfoot. Forcers newly arrived from the shuttle, their faces vaguely familiar, carried the supplies into adjoining rooms. Shouted orders, an angry voice, echoed from the hallways.

Marella and Hwang sat in a relatively quiet corner, looking unhappy, until they saw Kuhl come into the room. They waded to him through the confusion and debris.

"Did you get it down on cube?" Marella said. "Did you have any problems with the camera?"

"I've shot a few scenes before, Paul." He slipped the strap off his shoulder and handed the bag absently to Hwang.

"It just looked like you were having a little trouble with it," Marella continued.

"I usually use a set of my customized cameras, but they're too delicate to bring into a field situation like this. I told you I got the scene down on cube. There wasn't much to see. Our story's going to be the people here." He glanced at Frings. "Load the cube, copy it, then get it onto the shuttle for *Belfast* before it leaves. We'll handle all our shots that way: get them onto the ship as soon as possible, but keep a copy here for safekeeping."

"Yes, Citizen," Hwang said.

Someone rapped sharply on the door opening onto the corridor. Zierling, who had been speaking to Sidni Raviv, looked up, annoyed. "Sidni, see who the hell that is. First we're *persona non grata* and then—"

"It's help, Captain," Raviv called. A thick-bodied Chinese woman and a tall, slender man entered.

The man's skin was the color of soot, his hair tightly kinked.

"I was told you people may need help adapting your equipment to our power supply," he said in a deep, melodic voice. He held his hand out to Kuhl, who only then realized the black man had been speaking to him. Kuhl took the hand and briefly shook it.

"Allan Webber," said the black man. "This is my wife, Yuan Ch'ing."

"Pleased," Kuhl said, realizing he had been staring and that, in another moment, the black man would realize it as well. The conversation sure to follow would go something like this:

*Haven't you ever seen a black man before?*

*No. Well, in pictures. Most of them are dead now, and all of the others are in the LoSide. And we put all your wife's people on the other side of the world where, historically, they've always been. Very orderly.*

Zierling smiled at the strangers, either nonplussed or a better actor than he. She introduced herself, adding, "I'm the one giving the orders, I'm afraid."

"I'm sorry, I—"

"It's Brian's air of authority. We're very glad to get your help."

Webber looked around. "I can see that. They didn't put theirselves out for you."

"They?" Zierling echoed.

"Oh, the Hebes. It's just *tirtur*. Letting you know who's boss."

"I thought it might be something like that," Zierling said.

"Yuan Ch'ing and me get it all the time." He turned to her and said something in Chinese. She said something back, smiling. "She feels sorry for you," Webber said. "Maybe they'll accept you sometime. For now . . . the high priestess said something about you needing electricity?"

"I'll get Abe Hwang," Kuhl said. He found the old man in another room, peering into the guts of a wall socket.

"Do you think you should be meddling with that?"

Hwang stood and dusted off his knees. "I'm afraid I don't know enough about it to be sure."

"There's someone here who can help you out. A technician of some kind."

"Oh?" Hwang raised one eyebrow, grinning. "I haven't seen one since I was in the Sudd with the Aubrechts. You were there about two years ago, weren't you, Citizen Kuhl?"

"Of course," Kuhl said. (He had forgotten.)

"I almost slipped myself," Zierling admitted.

"Simon Weiss is against us as it is," Kuhl said. "There must be a lot of people here who feel as he does. If they do find out about the Night, after we've kept it from them . . . It's insane."

"It was the course of action laid out for us." But she looked unhappy herself.

The air in their rooms was merely stale now. The floors and walls shone. They sat on a formfit couch brought from *Belfast*. From the next room he heard people laughing, glasses tinkling.

"Don't you drink?" Zierling asked.

"I never acquired a taste for alcohol."

"It *is* an acquired taste."

"It seemed pointless to try to choke it down. I always had better things to do with my time. What are we going to do about the Terminal Night?"

"I wish there were something we could do about it."

"That's not what I meant."

"I know. If I saw a clear course of action better than the one the Synody gave us, I'd take it. But nothing is clear to me so far. Weiss tolerates us. So does this other one, his sister. That old Hebrew man looked at us as if we were angels. And then there's Webber. I thought you were going to run screaming from the room when he came in. And those kids in the little hats."

"You handled them pretty well."

"I've got just one trick, and I use it when I have to. If you're sweet to them they may think you're lying, but if you take their hand and smile it's almost as if they have something invested in you, as if they want to believe you're their friend. David Berry taught me that. I didn't think I'd be using the trick this much. I'll have to find another one soon." She frowned. "I'm supposed to act as plenipotentiary to their government. Is Weiss their government?"

"He acted as if he were."

"I can't see someone like Webber taking orders from someone like Simon Weiss." She stood and paced the floor, scattering debris left from the unpacking. "I can't see any of these people taking direction from anyone, including from Triumviratine Earth."

"We've been here less than twelve hours, Captain Zierling."

"You're right. It's too early to tell. But I have a gut feeling."

"Maybe there's something you're forgetting. They're still alive, which means they are somehow cooperating."

She nodded. "The Basques do the outside work and heavy labor. The Chinese take care of the agriculture. The blacks maintain the electrical and mechanical systems, except for the geothermal plant, which I guess the Hebrews operate. And the Hebrews somehow keep it all running together. So we're back to the original question. Somewhere along the line, Allan Webber takes orders from Simon Weiss."

"They have to in order to live."

"There's been many times in history when, given the choice, men chose to die instead." She shrugged and jammed her hands into her coveralls' slash pockets, stretching the fabric taut. "But . . . we won't settle this tonight. Damn it. I hate things being unsettled."

"You're not going to find any monsters here," Kuhl said quietly, standing. "That much is settled, Maya. I think your superiors told you that you'd find them here—somewhere out here, in space. But the Portals went everywhere. The enemy could be on the other side of the galaxy and never reach us. They might be extinct. Or disinterested. What would be the purpose of the StarForce then, if you're not interested in recontact for its own sake?"

Her gaze narrowed, her lips thinned as she glared at him. Then she turned away, her narrow back rigid. Kuhl put his hands on her shoulders, felt the smooth play of muscles there.

[No.]

Sara would have said that.

Maya was, conservatively, twice Kearin Seacord's age. She had been an infant when the walls of the citadels rose up around the enclaves. Fine lines gave her face the texture of old porcelain, and there were touches of gray in the smooth pelt of her close-cropped hair. But her step was light and her eyes were like Sara's, the color of a summer storm.

Sara was the perfect companion.

But Sara was not here.

She shrugged him off and, in the same motion, turned. She smiled, but without warmth.

It was Seacord's heart which closed like a fist.

It was Kuhl's mouth which answered her cool smile with his own.

"You're right, I should put it out of my mind," she said. "Let's go have a—" She caught herself. "Let's join the others."

Kuhl said, "All right, Captain Zierling."

The next day, Kuhl sent Hwang and Marella down to the agricultural tunnel they had passed through the day before.

"Try to get acquainted with the situation here," Kuhl told Marella. "I'll be doing some research. Any problems, get in touch with me."

He went back to his room and went through his bags, looking for the camera's operations manual. Sitting on the bed, Kuhl went through it, until someone knocked on the door. He pulled a meter-square schematic sheet for one of Jon Frings's sound mixers over the manual, then reached across the bed and opened the door.

Sidni Raviv stood in the doorway. "Someone outside to see you." She glanced at the schematic, its spidery lines and illegible legends. "You've been at that awhile, and it's late."

"If I understand how it works, I can get more out of the equipment. Who's here?"

"It's the man who was here yesterday. The black man."

Kuhl found Allan Webber in the kitchen off the main room, sitting at the table. Looking obscurely uncomfortable, he stood when Kuhl entered.

"What can I do for you, Mister Webber?"

"It's my two-in-ten. Thought I'd see how you were getting by. Looks like you've got most of fifty years of dirt off the floor."

"It's almost habitable," Kuhl agreed.

"You've got a basker outside, you know. Like a guard."

"We can come and go as we please, though. Two of our people went down to the agricultural section a few hours ago to film."

"Judy Weiss take you? Or one of hers?"

"Someone from Simon Weiss's office," Kuhl acknowledged. He was about to tell Webber to get to the point (as Sara would have had him do) but he clamped back on the words. The tightness in Webber's face indicated that there was, indeed, a point.

"I was thinking," Webber said, "not all of your people are down yet, am I right?"

"Twenty more Forcers are coming down tomorrow, and the rest of my team will be with them."

"It seems to me you'll be busy then, Mister Kuhl. They'll want to show you where the Portal was, the power plant—and how they kept it going all by themselves—down to the mining level, up the farm corridors. But me, I thought you might want to see something else before they got you all sewed up. I thought you might want to see where me and Yuan Ch'ing live. We could talk a bit."

"All right, Mister Webber."

"Al. I'll wait for you outside—we won't go out together. You go out your door, take one left and another, and I'll be waiting there. Bring your camera."

Webber's apartment was on the periphery of Liberty, itself a corridor on the edge of the colony, 450 meters long, two levels thick, forty meters wide. The only exit from the apartment was a translucent plastic door a centimeter thick. Sound carried through it clearly in both directions. The ceiling and two walls were naked rock that wept when the humidity controls malfunctioned.

"*Tirtur*," said Webber, "is a kind of prolonged harassment. The routine calls that come in the middle of the night when you're trying to sleep after one double shift and before another. The breakdowns in the apartment. Hot water, electricity, ventilation. Yuan Ch'ing woke me up one night because there was smoke coming right out of that vent over there. I work on the systems, I know there's no way it could have happened by mistake. Nowhere for the smoke to come from. Then, at work, you do a job and come back to it and find it's been done over wrong—and there's the supervisor standing there looking at it, waiting for you. Missing tools—they charge you for them, you know. A bolt dropped from a catwalk. If you remembered to wear your hardhat that day, it won't kill you, but it hurts. Of course, they don't want to kill you."

"Why, then?"

He signaled Aubrecht to come in close for the tight shot.

"It's Yuan Ch'ing and me, for one. The people in Liberty and T'ai-nan don't like us being together. But Yuan Ch'ing is their own and I'm a Liberty man so they won't hurt us. But in Masada they say it's wrong and they want to be sure we know. There's other reasons. Yuan Ch'ing doesn't like working in the farms. She wanted to learn maintenance work, like I do, so she came around to me. I taught her on her days off—two days in ten— and now she's as good at it as me, almost. But she'll never get certification for systems maintenance, and if one of the Hebes sees her on a job with me, he chases her off. We were married three years ago.'' He sat back in a worn and musty chair. ''You want another beer? How about a cigarette? Home grown.''

''No, thank you.'' The taste of the last brew was still thick on his tongue.

''You, Miss Aubrecht?''

''Thanks, I think I will.''

When Webber came back, Kuhl said, ''We'll return to what you were talking about in a minute. I want a bit of history now.''

''What I know of it, sure. Go ahead.''

''When did you start calling Relayer Liberty and the Hebrews calling it Masada?''

Webber looked at him uncomprehendingly. Then he laughed, the sound ricocheting from the low ceiling. ''Relayer is the rock itself, my friend. Liberty is *here*, and Masada—'' He shook his head. ''Look, draw yourself a picture. You've got the original colony, right? It's shaped like a cake, five layers through and nearly a kilometer across. The top layer is right below the surface. In the middle of the bottom layer is the power plant and right above that is where the Portal used to be. Within a year after they came here, more room was needed, if you can believe it, so they built a tunnel straight out from level three of the cake, northern quadrant. That's Biscay now, where all the baskers—the Basques—went to live. This is the second tunnel, Liberty, across the cake from Biscay. A vein of gold thick as a river used to run here. They took the gold out and my people moved in. That left the Hebes and the Chinese all mixed together, but gradually the Israelis, they settled onto the bottom two levels where they could keep a grip on the power plant. The Chinese moved to the top two levels. Now everyone's got a lot of room.''

''And where we live? The empty quarter?''

''It goes through level one and two, which was part of Masada until the die-back. We've got extra room in Liberty, and the baskers don't use the outside half of their tunnel. Up in T'ai-nan they took out the walls between every two apartments and spread out a little.''

''Wouldn't it make more sense to have everyone move back into the central core and close down the tunnels? You wouldn't have to push the air as far, you'd have less maintenance on your lines, and the compartments in the core seem to be better furnished.''

Webber chuckled. ''That's for damned sure. But, friend, it's *worth* it, not having the Hebes and the baskers around, staring and poking around and asking why you don't do things this way or that.'' He took another swallow of beer. ''And do you think they'd let a black man and his chink wife live in Masada? Course, it must be different back on old Earth. How many people does that ship of yours hold?''

''Seventy-five to eighty,'' Kuhl said.

''Maybe when you leave, friend, you'll have room for Allan Webber and his lady.''

''Where is Yuan Ch'ing, Mister Webber?'' Aubrecht asked. ''I thought she'd be here to talk to us, too.''

''You'd think after three years of marriage we'd be able to get the same two days out of ten off, wouldn't you? She's breaking her back over a hoe right now.''

''What reason do they have for not changing the schedule?'' Kuhl asked.

''They always have a reason. But I know it's *tirtur*. Now you know, too.''


It was late when they left Webber's apartment, and the corridor lights were dimmed to simulate night. The thin doors of the other compartments murmured with the life they concealed; Kuhl's footsteps rang on worn plastic; Aubrecht's camera banged rhythmically against her hip.

''What did you think of that?'' she asked quietly. ''Man's got a very *wide* case of statism, don't you think?''

''We're just supposed to take down what he says, not judge it,'' Kuhl said. ''Like bugs on a wall.''

''What we put on the screen, right. But we're entitled to our own opinions, too.''

''I suppose,'' Kuhl said, and left her hanging until she realized he would not answer more fully. But he had observed how Webber's tone of voice was like his LoSide friend Rag's when he was on a jag about the Peacemakers.

''I don't like this,'' Aubrecht said after a moment.

''What?''

''The dark. Are we going the right way?''

''We started at one end of the corridor; we just have to go to the other.'' But, in the semidarkness, the flimsy wall-panels and rough stone ceiling did look unfamiliar.

His eyes picked out movement ahead. His pulse quickened even as he thought, Don't be stupid.

''You scared the hell out of me,'' Aubrecht muttered as David Rosenthal stepped into better light.

"It is good to be alert in this place," Rosenthal said. "This is not a good place for you to be when the lights are dark. I'll lead you back to your rooms, if you like."

Kuhl followed grudgingly. "What makes this place different from anywhere else on Relayer?"

"The black men live here," Rosenthal answered simply. "If your skin is white, you are their enemy." He smiled gently. "It sounds very simplistic to you, but they are not complicated people."

They passed an invisible boundary; the corridor widened and brightened. "Now you are in friendly territory," Rosenthal said. He pointed, "Your rooms are that way."

"Thanks," Aubrecht said flatly.

"There is a thing to remember," Rosenthal said. His smile lacked both enthusiasm and sincerity. "You can never be their friend, but they can turn you against your true friends."

Kuhl said, "I'll try to remember."

# Chapter Eight

Frings and Marella had taken over one of the smaller rooms, cleaned it to antiseptic standards, and hung a *verboten* sign on the door. Inside were two small desks and three walls of shelving. Cameras, less readily identifiable gear, and spare parts filled the steel racks. Over one desk were arrayed the soft plastic pockets holding the recorded datacubes.

"You're doing a good job," Kuhl said, as if grudgingly. He plucked one of the cubes from its pocket and held it up to the light. The cube was completely transparent; the molecular distortions the editing computers read were too subtle for him to see.

"The crew works hard," Marella said. He hunched over the desk, probing into an audio recorder Alistaire had said she'd been having trouble with. "You're damned lucky to have them."

Kuhl put the datacube back in its place.

"Are we going to take a crew down to the council meeting?" Marella asked.

"Captain Zierling doesn't want it. I doubt Weiss would allow it."

"Of course." Marella put his tools away and closed the recorder's access cover. "Whatever the captain wants."

Heat flared in Kuhl's face, matching the temper he knew he was supposed to feel. "You just do your job, Paul, and I—"

"And your real work starts when you take all the cubes back to Manchester and start editing them down. I know; you've told me." He turned his chair to face Kuhl. "I've seen your work. It's the best being broadcast today. But I'm damned if I know how you do it. From what I've seen, you could have saved yourself the trip here. You could have just reviewed the material when we brought it back to Earth."

"That's not my way," Kuhl snapped. "And it's not my place to get my hands dirty. That's your lookout. I watch." He turned to the door. "Coming to the meeting?"

\* \* \*

The corridors leading to the meeting room were crowded with knots of people. Blacks, Chinese, Basques, and Masadans spoke in low tones not loud enough to reach others, filling the halls with their murmuring. Zierling put a gentle, welcoming smile on her face and kept it there as far as the double doors leading to the council's chambers.

At the door were Basques in gray shirts and black pants. David Rosenthal spoke to one, then broke off when he saw the Triumviratines approaching.

"Captain," he said, nodding correctly.

"Mister Rosenthal." The smile slipped. "If I had known there was going to be an audience, I would have come with a prepared text."

"You assume the council's decision will be to let you continue your mission?" Rosenthal asked.

"*Two* prepared texts."

"I'm afraid the crowd is here for Mister Kuhl. Rather, his documentary. It will be shown here after the meeting."

Kuhl's heart surged. He kept his face blank as Rosenthal looked at him. "And from their decision to allow the documentary to be broadcast throughout the four cities, you can perhaps assume the council's decision on your mission." He smiled, in the same way he had smiled in the corridor outside Liberty.

"I'm flattered," Kuhl mumbled, putting a little insincerity into it. The feature was Sara's, and the face on the screen would not be his, but reconstruction. There was nothing of him in the documentary.

And nothing of the Terminal Night, either, he thought. Nothing of what had happened to the ancestors of the people here, those who had been left behind after Relayer had been purchased.

"The meeting will start soon," Rosenthal said.

A Basque smiled at Zierling and held the door open for her and the rest. The meeting room was long and wide; the low ceiling seemed poised to crush them. Public seating fanned out from the low dais at the front of the room. Four flags hung on the wall behind the table on the dais; four men sat beneath them.

The hall was otherwise nearly empty. Two Chinese boys sat far back in the left corner, whispering to each other. Each had a notebook and graphite marker. Students, Kuhl thought. In the front row sat an elderly black man with bent shoulders and salt-and-pepper hair. A few rows behind him sat a striking, dark-haired woman. As Kuhl and the others passed down the aisle to the front row, he saw the woman's crutch propped against the seat alongside her. Only one foot was visible below

the hem of her flowing skirt. He looked away and sat between
Zierling and Paoli Marella, a few meters from the black man,
who looked his way and smiled.

Kuhl nodded and smiled back blankly.

The Euskaldun at the head of the table stood wearily. He was
no taller than any other Basque Kuhl had seen, but weighed at
least 110 kilograms. His face was a fleshy mask, his eyes black
beads.

"I call this session of the Select Council of Relayer to order,"
he said thickly, in English. "As the first order of business, I
move a change in the rotation of chairmanship of this panel so
Mister Weiss can be chairman." He sat down heavily.

"Second the motion," said the man from Liberty quietly.

"Those favoring?" Three hands went up.

"Opposed?"

Weiss's hand stayed down. "I abstain from the voting, Mister
Chairman."

"The motion is carried. The chair, Mister Weiss."

Weiss stood. "As the first item of business," he said, glancing down at the table, "I move we welcome the crew of the
Triumviratine starship *Belfast* to Relayer orbit and bid all citizens
of Relayer extend their full cooperation in the endeavors of our
visitors, so long as they do not interfere with the smooth functioning of our world."

"Second," said the Basque.

"Discussion?"

"Who determines whether they have interfered?" the Chinese
asked almost apologetically.

"We do, Mister Hua," the Basque said. "This is understood.
That's why we are here, to provide direction. But, Mister
Chairman, I believe we should appoint a liaison between this
council and the officers of *Belfast*." He beamed broadly at
Zierling, who nodded politely.

"This is an administrative matter," Weiss said. "I'll take
your recommendation into consideration, Mister Souletin."

"I move the question," said the black man.

The Chinese opened his mouth, then closed it.

"Those in favor?" Three hands went up.

"Those opposed?" The Chinese left his hands folded neatly
before him.

Weiss looked out. "Welcome to Relayer."

Zierling stood. "From the crew and passengers of *Belfast*, our
thanks. I hope our stay will be to our mutual benefit." She sat
back.

The meeting stretched on. One by one, Weiss read from a stack of hardcopy sheets before him: unresolved maintenance complaints, which he referred, individually, to Mister William Cleveland of Liberty, chairman of the council's subcommittee on life-support services.

"Never heard of most of these before," Cleveland said sourly, halfway through the presentation.

"They should be taken care of anyway, Mister Cleveland."

"Didn't say I wouldn't take care of them."

Kuhl kept a count of the complaints. He imagined the colony lurching and creaking along, leaking from a dozen seams, and knew the image was false. They could not have lasted in that state for a century. More likely, things were gradually, but inevitably, getting worse. He would ask Allan Webber about it.

When discussion began on the Formosan councilman's request for a variance in food allotments in observation of the Chinese New Year, Zierling leaned close to Kuhl. With mild surprise, he caught a scent of flowers from her. "Do you think it would be impolite to leave?" she whispered.

"You'll miss the featured attraction."

"I've seen it." She smiled. "I'm not sure I want to be around when they see it. Let them digest it before they ask us how we could have 'allowed' the war to happen."

He nodded. "It should be safe to leave," he said. "They don't seem to be paying much attention to us." He drew his legs out of the aisle. "I'll stay a while longer."

Her face did not reveal disappointment. "Later," she said. Marella stood to let her out, then, glancing at Kuhl—who nodded—followed her out of the meeting room.

A half-hour later Weiss opened the meeting to questions from the floor. The dark-haired woman staggered upright on her crutches.

"My name is Deborah Wenzel. I live on level three, room four-fifty-six," she said in a hoarse voice.

"We recognize you, Mrs. Wenzel," Weiss said. "Is this about the special facilities?"

"I know you people have a lot to do," Wenzel said, "but it's very difficult for me to get around the apartment with things the way they are." She colored, but added loudly, "Especially the bathroom. And with a small child at home it's not any easier, believe me."

"Do your neighbors help you, Mrs. Wenzel?"

"There's only so much they can do. They can't help me to—well, there's certain things they can't help me with."

"I understand."

Kuhl wondered how long the woman had been waiting to have the leg replaced. Weeks? Months?

Weiss said to Cleveland, "How long will it be now, William?"

William opened a thick, bound stack of sheets. He ran his finger down a page toward the back. "We have a special order down at the mill for that replacement cam for the *akavish*. Then there's a new run of parts for the hydroponics. Then I've got a full week set aside to run the railings for Mrs. Wenzel's apartment."

"And when would that be?"

Cleveland pursed his lips and flipped back to the front of the book. "April," he said. "First part of April. And, of course, we'll have the crew to install them then. Rip out the plumbing if we have to, and put it back in a better arrangement."

"Thank you," Wenzel said, her voice breaking. She hobbled from the room.

Kuhl felt a vague nausea, as if he had eaten something too ripe. Railings?

"Are there any more matters brought by the public? If not, the select council will go into executive session at this point." Weiss looked at the two boys in the corner. "That means you young men will have to leave."

Kuhl followed them out. The air in the corridor seemed somehow sweeter, the atmosphere less oppressive. He breathed deep and looked both ways, through the crowds, trying to remember the way back to his room.

Judith Weiss moved through the press toward him, her face a little less severe than usual.

"Good day, Miss Weiss," Kuhl said. "Our paths haven't crossed lately."

"I was looking for you." She nodded to the door of the meeting room. "Is it over?"

"They're in closed session. Your brother was chairman today . . . I assume because he's dealt with us the most so far?"

"The other councilmen always defer to him. By charter, the chairmanship rotates, but Simon has been acting chairman for seven years, and our father was before him. They're probably discussing you in there, you know. Simon knows about the tour you and your camerawoman took of Liberty the other day. With less than twenty-five hundred people here, there are few secrets, Mister Kuhl."

"It wasn't illegal."

"It was probably ill advised. We'll have to wait and see about it." She looked around. The guard at the door smiled absently at her. "Why don't you come with me?"

He followed her along the corridor. It was not the way he had come. "Where are we going?"

"Where there is a little privacy."

They went up through Masada, then into the Chinese quarter. The corridors here were wider, the lighting more subdued. Cooking smells perfumed the air, and from behind each curtained doorway came the musical and (to him) senseless tones of Mandarin Chinese. The Orientals they passed in the halls smiled and nodded deferentially as they passed, saying nothing.

On the upper level, cold air wafted from a set of steep stairs leading upward. She went first, keeping her balance on the eroded cement steps. He noticed for the first time the simple white shift she wore, not dissimilar from what Sara wore around the apartment, though cut unfashionably long, to well below the knee.

Whatever this is, it's no rendezvous, he thought. Just the idea made him smile.

But the room they came into was dark.

Then he saw the stars shining beyond the clear canopy. It was night on Relayer, and they were on the surface.

The padded floor of the dome was warm, but the air remained chill. Frost rimed the apex of the glass panels meeting a meter overhead. Judith Weiss knelt, tucking her skirt around her knees. Kuhl sat cross-legged.

"And this is Relayer, too, Mister Kuhl."

The sides of a shallow stone bowl rose around them. A thin wind blew down from jagged peaks and around the dome. Wisps of visible gases flowed across the curved glass, torn, and reformed by unchartable crosscurrents. He looked up, his chest tight. The constellations would not be very different here from what they were in Boston's skies, but he had never seen them through the perpetual cloudcover.

"Which one is the new star?" Kuhl asked.

"Pardon?" She looked embarrassed.

"Captain Zierling told me about the nova that appeared about seven years ago." Her reaction puzzled him.

She leaned back, arms stretched out behind her for balance, and shook her head. "Mister Kuhl, I thought you were the diplomat. I see I was wrong."

"I don't understand."

"I've spoken to your captain. She told me your ship's instruments confirmed that the 'nova' is not a true sun. There is no fusion occurring inside it. Therefore, it is not a nova."

"I suppose not."

She turned, still sitting, and pointed through the thick glass. "It is there. When cosmography was a younger science, it was thought the heat and light from stars was caused by the compression of the gases. No one knew about fusion then. Maybe this star glows through compression. If so, it will not be with us very long. A few thousand years, perhaps." She looked back at him. "Your captain asked me if I thought it could be a creation of the race that started the Portal War, or of the Outsteppers, who brought the Portals to Earth."

Kuhl said carefully, "I don't know enough about it to say if it's possible or not."

"Some of our people have their own theories about the star." Her look became distant. "It was the Basques who saw it first. Being a close people, and not thinking it important, they did not bring it to our attention until several weeks after it had become visible. It happened that was the week my father, also called Simon, died, and my brother became councilman of Masada. He believes it has some significance." Again, she seemed embarrassed.

"Well, *Belfast* has a few telescopes we can train on it."

"Citizen, there are those in Masada who are thoughtful, reasonable people, but who also believe very strongly in a God who intervenes in the affairs of men in material ways. Your revelation that the condition of our Portal is somehow unique among all the former colonies will be taken as further evidence that Relayer was singled out somehow, either for divine retribution or a divine experiment, to spare us from contact with the unrighteous. Since you brought news of Earth, both parties have found evidence to support their views."

"And your brother is one of these?" Kuhl asked. "He thinks that star was set in the sky for him?"

Abruptly, Weiss stood. "I do not believe God works in such a direct fashion," she said, "but my brother is, perhaps, closer to Him than am I. I tell you this so you will better know who you are dealing with. Simon thinks he has the support of our people . . . and more support than that, besides."

"Why tell me this?"

"Because not everyone on Relayer thinks as my brother does. Because his thinking may lead us into conflict with Triumviratine Earth. That conflict we could never win. If you understand us, perhaps the battle can be avoided. Your people do not yet understand us. I see the disapproval on their faces."

"We're not here to judge."

"Others, who will see Relayer through your eyes, will judge us. Why haven't you brought your cameras up here, to record this cold beauty? Why, instead, have you spent all your time in the black men's warrens?"

Kuhl's mouth tightened.

"I see I've offended your progressive sensibilities. On Earth, of course, there is no prejudice."

"I wouldn't say that."

Her voice was filled with pain and venom. What would she say if she knew about the Terminal Night? Kuhl thought. Your ancestors were killed, but it wasn't policy, don't blame us for it. Maybe it wouldn't make any difference if she knew. One more event in a history of similar occurrences.

"How much do you know of our history?" Weiss asked. "Did you know that when we were forced to leave Israel and we came here, we had to pay the wealth of generations for the privilege of carving a sanctuary from the cold stone? We started here with nothing."

"I know colonization rights to Relayer were bought by a consortium of four groups. Yours was just one."

"The others provided money, but it was our experts who designed the colony and who have kept it running for the century and a quarter since then. You saw the black men working in Liberty and I showed your employees the Chinese working in the farming corridor. You saw the Basques driving the *akavish* and tending the heavy machinery. But we keep them working together. We tell them when to plant, what to repair, where to dig. When you go to Liberty next time, you should keep in mind our labors also. There are twenty-one hundred people living on Relayer, which was built to hold seven thousand and expanded in our third year to hold over eleven thousand. Do you know how many live in Masada?"

Kuhl shook his head, jaw set.

"Four hundred. In our own land, we are a minority. It was not always so. After the Portal closed and we realized Relayer could not hold as many people as it had, it was we who sacrificed. One child per family. Or no children. Before the Portal War we numbered eight thousand. You look doubtful. Check the records we transmitted to *Belfast*. The story is there."

"What is it you want?" Kuhl asked carefully.

"To talk to someone not in the power structure, about Earth and about Relayer."

"Not just Masada?"

"Relayer."

Kuhl leaned back on his hands. "I'm going to disappoint you, Miss Weiss. It's true I'm an independent producer—I guess you know that—but the government maintains the distribution networks."

"You're still the one I want to talk to. I don't say I understand your world. I'm looking at things as if it were a century ago, and when I'm wrong, I hope you'll correct me." The tone, not arch, made for a surprisingly humble statement.

"I will," he said.

"My view is that Captain Zierling will file a report with her superiors on conditions here. They will from that determine the direction of future contact with us."

"That's my understanding also."

"And, while that process is going on, you will be producing your show about us. It may be broadcast before a policy has been decided on higher levels."

"Very likely."

"And, since your show will be an accurate presentation of life here, the policy, when announced, will not be at variance with what your audience has seen."

"Ideally."

"What I would like to know, Mister Kuhl, is if the policy will reflect conditions here, or if your broadcast will reflect the as-yet-unannounced policy."

"You're asking me if there's government censorship of my work."

"Yes."

Kuhl looked out over the harsh landscape. "Your brother was the one who called me a propagandist."

"I will make up my own mind, Mister Kuhl."

He smiled. "On the basis of what I tell you?"

"Partly. I have my own eyes, too."

"You have a difficult problem, Miss Weiss. Like you, I assume my broadcast will determine, if not policy, then the attitude of the general public about your society here. So we'll say for the sake of argument that you should try to influence me favorably. How do you know when I'm lying? You don't know anything about me or my world. And you don't know if *my* picture of my world is accurate. I say there's no censorship, and that I'm an artist who's fought successfully for my artistic freedom . . . but am I just a technician with an overblown ego? You have no way of knowing. It seems to me you have to show me what you want me to see, and hope for the best. And don't forget, if there is censorship it might be the opposite of what you seem to expect. Those scenes of Liberty might end up in the trash hopper.''

"That might be just what I'm afraid of. What will happen if you adopt a favorable policy? A research station here? Regular commerce? Maybe bring us back into the fold as a colony? No, thank you, Mister Kuhl.'' She looked away. He saw she was trembling, but it might have been the chill in the air.

"It seems to me that your brother—"

She turned back to him, eyes angry. "My brother would as soon you had never appeared in our skies.''

"I gathered that. Still, we are here. We have to be dealt with.''

"He won't deal with you. Believe me when I say that, Mister Kuhl. If he could have turned you away, he would have. And if he can turn you back now, he will.''

Kuhl shrugged. "He can't.''

"My brother is a very resourceful man.''

"And not altogether popular with you.''

She looked away again. Then she stood. "One doesn't have to be a journalist to discover we don't see eye-to-eye on everything.''

He stood up too. The curve of the dome was such that they had to stand closer together than they otherwise might have. "Would *you* rather we had never come here?''

"And never heard of our homeworld again? Never known what had happened? No, I don't wish that. Masada is where we live, but there is a part of Earth that will always be our home.'' Her gaze grew distant. "I would like to see it one day.''

"You can. I know part of Maya Zierling's mission is to bring at least one ambassador back from Relayer.''

"Simon needs me here.'' She started down the steep stairs.

"Miss Weiss. I meant what I said. Show me what you think I should see. For at least the first few weeks, and maybe for the entire time I'm here, I don't know where to look or where to find the information I need. And that information is, I guess, everything there is to know about your people. I have to rely on those who offer to show me what conditions are like here.''

"Like Allan Webber?'' she asked, her voice full of contempt.

"Or like you.''

She paused, considering. Then she nodded. "All right. Tomorrow, ten in the morning, I will show you. Bring your crew.''

"We'll be waiting,'' Kuhl said.

Footsteps echoed up the stairwell. Weiss's eyes widened in

surprise, then her look turned to anger as the boy charged around the stairwell below. He ran into Weiss, head down, and she grunted. Kuhl recognized the dark-haired boy; he had seen him a few times before, in the corridors near the empty quarter.

"Miss Weiss, I'm sorry, I didn't see you there, I—"

"Sam, I told you never to . . ."

He was very young and looked very frightened. Weiss put her hand on his head. "What's wrong?"

"I knew he was with you," he stammered, glancing round-eyed at Kuhl. "And Neil—"

*"No names,"* Weiss hissed.

The boy gulped. "Sorry. But he *took* her. The captain, back to the big meeting room. Ha—*someone else* told me to tell you the other *dar* are looking for Mister Kuhl. The one who calls herself a Jew, she wants all of them in the empty quarter because no one knows what's happening."

"Where's Maya now?" Kuhl demanded.

"Just in the big room," the boy cried. "They didn't hurt her. Neil and the others said they wanted her to answer questions and she came with them."

"She can't have been in there more than a few minutes," Weiss said. "We just left there. What does it matter?" But there was an undercurrent of concern in her voice.

"There's something else," the boy said. "Some of the other *dar* tried to go with her, but they were turned back at the meeting room door. The baskers said there wasn't any more room."

"What's going on?" Kuhl said. A long time ago, Sara could have let him see from one side of the world to the other; now a closed door kept him from knowing what was happening to Maya Zierling.

"The best place for you is back in your quarters, as Miss Raviv wants," Weiss said. "Let's go."

The boy turned and ran down the stairs, taking them in awkward leaps, four and five at a time. Weiss and Kuhl followed almost as quickly.

In the main corridor, Weiss turned to Kuhl. "The boy will take you back to the empty quarter. I'll go down to the council chambers and see that your captain is . . . comfortable."

The boy nodded and took a step away, but Kuhl stayed where he was. "We may as well go without the secret-society camouflage, Judith. I heard you call the boy Sam. Neil Wolfram is the one who took Maya, and I think you know more of what's going on than you say. I'll go with you."

Anger flared in her face, then subsided. "Mister Kuhl, I really do not know what is going on here. If both Sidni Raviv and my friends think you would be better off behind a locked door, they may well be right."

"It sounds as if your brother is demonstrating some of that resourcefulness you mentioned. I have my own resources, Miss Weiss."

"If I was sure we had more time, I would argue with you." She turned to the boy. "Sam, you go home now."

"But—"

"*Go.*" He disappeared around a corner. "You're a bad influence," she told Kuhl.

"So I've been told."

The corridor was empty. So too was the main hall which bisected this level and led to the ramps to the lower levels. From behind the fabric curtains hung across the apartment doorways came low whispers, an electronic hum, a muted voice. Kuhl cocked his head, his ears straining for the sound.

"They're still watching the film," he said.

They descended through the deserted halls.

When they reached Masada's level, the rumble of angry voices came to them. The halls for a hundred meters around the council chambers were packed with an angrily muttering mob. The press reluctantly parted for Judith Weiss. Kuhl put his head down and followed her.

Television monitors had been set up on either side of the double doors leading into the meeting room.

"And this is Belgrade, our Capital," Kuhl heard his own voice say. The white ceramic walls rose to fill the static-streaked screens.

"*They* got along all right," the black alongside him said. On the screen, gaily-clad citizens waved to the Relayermen. "Yeah, while we worked for the Hebes down here." He shot a glance at Kuhl.

He had reached the doors.

"Don't you know who I am?" Weiss angrily demanded.

The Basque shrugged and spread his hands.

"I demand to see my brother!"

A new sea of faces flickered onto the screen: the audience inside. He saw their angry, or hurt, or mystified looks in two bleary dimensions. He heard their shouts through the speakers and through the floor.

Weiss turned away from the Basque guard, her face red with repressed rage.

"We're going back to the empty quarter now," she told him. "No arguments, no discussion."

He opened his mouth to speak—

*"Please."*

—and closed it.

"All right," he said.

"It's all lies!" the television cried.

Weiss's head jerked toward the sound.

"Tell them what happened *after* the war, *dar!*"

It was Neil Wolfram's voice.

His face filled the picture: sweat-streaked, the tendons standing out on his neck, eyes wild.

"Tell them about the new holocaust."

[Sara, cut the transmission. Cut power to the chamber if you have to! Just—]

He strained, listening for her response above the strident voice. Then he—

He shivered.

Useless.

*[Damn you!]*

"Tell them about the Terminal Night, *Captain*," Neil Wolfram sneered.

"He *told* him," Weiss breathed.

Kuhl swung on her. "What are you saying?"

She clasped his wrist with strong fingers. "Now. Out of here."

"Maya—"

"Your captain is very capable," Weiss said.

Wolfram's voice would not stop. "You've told us about the monsters who marched through the Portal. Now tell us about the human monsters who murdered a billion *more* men—*our* fathers—so you could live safe within your white walls."

Maya Zierling began to speak. Her words were swept away.

Kuhl barely heard her dead voice recite, "We estimate that four hundred million people died. Severe dehydration from both the poisoned water supplies and the lack of fresh water in the chaos that followed. One hundred million more, maybe, before we could rebuild the distribution lines in the Welfare Reservations."

He followed Weiss into the crowd.

"The man who did it, he was crazy. He was found and tried—"

Weiss stopped. Kuhl looked around him.

"There was nothing we could do. It was too late—"

"This is the man what made the film," said a face Kuhl had never seen before. The faces surrounded him. "This is the man what lied."

"—they were already dying—"

Weiss shoved the man in the chest, then looked around, her mouth set.

"Remember who you *are*," she hissed. "We survived for a century here—"

"No thanks to his kind!"

"—because we forgot our hatreds."

"—there were millions of bodies in the streets. There was nothing we could do."

"I haven't forgot how much I hate you, woman! You—"

The woman who had shouted was far back in the crowd, but Weiss found her. "You will let us through," she said firmly. "You will all let us through. Go back to your homes. What's done is one hundred years done."

"All our people back home are dead." The cry ended with a wail.

"Some of them are those who killed," said Weiss. "Our nations no longer exist. There is inside and outside. Now let us through."

She took a step forward. No one pushed her back.

He followed.

Someone jabbed his ribs. His eyes watered when pain flared in his left instep. Someone tugged on his arm and he nearly went down. But he followed Weiss to the opposite side of the hall. A maintenance door opened on a narrow, deserted stairwell leading downward.

"Why are you helping me?" Kuhl asked, when he got his breath.

"I think this is a very bad time to ask me a question like that."

The metal door at the bottom of the steps was locked. Weiss took a ring of keys from her pocket and started flipping through them. Kuhl put his hand to the door. The metal jumped under his touch. Only part of the vibration was his hand's trembling.

"Who told Wolfram?" Kuhl said. His throat was tight.

"Stand away from the door."

"You said someone told him. You knew it was going to happen. You took me away, filled my ears with that talk, to keep me away from Maya."

"You're being ridiculous."

He grabbed her shoulder and spun her around. Her head bounced against the metal door; she winced. "*Damn* you—"

"Tell me."

"I'll tell you nothing. No one asked you to come to our world. What happens to you when you're here is your own responsibility. Your lies are also on your own heads. For now, be glad I am with you. I know Neil, yes. I know his plans. His people will be moving through the halls now, making the people think about what you did."

"*I* was three years old."

"Your people."

"There *is* no more 'your' and 'my' people! Why don't you understand the way the world is?"

"*This* world is very different. Stand aside."

He stood back, breathing hard. Useless. He clenched his fists.

Weiss pushed him out of the way and fit a key into the old-style lock. She pulled the door open.

Sweat stink and hoarse shouts rolled over him. Then she said something—he couldn't hear what—and opened the door wide. He plunged in after her.

The crowd roiled in the narrow corridor, yelling, cursing, waving their fists at the line of Basques blocking their way into the empty quarter. Glass shattered; the hall grew dimmer.

A black shouldered Kuhl aside; he staggered; another one pushed him again, away from the door.

"We want to talk to those demons!" one of the blacks shouted.

"Let us through!" said another.

And another, "They're not one of us! You are!"

"No one comes through," one of the Basques growled, " 'Brother.' " He shoved the black.

The crowd surged. Kuhl did not see the blow, only heard the sound of flesh hammering flesh.

"*Wait!*"

Kuhl turned. Other heads turned. He was shoved again, a wedge of black men forcing their way to the front of the mob. They opened a path for a bearded, bald black man whose neck and shoulders were heavily draped in beads and chains. But it was the man standing alongside him who had spoken.

"You've got to wait, and think, and see what you're doing to yourselves," Allan Webber shouted. He put his face close to the Basque's.

"You hate us, yeah, but you've got to live with us. You remember that." He turned to face the mob. "And you got to remember that if you break some lights, maybe we can't fix them again, and if you break a man's head, maybe you'll need that man someday.''

The crowd murmured angrily.

''Move on, then,'' said the Basque, and shoved Webber from behind.

Webber turned, arm upraised. ''Didn't you hear what I'm trying to—''

The Basque knocked Webber's arm away. His fist sank into Webber's belly. Kuhl heard the breath rush out of him across all that distance.

The mob surged like a tide.

Someone tugged his arm. Kuhl jerked away, then saw it was Weiss.

Somehow she found the door again, dragged him through it. He pulled it shut after them.

''Not that way,'' she gasped, hands on knees. ''Savages.''

Someone pounded on the door, then the sound went away.

''We've got to go back.'' As soon as the words had tumbled from his mouth he realized how absurd they were. ''A man I know . . .''

''No one *I* know. You won't find any Jews in that mob. We know what's at stake. Our world can't afford this kind of . . . savagery. Besides, we're used to being exterminated by you Gentiles.''

There was no irony in her voice. Kuhl did not mention he had seen many Masadans in the crowd.

''Come back this way,'' she said. ''I think I can get us closer to your rooms before we have to go back out into the pedestrian corridors.''

He followed her back up the stairs, then through a narrow doorway and into a tube crowded with cables and pipes. They came out into another stairwell, by another door.

''This is as close as we come, unless you are willing to try to crawl through the ventilator shafts. And I think you are too stout for that.''

''It sounds quieter here.''

She shrugged and opened the door.

Ribbons of smoke twisted along the ceiling. Someone shoved against him and he rolled with it, sliding along the rough wall. Weiss took his hand. He couldn't see her; there was too much in the way.

Up ahead, a sweating, thick-bodied man floated up near the overhead lights, bobbing on the shoulders of the men under him. The man had a screwdriver and was popping the lenses from the overheads, dropping them down to the others below. The unrefracted beams cast his face into nightmare planes of pure dark and light.

Someone pushed Kuhl into the wall. The bare-chested man standing on his feet was laughing, swinging a bottle around. The alcohol stung Kuhl's eyes. He licked at it, tasted it, then shoved as hard as he could. The man went down, somewhere, but there was another one beyond him, and then another. The tide surged against him, alternately crushing him against the wall then leaving a vacuum into which he stumbled. Weiss was at the end of their linked arms, her hair sweat-plastered to her face.

He recognized the corridor now. They were near the empty quarter, not far, not far. And maybe the crowd was a little thinner, the pulse of angry voices coming now not from all around him, but from behind him.

They turned a corner and the corridor was abruptly clear, as if they had passed through an invisible wall. He looked around the corner, breathing hard. One of the overhead lenses shattered, showering powdered glass. Coils of smoke curled toward him, but he couldn't see where it was coming from. He was far enough away, now, to hear the chant, in recognizable English, to burn, to tear. Underlying it like a backbeat were the melodic words, *Sh'ma Yisrael, Adonai Elohenu, Adonai Echod.*

The beast in the corridor had a thousand legs and hundreds of sweating faces turned toward the harsh light. A man it had devoured lay only a dozen meters away, on the fringe of the monster. The wall was smeared red behind him. His fingers twitched. Then the crowd surged forward and swallowed him.

Weiss called him away.

The Basques stood shoulder to shoulder around the curve of the hall, and they wore the black and gray uniform Kuhl had seen before. They were not armed, but he looked at their thickly veined hands and saw that it did not matter.

Weiss spoke to one of them, then gestured to Kuhl. The line parted and they passed through. The door to their quarters was open and beyond it, further down the hall, was another line of guards.

"You will all stay here until I come for you. No one else."

Kuhl worked spit into his mouth. "Thank you," he said when he could.

She nodded curtly.

"But what if you don't come back for us?"

"No one will be hurt," she said matter-of-factly. He wondered if she had seen the broken man, if it mattered.

Then she said, "There is always your ship."

The light in the corridor changed in quality. She looked up, her face shadowed now. The lights behind them had gone out.

"What is—?"

Darkness.

He heard her breathing, rapidly, like an animal, in the sudden night. Then the shouts.

The beast roared all around them.

A hand on his back, coarse and heavy as stone: an Euskaldun shoved him through the door to their living quarters. He was pushed a little further, blundering in the dark, until the table they kept in the common kitchen banged him in the hip. He sucked in his breath, bit his lower lip, and sat on the table.

Commands were called back and forth in harsh Basque. Furniture scraped across the floor, a flame flickered and died in a cupped hand, someone cursed in a language he didn't recognize, and the the pounding on the door began. It sounded like the tide coming in on the Jersey shore, and he shivered.

Weiss groped across the room. "Be quiet please," she said. "Please be quiet and they will go."

And, after an eternity that lasted just long enough for his heart to beat a hundred times, they did go.

The silence that came to the room was deeper than any he had known before. Even the wind from the ventilators had gone quiet. In its place he heard their quiet breathing: himself and the five in his crew, Raviv and Krause and a half-dozen Forcers, Weiss, about ten Basque guards called in from the corridor outside.

"I'm going to work on getting some lights," said Krause. His clothing rustled. He padded slowly across the room, to the short hall leading to the cubicle they had made a storeroom.

"You will find no lights, mister," Weiss said. "If the air circulators are out, the power failure is not localized."

"We've brought our own resources," Krause answered from the darkness. "Who's near me who can help? DeRienzo?"

After a few minutes, Kuhl heard them in the other room, ransacking the orderliness they had established just the previous day.

One of the Basques muttered in his own language and was answered by low laughter. The animal scent of their leather boots was sweet.

Aleydis Aubrecht whispered to her sister, who sighed raggedly.

On the floor in front of the table, Jon Frings spoke in a thin monotone to Paoli Marella. Between them sat Kuhl and Weiss.

"We've had a few major power outages before," she said loudly, startling him. "The one right after the war was the longest. It lasted six days, and by the end of that time the air was stale. It was still breathable, of course. On average, there's been a power failure every two years since then. They never last more than a few hours, at most."

"But were any of them caused by sabotage, Miss Weiss?" Sidni Raviv asked. She held taut the edge of fear in her voice. "Was it done by someone looking to do the maximum amount of damage, or was it just through general decay?"

"What has happened is not sabotage," Weiss answered. "If it were, whoever had done it would have to try to live with the consequences."

"That's never stopped terrorists before, has it?"

"There are no terrorists on Relayer, Miss Raviv."

The Forcer subsided, the silence stretching onward, casting its shadow in the darkened room.

Then Raviv said, "We should call *Belfast*. A squad of Ground Patrol would bring order down here."

"And you have such, on board?" Weiss asked. "And yourselves, handguns?"

"We told you no. And no doubt you've gone through our stores and luggage to see for yourself."

Kuhl felt Weiss's tension across the short centimeters separating them.

He sighed, then his breath caught in his throat as pearly light shone around a corner. Krause came in, his face lit from below by the bundle of luminescent cloth in his arms. He dumped the outsuits on the table behind Kuhl. Their glow was no brighter than twilight, but Kuhl blinked nonetheless.

"This evens things up a little," Krause said, looking pleased with himself. Smith DeRienzo, the other Forcer, came in behind him and dropped another armload of activated suits.

"I think we should call *Belfast*," Raviv said. She came over and pushed the suits around, looking for the one with her name stenciled on the breast. "You'd be a hell of a target walking around in one of these things."

"We won't call *Belfast* until the captain's told us to do so," Krause said. He threw a suit to her. "Here's yours. Finding the captain will be our first priority. Miss Weiss?"

She stood. "At this time, Relayer has no air, heat, light, or communications. Only the last two are critical if we're to make repairs, and find your captain.''

"I was thinking of a trade-off myself," said Krause.

"Who put you in charge?" Raviv said sharply.

"No one is in charge but Captain Zierling." Krause looked at Weiss, his face apologetic. "Someone should explain that the StarForce is a paramilitary organization, Miss Weiss. Shipboard— and this counts as that—there is a captain and there are a number of Forcers, all of whom are equivalent in rank, though one may follow the orders of another according to assignment. Therefore, I have no authority to make any kind of deal with you. Nevertheless, I'll make one.''

"I have no authority either. But there's work to be done. I would suggest you give one of your suits to each of Captain Echibaru's guards. They will go first to the council's chambers, where Captain Zierling was last seen, and hopefully find her there still. From there they will go to strategic points on Relayer, hoping to assess damage and coordinate repairs.''

"That sounds all right to me, except for one point: The suits stay with StarForce personnel.''

"I don't go along with any of this," Raviv said. "We should call *Belfast*.''

"The only thing Berry can do is sit on his hands. He doesn't have any more authority than we do. Maya left him in charge of keeping *Belfast* running. That's all.''

Raviv subsided sullenly.

"It is settled, then?" Weiss asked. "Captain Echibaru and his men number eleven. An equal number of yours and—''

Krause shook his head. "One of our people will stay here. And I think some of the guards should stay behind to watch over them. I'd rather stay barricaded in here myself and wait for help, except I think *we* are the help. Five of us will go with the Basques—six, if you want to go.''

Kuhl stood. "I'll go with you. One of those suits is mine.''

"That's a volatile, dangerous situation out there," Krause said.

"And your outsuit doesn't make you invulnerable to it—to the contrary, as Sidni pointed out. And you didn't bring any weapons with you?''

"You know we didn't.''

"So if there's any problem, the Basque guards will have to handle it. They look better equipped for it, physically, than any of us, Krause.''

"I still can't ask any of your people to take the risk.''

"You're not asking. I offered my own services," Kuhl said.

"I'll go with you," said Marella. Frings nodded, too.

"We're leaving this place almost defenseless." Krause looked around. "And the Basques aren't armed any more than we are, are they?"

The Euskalduns' faces looked grimmer than usual in the half-light. "There are no weapons on Relayer," said one of them even stockier than the rest. He wore a complicated insignia on the right sleeve of his tunic.

"I am Captain Mattei Echibaru," he said. "We fight well. Our hearts are our weapons."

Krause grinned uneasily. "If that's all the ammunition we have . . ."

The humor was lost on Echibaru. "It is enough," he said darkly. He turned away and called orders to his men.

"The talk of violence is academic, I think," Weiss said. "Listen."

Kuhl heard nothing, but this time understood what it was the silence told him.

"The disturbance is over," said Weiss.

# Chapter Nine

Marella lifted the horse collar over Kuhl's head and helped secure it. The helmet would have been a needless encumbrance, but the collar held the radio transceiver and batteries.

Marella looked over his shoulder, to where the Basques were methodically demolishing furniture to provide themselves with clubs and batons. "What the hell are you up to?" he whispered. "When you suggested we go along, I thought you were giving us the chance to really dig into the heart of the situation here. This is real statism, real race hatred. Why aren't we bringing our equipment?"

"No one would allow it—not Krause, Weiss, or Echibaru. There are a dozen reasons against it," Kuhl said. "Chief among them is that it would inflame the situation even more. And we would be the primary targets."

"And because it would inflame the captain? Brian, recording the riot, or at least its aftermath, is the difference between a dry documentary and the chance to present an actual bit of history."

Kuhl said, "No."

Marella nodded, tight-lipped. "Well, you did give your word to the captain, didn't you? So much for that 'art' you tell us about at every opportunity."

"I'm doing what I think is best. We'll get the story later."

"The story of the event, not the event itself." Marella shook his head. "You know, after all I'd heard about you . . ."

"You can still stay behind, Paul. No one'll think any worse of you."

The double meaning did not escape Marella, who glared. "I'll go."

The Basques herded the Forcers and Kuhl's team to the back of the room, then arrayed themselves in a semicircle facing the door.

One of them opened it.

An acrid tang wafted in through a deep silence. Then came a groan, impossibly loud. Captain Echibaru stepped forward to

catch the man as he fell through the doorway. Cradling t
man's head, Echibaru lowered him to the floor.

He was a Chinese, his face a mask of blood. It bubbled fro
his nose and oozed sluggishly from a jagged cut starting at t
corner of his right eye and ending on the right side of his nec
Echibaru twisted the man's head and probed the cut with h
finger. The Chinese whimpered.

"Not very deep," said the Basque. He lowered the mar
head to the floor and gestured for two of his men to drag hi
inside. "He will be all right."

Kuhl looked away, a sharp taste surging into his throat. A
Hwang stood behind him, looking over his shoulder, eyes shi
ing and alert. "Why don't you talk to him," Kuhl said, "fi
out if he's hurt inside."

"In Chinese?" Hwang looked surprised. "I don't spe
Chinese."

"See if you can do something for him anyway," Kuhl snappe

He joined the others in the corridor outside. Ropes of bl
smoke twisted along the ceiling. Misshapen shadows jerk
along the walls whenever the suited Earthmen moved. The pa
suit-lights picked out scorch marks, graffiti spatters, less reco
nizable stains.

"We ought to paint targets on our chests," Raviv muttered.

Krause hadn't heard. "Let's start," he said. "Sidni, you a
Brian will go with two guards to the power plant, via t
council's chambers."

"I will go with them," Echibaru said. He smiled at Ravi
who frowned in return.

Krause said, "Citizen Frings, you and Forcer Webster w
head for the air circulation plant with Miss Weiss and tw
guards. Citizen Marella and Forcer Fountaine will take the lo
way around, through the agricultural tunnels and then up to t
top level and the communications center." He glanced at Echibar
"Can you send three guards with Fountaine?"

Several Basques stepped forward to volunteer. Echibaru d
tailed three of them to go with Fountaine, a stocky blonc
woman taller than any of them.

"That leaves me and one guard," said Krause. "Captain,
any of your men speak English?"

"Arrigua," Echibaru said. He turned to the Euskaldun. "Yc
will go with this man."

"Where are we to go?" Arrigua asked.

"Your own headquarters," Krause told him. "Then on to th
meeting room. Sidni, you'll wait for us there, or we for you."

\*   \*   \*

Kuhl heard footsteps behind him; they were echoes of his own. He shied from moving shadows; they were his own. Echibaru glanced over his shoulder and grinned coldly. Kuhl returned the look.

Raviv walked alongside him. "This is crazy, Brian. I don't even know where we are."

"I think the council's meeting room is just below us," he said, his voice echoing from the walls.

"That doesn't make me feel any better."

"We will protect," said Captain Echibaru. He cradled a thick table leg. His head turned metronomically, scanning the corridor. The other guard trailed a dozen meters behind, poking a thin metal rod at the doors they passed. None could be locked, but all were firmly closed. If anyone waited behind them, they stayed hidden.

"Do you think the captain is all right?" Raviv asked, her voice hushed now.

"We'll know soon enough."

"You looked worried about her."

"Just concentrating," he said pointedly.

"Quiet, now," Echibaru said. He stopped. Kuhl heard it then, a rustling from up ahead, like bugs in a wall.

Twenty meters further on, this corridor met another in a T-shaped intersection. Past the juncture the hall branched into two ramps, one leading up, one down. The floor at the intersection was littered with crushed glass sparkling faintly in the light from their suits.

Echibaru turned around, finger to lips, and gestured for Kuhl and Raviv to wait where they were.

The two Basques stepped soundlessly onto the glass. When they had reached the intersection they paused, then sprang forward. Someone shouted, and running footsteps echoed. Kuhl ran across the glass and reached the other hall in time to see several men disappear down it. The younger Euskaldun started after them, but Echibaru called him back. He said something in Basque, then translated, "It could be an ambush up ahead. Looters." He spat onto the corridor floor.

"How do you know they're looters?" Kuhl asked.

Echibaru said, "Blacks. And this is a Jew dormitory hall."

The overhead light fixtures were smashed; one lens hung precariously. Echibaru scythed it down with the table leg. It exploded at his feet. Sweat gleamed on his face.

"Let's go down to the council's rooms," Raviv said.

"In a moment, lady." Echibaru stepped forward, his club swinging easily from one hand.

"*Attention!*" he shouted. "In this area you will come into the hall, please. This is Captain Mattei Echibaru of our police forces demanding you come out at once."

He waited. Raviv started to say something, but the young guard's venomous look made the words dry in her mouth.

After a minute had passed, Echibaru said over his shoulder, "You will please stand there where we can see." He and the other guard went to the first door on the corridor. Like most others on Relayer, it had no lock. Echibaru tested the knob anyway, and smiled.

The guard knocked the door back on its hinges and rolled right. Echibaru hunched over and charged left. A woman's wail cut short almost before it had begun.

Kuhl ran forward—Raviv called for him to come back—his legs pumping against the restrictive fabric of the outsuit.

The apartment was ruined. Tattered murals clung lifelessly to bare rock walls. Musty furniture lay splintered on the worn plastic floor. The door behind him sagged from one hinge and the glass-fronted wood cabinet behind it had collapsed.

A woman sat on a couch with slashed cushions, head down and shoulders shaking. Purple bruises showed through the torn sleeves of her coarse brown dress. She looked up briefly when Kuhl entered; both eyes were closed, one swollen, one teary. The young Basque stood alongside her, one hand resting lightly on the back of her neck.

A stained curtain hung across the arch leading into the next room. Echibaru backed through it, his club across the throat of a young black man. The black gasped as Echibaru turned around and yanked him off his feet. Echibaru let him sag to his knees. Blood flowed freely from the black's nose, but he did not try to wipe it away. He looked around the room without moving his head. His eyes narrowed when they rolled Kuhl's way.

"You see?" Echibaru poked the club into the man's shoulder blade. "A marauder."

"*Tol'* you, just wanted to get away from the crazy men," the black moaned. "Skullcappers they were. A lot of them."

"And the apartment?" Echibaru hissed. "This woman does not housekeep well?"

"It was *like* this." He struggled to his feet, breathing hard.

"Hands in pockets and keep heels together," Echibaru said. He turned to the woman. "The man lies, or is he your guest?" The woman did not look up. "Madame Jewess!"

One eye opened, dull and filmy. "I've never seen him before,
and I didn't ask him in. He came after. Maybe fifteen minutes
ago. I don't know."

"After what, please?"

"After the . . . blacks."

"This man among them?"

She looked more alert, shaking her head. "No, not him. I
remember what they looked like. I will remember for as long as I
live."

"Why don't you tell him it wasn't the blacks, then? Why
don't you tell him it was some of his own greasy—"

Echibaru plunged the table leg into the black man's stomach.
He folded, gasping. He had not cried out.

"Your name, black man?"

"George Carter," he ground out.

"George Carter, you will go to the detention hall now. I will
be there in one hour, and will find you there. If I do not, I will
find you where you are. You understand?"

Carter nodded. Echibaru nudged him in the ribs with the toe of
his leather boot. "Speak."

"*Understand.*"

"Good." Echibaru looked up. "Situation is controlled now,"
he told Kuhl. "We will go to the council's chambers now."

The hall outside the meeting room was littered with glass;
sweat stink and blood's copper tang hung in the stale air.
Dozens of men and a very few women sat cross-legged along the
walls. They moved uneasily away from the Forcers' suitlights,
murmuring.

Basque guards waited outside the meeting room doors, hunched
around a portable heater more for the light it gave than its
warmth. When they saw the approaching suits' glow they stood,
eyes round. Echibaru spoke harshly, then laughed. One of the
guards slapped Kuhl on the back and put his arm around his
shoulder, saying something Kuhl didn't understand.

A dozen meters further along the corridor, on the fringe of the
light, Basques stood with arms crossed around a group of about
twenty blacks and Chinese. Another group under guard consisted
of white men. Kuhl recognized one of the glaring, upturned
faces: one of the group who had been with Wolfram on Kuhl's
first day here, when Wolfram had visited Zierling. A bruise
purpled the young man's forehead.

Raviv moved closer to Kuhl. "It all happened too quickly. As
if a wire snapped somewhere." Kuhl started to nod, but she

said, "I mean, as if someone were waiting for it to happen. As if it were planned."

"Maybe it was," Kuhl said after a moment.

Echibaru came over to them and smiled down at Raviv. "Young lady, your captain is sound and safe within. She never left this place and the rabble never touched her because of the presence of my brothers."

Raviv grinned, relieved. She stepped toward the door, and one of the guards stepped in front of her. Echibaru put his hand on Kuhl's shoulder.

"There is no need," Echibaru said. "We will go to the power plant now, mister and young lady?"

"In a moment." Kuhl tried to knock Echibaru's hand away but it was like brushing at a tree limb. The hand on his shoulder closed. Tears started in Kuhl's eyes.

Echibaru put his lips close to Kuhl's ear. "Do not force me to be strong with you in front of my brothers. We would both regret it afterward."

Kuhl stepped back. Echibaru let his arm fall to his side. "Let me see her," Kuhl said under his breath, smiling for the benefit of any who watched.

Echibaru smiled too. "You think I would deceive you?"

Raviv said, "Captain . . . the whole *point* was to speak to her, to receive her orders."

Echibaru barely glanced at her. "She will provide no guidance for a time, I understand." He looked into Kuhl's eyes, then jerked his head toward the door. "We will see for ourselves. Come in, you and the woman both. I will allow it." He opened the door for them.

*"Who's there?"*

It was a woman's voice. After a moment he realized it was her voice.

Pale green light flowed from a portable lantern sitting on the table below. Its sluggish illumination did not reach the shadows lying over the rows of seats at the back of the hall.

Echibaru crossed his arms over his chest and leaned against the doors. He nodded. "I will wait for you."

"Captain?" Raviv called. She hurried down the aisle. "Maya?"

Souletin and Cleveland, the councilmen from Biscay and Liberty, sat at either end of the head table. Kuhl's glance lingered on them for a moment—took in sweat-stained clothes, drawn faces and withdrawn gazes—then settled on Maya Zierling.

She sat between them, shoulders hunched, her eyes locked on

the sheets of light trapped inside the lantern. Her dry and blackened lips were slightly parted.

In the darkness behind her, a half-dozen Basque guards lingered near a shadowed exit Kuhl had not seen the last time he had been here. That was only a few hours ago, he realized, disbelieving.

He licked his lips. "Maya?"

Her head jerked up. Her lips formed a syllable: You. Merely that, but his skin crawled.

"Captain," Raviv began, "we've got teams throughout the colony, setting up a communications net and just as soon as you . . . as you . . ."

"You." Zierling slowly got to her feet. "Told. Them."

"I didn't," said Kuhl, knowing already it was useless.

"Destroyed everything." Her head swung loosely to Washington, to Souletin. "For you, too. *Trying* me for something that happened when I was a Forcer fresh out of the egg. It's ruined for you, too."

Souletin said to Kuhl, "She has said this many times in the last hour."

Kuhl looked away from her, to the Basque. "Where's Simon Weiss?"

"The power plant. He has duties there."

"He's done enough here," Kuhl said. "Maya, come with us. We'll bring you back to the empty quarter, get you back up to *Belfast* if you want."

"Maya, you have to—" Raviv began.

"Go with him," Zierling grated. "Get out of here."

"We have to know what to *do*. If not . . ." She shrugged helplessly.

"If not you have to know who's in—" She broke off. Her shoulders slumped, face fell, and Kuhl saw the Zierling he had expected to see when he had come to this place: tired, beaten, but the same woman he had known briefly. "Who's . . . in charge," Zierling finished.

She sighed.

"I'm very tired, Sidni." She shook her head. "You said something about teams?"

"Combinations of Basques, Forcers, and Citizen Kuhl's people are going to the vital areas and providing communications and light. Miss Weiss suggested it."

"*Belfast?*"

"We were waiting to hear from you before we contacted

them. And, with the colony's systems out, we might not be able to anyway."

"That's all right. It looks like we're in no immediate danger. Sidni, we'll go back to our quarters. Plan things out."

"Yes, Captain." She smiled, relief plain on her face. "I'll tell the others you're all right. We were afraid . . ." She shrugged, smiled again, and withdrew a few meters.

"Any orders for me, Captain?" Kuhl said a little stiffly.

"I don't have the authority to order you to do anything. Certainly not what I have in mind, Citizen."

His chest grew hot and tight. "I had nothing to do with that, Captain. I gave you my word I wouldn't tell anyone."

"So you did." She walked over to Raviv, leaving him alone.

"Bitch," Souletin commented.

"Basker," Kuhl said. "Nigger. Chink. Hebe."

"Murderer," Souletin returned passionlessly.

Kuhl walked to the back of the meeting room. Echibaru rose from a seat in the rearmost aisle and opened the door for him. "I told you the truth."

"She's better now. Where's Wolfram?"

"The little one is not coming with us?"

"No. Where's Wolfram?"

Echibaru contrived to look disappointed. "Too bad. Where now? We can bring more men. We don't need all these here to watch over those cattle." He glared fearsomely at the huddled figures.

"He got away from you, didn't he?"

Echibaru was silent for a moment. Then he said in a low voice, "There is nowhere he can run. Everyone is looking for him."

"Even Simon Weiss?"

"Especially him." He turned to Kuhl, grinning. "You think this was directed at you? *You* were directed at *Weiss*."

"They told me Weiss is at the power plant. I want to go there."

"Then I will bring you."

"We won't need anyone else."

Echibaru looked indifferent. "No. Come this way."

The heater's dim light was soon lost around a corner. Kuhl's suit glowed brightly as they turned down a side corridor, then down another, narrower hall. Kuhl thought he recognized the passage; Rosenthal had led them along it to Weiss's office, two weeks before.

"You don't mind herding them like cattle, do you?" Kuhl asked.

Echibaru seemed thoughtful for a moment. "Man to man with you?"

"Go ahead."

"They are cattle. And the Jews worst of all, though they hide it, strutting like chickens. The black and yellow men are worthless, but we owe the Jews for one thing."

"Bringing you here?"

"No. I don't thank them for taking us away from our lands . . . or our grandfathers, who were weak. I bless them every morning for the time they died by the hundreds." He glanced at Kuhl, smiled, raised one eyebrow. "I am surprised you were not told this. They tell us day after day. When the Portals closed, this rats' warren could not support us all. Terrible times, with not even enough air for everyone to breathe. There were then more Jews than any of the rest of us. Some of the old of all the nations killed themselves, and the women bore no children for ten years."

After a full minute, Kuhl asked, "How many?"

"A thousand, I think. Hundreds. Some of our old men, too. The ones who gave up our nation. Better off without them. Do not believe they did it for us; they did it for themselves. And they hate us as much as we them—*more*—because we are strong, and because we are not Jews."

As they walked, Kuhl studied Echibaru from the corner of his eye. The Basque stood less than 160 centimeters tall, but he massed at least as much as Kuhl. He could kill with those hands, those arms . . . those eyes.

But Kuhl said anyway, "It was your men I saw start the trouble, up on the second level. They went into a peaceful crowd and turned it upside down."

"It was Wolfram's men. We controlled the situation."

"I know what I saw."

"This is a serious charge not to be made lightly," Echibaru said. "In a time of confusion, a weak eye can see many things. You saw what you expected to see."

They came to a downward-leading spiral staircase. Voices buzzed from below; machinery clanked and hissed. Kuhl put his hand on the rail and, seeing how long a drop it was, gripped hard.

"The power plant is immediately down," Echibaru said. "The rest of your way is simple." It was a dismissal.

"You'll need a light to get back." Kuhl fumbled at the fasteners of his glove, but the Basque shook his head.

"I know the corridors. And you do not, mister. Better to keep an eye ahead and the light around you." He smiled. "This advice I offer you freely."

Kuhl watched Echibaru's back until the shadows swallowed him.

Kuhl entered the power plant on its control deck, overlooking the main floor. A half-dozen black men dressed in worn white suits sat with their backs to the wall or lay on the tiled floor. Blood and lymph seeped through the cloth bandages on their faces and hands. The sour stench of their burned flesh hung in the unrecirculated air. A Chinese woman moved among the injured, rearranging dressings, offering water from a plastic bottle.

A white man stood stiffly at the front of the room, watching over banks of dead indicator lights and dials with needles pegged firmly at zero. He looked up as Kuhl entered, then looked away.

Beyond him, a window running the width of the control deck overlooked the main floor. A hundred dim lanterns, maybe the colony's entire store, lit the heat exchangers and turbines crowding the stained cement floor. Workers swarmed, shouting. Smoke drifted, thick in places; steam hooted.

Kuhl watched a moment. He thought he spotted Marella, and then Hwang, who shouldn't have been here.

"Is Judith Weiss down there?" Kuhl asked.

"In the rear quarter."

"How do I get down there?"

The technician pointed to a steel door at the far end of the room.

On the other side were lockers and a set of narrow stairs. He stripped off his suit and hung it in an empty closet. He smoothed the stained and wrinkled singlesuit he wore beneath, then went down.

He tasted the acrid smell of burnt insulation. Sparks drifted down from the catwalk where a welder worked. Rivulets of water streamed across the pavement. Chains rattled, a vent hissed, and a fresh stink of burning oil broke over him.

"Glad you made it, Brian," Marella said, coming up to him, hand extended. Kuhl took it, vaguely surprised. "It was a mess up there," Marella said. "We found about a dozen people with injuries. They were minor, I guess, but there was a lot of blood.'' He hunched his shoulders, as if remembering. ''I got my hands dirty.''

Kuhl nodded, recalling the man he had seen slumped against the wall a thousand years ago. What had happened to him?

''I guess what I'm trying to say is, I couldn't have helped if I'd had my hands full of a camera,'' Marella finished.

''In any other situation you would have been right, Paoli.''

''Maybe. You found Captain Zierling?''

''In the council chambers.'' Kuhl's mouth tightened. ''When things get a little more settled, we have some questions to ask.''

''Beginning with Simon Weiss, I suppose.''

''That's right.''

''I'll hold him down for you.''

They found Jon Frings and Abraham Hwang kneeling over an open floor grating. In the access tunnel beneath, a pair of bare-chested men worked. Dry steam burst freely from the pipes lining the walls. Kuhl wiped his upper lip with the back of his hand.

''How's it coming, Jon?'' he said.

Frings looked up, startled. ''All right, Citizen Kuhl.'' He smiled nervously.

Don't become their friend, Sara would have said. You're trampling your personality profile.

But Sara wasn't here.

This isn't her world either. She couldn't help me here. The realization oozed over him like a slow tide.

''Miss Weiss was right,'' Hwang said over his shoulder. ''About some things, at least.'' He groped for the wrench along-side him and, without being asked, handed it to one of the men below. ''Strength in simplicity. Most of these switches are mechanical, and most of the parts can be fabricated with a mechanical press or lathe.''

One of the workers looked up, his face glistening like polished wood through a sheen of sweat. ''Your technology doesn't have the answers to everything.''

Kuhl knelt alongside Frings. ''What happened to the lights?''

''I've heard bits and pieces,'' Frings said. ''There's a shaft extending way down into the mantle—the glory hole, they call it—that's capped by a valve that either diverts the steam to one of two banks of turbines or vents it to the surface, when the pressure builds past a certain point. So the valve froze open and they lost all the pressure in the hole. It'll be at least ten hours before they build it back up to working torr, which will give them time to repair the subsystems taken out by the fire, I guess.''

"No secondary systems?''

"Not for fifty years, it seems.''

"Was it sabotage?''

"No one's told me anything about that,'' Frings said, "but no one seems to know how the fire started, either.''

Kuhl straightened and turned to Marella. "I think things have quieted down enough so that we can get back to work. I'll find Weiss and get his permission.''

"I saw him down by the glory hole,'' Marella said.

An electric tractor towing a train of three parts-laden carts hummed past him, horn blatting. Black men in dirty white overalls ran after it.

He stepped aside for the next tractor, but it pulled alongside him, engine whining. "You the one who talked to Allan Webber?'' The bald man's head gleamed.

"I know him,'' Kuhl said.

"He told me to look out for you,'' said the black man. "Get up here.'' He shifted on the tractor's bench seat to make room for Kuhl. The vehicle jerked forward. "Headed down to the glory hole? Hey . . . I can't look to see you nodding, friend.''

"Yes, I am.''

"Al told me you were a man of few words. He said, you see the one with a face like a mask, he's our man. He meant your eyes. He said they never change. That so?''

"Is Allan all right?''

The man glanced at him. "Why would you ask that?''

"I saw you and him in the riot.''

"Dangerous place for you to be. So's this, I guess. There's more than one person who'd be happy to break any Earther's arm if they weren't so busy trying to get the world running again. Your arm, especially, after you've been telling everyone how impartial you are.''

"But I didn't—''

"Hey, you don't have to tell me 'bout it. I know the things a man has to do to live. But they'll think of coming after you later, you can be sure. When the smoke clears, no part of Relayer will be good for you. I tell you that because Al would have. He's dead. Basker broke his head for him. So I broke the basker's arm for Al. Wasn't a fair trade.'' He sighed. "I liked Al.''

"You're sure he's dead?''

"Saw his brains on the floor.''

Kuhl choked back bile. "And how many others?"

"That basker, next time I see him. But no, none others I know. A lot of people broken up, though. Three of the hospitals are full and the Jews' hospital is getting there."

The tractor spun down an aisle between two banks of turbines. At the end of the lane, another black man flagged them down.

"Jews don't want you any further than this, James," the man said.

"Their top man in there?" the bald man asked.

"That's right."

"Then take our man in, here." Her jerked his thumb at Kuhl. "This is the one Al told us about."

The other man's eyes narrowed. "Isn't this their camera-artist? I'm not taking him anywhere. You heard how they killed our people—but not through him."

"This man here never killed anyone in his life. You do as I say, Clifford."

The man hesitated. Then he said, "All right."

They walked across yellow crosshatchings painted on the floor. Overhead, the ceiling bowed upward to accommodate a nest of twisting pipes. One conduit, broader than the rest, stabbed downward to meet the floor. Scaffolding and ladders wrapped it. Heat had painted glossy designs on its skin. Technicians swarmed around its base, inside the railing hung with warning signs.

"Far as I go," said the man alongside him. "They don't like us inside the restricted zone."

"Thanks," said Kuhl. He swung a leg over the rail.

Someone flung Hebrew at him. Then, in English, "No closer!" Kuhl shrugged him off.

Chains rattled across pulleys. Backs strained, pulling the valve out of its niche. Water vapor blew around it. Simon Weiss pushed at the misshapen component. Metal squealed, it came free, people danced away from it as it rolled heavily across the floor.

Simon Weiss looked over his sooty shoulder, saw Kuhl, and glared. Ash formed a star-burst pattern on the open hatch beside him. Kuhl felt the heat from it on his face. The valve—a meter in diameter and weighing at least three hundred kilograms, he judged—had fallen in on itself like soft candy.

"You can't cast something like that," Kuhl said. "How many did you have in reserve when the Portal closed?"

"*Dar*, I tell you now—" Weiss broke off, looking past Kuhl. Kuhl turned; his stomach clenched.

The Masadans murmured in surprise. One of them moved to

stop Zierling from entering the restricted zone. She stopped him
with a glance. Another was not so quick-witted. The captain
said, "Excuse me," and shoved him hard in the chest.

Color flared in her cheeks. Her mouth was hard. Cropped hair
gleamed and epaulets shone in the uncertain light.

She stopped meters from Weiss.

"I just wanted to say how sorry we were to see this happen,"
she told him levelly. Her voice carried distinctly the length and
breadth of the power plant; quiet descended behind her words.

"As you know, Councilman," she continued, "when *Belfast*
was outfitted we thought you would need supplies. I would like
to offer you any assistance my ship, and Triumviratine Earth,
can give during this disaster."

Weiss slowly descended the ladder. He said nothing.

"We have portable lights," Zierling said. "The ship can
transmit power to a receiver we will provide. We have concen-
trated food, a water purifier. Taped books and a press. Several
medicians and their stores are waiting for your word." She
smiled thinly, the cords in her neck taut. "A few more bottles of
that vintage from the Carmel wineries. And, of course, whatever
technical expertise we can offer in this trying time."

She extended her hand to him. Even the machines seemed to
hush.

After a moment, Weiss took her hand. Zierling held it.

"Wolfram," she said, her voice lower. "We want him. We
want to know—we want to talk to him."

Weiss's look was cold.

"A request," Zierling said. "From one sovereignty to another."
She let Weiss's hand go.

"He is a fugitive," he said. "When he is found, he will be
dealt with according to our laws and customs."

Zierling nodded.

Kuhl stepped out of her way. She brushed past him, her face a
mask, their glances never meeting.

Weiss stared after her. Then he clapped his grease-stained
hands together brusquely. "There's much to be done! We work
to live!"

He turned to Kuhl. "You wanted something of me?"

"Now that the emergency is over, Mister Weiss, permission
to record the recovery effort."

His look was sour. "Granted," he said curtly. He looked
around. "David!"

Rosenthal hurried over.

"David," Weiss said. "Find the apostate. Find him, and when you do, *cherem*."

Rosenthal looked shaken. "Simon, the rabbis would never—"

"I will make the judgment. The judgment will be *cherem*."

Rosenthal walked away, calling for some of the other Masadans to join him.

Simon Weiss's eyes smoldered in an impassive face. "We deal with our own," he said. "We have since the beginning. We do not need you to dispense justice to our own people."

"But you do for other things," Kuhl said.

Weiss shook his head, a jerky side-to-side motion, his fists clenched at his side.


"Someone to see you," Sidni Raviv called through Kuhl's bedroom door. He looked up from the piece of stretched canvas and reached for the doorknob.

"Thank you, Sid, I—" But she was already gone. She had been distant to him in the week since the disturbance, and she did not smile anymore—at least not for him. And he hardly ever saw Zierling. Kuhl draped a cloth over the painting and pushed the easel into the room's sole unoccupied corner.

Judith Weiss waited in the common room. She stood as he entered, handing him a thin sheaf of hardcopy.

"A report on the failure of the geothermal plant," she said. "I gave one to Maya Zierling, also."

"Thank you." He started to page through it.

"It was a maintenance failure, as we'd thought," she continued. "There were structural flaws in the valve that should have been detected and repaired before it failed."

"And Neil Wolfram's men had nothing to do with it? Or the Basques?"

She said, after a moment, "There were gauges, indicators. The report also notes that Neil Wolfram and some of his followers were in the plant at the time and distracted the workers. There are no automatic failsafes, not anymore. The man who was monitoring the gauges was . . . fighting."

"But not sabotage?"

"If *Belfast* had not been able to manufacture another valve, it might have been the death of us. You know that. Neil would have known it. It was not sabotage. He would not want to harm his own people."

"Just kick them around a little bit." Kuhl folded the papers lengthwise. "Did you ever find him?"

"This morning."

"Will Simon let Maya talk to him?"

"No."

"She won't—"

"He's dead. He was found dead, in a maintenance corridor."
Kuhl's heart hammered. "How?"

"He hanged himself. His neck was not broken. He strangled.
I saw him, the face swollen . . ." Her eyes were dry, but her
lower lip trembled. "The face was swollen, like dough. But I
could tell him, by his eyes."

"I'm sorry," Kuhl said after a moment.

"No, you're not. I don't blame you. On Earth, you would
have exiled him or executed him. Here, every life is precious."

"Then why did he kill himself? I haven't seen any jails here,
either. Echibaru still has some people under house arrest, but
that's no reason . . ." She had turned away. "Judith, what is
*cherem*?"

"Shunning," Weiss said. "It is . . . like exile."

"I see," Kuhl said, but he didn't see. It was just another piece
in an exceptionally large puzzle. "What did he want?"

"By . . . agitating?" She shrugged. "He accused Simon of
being weak. He thought you shouldn't have been allowed to
stay."

"I don't understand how he thought it could work."

"Maybe he knew it couldn't, but he had to do something
anyway, when he saw you come into our skies and threaten to
take our way of life away. And it will happen. But does it matter
now?"

"The only thing that matters is who told him about the
Terminal Night."

"I don't know," said Weiss.

"Would you tell me?"

"No." She went to the door.

Kuhl followed her. "Simon was really rocked by this, wasn't
he? He won't answer our questions, won't speak to us, and the
word is he doesn't leave his offices or apartment much anymore.
No one sees him—hard to do, in a place like this. Has he heard
that the Wenzel woman got a prosthetic leg from *Belfast*'s
medicians? Has he approved the plans for the solar plant on the
surface? Or the upgrade of the ventilation systems?"

"Why don't you go to his office and ask him yourself?" She
opened the door to the corridor.

The Basque guard standing just outside nodded curtly to her.

A few meters beyond him, a half-dozen young men waited.
They were always there, Basque or black or Chinese or Jew, and

their eyes were always the same, though the faces varied from day to day.

"Tell us another lie," one of them shouted.

"*Liar!*"

"I think I'll stay here," said Kuhl. He closed the door after her.

Someone rapped on the door of Kuhl's cubicle. Before he could answer, the knob began to turn. He had time to drape a cloth over his painting and push the easel into its place in a corner.

Marella came in, smiling. "This is number seven-hundred-twenty," he said, closing the door behind him and tossing a datacube onto the narrow bed. "You've been spending a lot of time in here," he observed neutrally.

"That's my business." Kuhl ran a hand through his hair. "Any difficulties today, Paoli?" The tone was grudgingly conciliatory. Was that the right note? Who would know?

"We did the Basque children at play today. Alistaire got beaned with a rubber ball. She'll get over it." He glanced at the cube. "Seven-hundred-twenty," he repeated. "Except for the twelve hours of recording time we're holding for our departure, that's the end of it."

Kuhl took the cube into his hand. In its warm, glassy facets he could see nothing but the distorted image of his own palm; but for the computers in a production studio, the matrix contained sound and light reduced from disordered wave-patterns to orchestrated molecular distortions.

Marella chuckled. "On the walk back here, Aleydis was saying she was bored already. Myself, I think I'll spend my last week relaxing. We've earned it." He sat in the chair in one corner of the room. The compartment was small enough that their knees nearly touched, and Marella's elbow jogged the easel. He snatched his arm away from it. "Don't want to disturb the work in progress," he said. "I didn't know you painted."

"I have for years. Not that the results would show it." He handed the cube back to Marella, who pocketed it. "When can you send that up to *Belfast*?"

"The shuttle that brought down the kids' recreational equipment isn't due to lift off for another hour and two-tenths. A case of twelve cubes will be on it. Unless you want to screen any of them first?"

"I told you I'll wait until we're back home. I always work that way. I'll view the seven or eight hundred hours in a forty- or forty-five-day stretch. Then I'll go back, saving the scenes I remember. Then you and I will link up and string it together. That's when the real work begins.''

''I can come to your Manchester studio,'' Marella offered. ''After all,'' and he grinned lopsidedly, ''I don't mind traveling.''

''We'll do it as I outlined: by remote. It works that way. You don't tamper with something that works, Paul.''

''All right.'' Marella stood. He paused, and Kuhl could almost feel him trying to come up with a line that would prolong the conversation, one that would reach him—and he heard Sara say, Stay inside the parameters. (And what if Marella went to the address in Manchester? He did not know what Marella would find, but it would not be Brian Kuhl.)

So he said, ''You're worried, aren't you, Paul? Afraid I'm going to butcher your scenes?''

He frowned. ''We may not get along, but I know you're the best producer on the air today.''

''Then it must be you're afraid of the government censors I'll have at my elbow. 'Trim there,' they'll say. 'Lie here. Ignore this.' '' He kept his face calmly speculative and clenched his fists.

''The thought had crossed my mind,'' Marella said. ''It's been on all our minds.''

''And you've all worked the Public Information desks.''

''That's different.''

''Is it?''

''People consider the source.''

Kuhl shrugged. ''I don't think people are that attentive or interested. But perhaps you're right. In which case, what can you do about it, standing at my other shoulder? Nothing.''

Marella said nothing, searching for new words. Then he left without saying anything, slamming the door behind him.

If Sara had been here, she could have told him the words to turn Marella around, not merely turn him away. She could have told him, too, who had given Neil Wolfram the word on the Terminal Night; and what Marella said about him after the door was closed; and whether they still suspected him of putting the word in the suicide's ear. She could have told him everything.

He turned back the cloth covering the easel. The face staring from the canvas was not quite hers. The hair, like the eyes, was the color of storm clouds. Shadows suggested high cheekbones, and implied as well the faint lines and hollows of age. The mouth frowned.

He wondered if the angry young boys still waited outside his door, if they still blamed him for being someone he never was, for something he had not done.

Why don't you go out there and find out? she would have asked.

She was not here to tell him how to explain.

Because I'm afraid, he would have answered.

He moved the easel closer and slid his palette from under the bed. He daubed the brush in flesh-colored paint and touched the camel hair to the corner of the mouth, trying to urge it from a disapproving frown into the suggestion of a smile.

# Chapter Ten

Kuhl woke up thirsty, the sweaty, twisted sheets smothering him. He fought them off and ran his hand through his hair.

When he came back from the common bathroom, Aleydis Aubrecht was waiting outside his room. Kuhl grunted as she dumped a pile of wadded cloth into his arms. She put a padded sack on top of it.

"Suit, helmet," she said. "Krause is flitting back and forth. He said he'll get to you eventually if you need help putting it on."

"I think I remember," Kuhl said slowly.

"You didn't *forget*, did you? That today's the last day?"

"Of course not," Kuhl snapped. And he had not forgotten, merely been overwhelmed by the carry-over from the dream: empty sands, buzzing flies, the drain of imagined thirst. He went into his room and unfolded the outsuit. Over the next half-hour he put it on and then, dissatisfied, took it off again.

He looked at it, scowling. But it *was* his. He recognized the patch behind the left knee and the spot on the back of the helmet. He had scratched it in taking it off, his first day here.

He put it on again. It was easier this time, the seals and connectors more comprehensible, but he was still frowning when he was finished. If he cinched the ankle- and wrist-straps as far as they would go, the suit was still looser than he remembered. When he inhaled deeply, his chest met no resistance. He smoothed the fabric and wondered if Krause had belts for the outsuits.

The boots fit, though, and then the gloves when he tried them on. He had lost some of Kuhl's weight. Then, he thought with vague uneasiness, Do I still look like him?

Then, smiling to himself, To these people, who else would I look like? It was all over anyway. The shuttle would lift in two hours. Most of his clothes and equipment were on their way to the garage by now.

Marella looked in the open doorway. "Get your suit on by yourself?"

"I managed," said Kuhl. He looked around his room, checking for things he may have left behind. A personal duffel sat on the end of the stripped bed. His paintings lay in a corner.

"We're leaving this place better than we found it," Marella said. He caught Kuhl's glance. "The rooms *and* the colony. You look better, too. Healthier."

"I lost a few kilos. I'll put it back on in the studio. Is everything set at the landing strip?"

"Alistaire and Abraham are there now, setting up the cameras. The Relayermen will operate them, as we planned, then juice the pictures up to *Belfast*. We've rehearsed it a few times. Nothing will go wrong. And, if it does, you can always animate it, once you get back to Manchester."

"And the ambassadorial team? How will you be handling that?"

Something flickered in Marella's eyes, something close to resentment. It was gone before Kuhl could frame a reply to the retort he had expected. Why aren't *you* handling it? Marella might have asked.

"Most of it will be left to the media crew waiting for us at Manaus. We'll get a little something for the departure sequence. Aleydis has kept her hand-held camera unpacked and she's got two cubes, one for back up."

"You seem to have thought of everything."

"Aleydis set most of it up. She's been working very hard, the last few weeks in particular."

"Maybe she had to work hard here, but she won't be in Manchester with me when I refine seven or eight hundred hours of raw material into a few hours of finished product, Paul."

"Paoli. It was my father's name. You always forget that when you're being arch." He glanced at Kuhl's bag. "Want me to take that out for you?"

"I can manage."

"All right." Marella backed out of the cubicle, looking as if he had swallowed something sour. "But I will be *very* interested in seeing what comes out of that studio of yours."

So will I, thought Kuhl.


Kuhl went into the common room, where the others had gathered. They had pushed the furniture up against the walls to make standing room for his six-man crew and the forty-odd Forcers who had spent two months here. The scent of the outsuits, plastic, and stale sweat thickened the air.

Zierling came in from the corridor. Her outsuit made her

shoulders seem unnaturally broad, her face unusually delicate. She cleared her throat and a dozen conversations ceased.

"We've got two shuttles waiting on the landing strip," she said. "We've got every working vehicle on Relayer mustered to take us out there. I've been on line to David Berry, and he says *Belfast* is ready to take us home."

A ragged cheer went up.

"This place isn't what we expected it to be," she said. "No way it could have been. It's a small culture—or cultures"—her smile was fleeting—"and they've had to adjust to hard times the best they knew how. Abe Hwang was telling me about bonsai last week. I guess that's what we have here. It may look . . . twisted, to some of us. But it lives, in miniature, and we can't fault them for that. You've all done a good job for me and the StarForce. Now we don't have to worry about this place anymore. Let's get up to *Belfast* and go home."

Two lines of Basque guards, twenty or thirty in all, waited in the corridor outside. Their faces were as neutral as their severe clothing. Behind them stood the young men shouting their slogans and beyond them, out of sight, a ragged crowd lining the walls of the hallway.

A half-dozen Basque guards marched in front of the Triumviratines, a half-dozen behind, the others pressing in on either side. A gray-clad arm jostled Kuhl. He glanced at the Euskaldun, who fixed his gaze ahead. It happened twice more before the corridor opened out into a main thoroughfare, seven meters wide and half that high.

A group of Chinese children, ranging far from home, moved aside for them, then fell in behind. They were joined by others, laughing, shouting in their languages. Before they had gone a hundred meters, adult men and women from all Relayer's nations started to trickle in from side corridors, lining the routes, silently watching as the Triumviratine citizens passed.

A Basque shook his fist and cursed. The woman beside him held her finger to her lips to quiet him.

"*Sh'ma Yisrael, Adonai*—"

"Hey, take us with you, friends!"

"*Dar!*"

"When will you come back?"

Abraham Hwang moved up alongside him. "I will not miss this place," he said quietly, "but I am glad I came here."

Kuhl said nothing. Hwang looked at him curiously. "And you, Citizen Kuhl?"

He shrugged, as if irritated. Kuhl would not have admitted he did not know what his thoughts were.

*"Liar!"* someone shouted.

The corridor to the garage was blocked. Simon Weiss stood in the center of the corridor, flanked by David Rosenthal and a dozen other Masadans. The shouts of the crowd dwindled to silence.

"Captain," said Simon Weiss into the quiet, "I speak to you unwillingly. Yet, I am the elected Councilman of Masada and, beyond that, Chairman of the Council. I have my duties."

Zierling's mouth tightened. "Mister Weiss, *Belfast* appeared, unexpected, uninvited, and unwanted, too, as we soon found out. That's something that was beyond your control, and mine. All we've done, before and after you tried to make things difficult for us here, is to learn about you and extend a helping hand."

"It is bait for the trap that will bring us into the Triumvirate," Weiss said.

"I can't convince you that's not true. I won't try. The fact is, the majority of people on *both* our worlds don't care one way or the other whether you're a member of the Triumvirate or not."

"You are mass murderers!" Weiss hammered the air with his fist. "Again and again the entire world is made into a graveyard. The unrighteous can wallow in the ashes of their own dead. *We cannot.*"

Kuhl looked around. He saw the faces of those around him, citizens and Relayermen both, darkening.

"We're just parrying for the benefit of the audience," Zierling said, sounding tired.

Weiss looked around him. Rosenthal took a step toward him, as if he were about to speak, but said nothing.

"It has ever been the duty of the Jews to lead man on the path from Creation to the Kingdom of God, and the aim of the unrighteous to murder us along the way. We the soldiers of God, you the partisans of Satan. It has been that way for six thousand years. And that, Captain Zierling, is not empty rhetoric. It is the truth as revealed to us in Masada. It is what I believe. History bears me out. Now there are no Jews on Earth. In that sense, you have won."

"There are Jews on Earth," Zierling said.

"As a nation? They are Jews in name only, carrying out what are, for them, empty rituals in the amusement park you call Jerusalem. I have studied the transmissions from your ship's computers. I know this to be true."

"Simon . . ." Rosenthal said nothing else. His jaw was set, his eyes downcast.

"There are those among us who wanted me to sue for a peace between us," Weiss said. "They wanted Masada preserved—as a pastown, a reservation, an amusement park, it made no difference. They wanted me to ask that you leave *us* alone and let our sons worry about the threat of your world's power hanging overhead. *This I will not do.*"

Rosenthal looked pained as the crowd rumbled angrily. "Simon, you said—"

Weiss silenced him with a look. "For your treachery, David, my smaller one." His gaze swung back to Zierling. "The message you will bring back to your masters is this: I have taken up the duty my fathers cast down when they fled from your world. Before your ship came, I could take up that mantle only in spirit." His eyes flamed. "But now my *flesh* will walk again in Jerusalem."

"*Belfast* can bring you there," Zierling said.

"On *my* terms!" His voice crashed in the corridor. "When Jerusalem is our city, and not your toy, will I walk down its ancient streets and kneel at the Western Wall."

Zierling looked around at the Basque guard standing alongside her. "Do the people in Biscay feel as strongly?" she asked Weiss.

"Go," Weiss said as if he had not heard. He stepped aside, pointing down the hall. "Bring that message to your masters. We in Masada will one day come to them. Until that day, you are unwelcome here."


Standing in the garage air lock, waiting to cycle through, Kuhl braced himself for the slap of cold, lifeless air.

The steel door slid aside. Warm, oil-scented air rushed in. The brightly-lit chamber resounded with the clatter of gas-fired engines and the roar of their exhaust.

A tractor towing two carts of outsuited Forcers rolled across the garage floor and into the main air lock leading outside. Other Forcers clambered into a waiting *akavish*. A second machine knelt clumsily to accept more passengers. Basques trotted across the floor, shouting orders.

Krause walked over to him. "Brian, you'll be going in that spider that just came back from the strip. You, your people, the diplomatic party, and me. There was a last-minute shake up in the diplomatic party. Did you know about that?"

Kuhl shook his head.

"It doesn't matter, I guess. I gave Aleydis the new names so you can identify them at your studio. This way."

Up close, he saw the *akavish* was the same one which had brought him here. Some of the more corroded hull plates had been replaced with ceramic panels made aboard *Belfast*. Their pearly luster was already streaked with hydraulic fluid.

Aleydis descended from the ladder leading into the machine's belly. "I've got our gear tied down up there," she told Kuhl. "I was out at the strip an hour ago. The camera crew is ready for us."

"Do they know what they're doing?"

"They'll do the job," she said. "Have you seen the diplomatic party? Damn it." She jerked her thumb over her shoulder.

Kuhl looked, his eyes widening slightly, his face growing cold.

"It's like Earth's a penal colony or something," Aleydis said from somewhere far off. "Like we're Botany Bay or something."

There were six of them, the most *Belfast* could bring to Earth, sitting close together on crates stacked alongside an *akavish*.

Judith Weiss looked up from where she sat, between Allan Webber's widow and a Basque couple. Her eyes met Kuhl's, then Kuhl looked away at those with her.

He did not recognize the two black men in the party, sweaty and uncomfortable in their oversized outsuits. The Basque couple sitting next to them spoke intently to one another. Beneath nimbi of gray hair, their faces were lined with age.

Kuhl turned to Aleydis. "Get David Rosenthal for me. Then find Zierling."

"Hey, there's nothing we can do, and I've got to—"

"Get them. Until I talk to them, this spider doesn't leave. Tell them both that."

She shrugged and walked off.

Kuhl went to Judith Weiss. She looked up at him, her face drawn, her eyes sleepless.

"What is he doing?" Kuhl asked.

"You know what he's doing." Her voice, too, was blurry and unfocused. "Did he 'exile' you? He said he would."

"He threw us out as we were leaving," Kuhl said. "Zierling can't allow this. He's just getting rid of—what, the troublemakers?"

"The captain already knows. There's nothing she can do."

The Basque man moved so Kuhl could sit next to Weiss. "You said he wouldn't let you go."

"I misjudged him." She smiled bitterly. "It's happened often, lately. This morning, David and I told him what he should do.

To try to heal your image of us, after what Neil and his gang did. He . . . invited me to go.''

"And if he did have a say about our coming back, you'd be exiled on Earth forever.''

"He would . . . regret it, in time.'' She shrugged. "But he doesn't have any say.''

Kuhl looked up and saw David Rosenthal approaching. Kuhl stood, but Rosenthal brushed past him.

"I wanted to say good-bye, Judith,'' he said. "I've spoken to Zierling. She said it might be a year—a little more, a little less—before we see you again.''

Kuhl said, "There has to be a way for her to stay, if she doesn't want to go. We don't have to take her. There's no way Simon can force us to.''

"I said he invited me to leave,'' Judith Weiss said. "I could stay . . . but I will go.'' She made a sound that was not quite a laugh. "This . . . is not quite what we expected, is it, David?'' Her eyes glistened.

"He is closer to God than we are,'' Rosenthal said stiffly. "He is the *Navi*.''

"Good-bye, David.''

After he had gone, Weiss looked at Kuhl. "You want to ask me if Simon is mad. The truth is, I don't know. Who am I to say that David isn't right, or that a star was not set in the sky to light the way for Simon?''

"You don't believe that.''

"Many do. It doesn't matter.''

The silence between them lengthened. Then he said, "You're the best choice for an ambassador to the Triumvirate. Your mind is open enough so you can learn, bring the knowledge back here. But I know you'll miss this place. I'm sorry.''

She said nothing.

"You will like it,'' Kuhl said. "Earth.''

She looked at him. In her eyes hid a wounded look. "I've heard you speak about it, but do you feel for it, as I love Masada?''

He tried to remember.

Finally he said, "A part of it.''

# III.

# ILLUMINATION

I do not mind lying, but I hate inaccuracy.
—Samuel Johnson

# Chapter Eleven

The Manaus terminus rustled and buzzed with a hundred new conversations. A man who looked like Aleydis or Alistaire Aubrecht bustled past him.

"Abelard!" he heard Aleydis (or Alistaire) shout.

Kuhl stood in the center of the terminus, tapecase and personal duffel growing heavy in his arms. Frings strode by, arm around a woman who held a child's hand. Frings slowed, seemed to be obscurely embarrassed, looked as if he were about to speak— then the woman tugged on his sleeve and Kuhl turned away, as if looking for someone.

"Citizen Kuhl?" said a voice from behind him.

He turned gratefully, but his smile faded as he saw the camera hovering over the stocky man's right shoulder.

"I'm Constantine Violano," the man said, extending his right hand. "With the local information desk. First, let me say how much I enjoyed your Asian documentary." He winked broadly. "I managed to get a look at a copy—just how we'll let stay a secret, eh?"

Kuhl smiled tiredly, but his gaze flickered back to the camera lens. What would he say, what would he do when—?

"Can you tell the Manaus audience a little, please, about what you found on Relayer, Citizen Kuhl?"

Where was Sara when he—

(And so he remembered.)

He pressed his tongue against the pressure switch in the roof of his mouth.

[Welcome *home*, Kearin.].

"Citizen?"

[What do I—?]

["I have a whirl of impressions in my head, Citizen Violano . . ."]

"Citizen Violano," said Kuhl, "I have a whirl of . . ."

\* \* \*

145

In a visitor's apartment on Sub One, Brian Kuhl set his suitcase by the door and lay gratefully on the bed.

Sara watched him attentively from the bathroom door, drying her hair.

"It was different this time," Kuhl said, staring into the cool blue ceiling. He rolled on his side to face her. "Without you."

"Did you miss me?" She set the towel down, then slid her sheer gown over her head.

"Always," he said, after only a moment's hesitation.

She smiled. Then, smiling, she sat on the edge of the bed and drew her fingers across his forehead.

He felt nothing.

Her smile vanished. "You've changed."

"Maybe a little," Kuhl said.

"Close your eyes. Tell me everything that happened."

He closed his eyes; still he saw her. Her face was lined, her hair gray and cut brutally short.

"Don't be troubled," she said. "Tell me all about it. I'll remember everything."

Kuhl paused. Then he said, "21 February 2166, approximately 16.32, personal communications were lost. Shortly thereafter, accompanied by . . ."

Sara stroked his forehead, listening to every word.

In a conference room on Sub Three, the walls fell away in a swirl of airy static. A starfield coalesced about him, and within it one point grew larger than the rest. It swelled, becoming a world with bloodied polar caps, harsh plains, tortured mountains.

"This is Relayer," said Brian Kuhl, "a world tormented by a hellish environment, a tragic history, and by self-hate, prejudice, and statism . . ."

He looked up into the blue ceiling. Sara peered at him through her stalk-mounted eye, then withdrew. Then her face appeared above him.

"Sara?" Only his lips moved. His throat, dry as paper, could not force the words out.

She smiled. Then he saw it was Candace Carpentier. Seacord felt her take his hand in her warm fingers. "I wanted to thank you personally, Seacord, since I took the time to send you personally."

His brow furrowed. His thoughts were mired in a postoperative drug quagmire. Sara flushed the garbage from his system. In its place came a flood of healing accelerants. Sculpted flesh restored, bruised bones straightened, he breathed deep into lungs freed from smothering layers of fat.

He smiled to be Kearin Seacord again.

"What was it like, being there?" Carpenter asked.

His smile faded. "My report . . ." Ten days under hypnotics and chemical stimulants, dredging forth every sight and conversation from the two months on Relayer—

"I've read your report," she assured him. "But, what was it *like?*"

Seacord thought a moment. Finally he decided, "Not much different from here."

She took her hand away from his, her gray eyes clouding.

"Thank you," she said again, but now coldly, and then her face disappeared from his field of view.

Seacord struggled to sit up, white points of pain blossoming in his belly and across his shoulders.

"Be still now," the Datalink said. Its fragile arm could exert no pressure as it pushed on his chest, trying to restrain him.

The room wavered drunkenly, and he saw for the first time that Brace and Spencer Swan were here in the operating theater, too. Swan looked grim.

Brace wheeled his chair over to the recovery table and grasped Seacord's forearm in drystick fingers. "Kearin . . ." he hissed.

"What's the decision?" Seacord said, turning to Brace.

Brace just shook his head.

"What's going to happen out there?" Seacord shouted after Carpentier. "What's the good word on the Force?" Brian Kuhl demanded.

The door opened. Carpentier walked through, her back ramrod straight, her shoulders square. Swan looked over his shoulder, his eyes narrowed, his mouth set, then the door closed on them and they were gone.

Seacord lay back. His chest heaved. Perspiration ran in icy rivulets along his rib cage. "Brace, what's the good word on the whole thing?"

"That is the question you never ask," Brace said. The Datalink's arm came close, shooing him away. He rolled back. "You just gather the data."

The fragile arm stroked Seacord's right biceps. He felt a cold sting.

"Sleep," Sara told him.

The night breathed warm on him. Seacord rolled over onto his back and pillowed his head on his arms. He looked out the bedroom window, out over the Hub, to the Suffolk slab's glittery cliffs. He sighed.

Sara said softly, "Restless? Do you want to talk?"

He swung his legs off the bed. The wood floor was cold underfoot. "Wardrobe light," he said.

"Kearin?" But she put the light on for him.

In the back of his closet he found his old black singlesuit and his black walking boots. He brushed off the dirt clinging to the tread.

As he was putting on the clothes, she said, "It's only been a week since the debriefing. What if Brace needs to know more about Relayer?"

"They always call me back within two or three days."

"This time might be different."

"It won't be any different. What does Brace know about that man we . . . about Damien Rosendahl?"

"He wouldn't want me to tell you. Are you going out? Where are you going?"

He said nothing, just started toward the door.

"What if Justin Izzo calls again?"

"I left *Palisades* for him in Suffolk. I told you where, Sara. Don't play with me."

"But don't you feel too weak to go out? They made you lose a lot of weight last week."

"I'm going out. Now, close your—"

"*Kearin!*" she shouted before he could finish, shouted loud enough to drown him out even to her own ears. "Kearin, I'm afraid if you make me close my eyes I'll never open them to see you again," she said, all in a rush.

He let his breath out in a slow, ragged sigh. "Sara . . . close your eyes."

The apartment did not feel any different once she had gone out of it. She would come back after he left, not knowing where he had gone.

It had taken a long time to train her to do that, subtly, so she never knew.

But, when he went into the living room, he found the Datalink unfurled and glowing. A message (set there before she had left the apartment) phosphoresced the length and breadth and depth of the holograph field.

*Don't leave me. Don't leave me. Don't leave me.*

He climbed the stairs to the roof and powered up the skid.

* * *

Jersey Sector again.

Brace had brought him out of the Jersey Lo seven years ago, given him a new name, the apartment in the Hub, given him the hours and the time to develop from a charcoal-and-paper dabbler to an artist whose name was known in cities he had never heard of when he'd lived in Jersey. Brace had given him a life. The only cost was to live another life from time to time, and to give up his life in Jersey.

He had paid that price only until he had discovered the way to close Sara's eyes to his departures.

If Brace found out . . .

But Brace would never know.

Seacord went back rarely now, just when the press of memory grew too great and had to be released. He had been born a lakker in the Jersey Lo. It was Jair who had found him, on the day after the Terminal Night, and raised him as his own son. It was Rags who had been a brother to him, and it was in the Jersey Lo that he had, for the last time, been sure of who and what he was.

He came in low, skimming the brackish water of Arthur Kill, below the sensors along the tops of its concrete banks. The Jersey citadel loomed on his left, massive and alien as a captured moonlet. His heart surged when he saw it, familiar sight of twenty years—though, then, seen always from below.

Seacord shifted his weight and the flying platform banked left, skittering across a lagoon he knew of, then up into the ten-meter-wide throat of a coolant intake. After a hundred meters the tunnel opened up, becoming a channel. He flew up a steep side and into the moist-smelling, ghost-lit cavern under Jersey's foundation. Behind him, the water slapped inward to the heat exchangers at the heart of the city's environmental system.

He stepped off the still active, hovering skid. Around him stretched a twilight forest made up of ten thousand pillars anchoring the citadel to the Staten Island bedrock. They merged seamlessly into the underbelly of the city, forty square kilometers of cement and ceramic punctuated by conduits and access doors frozen with a century's rust. No one, citizen or lakker, ever came here, to the world between two worlds.

The *sitra achra*, he thought. The real thing, this time, not some creeped philosophy.

Raw sewage and ozone perfumed the air. The ventilator mumble, machine clangor, and full-throated roar of the support systems for fourteen million souls were not so much heard as felt in his chest.

He touched a control toggle on the skid and, inert, it sank

squelchingly into clay made of brine and pulverized brick. With the side of his boot, he swept mud over the place it had gone under.

He looked around him, picking out a trio of landmarks, fixing the position of the buried skid from them. Nobody would find his ticket back to the Hub, and if they did, he had pried the registry chip out of it.

He started walking, the maintenance lights which flickered from every fifth pillar showing him the way. The crushed skeleton of the old city slid underfoot, bricks scraping, metal twisting and squealing. Two hours brought him to the citadel's northern perimeter. Out past the overhanging lip of the Jersey slab, the sun was melting the night sky to dawn streamers. He looked around for three other landmarks, found them, and from them a certain spot.

He overturned a particular twenty-kilo shard of concrete and scooped out a few handfuls of mud beneath it, revealing a battered metal box. He lifted it free of the muck, set it on top of the slab, and opened it.

Inside the box were a bundle of worn clothes, a citizen's identification band, and some wire and other oddments. He lifted these out and set them on the slab, alongside the box.

On the floor of the box was a bit of neatly folded paper.

*"God!"*

He slammed the lid and clamped his trembling fingers around the box. His breath came in shuddering gasps.

It was over, he thought.

He pushed the box away and sat on the slab, looking at it, arms wrapped across his fish-flopping gut.

Then he admitted to himself what he had realized the moment he had seen the paper, which he had not put in the box.

So, he drew the box to him and opened it. He unfolded the paper and held it close to his face so he could make out the small, precise lettering.

Come upstairs, it said.

He sighed and dropped it in the box. It was unsigned but he knew whose work it was, had to be, and it was all over. He stood, squared his shoulders, and looked around. A few dozen meters away, steps grew from a pillar like bracket fungus on an oak. The access hatch at the top of the ladder gleamed.

It was open.

He climbed the ladder.

He emerged in an alcove adjoining a service corridor. Steam wafted from old pipes. Indecipherable legends were stenciled on conduits and monitor boxes. The tunnel, closed on one end by a steel grate, on the other by a heavy, rusted door, was empty. His path was unclear.

He started toward the door and, as soon as his back had turned, heard a faint sizzling behind him. He looked over his shoulder and saw Brace sitting in his wheelchair.

"I expected to find you here," Brace's image said dryly. It was not idle conversation. Instead, it was a reminder.

I can hurt you, Brace was telling him.

Bile surged into Nem's mouth. He fought it back; it left a burning trail all the way down his throat.

Brace's eyes stared into his own. Seacord looked away.

"If it matters," he said softly, "I'd decided this would be my last trip in."

"Nothing you say matters," Brace said. "Most unforgivable of all is your stupidity. You know the Datalink's capabilities, but apparently you don't know your own limitations. Your reprogramming attempts were reported while they were still in progress. The appearance of your friend, in Suffolk, was very poorly played."

Seacord stared.

"We sent him back to Jersey. You were foolish to come here after that indiscretion, Kearin." Brace shook his head. "Would you go back to the LoSide now, and stay, if you could do so without interference from me?"

"No," Seacord said without hesitation.

Jair was his father; Rags was his brother. But he remembered the sleepless nights, the hungry days, the bitter months and crushing years.

"No," he said again.

"I didn't think so. Keep this in mind: the Datalink will not allow you to come here again. Any attempt to come here will be severely met."

"I understand. Will I . . . still work for you?" Will you let me live in the Hub? Will you let me live? he thought.

"If you weren't going to work for me, you would be thrown out like garbage. That was your friend's expression, wasn't it?"

I know everything about you, Brace was saying.

"There's a job for you now," Brace said. "It's an offshoot of the Relayer mission. You'll have a different identity, of course. Change into more suitable clothes. Take public transportation back to Boston. I'll see you in my office in six hours."

"I can be there in less than one."

"*Six*. Take a room in Suffolk and sleep for five hours. You look like hell. If you find you can't sleep, think instead."

They were taking the Hub from him.

"Your home in the pastown is being modified," Brace said. "You will never do this again."

The image gazed at him.

"How long have you known?" Seacord dared.

Brace looked at him with naked contempt. "I have always known. Remember that: I have always known. I've just waited until now to tell you."

His image faded. The portable projector mounted on the wall behind him became visible. Then, with a serpentine hiss, it too faded.

Seacord looked over his shoulder. Where the rusted door had been was now a table piled with fresh clothes. Behind it was a corridor, the way clear.

# Chapter Twelve

Lightning flickered, illuminating the slice of cloud cover wedged between the ranks of apartment blocks fronting the alley. Droplets pattered audibly on the stiff shoulders of Loren Middlebrooks's tunic. The kinetic energy of each falling drop painted rainbows on the black material. In a moment the whole suit was aglow with shifting patterns.

Maya Zierling tugged on his hand.

"Come *on!*"

He held back, grinning. "It's just water."

"I don't like it. It's wet."

"Welcome to weather. We're almost there."

She looked around. The block looked like any other they'd walked that night. "How can you tell?"

"There're signs." He saw it in broken streetlamps and dangling spy eyes. Just a little more vandalism than the norm. The pattern was familiar to him: first, stepped-up surveillance to catch the vandals; second, failure; third, resignation and decreased maintenance. Then the floating happy club would move in, until the Peacemakers sniffed it out again. Kearin Seacord had closed this one down twice already.

Well, not tonight.

"Over there, Brushes."

She squeezed his hand so it hurt.

The big man stood from the doorway as they approached. From a distance, his yellow singlesuit resembled a Peacemaker's garb. Up close, the illusion dissolved. (They could never pinch him for impersonation.)

[He has a weapon. Mark-IV staplegun, over and under. But the clip is empty, and, of course, I'm not transmitting any power into it.]

[Probably found it in a discard canister.]

[Massing four-and-three-tenths kilograms, it makes a serviceable bludgeon. Be careful.]

[I will, Sara.]

Middlebrooks dropped Zierling's hand and walked straight to the guard, stopping a meter away. "Inside?"

"Say again?" said the guard. He hooked his thumbs through his fishnet belt, bringing both hands closer to the pistol tucked against the small of his back.

"We want to get happy."

The man's face changed from slothful stupidity to something more carnivorous. "You got the time? Or hours? No transfers through the link, you know."

"Save that for the tyros," Middlebrooks said. "I've got time." Very slowly he reached his right hand up to the left shoulder of his jacket. He parted the fabric, somehow, and took out a stiff, flat pouch a centimeter wide and eight centimeters long. The white stuff inside glittered like hazy memories.

"This'll buy us in." Middlebrooks tossed it to the man, who nipped it out of the air.

"Got to test it."

"Do it when we're inside. You don't like the cut, come and find us. Don't lip-taste it, though. It's pure."

The man grunted. "Sure. It's all pure."

"This is. It's not out of the LoSide, it's out of the agricultural tracts, direct. Let your test-bench tell you—when it comes down from orbit."

"I'll do that," said the guard. The pouch disappeared somewhere into his singlesuit. When he stepped aside, the door behind him opened. "Basement, room forty-three," he called after them.

The hall was narrow. Middlebrooks had to step aside to let a young woman pass. She was dressed in worker's coveralls and carried a toolsac. If she thought him oddly dressed, her look did not betray it.

An apartment door opened behind them. A hobberknockered younger ran out, shouting something about visiting upstairs. His father (presumably) warned him not to go outside.

"Everything is so close," Zierling said. "Not like Aztlan."

"What about that place you said? Relayer?"

She bit her peach-colored lower lip. "I talk too much. Something in you brings out things I shouldn't say."

"It's serious? I saw about Relayer on the screen. Loosen up. Want another kiss of time?"

Her eyes darted both ways down the hall. "Here?"

"Anywhere, Brushes." He stroked the two narrow swaths of hair, then cupped her head and drew her almond-flavored lips to his. When they parted, her face had darkened from the rush of blood.

"Give it to me like you did the last time," Zierling said.

"Here?" He mocked her.

"Do it."

Another secret pouch, then more time. He rolled the black capsule in his palm, then put his hand to his mouth. She put her arms around his neck and kissed him open-mouthed. He pushed the capsule between her teeth with his tongue. She let this kiss linger, too.

"Now you," she said, her eyes already glazing. "That way."

"I'll get a double dose."

"You can put the handle to it, can't you?"

"Yes."

She opened her mouth. He placed a second capsule on her whitened tongue, then took the kiss. She pushed it into his mouth slowly, teasing him. When it was on his tongue he pushed it up, against the back of his upper teeth, against the roof of his mouth, through the stoma Brace had had him fitted with. The pill felt huge, nestled in the mouth pouch.

He flicked his tongue against his teeth, rubbing the trace powder from her tongue off of his. It burned like an open wound on his palate; he felt the surge of bloodheat in his face and gut.

[How much of a dose am I getting?]

[The antitoxin should be able to handle it. I'll monitor the serum levels, Loren.]

He groaned breathily. She smiled. "You like that," she said.

"You do a lot of things for me I like. How come a starship captain is bothering with a very bad man such as myself?"

"When I said you were a bad man, you said you were just trying to pay the habitation tax for a wife and two kids."

"Two wives and a kid." He smiled. "But there's just me, in truth. And habitaxes. They're higher for us entrepreneurs, you know."

"What does Suffolk Administration think you entrepreneur?"

"Toys." He put his arm around her narrow waist. The gauzy, vat-grown fabric of her dress made a sound like muffled, breaking glass when it shifted. "What does Aztlan think you do for happy times?"

She stiffened slightly. He purposely misinterpreted it, holding her tighter, putting his face into the scented hollow of her throat. She reached behind her and got his small finger, drew it back so he had to let go—but, without hostility.

"Let's go down," she said.

"Anywhere."

"To the happy club, sport."

The walls of the darkened drop-tube were painted black, so they could not tell how far they fell. The doors opened on a narrow corridor. A shimmering curtain melted aside for them.

"Take your coat, sire?" The young woman extended her metal-gloved hands.

"It's worth your life," Middlebrooks said matter-of-factly. (She shrank back.) "When does the show start?"

"A quarter-hour, sire."

"Show us to a private booth."

"This way, sire." She flowed away from them, between glowing gasjets, balloons painted with leering skulls, and metal-tabbed animal skins flapping on invisible gusts of magnetism. The oddments drew attention from cracked basement walls and dewy overhead pipes.

A ramp led downward. They passed through a crystalline curtain and into a room big enough and dark enough so that the opposite wall could not be seen. Tables, each separated from its neighbors by one-way privacy screens, ringed an open space about twenty meters in diameter. The floor there pulsed like a black sea.

[Another hologram. Their power consumption is enormous.]

[Remember I've been here before. Now, don't distract me.]

They passed several booths on the way to their own. In them:

—An old man and four nearly identical blond men ate a feast of broiled fowl, a dozen species of vegetables, and less readily identifiable black-market foods.

—Two women in severe singlesuits bent forward in earnest conversation.

—Three men made slow love to the two women presented on the oiled table before them.

"*Rapid*," Zierling said. "You *do* know how to have fun."

"This is as rapid as the ones with limited imaginations—or limited hours—get. More to come, love."

The hostess showed them to a table on the periphery of the open floor. Once inside, the other booths disappeared into random patterns of diffracted light.

Plush cushions, dry but moist-feeling, surrounded the genuine wood table. The commlink cover and keypad were also wood. Food, drink, or toys could be passed into the booth through an inlaid door in the center of the table.

"What now?" Zierling asked. She stretched out on the cushions, the dress falling open, making promises Middlebrooks did not want to be kept. He looked away, frowning over the keypad.

"Aqua vitae."

"Slow."

"When the time rushes in on you, you'll be glad you didn't have any liquor on top of it. Listen to a man of experience."

She smirked. "I have experience, too."

"I know."

She looked expensive. The shimmering, crackling fabric of her dress, woven in Aztlan, remained rare in the terrestrial citadels. The cut of the garment was unusual, too: a kind of peplos such as Athena might have worn, the fabric folded around the vaguely eccentric body, caught at each shoulder by an ornamental pin, leaving the arms bare, open down the right side. A wide belt, concealed by an overfold, held everything together.

Her hair glittered with metallic sprinkles and her eyes sparkled with time. But no amount of ornamentation could conceal the age stealing into her face. The drug was burrowing out from the inside to meet it. Even the StarForce's medicians could prolong the useful life better than delay the inevitable end. She was seventy, she looked forty, but sometime soon the whole physiological mechanism would just fall apart and all at once she would be close to death, and look it, and feel it.

"What's the matter?" she asked, sitting up and reaching for his hand.

"Just wondering if you like this place. Maybe it's too rapid. It's different from that place I found you in last month."

"Who wants to spend any time in a sports club, once you know about these places? Besides, I'm too old to use the *sesta* without pulling a muscle, but I'm not ready to sit back and watch you young people play."

He took his hand away, as if she had made him hurt or angry. "You mention that a lot. Age. Like you hate me for being as young as I am."

"You're good for me. No . . . you're very bad for me, with these endless hits and rigorous nights. Maybe you're trying to wear me out, Loren." She smiled carnivorously. "But you can't collect the death benefit unless you're a Forcer, you know. We don't take care of anyone but our own."

He reacted again, turning the anger up.

[Would Middlebrooks be angry? You're stepping in and out of the matrix.]

[She'll think it's the hit of time she gave me.]

[That's not the point. Is something—?]

He cut Sara off. [*Shut up*. You're distracting me. We'll get what we need tonight, or not at all. Her leave's over in five days.]

With seeming reluctance, he let her take his hand again. "Maybe I am a little mad at you—because you remind me of someone on *Belfast*."

Me? he thought. (He nearly shook his head.) Kuhl? He kept his face neutral.

"His name was David Berry," Zierling said. "He was about your age, I guess. Something . . . happened. We complemented each other somehow; he had youth and I wanted it, and I had power and he wanted it. What we had lasted as long as it took us to realize we couldn't share the two things we needed to share. So, when *Belfast* came back, we let it go. The Force covers a lot of territory; I won't see him again."

"And he put you onto time?"

She looked at him sharply. "Why do you think that?"

"I can see you haven't been using time very long. It's still an event for you, not a part of your life, like it is for me."

"Well . . . it *was* him. I'm not sure if I should thank him for that or not. I was perfectly happy by myself, you know, before I met him. I had been for years. Then it all went to hell. I was sloppy on the Relayer mission because I was thinking about him. Sex has no place on a ship. It's too confined, there's no escape valve for the pressure. When I make commandant—and I will—I'm going to segregate the crews even more than they are now. Breaking them down regionally isn't enough. We'll do it by sex, too."

"You mean, if they want it or not?"

"On second thought, we'll just eliminate the men altogether. You kids." Her eyes unfocused all of a sudden and she blinked hard.

"It's hitting you, telling you it's there," Middlebrooks told her. "Roll with it." Two thin goblets of clear liquid appeared on the table. He pushed one to her. "Take that. It smooths out the rush, makes it last a little longer."

"You look funny," she said muzzily. "And I've been talking a lot."

"It's the rush. It—" A chime, clear and crystalline, sounded. [Grin. *Anticipation*.]

He smiled broadly. "Oh, Brushes, this is where the ride gets rapid. Come here and sit with me."

She slid across the cushions to sit alongside him, where they could look out across the open floor.

The floor was heaving, boiling, throwing out sheets of ebony like negative images of flame. He draped his arm across her thin shoulders and felt her trembling from the drug.

[Is she all right, Sara?]

[I can't monitor the narcotic levels in her blood, but from what you've given her, she hasn't received a debilitating dose. Don't give her any more, though. Her defenses are coming down, but the next stage is free association and incoherence.]

[Watch out for her.]

[I'll monitor her surface and internal temperatures. My visual receptor is blocked.]

[Was David Berry one of ours?]

[I do not know, Loren. Does it matter?]

The floor exploded. Gouts of blackness flew upward, to melt into the indeterminate ceiling. Rings of color spread from the center, dissipating as they reached the booth.

They faded to white, achieved definition, became a circular pit fifteen meters across and three meters deep. The floor was stained and pitted, the walls faintly concave. Circular metal doors were set at ten-meter intervals.

A cloaked figure stepped through one door. From within the shadowy confines of his hood, he surveyed the surrounding tables. Then, with glistening metacarpals, it threw back its hood. A death mask stared with lambent eyes.

[Cheap theatrics.]

[Stop trying to reassure me, Sara.] His heart thudded. It was not the facade that frightened him, but what lay behind it.

[You weren't this frightened the first time.] Sara sounded concerned. [Is it the time in your blood?]

It was that the first time he had thought how similar this was to a street show in the Jersey Lo. He remembered flashing steel, a ceremonial cut, and long drafts of brew afterward. Now he scented the animal desperation in the air. It penetrated the privacy screen around the booth and made the air heavy. It was the clerks and administrators and programmers around him, waiting for a tangible enemy to appear. The Triumvirate had no enemies and its citizens no rivals, except, comfortingly, here.

"Death," said the figure conversationally, "is an ending. Fear is the beginning of an end, but the road may be long. The road you travel with the cockatrice as your companion is endless. The cockatrice." It raised one draped arm and pointed. One of the steel doors ground open ponderously.

And it was knowing what was coming next.

He gripped the seat, knuckles whitening.

And it was remembering a glossy photograph, a tattered hull, a soundlessly screaming mouth in a twisted face, a starry backdrop.

"I don't—" Zierling started to say.

It burst from the entranceway like a tide, surging across the floor on too many legs sprawled at impossible angles, churning stroboscopically; he saw jaws, talons close on the empty air where it perceived a man to be, there on the battle floor.

"The man who faces fear is to be admired," said the death figure.

The cockatrice spun like a whirlwind and struck again with a storm's fury, uselessly.

"But the man who succumbs to fear comes to the end of the road, and the terminus."

Death faded into a miasmic cloud. Behind it lay a second door, now squealing open on neglected hinges. The man lingered in the open portal for several heartbeats, then stepped into the light. He was tall, heavily-muscled, wearing a well-tailored loin-cloth and a vaguely confused expression.

The cockatrice pointed its broad head toward the ceiling and parted long jaws filled with teeth. Its roar was silent. Silently it slid along the curved wall, eyes locked on the man.

Sweat gleamed on his skin. He took a single step back, but the door behind him had closed.

[Is it *real?*]

[It is no hologram. It has body heat, eighty degrees centigrade. It is no terrestrial animal.] And, anticipating his next question: [The man is real also. I've identified him as a transportation officer working in Hatteras Sector.]

[When we closed this place down last time, we never saw it, never knew for sure—]

"Loren, do you know what that *is?*" Zierling breathed.

"Yeah."

He could not focus on it, as if it were cloaked in a thin mist that followed it as it stalked on six sinuous legs. The form was vaguely feline, but again not; his first impression was only of disquiet, as if his body intuited it shared no common ancestry with the cockatrice. Its greasy gray hide shifted with each step, and it left moist tracks on the stained floor of the arena.

The head was too wide, the snout too long, as if a panther's skull had somehow melted and run. There were no ears. The red eyes, glowing from beneath an overhanging shelf of flesh, were a match for those of Death in his holographic personification.

The man's footsteps carried clearly to their booth, but the monster padded silent as a nightmare. Again its jaws parted, again it soundlessly screamed its rage or satisfaction or some-thing completely different. The lambent eyes never left those of the Hatteras citizen.

[We have to stop this.]

[According to StarForce studies of the cockatrices in captivity on Aztlan, they do not kill. And your mission with Zierling takes precedence in any case.]

It sprang, covering the intervening fifteen meters before the sacrifice could react. There was the sound of a hammer on meat, then the man was down, blood flowing from nose and mouth, and the monster was on the other side of the pit, restlessly pacing, never still, never fully definable.

Zierling gasped. She put one hand to her nose and one to her mouth, as if she had been struck.

"This is . . ." Middlebrooks closed his eyes to slits, trying to think.

["This is just the start, Brushes. Keep watching."]

"Keep . . . watching. This is just the start."

The man staggered to his feet, head lolling. Blood streaked his chest. He wiped at his face, then wiped his hands on his breechcloth. A wide print blazed on his face, beneath the blood, but the skin seemed unbroken.

The cockatrice struck again, in the same pattern, but this time Middlebrooks saw the arm snake out, saw the heavy pad flatten against the man's side in a burst of kinetic energy.

The sacrifice staggered, but stayed on his feet. His right arm lashed out reflexively, but the cockatrice was already somewhere else.

Zierling breathed hard, face mottled, hands linked in her lap. Sweat beaded her upper lip, ran down her naked arms. "It's going to kill him. It's going to kill him. How can they let this happen?"

"Peacemakers don't know about it," said Middlebrooks after a pause. "And . . . I've never seen one kill before. It just makes you wish you *were* dead. You should know about these cockatrices, right? They were sent through the Portal to stir everything up. Terrorize. You just watch."

The third time the monster came in, it was slower, each lope distinct, the fluidity of motion gone. The fleshy club at the end of one forearm looped out—and this time the sacrifice caught it, wrapped his arms around it and turned, dragging the cockatrice with him, slamming it into the wall once, and then again.

The background murmur from the booths became a roar.

The man swung one leg over the squirming creature, pinning

it to the floor. The head whipped around, the snaking legs beat ineffectually.

Sweat and blood running freely, grinning, the man raised his fists over his head and brought them down on the beast's head.

The skin split, audibly.

Middlebrooks's pulse surged. He felt Zierling grow rigid beside him, heard her gasp as if from the other side of a black void.

Gray ooze flung upward from the tear in the cockatrice's hide. It caught the man in the face and he threw his hands up to wipe it away. His foot caught on the creature when he backed away from it and the skin split again, messily, and the man tripped and fell down hard alongside it.

They lay next to each other like spent lovers, the cockatrice oozing across the floor, its sides heaving. The man gasped, arms cradling his head.

Then he screamed as the cockatrice's hallucinogenic lymph slid through his pores and into his bloodstream.

The cockatrice's head came up, suddenly alert. Then it got to its feet and padded across the floor of the arena. A door opened to let it escape.

The sacrifice screamed, back arching, arms beating a tattoo on the stained floor, gray gelatin streaming from eyes and mouth to mix with the foaming spittle, blood, and sweat.

"What is the worst thing that ever happened to you?" Death's whisper seemed to come from directly behind him. "What is your greatest fear? This man walks that road."

Middlebrooks watched for the requisite length of time, and then two women wearing metallic gloves entered the arena and took the offering away.

Her apartment, in a transients' block on the other side of the city, was nearly the size of his home in the Hub. She had been living in it for two months, but except for a small sculpture of *Belfast* executed in wire, and the uniforms scattered around the room, she had left no mark on it.

"This your ship?" He poked at it, and it wobbled on its stand.

"David made that. Don't touch it."

"Hey, sure." He flopped onto a couch.

"What happens to him?"

"Who? The man in the pit? They put a few hundred hours into his account and he goes away with a hell of a story to tell—if there's anyone he can trust to tell it to."

She walked across the room tentatively, then sat at the opposite end of the couch, her hands in her lap. The peplos lay in a wad at the end of her bed; now she wore a plain, unrevealing nightdress. Her skin was faintly gray; she was coming down off the time.

"Outside of the couple we have in captivity at Aztlan, they're supposed to be extinct," she said hollowly. "They couldn't have lived this long in a natural environment."

"I guess whoever sent them built pretty good. I've been hearing talk for years about how they're all over the LoSides. Not many of them, but spread out, doing the thing they were designed for—giving nightmares. After the poisons and rockets they sent through the Portal, and then these things, I guess the next step would've been an invasion force."

"I could've done without seeing it."

He grinned. "Hey, I told you it was rapid."

She stood abruptly. "It's all a game to you, isn't it? After a few hours or days he's able to go back to his job, so in the end it doesn't matter, does it?"

"Hey, he volunteered. They don't grab people off the street to do that. And the time we paid to get in goes partly into his pocket. He's got no complaints."

"Would you do it?"

His grin turned to a wan smile. "*Watching* is rapid. *Doing* is merely intense."

"Well, you might not have a choice in it, Loren. Then we'll see how rapid you are."

"Hey, what are you—?"

"I've been out there in the Deep. The signs are there. They're coming back. And this time they'll be coming from all over the sky, not a tunnel through space we can squeeze shut."

He started to laugh. "Yeah, right."

"We're going to be the only thing standing between them and you, Loren. We can't wake Administration up to the threat because they're like you, rooted in the past, or the present, anything but the future."

"I get along. You've seen these monsters, huh? You've seen them on the road back to here?"

"I've seen the signs," she repeated. She sat down again, closing in on herself. Sara urged him on.

"Well, you can take care of them, right? You're tough, Brushes."

"We're nothing to them. They've built a sun."

"Hey, you and me could build one if we—"

Her hand shot out, fast as the cockatrice's pad, smashing into his cheek. Blood welled in his mouth.

"Not many people do that," he said dangerously.

"That was for letting me think I could talk to you. I talk, but you aren't listening."

"So? What do I know about stars? Or monsters from the other side of the Portal? They were here once and left the cockatrice behind. So, they'll come again. What can I do about it?"

"Nothing."

"Right."

Her shoulders slumped a little. "It was that white powder in me, making me say too much, too crazy."

"Really got me creeped. But it does that to you, Brushes. You've got to slide with it. You've got to slide with everything that comes to you."

She looked at him, her deep gray eyes deeply confused. "That's what you do. Nothing affects you. The cockatrice could've killed him, and it wouldn't have mattered to you."

He shrugged, looking vaguely uncomfortable.

"You remind me of someone on *Belfast*."

"Berry, right. You told me about him."

"No. After him. Nothing started with him because I never felt I could trust him. His eyes never changed."

"I don't know anything about that."

"It was useless."

"And with me?" he asked with curiosity, but with no particular emotion. It was just the right note.

She just smiled. "Let's go down."

It was the last time.

# Chapter Thirteen

It was a long walk back to Middlebrooks's apartment on the north side of the citadel. Dawn was striking through the corridor windows by the time he reached his door and told it to let him in.

Brace waited for him.

His image, here, was merely incongruous.

"It went well?" the hologram asked.

Middlebrooks nodded wearily and sat in a chair by the door. The studio apartment measured just five meters by ten. Its bare white walls reminded him of his apartment in the Hub. He wondered if the alterations Brace had told him about were completed, if he would ever be allowed to return there.

"What did she tell you tonight?" Brace asked.

Middlebrooks rubbed his forehead. "I don't know how much is her suspicions and how much is hard fact, but she really believes—or knows—that the light in Relayer's skies, the nova, is associated with the aliens who launched the Portal War. Or with the Outsteppers themselves. Or some third party. She told me that much, but afterward she was sorry she had."

"She no longer trusts you, then?"

Middlebrooks was reluctant to agree. "Not as much as at one time," he admitted.

"Perhaps the mission should be curtailed," Brace said. "If she never saw you again she would be disturbed by the abruptness of the falling out, but not suspicious."

Middlebrooks stood up. "I believe her. And she believes what she's telling me."

"Of course," said Brace. "Why would she lie to someone like Loren Middlebrooks?"

"What about Carpentier? Has she been reviewing my reports? Has she—?"

Brace rolled his chair forward. The thin, spoked wheels left tracks in the rug.

Middlebrooks's pulse surged. Brace was really here.

165

"You were about to say something?" Brace asked dryly.

"If the report is right," Middlebrooks said, "then we could be in great danger."

"We could," Brace said.

*"Why are you here?"*

Brace smiled coldly. "This is an extraordinary situation," he said. "Your life as Middlebrooks is ended. There is a new assignment."

"Now?"

"No morphic surgery or sleeplearning will be necessary. The mission should last less than thirty hours. If it shows signs of going beyond that, adjustments will be made." Brace reached into a pouch hanging from the arm of his chair and extracted a stiff paper envelope. He handed it to Middlebrooks.

Inside were sheets of hardcopy covered with densely-packed type.

"Your new maxtrix is a Baja Sector citizen named Sim Winter," Brace said. "His appearance matches the face you're wearing now. He is a low-level functionary for Baja Sector Administration, but he is also an historian and a member of several North American historical societies. His specialty is statism in the periods immediately preceding and after the Portal War." His eyes narrowed. "You see where this is leading."

"She'll *know*."

"Zierling did not know, and as Kuhl you were closer to her than you were to Judith Weiss. Your appearance, mannerisms, and gross physiognomy are different from Kuhl's. If there are any passing resemblances, and if Weiss notices them, they'd fall under Occam's razor—that, indeed, there are often resemblances among people who have never met." He pointed to the hardcopy. "The minimal background you will need is in that file."

Middlebrooks hefted it. The pages rattled faintly and he willed his hand to stop trembling. "We've never done it this way before."

"The press of time dictates it; the ease of the mission permits it. Judith Weiss will be in Suffolk this afternoon, on her way to the Jerusalem pastown. It's arranged that you'll be her guide. You will discover what she wants there."

"That's all?"

"That is all."

"It's *natural* that she go there," Middlebrooks said.

"You will learn the extent of her interest, discover if it is as single-minded as she professes it to be. As Winter, it's natural that you would do so."

"Why not another operative? There's still more I can learn from Maya Zierling."

"We have already established that is not so," Brace said. "Are you regretting your decision, Kearin?"

"What decision?" But he knew what Brace meant, and his heart grew cold.

"Your decision to stay. You question your assignments now. What happened to you on Relayer? Was it too much like the Jersey LoSide? Do you think on those years of your life with nostalgia?"

Middlebrooks said nothing.

"Answer me."

"Relayer is like here," Middlebrooks said. "I saw that. They've made each other into enemies because they need an enemy to keep them going. But there it was out in the open. There was blood. There's no blood here."

"We have real enemies," Brace said. He rolled himself forward. From the chair's side pocket he produced a pearly citizen's identification band. He put it in Middlebrooks's hand.

"Put this on," he said. "I understand you can do it without the help of our machines."

Middlebrooks felt his face grow hot.

"You may have changed," Brace said, his face less than fifty centimeters from Middlebrooks's own. "What has not changed is this: The reason for a mission, the disposal of the information, remain my responsibility not yours. Remember that, Sim Winter."

Winter put Middlebrooks's clothes into a duffel bag and set it near the door. Ten minutes' work, and it was as if he had never lived in the stuffy basement apartment. The only thing he would leave behind was a scar on the bathroom doorframe, indirect result of a bleary night with Maya.

There was a Datalink near the bed, a basic model with keypad and flat screen mounted in a gray plastic case. He sat on the bed and looked at the gray screen imperfectly mirroring Sim Winter's face.

Maya'll wonder why I haven't called, he thought. She said she worried that the time in him would get him into trouble on the way home. So, usually he slept with her.

She'll be worried.

But (Brace was right) perhaps not very much.

He'd punched in the code before deciding to do so.

The screen engaged, lightening to bone white. It remained that way for nearly a full minute, then a legend unraveled across the pixels:

COMM: SHUNTED TO TVS *BELFAST*.
TRANSLUNAR CHARGES APPLY.
SHUNT CALL?: (Y/N)

The message hung on the screen, black-on-white, with clarity and finality.

He tapped a key and the screen returned to darkness.

Sim Winter took his duffel and left the apartment.

# Chapter Fourteen

"Take this, Citizen. It will open your mind."

Sim Winter took the scrap of hardcopy which had been thrust at him. He glanced down at it—WATCH THE SKIES! it proclaimed—then up at the white-haired, wrinkle-faced woman who had given it to him.

"There's great danger if it's allowed to go on," she said, her eyes lively. The murmur of those waiting on the tubetrain platform nearly drowned out her fragile voice. She was, he thought, the oldest person he had ever seen, certainly older than the citadels themselves. Her bony fingers plucked at the chain hanging at the open neck of her tunic. The overheads glinted from a token, an open ring nearly obscured by a silver cross.

She held it away from her neck. "That's the old symbol of the Portal you know—closed off, the way we want it. Can I interest you in one? They run to six hours, for the better ones. It helps to pay the cost of the handbills," she added, apologetically.

"I'm late for an appointment," he said. He looked past her shoulder, to an alcove on the other side of the platform. With their polarized visors, it was impossible to tell if the two Peacemakers there were looking in his direction.

The woman's face fell. He lifted the handbill, said "Thanks," and reentered the human current running through the Suffolk terminus. He kept his head down when he passed the Peacemaker's station, but one of the policeman stepped in front of him.

"Was she bothering you, Citizen?"

"No . . . not really." Winter offered the brochure to the officer. "She gave me this." He caught a glimpse of garish colors and crude lettering before the Peacemaker's mitt engulfed it.

"If she's not harassing the citizenry, there's not much we can do." The muffled voice sounded regretful. "She didn't sell this to you, did she?"

"No, just handed it to me."

"Well, she doesn't need an entrepreneur's license for that."
The Peacemaker took a step back, dismissing him.

Before he left the corridor, Winter looked over his shoulder.
The old woman stood where he had left her, a small island in the
stream of passersby.

Universal and ideographic signs directed him to a transients'
restaurant. The brightly-lit interior was nearly empty. He pushed
through the bursar's one-way gate and paused.

[Sara . . . this will never work.]

But Judith Weiss looked up as he entered; then, incurious, she
returned to the conversation with the others sitting at her table.

Each step across the undecorated ceramic floor seemed loud to
his ears. Judith looked up again as he approached the table.

Her hair was fuller, her face less sallow. The vertically striped
singlesuit would accentuate her height when she stood, Winter
thought; it fit her much more closely than anything she would
have dared wear on Relayer. Al Webber's widow sat next to her.
The man with them looked up, then stood.

"You must be Citizen Winter," said Spencer Swan, reaching
for Winter's hand.

Winter took his hand, waiting for the cry of recognition, but
only for a moment. Idiot, he thought. Swan had never met Kuhl,
and Sim Winter looked nothing like Kearin Seacord. But had
Carpentier put two agents on Judith? And, if she had, why
hadn't Brace told him?

Unless Brace didn't know . . .

[Sara, could it be coincidence that he's here?]

Whole decaseconds passed without response. *[Sara?]*

He put his hand to his ear as if brushing at his hair. He heard
it then: the long, low hiss of a carrier wave carrying no signal.

"Citizen Winter?" Swan pumped his hand some more.

"Oh, very glad for the acquaintance," Winter said with appar-
ent enthusiasm. He peered at Swan's face. "You . . . you're not
from Relayer, then?"

Swan grinned. "No place more exotic than right here in
Suffolk, I'm afraid. From Tasman, originally. I'm with Security
Affairs. Just met Citizens Weiss and Webber here and thought
I'd keep them company while they were waiting for you."

"Oh?" He looked dismayed. "Am I late?"

"Not at all. Here, sit down," Swan said, and made introductions.

"Do you specialize in any particular period, Mister Winter?"
Weiss asked.

"Oh, immediately preceding and antecedent to the Portal

War. Say, 2045 to 2055 or '56.'' He grinned foolishly, disarmingly.

'' '45 was the year my world was settled,'' Weiss said.

''Oh, I know. But—'' He paused, then looked embarrassed. He dropped his voice to a conspiratorial level. ''My specialty is, in fact, more the effects of the war on this world, and not so much the colonization and exploration efforts. Oh . . . that was what you were interested in, wasn't it?''

''Yes it was, Mister Winter,'' said Weiss. She sounded weary of him already.

Bird-like, he turned his head to Yuan Ch'ing Webber. ''So, you've been here, what is it, about two months now? How have you enjoyed it thus far? Where have you been?''

Webber smiled back at him and nodded, saying nothing.

''Yuan Ch'ing is only now learning how to speak English— your Universal,'' Weiss said. ''As for where we've been, I think it would be about fifteen cities in the last two months. Most of the time it's been just Yuan Ch'ing and me. They've split our group into three.''

''And what has impressed you most?'' Winter asked eagerly.

''The sameness of it all. I'm hoping Jerusalem will be different, a vacation for us.'' She looked at Swan. ''Is there time for Yuan Ch'ing and me to eat before we leave for Jerusalem?''

Swan checked his banglewatch. ''I'd think so.'' He pressed his palm to the table. A menu glowed in front of his place. He showed Judith how to do it.

She frowned. ''It's so difficult to read.''

''The character-set is basically the same,'' Winter offered. ''There are a few more than were in use in the last century, adopted from Cyrillic and Arabic. And—oh, maybe you should help her, Citizen Swan. We use the positional—never mind. When does the train leave?''

''Seventy-five minutes from now.''

He pushed away from the table. ''Be along shortly.''

On his way to the nearest Datalink kiosk he tried calling Sara's name once more, to no result.

He found a communications booth a hundred meters back along the corridor. He slipped inside gratefully, then, with his fingers poised over the keys . . . stopped.

What was Brace's access code?

He didn't even know if he *had* . . . Well, of course Brace *had* to have one. If you lived in a citadel, if you wanted to eat, you had a citizen's code.

He had never needed it before. Brace always came to him.

Winter keyed for assistance, and found zero Suffolk residents had "Brace" as either given or surname. He let his hand fall away from the keypad. It was hopeless. And ridiculous.

He'd have to abort, return to Black Rock. Would Sara let him down to Sub Five? Of course she—

In response to no action Winter had taken, the screen cleared. Brace looked out at him from the phosphors.

"I've been waiting for you to try to contact me," Brace said. "I asked the Datalink to connect us whenever you tried to use a communications circuit. You have a problem."

"Don't I know it. I—"

"No doubt you were alarmed," Brace said. "It's a hardware problem on our end, and of no danger to you. Have you met with Weiss and the others?"

"What kind of hardware problem?"

Brace's look was, for a moment, blank.

In that moment, a cold wind swept along Winter's spine.

"You're lying to me," Winter said.

"Yes," said Brace.

"What's the real reason I'm out here without support?"

"You're asking questions again, Kearin. You need to remember not to question me."

Remember I can send you into the LoSide, Brace was saying.

Winter just stared into the screen.

"You're in no danger," Brace told him after a moment.

"Spencer Swan is here."

Brace, for the second time, looked blank. "Who?"

"The operative who came with Candace Carpentier to Sub Five. He apparently met Weiss here, at the terminus. He's representing himself as a Suffolk SA employee."

Brace raised one eyebrow.

"Is he?" Winter asked.

"No," said Brace, frowning. "What are his intentions?"

"I don't know. But he's indicated he won't be accompanying us to Jerusalem."

Brace's face cleared. "Then we can investigate and contain the problem, if problem it is." Emotion flickered in the lined face. "He's in *my* sector, damn him. And this time without Carpentier."

"And you want me to go to Jerusalem. What's the difference?"

"That's another question. Are you sure you made the right choice?"

"Carpentier's right hand is here. My right hand, Sara, isn't. I'm not leaving this booth until you tell me what is going on,

Brace. My life has been confusion since Carpentier came to Sub Five.''

''When you return to Suffolk, contact me at this code.'' He recited the twelve-digit number. ''I'll bring you in when I hear from you. Understood.''

''I'm *not*—''

Brace blanked the screen from his end.

Winter hammered the access code into the commlink.

No response.

[Sara?]

No response.

Sim Winter returned to the restaurant.

After a meal he did not taste and conversation he did not remember, Winter and the others walked out to the BoreLink platform.

It's no more difficult than the Relayer mission, he thought. I survived that.

A tone sounded across the nearly-deserted platform. The tube train hissed through the air lock leading from the evacuated main artery. Its black corrugated skin split, spilling light from within. As the other passengers moved forward, Weiss turned to Spencer Swan.

''Thank you for making the city a little less foreign to us, Mister Swan.''

''Even though it's like all the others, Miss Weiss?'' He smiled. ''You're very welcome.'' He nodded to Webber's widow. ''Yuan Ch'ing, enjoy the rest of your stay here.''

''Thank you, Swan,'' she said musically, and unexpectedly.

Swan took Winter's hand again. ''Good meeting you also, Citizen. See that nothing happens to them, will you?''

Winter looked confused. ''We're not expecting any trouble, are we?'' He grinned nervously.

''I don't think the unexpected would bother you, Citizen Winter. I think there's more to you than you let on.''

Winter kept the clown's grin on his face.

''Flatterer,'' he said.

The BoreLink tunnels laced together the three hundred citadels, the saline-filled tubes within the walls conducting messages from one lobe of the Datalink to another, carrying incidentally less-complicated audiovisual signals between the cities' slower-thinking human inhabitants. The cargo and passenger trains were scheduled around the migrations of millions of computer-controlled inspection robots and repair drones. A tectonic shift six hundred kilometers west of the Azores brought the automatons out in force. Their train was diverted north, making an unscheduled stop in Manchester, then south again, overland briefly, paralleling Hadrian's Wall, then across the Channel, to Berne, Corse, and nonstop from there to Jerusalem. The journey took nearly three hours. A carefully-modulated voice emanating from the soft, curved walls apologized for the delay.

Sim Winter, Judith Weiss, and Yuan Ch'ing came up from the Jaffa Gate, in the shadow of Suleiman's walls. Moist heat beat down on them. Sunlight refracted unevenly from cultivated hills, the citadel looming at their backs, the stone blocks rearing ahead of them, at the end of a dirt road. Weiss drew her breath in a long, drawn sigh.

"The Talmud says there are ten shares of beauty in the world, and Jerusalem has nine," she said.

The pastown lay completely outside the walls of the Palestine citadel, which stretched westward for fifteen kilometers, to a smaller historical reserve at Bet Shemesh. Palestine's LoSide was a constellation of camps tucked below the horizon.

The Old City sprawled on the gentle slope, a fragile pile of stone that had weathered nearly three thousand years of climate and conquest. The Dome of the Rock and El Aqsa Mosque glinted, but their brilliance paled before the funhouse-mirror slopes of Mount Scopus.

Weiss turned away from the sun's light playing on the glazed hillside. "My brother was right," she mumbled.

Yuan Ch'ing took her arm and urged her forward, smiling mutely, reassuringly.

Winter sought to keep the sympathy from his voice.

"That happened long before Relayer was colonized," he said. "It was toward the end of the statist wars in this region . . ." Weiss stared at him, and his voice trailed off. "I had assumed you knew," he added weakly.

"It is one thing to know, and another to see and feel. After so long, nothing grows there still."

"But . . . the soil is fused."

"Couldn't something have been done?"

"It reminds us of past conflicts. That is the last and largest monument to the wars that ended with First Contact," Winter said, subdued. Then, more animated, "Would you like to go there? There is a fine—"

"In 1967 we entered through Saint Stephen's gate and Jerusalem was ours again for the first time in eighteen hundred years. But before two generations had passed, the Syrians, wearing United Nations uniforms, were pouring over those hills.''

"It was the *Israelis* who detonated the devices.''

"And if that had been enough we would never have been exiled to Relayer. We have not been able to live here in peace since King David made this his capital. How many, here in Jerusalem, died in the Terminal Night?''

"I may not be so well versed in the Arab-Israeli Wars, Citizen, but I know something about the Terminal Night. The madmen responsible for that were punished, and the faults in our system of government that gave them so much power have been revised.''

"When we were children, my brother would tell me the story of the Holocaust, so we could appreciate how fortunate we had been to have even Relayer as a home. He told me how the Europeans and Americans had crushed the evil of Hitler, forgiving yourselves for his acts, putting the blame on a single, deranged animal, and completely forgetting that time's anti-Semitism. I see that's happened again. There's no reason for you to learn that lesson of history. You're not the ones who suffered a second time, and will suffer a third. I know your history better than you do, Mister Winter.''

"A version of it, certainly,'' Winter said stiffly. "I'm sorry if I offended—''

"You're nothing,'' Weiss snapped. Then she put her head down, a slow flush rising in her face. She looked around her, at the passersby who had lingered. They moved on reluctantly.

"I'm sorry,'' she said so softly Winter could barely hear. "You are my host, and I was rude. I think I've seen nearly enough, for now. Maybe I can return another day, when the . . . surprise would not be so great.''

"I understand.''

"But . . . there is a place I promised my brother I would visit. Does Or Ha-haim Street still run near here?''

A dirt road led uphill to the Jaffa Gate. The dust they kicked up settled immediately and did not cling to their clothes, but the oppressive heat suffocated. Winter's singlesuit was damp by the time they reached the gate's environmental field.

A Peacemaker waved them through the entrance without inspecting their citizens' bands. A second guard barely glanced at their entry passes. They were inside. Conditioned air and the shadow of David's Tower cooled them. The walls pressing close to the cobblestoned street blocked the sight of the centuries-old nuclear battleground to the west.

David Street surged with crowds in a bewildering variety of dress. Old-style military uniforms clashed with polyester skirts and Bedouin abas. Skullcaps and *ighals* bobbed. A Peacemaker riding in an open-deck freewheeler was most incongruous of all. A man in beggar's clothes, squatting near a gutter, hopped back to avoid the transport's soft tires. He shook his fist at the peace officer, who ignored him, and then went back to hawking statues from Hebron, coins from Gaza, pieces of a building block from Jericho.

The contrast with the Boston Hub and other pastowns he had visited stirred Winter and made him vaguely uncomfortable. The Old City resembled the Jersey Lo more than any place he had seen—and that not very much. How to act here? It was all uncontrolled.

(But he remembered the sign hung at the gate. Jerusalem had no residents; it closed for maintenance for the four hours before the dawn of every day.)

The walls were as anarchic as the actors in their native dress. Structures built to last eternities leaned drunkenly, outrageously against one another: Crusader arches, a Roman square, Byzantine paving stones, a store built by an Ottoman shopkeeper, a Muslim mosque, an Armenian apartment. Most recent were the camouflaged Datalink kiosks at nearly every corner, something else he would not have found in any other pastown.

The wall built by the Ottoman sultan, just four kilometers around, kept everything from flying apart into a dozen different centuries. But only its facade was genuine; silicon-nitrogen ceramic made up the load-bearing structures. The story was the same for most of the interior structures. Winter saw the realization of deception come to Weiss's face as she struggled with the signs written not in English, Hebrew, Arabic, Aramaic, Turkish, or Armenian, but in Universal.

At the confluence of David Street, the Street of the Chain, and Suq Khan Ez-Zeit, the ancient walls stepped back, forming a square filled with actors in their Bedouin and Hebrew roles, selling lengths of hand-woven cloth, wicker baskets, polished trinkets, maps of the Old City on squares of stiff paper. The Temple Mount came into view again, just 250 meters distant. Beyond it, Scopus's glitter caught Weiss's eye and held it.

Winter moved in front of her, blocking out the heat-glazed slopes. He pointed. "The street you're looking for is a few hundred meters that way," he said.

* * *

The heavy stone walls of No. 6 Or Ha-haim Street had been built to withstand invaders and terrorists, chilling nights and torrential rains; none of these existed anymore in Jerusalem. The plaque alongside the door, giving street number and a name (Herzl), was tarnished into near-illegibility.

"Is this the place you wanted?" Winter asked.

Weiss stepped forward and rapped on the wooden door. It was opened a few moments later by a dark-haired girl wearing a simple turquoise shift. A red bandanna held her hair away from a sweating face. She looked at the strangers uncertainly.

"We've come to see the museum," said Weiss.

The girl looked at Yuan. "Even her?"

Weiss's face hardened, but her voice was gently firm when she asked, "Are we the only ones who can learn from the history of our people?"

The girl shrugged and stepped aside for them. Winter ducked his head to enter the dim interior.

The scent of woodsmoke clung to the walls. The wooden furniture looked fragile. Doorways led to other rooms.

"You don't stay here by yourself, do you?"

"No," said the girl.

"Who lives here besides yourself?"

She shrugged.

"What's your name, child?"

Unwillingly, she said, "Dara."

"Is your mother or father here, Dara? I'd like to speak to them."

"They live in the citadel. My grandfather is here. He's sleeping. Are you *Ivri*?"

"Very much so. My name is Judith Weiss." She introduced the others. "Can we see the rest of the house?"

"Better to come back another time."

"But we've come from very far away," Weiss said.

The girl thought a moment, then shrugged again. "You'll have to be very quiet."

In the bedroom, fragile cribs and beds crowded the flagstone floor. Small tin stoves sat in the kitchen alongside wooden buckets of coal. A gilded mirror, fogged with age, hung in a second bedroom. The bed was made of wooden boxes and boards.

They passed through a narrow courtyard, into another room. Along the walls were ranked quills, reeds, and stiff paper; a grinding wheel; a shoemaker's forms.

On the way back, they lingered in the courtyard.

"The house takes its name from here," Dara recited. "The Old Yishuv Courtyard Museum. When Jerusalem was reunited in 1967 this was set up as a museum for how life was lived before the city was struck into two pieces."

Weiss smiled gently. "I know," she said.

Winter sat on a wood and stone bench and studied the clump of white gardenias by his foot. He frowned; it was just a house.

"Dara!" A man's hoarse voice called from inside the house. The girl dashed inside.

"You haven't been here before, Mister Winter," Weiss said, more a statement than a question.

"This is the first time I've been to Jerusalem," Winter admitted. Weiss frowned, and he added, "Perhaps the government should have found another historian to accompany you, someone specializing in the nationalistic era following the Second World War. I believe the thought was that you would.be interested in how the world has changed since the Portal War."

"There is time for everything. I will be on Earth for many more months." She looked around the courtyard, a narrow slice of gardened tranquility, isolated from the rush and babble outside. "The name of the museum comes from the Jews that immigrated here from Europe in the eighteenth century. It has been a museum since 1967. Your culture seems to value stability. Certainly there's something to be said for a long tradition like that." She sighed, then looked at Yuan and smiled sadly. "You're not very happy, are you? But you would have been unhappier staying behind."

"Why is that?" Winter asked.

Weiss seemed not to have heard the question. "I have to see the Wall before we leave," she said, half to herself.

Should he take the direct approach? "Miss Weiss, why did you want to come here? There is the Israel Museum, and the old Knesset Building . . ."

"This place shows how we lived. It's not your image of how we were. It's not . . . under glass."

"Of course not," said a voice.

Dara led the old man into the courtyard. His feet, hidden by the folds of a black robe, glided silently across the paving stones. A face framed by unruly white hair seemed to float above the high, stiff collar. He sat heavily on the bench, alongside Weiss, the breath wheezing from him. His face was red with exertion.

"We don't get many visitors to this part of the Old City," he said, when he could speak again. "It seems as if everyone who's wanted to see the place already has, old people like me. The young ones don't want to come here." He raised a fluttering hand to his head, patting his skullcap into place. "And then there's you." He looked at Yuan, then glanced at Winter. "You're not Hebrews. You don't look at home here." To Weiss, "But you . . ."

"I'm from Relayer, elder," Weiss said.

"Relayer?" He frowned, concentrating. "I remember my father telling me about that place." He looked at Weiss, suspicious. "How can it be you're back here in the Old City?"

"The ships . . ." Weiss began.

Dara tugged on the old man's veined hand. "I told you about that, Eliahu. They were saying that the ships would go out to all the old colonies." Her face had grown pale. Her gaze flickered to Weiss, then away.

"I remember that now. I didn't hear anything about them coming back." He looked at Weiss again, and then smiled broadly. "I see the proof they did, though. What's your name, girl?"

Judith Weiss told him.

"I saw her on the screen last night," Dara said gravely in her high voice. "She was inside Relayer."

Herzl looked down at his grandchild. "What's this, child?"

"There was a show on the screen. I saw it at Mother's house." Dara looked at Weiss. "Eliahu doesn't even have a commlink here. The show was three hours long so I didn't watch all of it. There's going to be more tonight."

Weiss sat back a little. "I didn't realize it would be so fast."

"We can set up access for it," Winter offered. "You can see last night's program, too, but there'll be a surcharge."

"Yes. . . . Dara, what did it say about us?"

Eliahu Herzl put his hand over Weiss's. "Don't concern yourself with their pretty pictures and flowing words. They're all lies." He lifted his hand; it swept in an arc to encompass the surroundings.

"Tell me, Judith, what do you think of our little house? *It* is real."

She smiled faintly. "It doesn't seem to have changed since Relayer was settled."

He laughed. "For far longer than that has this house stood still."

Weiss glanced at Winter before she said, "I'm surprised the

government allows you to go on. They seem to have a policy of turning away from the past."

The old man nodded. "You're a stranger here—and how strange it is to say those words—so you see the Peacemakers in every city, the same uniformed officials, the communications links and subterrene trains welding everything together, *tight*," he knotted his bony hands together, "like this." He lay his hands in his lap again. "But it is all surface. You see layers of bureaucracy and you cannot know how thin they are, and how they struggle with one another. Imagine two blankets, each trying to cover the other. Soon there is only a tangle." He looked up at Winter, smiling. "You are Judith's escort? From the security division, perhaps?"

"I'm an historian. And I work for Administration as a researcher."

"Then, as an historian and official, you have seen our government from both sides. It is like two blankets, isn't it?"

"I hadn't thought of it that way."

The old man turned back to Weiss. "When our nation was founded—and it doesn't matter if you say that was when David was king, or in 1948—a nation was a simple thing. thing. A territory, and the people in the territory, and the men who led it. We still have nations—you've been told otherwise— but they are elusive things. It is a jurisdiction, the subordinates in a department, and the policies that govern it, written or not. There are many more nations than ever before." He grinned again. "And because the borders are so ill-defined and ever-changing, you can make your home in the place between the nations and be apart from them. So that is the answer to your question. I'm not so old I'd forgotten it already."

"You're not doing anything wrong here," Winter said. "Not that I can see."

"I agree with you, historian. But are we contradicting policy, reminding people that past ages were not all chaos and wars?" He shrugged. "I should be thankful the Old City was not buried under that monstrosity in the west. There was talk, when they were building it . . . But we had friends then, and have friends still. I go there every night and sleep in the room my daughter has set aside for me in her apartment. What do I call your mother's home, Dara?"

" 'The end of the world,' " she replied instantly. Eliahu smiled.

"Why?" Winter asked. The old man reminded him of another old man, one who lived in Jersey in a house full of books scavenged from the entire Lo. Jair would not have had to ask what the old man meant.

"It's the end of the world because there's no future there," Herzl said. "Or because it is the future. My father lived here when the War through the Door came and went like a terrible burning wind. He thought it was the end of the world, and so did everyone else. But the world is still here . . . and the world before the war is gone. So maybe my father and the others were right. The world *had* ended, just as it did when the Door to the Sky was built, and when they dropped the first atomic bomb, and when the holocaust came, of course. The world ended frequently then." He put his hand on Weiss's knee. "There are worlds under your feet, girl, each buried under the ones that followed. Once they're submerged, they never surface again. You can never regain the past once the present has come. But here the present has never come, so we live . . ." His voice trailed off; he shrugged. "There are other places like this. Not many. You should see some of them before you leave. You are going back to Relayer?"

"On the next ship that goes there."

"Your family is there? They did not come with you?"

"My brother. He is the one who remembered Or Ha-heim Street and told me to come here."

The man smiled. "That's good. Maybe he'll come here one day and I'll meet him, too." Eliahu put his hands on his knees and stood. "But for now, young lady, I'm an old man and I need my rest."

Weiss's face registered surprised disappointment. The old man saw it, and pressed his lips together, thinking. "Dara, go get my book."

"What book, grandfather?"

"*Any* book, child."

She ran back into the house.

"You've come a very long way and I may have been a disappointment to you." Dara came back and pressed a leather-bound volume into his hand. It was scarcely bigger than his palm. "Keep this. It's older than the dream of your world." His gaze wandered. "Such a crazy dream that was," he mused. "Anyway, take it. Remember everything I said, in case I'm not still with the living when you come back. And—your brother's name?"

"Simon."

"Share your gift with Simon, as he shares with you, brother and sister."

"I will," Weiss promised.

"Come here, granddaughter." He put his hands on her cheeks and kissed her forehead. "Go now. Dara! Take them into that place they call Palestine."

"But, Eliahu—"

"Don't whine. You were whining all morning, telling me you wanted to play with that boy, Michael, instead of watching the door while I slept."

"Citizen, we can leave from the terminus outside the Jaffa Gate," Winter offered.

"Don't be a crazy man. There are no restaurants here, no beds, no showers, nothing to make it fit for human habitation. Go to the citadel and wash the dust off yourselves. And if you can find your way onto the Wall, look east and you can see the Old City laid out before you. It's worth the trip just for that."

"I was going to see the Wall before I left, Eliahu," Weiss said.

"Dara! Take them to Herod's temple, first. And none of your whining, child. I'll give you candy when you get back."

The surface train was crowded, tourists on their way back to transients' rooms in the citadel. The historic dress some wore seemed affected and vulgar in contrast to the clean, Mondrian lines of the train's quiet interior. Hills dotted with olive trees slid past the polarized windows.

Dara sat across from Winter, her hands twisting restlessly in her lap. When he smiled at her she frowned and stared out the window.

"I'm sorry I was rude to you before, Mister Winter," Weiss said from alongside him.

"You've already apologized."

"It is . . . hard to be away from my people."

I know, he thought. "I understand," said Winter. "May I see the book Citizen Herzl gave you?"

The binding was rough and warm to his touch. The pages were trimmed raggedly and, when he opened the book, told him nothing. The graceful, tortured characters of the Hebrew alphabet were meaningless to him. "What is it?"

"A history of the Marranos. They were Spanish Jews who converted to Christianity to escape persecution, but they continued to practice their faith in secret."

He nodded, continuing to turn the pages of the book. No illustrations. It was a dead thing in his hand, telling him nothing. He glanced over his shoulder, marking the position of the surveillance camera at the end of the car. Weiss reached for the book, but he said, "I'd like to hold it a while longer, if that's all right. In the period of time I study, there were few books. By then, everything was being put on magnetic media."

She nodded. He turned the pages of the book, feeling vaguely foolish. Was Sara watching now? But, if she were not, the camera's memory could be tapped later. It would be equally simple for another escort to take the book and copy it later, but Winter felt obliged to contribute some sort of data during the course of the mission. All he had learned thus far was what he could have surmised: Judith Weiss was lonely.

But no barriers of language or form separated her from the body of Triumviratine citizenry. Winter watched Yuan Ch'ing, chin resting in her hand, staring blankly out the window. She knew some Universal or English, enough to communicate basic needs, at least, but she remained silent. Had the government offered her sleep tutoring? Had she refused?

He bit the inside of his cheek to conceal his frustration. Where the hell was Sara? Brace had told him nothing.

"Excuse me a moment," he said. He had to try to reach her again.

Weiss twisted in her seat to let him into the aisle. "I think we're nearly there, Mister Winter."

He smiled bleakly. "Can't wait."

There was a terminal in a booth at the end of the car, but he went past it, to the next car, out of Weiss's sight. He let himself into the booth and punched Kearin Seacord's communications code.

The signal flashed forty-five hundred kilometers westward; whether through saline conduction tunnels or via satellite, seconds passed.

Come on come on come on, he thought.

"Kearin Seacord's residence, in the Hub in Boston. Artist working in—" The screen displayed a recent oil painting.

"Sara, it's Sim Winter. Sara?"

The spiel stopped abruptly. After another second the painting was replaced by her face. A wave of relief dizzied him. "Sara, I'm so—"

Her look, a simulation of anger and confusion, stopped him. "Loren, what are you doing in Palestine Administrative Tract?"

"I'm not Loren. I'm Sim Winter."

She frowned. "It's me, *Kearin*," he insisted.

"The Middlebrooks matrix was to have been terminated six hours ago, but you still wear his face. Who is Sim Winter?"

"Sara . . . are you all right? I lost internalized communications with you a few hours ago and then—"

"I just ran a diagnostic review for the last twenty-four hours. There has been no systems interruption."

[Can you return to internalized commlink now?]

Her look grew more angry. "You're the one who made the rule there was to be no in-comm unless you were in the field."

"I *am* in the field. There's something wrong with your—" He sagged against the door of the booth. "There's never been *anything* wrong with you before."

"Are *you* all right?"

"I . . . am confused. Look, contact Brace and tell him I'll be back in Boston within a few hours. And tell him *I* think your malfunction has not been remedied yet."

"There is no malfunction."

"Just tell him what I said, please."

She pouted. "Very well. But, Kearin, I insist you return to Boston immediately. There is a tubetrain scheduled to come here via Manchester, leaving Palestine in four minutes and sixty-five seconds. I will delay it until you arrive." She apparently saw his hesitation. "I *insist*."

Resentment flared for an instant—*she* was supposed to serve *him*—but then he realized he was grateful for Sara's direction.

"I'll be on the train," he said, "and when I get there—"

Someone tapped on the door of the booth. Looking over his shoulder, he saw Yuan Ch'ing. She smiled, waving for him to come out.

"I've got to go," Winter said, breaking the connection.

"Palestine in forty-five seconds," said an inflectionless voice from near the ceiling. In the booth, he had not heard the announcement.

The train plunged on, into the walls of the citadel. The window darkened, internal lights came on, and deceleration urged them back to their seats.

[Sara, are you there now?]

*What the hell was happening?*

There was no one to tell him.

Peacemakers ringed the debarkation platform. Winter's heart stuttered . . . until he realized they were not for him. (Why should they be? he thought, catching himself. Ass. But the situation creeped him. He could not shake it.)

Nearly invisible alongside the peace officers' gaudy auric uniforms, a half-dozen demonstrators moved among the travelers stepping from the train. All wore the closed-Portal symbol he had seen in Boston. One man clattered with the weight of chains hung around his neck, wrist, and waists. Skull-shaped metal cutouts depended from the links.

"Take this, *please*," he said, thrusting a translucent plastic panel into Winter's hand. "You *must* read it." His eyes were glazed, whether from time or fear Winter could not tell.

"Get away from me, please," Weiss said to another demonstrator.

Warmed by the heat of his palm, the display came to life with a miniature, two-dimensional scene of a skyline on fire.

THE WAR
IT CAN RETURN
OUR CHILDREN WILL KNOW
THE PAIN WE HAVE BEEN SPARED
DO NOT TEMPT THE DESTRUCTION AGAIN
CLOSE THE DOORS TO THE STAR-DEATH—NOW!

(The words rolled up the tiny screen and out of sight.)

The fiery backdrop changed. A velvet sky, a chiaroscuro plain. On the verge of handing the object back to the demonstrator (who was now moving on), the image held him. The tarnished spider-shape, the man in armor standing alongside it . . .

*"Where did you get this?"* The thing fell from his hand, splashed into crystalline dust. He caught the man's shoulder and spun him around.

The fear was clearer now in his eyes. "What do you—?"

(From the corner of his eye, Winter noted and disregarded Peacemakers converging.)

"That scene from Relayer, where did you get it?" He had not relinquished his grip on the man's shoulder.

"It was on the screen, everyone saw it, I took it off the screen, it was last night, we were warned." A line of spit started at the corner of his mouth.

Winter let him go; the man rubbed his shoulder then, continuing the motion, wiped the spittle away with his sleeve.

A gold uniform loomed at Winter's side. Another took up position behind the demonstrator. Wireguns stayed sealed in their holsters, but the articulated gloves flexed.

"What's the problem here?" came the officer's mechanized voice from beneath the inscrutable black visor.

"I didn't do anything wrong," the demonstrator blurted. He was younger than Winter had first thought, probably not more than a few years out of crèche. For a moment he regretted—

He stole from us, he reminded himself.

"That viewpanel he's handing out, it's got pirated copy on it," Winter said. He toed the dust at his feet.

"It does not!"

A Peacemaker put a warning grip on the boy's forearm.

"What's it all about, Citizen?" the mechanical voice asked.

"There's a scene in there, illegally copied. It's an infringement." What would their faces, behind the visors, reveal?

But they didn't ask him why he should care. Instead, "Do you have any more of those with you?" one asked the demonstrator.

"Some," he said unwillingly. "But it was on the public channel, and anything on the public channel you can use. We're citizens, it's *ours*."

"The producer's an entrepreneur," Winter said curtly. "I know him . . . by reputation. He's not an agent of the Triumvirate."

One Peacemaker put a hand to the side of his helmet, head cocked to one side. "Datalink confirms that much of it, Jeanne. Let's see one of those panels, friend."

The demonstrator rummaged in his pockets. He lifted his gaze from the floor long enough to favor Winter with a hating glance. Winter looked away.

"Bring all of them down to the Grid, the commander says," said the Peacemaker who had just spoken.

The Peacemaker he'd called Jeanne signaled. The other guards stepped away from the walls. One of the protestors went limp when she was grabbed from behind, but it made no difference to the peace officer's augmented strength.

"We're only trying to save you, save us all!" the young one shouted as they took him off the debarkation platform. "The monsters will come back and lay waste to us all!"

Weiss, Yuan, and Dara Herzl waited for him by an exit.

"What did they want?" Weiss asked, subdued.

A couple walked by arm in arm, laughing at what they had seen—"Damned anarchists got what they wanted, anyway."—and favored Winter with a smile as they passed. He pretended not to have seen.

"Apparently there was a broadcast yesterday of a documentary on the mission to your world. It's stirred up a few people who were probably off the beam in the first place."

Weiss's mouth quirked. "Are they worried about us retaking Jerusalem?"

"No. About whatever waged the Portal War following you to Earth."

She paled. "Oh."

"But it translates to fear of you, in an abstract way. It's a bad thing."

"So you acted against it."

"I reacted—to a crime against Brian Kuhl."

"You know him?"

"Only his work. He'd done studies of postwar ecological changes, so our fields of interest overlap. I'm not sure I approve of him putting himself outside the government and society as he's done—not that he needs my approval—but it took courage to do so. That boy is stealing from him by what he does."

Weiss looked at him for a moment. "I think Kuhl would have appreciated it." Then she smiled. "No, that is one thing he would *not* do. But he would have agreed with you."

"You've met?" Winter displayed confusion. "Of course you've met him. You probably know him."

"I could have known him, perhaps, if we'd had more time. He's a very difficult man to know, I think. And now he's cloistered in his studio in England."

"You sound disappointed."

"No . . ." But she seemed to considered the possibility. "No, I wouldn't say that, Mister Winter."

They went up into the alabaster streets, so similar (he supposed; it didn't really matter) to Suffolk's. A few pedestrians walked quickly along the narrow streets. An enclosed freewheeler, doors stenciled with the Peacemakers' dove, trundled away. Carrying the protestors, probably. He felt a twinge of regret, which dissolved when he looked at Weiss again.

"I think you were wrong," Dara Herzl said abruptly. "They're right. What are we going to do when the monsters come back and bring more bombs and gases?"

"They won't come back," Winter said. When he looked up, he could see just the slab sides of the alabaster buildings, the bright splashes of paint flowering around their windows; beyond them, the sky was a perfect, pearly shield. "Aren't you hungry? We'll take you to dinner."

"I've got be go home. But I'll take you to a restaurant near the BoreLink station."

"Thank you," Yuan Ch'ing said, surprising them all. She smiled. "I understand some, from my husband."

"Where's he?" Dara asked.

"Dead now," Yuan said.

"Oh." Dara said haltingly, "I'm sorry."

"He is full of peace." Yuan glanced up, then held out her hand, palm up. She smiled. "Rain."

"I was starting to think it never did that here," Weiss said. "I . . . we've never *seen* rain before."

Dara started walking faster, short legs pumping, heels clacking on the street. "It's just up a few hundred meters." She started back toward the wall surrounding the Palestine citadel.

Apartment blocks gave way to smooth-walled manufactories connected by overhead walkways. The rain turned from spatters to a consistent drizzle. No one else was on the street. A skid hissed overhead, then another. The street rumbled: the train they had taken in, returning to the Old City.

"Here." Dara turned abruptly into a narrow, open doorway. They went down several steps, into a tunnel a few dozen meters long. A stiff wind blew rain into their faces from the other end. Dara looked miserable, Weiss and Yuan delighted, as they came into the street on the other side, into a sudden downpour. Drops exploded on the pavement; rivulets sheeted the sides of the factories around them. The hammer of machinery pounded against the humid air. On the other side of the roadway, tables and chairs were arranged behind an environmental screen, under the overhang of a looming factory. Workers in dirty gray singlesuits crowded the restaurant. Their skids hovered outside the environmental field.

Winter stepped out into the rain, and felt the hairs on the back of his neck rise. He looked up, behind him, and saw the wall of a factory laid bare. Alabaster panels had been stripped away, revealing a Mondrian pattern of communication lines and power grids. A scaffolding clinging, crab-like, to the side of the building supported welding stations, lockers, and more workingmen. Rain splashed and hissed against a portable environmental field. Laserlight flared as a weld was made. Fine carbon ash drifted down, mixed with the water, and stained the street.

"Come *on*!" Dara shook her wet hair and growled, *"Grand-father!"* She started across the street at a dead run.

Winter watched them replacing the building's guts for a moment more. If the Portal War did return (more savage this time, because it could not be turned off, because it would have to be *fought*) what was the point of it all. He remembered Relayer. And Zierling. Dara Herzl, and the young demonstrator with frightened eyes. (And the cockatrice's amber eyes.) Parts of a puzzle he could not define, let alone put the handle to.

The rain suddenly abated as a vagary of wind spun the drops away. With it came a quick change of pressure. He looked up, startled, and the scaffolding, which a moment ago had been safely secure and distant, a part of the backdrop, now loomed overhead.

*[Kearin!]*

The internalized shout galvanized him more than the arching sparks, the crackling power field, the screams of falling workmen, the thirty metric tons of metal descending on him at a leisurely 981 cm/sec$^2$.

*[Move!]*

Hopeless, he thought.

He took a few hundredths of a second to take it all in: Dara safely across the street, starting to turn back to look; Weiss on his right, a meter ahead (not far enough; the shadow of the beast fell across her); and Yuan Ch'ing—*where was she?*

He felt the scream of metal tortured by uneven stress loads, the whistle of air, so he launched himself across the space to Weiss, so short a distance. Hand to arm, his body behind it, driving his shoulder into her side, felt ribs and breast, then the breath bursting from her—then no longer any resistance, airborne now, a question of physics and of how far his will and impetus would carry them.

It exploded behind them, scattered metal, the smack of flesh on pavement, chime of tool on pavement. Then he and Weiss hit the ground together, breath gone.

He opened his eyes to see hers squeezed tightly shut and her face bloodless.

He rolled onto his back, the rain on his forehead, running down his cheeks.

A limb of the scaffold reared over him, a serpent struck dead in mid-strike.

The rest of it was all over the street.

Sounds bracketed him. Moans and whimpering ahead. Shouts from behind him, the restaurant, the workers running from it. From the decapitated power source, gouts of sparks flung skyward, lightning gone wrong.

Near it was a gray-clad arm. The hand held a straight-edge. The body was—he didn't know where the body was.

Blood crawled across the street.

Some of the moans stopped.

Weiss stirred under him, weakly protesting his weight.

Winter found he couldn't stand, so instead he slid his butt around on the pavement to face her, so she wouldn't see, but she saw it in his face.

"The little girl?" she whispered.

He shook his head. "Yuan Ch'ing."

Her tears mingled with the rain and grit on her face. He folded her into his arms without thinking.

Thinking, [Sara, you answer me *now*, damn it! No more of this!]

A worker, her face so full of heart that Winter felt a fresh surge of grief and his own tears start to come, gently put her hands between them, trying to help him or Weiss up. Winter just shook his head, mouthed a syllable. "No."

The woman nodded. She went away.

Weiss struggled in his grasp. He hugged her tighter so she would not see.

A coveralled worker lay face down in the street, his face covered with grit, his chest impossibly flattened where the scaffolding had fallen across it.

His blood had run in broad rivulets to where Yuan Ch'ing lay. Her wide eyes stared into the rainswept sky.

Ambulances rolled through the thunder. Peacemakers descended like a flock of angry doves.

# Chapter Fifteen

Steel mesh broke the detention grid's eight thousand square meters into individual cells three meters square surrounded by a meter of open floor on all sides. The grid, Sub Two in the Palestine security complex, had been built with the citadel in a more disorderly time. Winter could look through the wire walls and see he was the grid's only occupant. The slumped shoulders of the Peacemakers pacing the catwalks overhead betrayed the boredom which visored helmets concealed.

[Sara, when I get out of here I'm going to dismantle you.]

He had not heard her voice in twelve hours, since that moment in the rain-wet, blood-slick street. They'd loaded Yuan Ch'ing into a cabinet mounted on the back of a Peacemaker's skid, not bothering to turn the stasis-field on. The medician called for Weiss had, seemingly, been unnecessary; she complied when the Peacemakers urged her to her feet and led her away.

Winter had moved to follow. They asked him name and purpose, called the Datalink for routine verification—

And here I am, he thought.

He locked his fingers into the yielding mesh and rattled it experimentally. It gave freely from its anchor points at the four corners of the floor and above, at the top of the truncated pyramid. It was cheap, quickly-constructed, and inescapable. If he tried to climb, the walls would merely sag under his weight. And, beyond the cage were a half-dozen peace officers in this room, then a blast door, a corridor, another door, another corridor, and so on from the heart of the complex to the surface.

The blast door rumbled open, the sound reverberating from the faintly concave walls. He looked that way, squinting against the harsh light from the hall beyond. A woman in civilian clothes moved away from the light, conferring with one of the Peacemakers. Both descended from the overhead walkway to the floor of the grid.

They stopped in front of his cell. The woman, his height or a little taller, stared at him for a moment.

"Your name is Sim Winter?" she asked.

"Yes."

She smiled, as if he had shared a private joke. She nodded to the Peacemaker, who touched the key hanging from his belt. The anchor points at the floor opened and the mesh rose hissing until it hung overhead like a canopy. He ducked his head as he walked under it.

"Come with me," said the woman.

They entered the corridor, turned off it almost at once, and were in unfamiliar territory. The woman's mouth was set, as if she were faintly annoyed; her heels clacked on the patterned floor; Winter hurried to keep up.

They passed several closed doors, an intersecting corridor, and came to a drop-tube. He hesitated. Free?

"Come on."

The platform descended, and his mouth went sour. One level, two. Three. Sub Five.

The tube doors opened on the familiar white corridor, lined with sensors.

"What is this place?"

The woman smiled. She waved him through the door on the other end.

There was no wood-paneled receptionist's office. Instead, he found himself at the top of a bowl-shaped room twenty meters across. Brightly-colored steps floating atop the soft, undulating floor led down to a ring of cushions surrounded by columns of blinking arrays extending to the ceiling. Winter and the woman went down to the office.

The man waiting below waved for Winter to sit. Gray hair framed a heavily-lined face. Loose robes concealed a muscular frame; Winter noted the muscle-corded hands when the man reached for a cigarette.

"You are Sim Winter," said the man, "a simple historian. Smoke?"

"No. What is this place?"

The woman, standing alongside Winter with her hands behind her back and feet apart, laughed deep in her throat.

"My name is Kendall Abruzzese. I'm the Security Commander for Palestine." He waved his hand at the woman, the cigarette trailing mauve smoke. "This is . . . well, it doesn't matter who this is, does it?" He shook his head. "You've been poorly treated." He glanced at the woman. "I wouldn't treat you that way."

"I hope not," she said.

"I don't understand any of this," Winter said truthfully.

"Sim—I'll call you Sim because we both know your name is meaningless—I'll try to be delicate. The jig is, as they say, up. You have been found out. Your adherence to the Winter matrix is admirable, but useless." He leaned forward, staring intently at Winter. "Now I want to know what the hell you were doing in my sector with a matrix that seems to have been cobbled together for a younger's crèche assignment."

Winter opened his mouth, then closed it without speaking. Winter had nothing to say.

Abruzzese glanced at his operative. "What would you do if your matrix had been burst?"

She shrugged. "It's never happened."

"Never happened to this one before, either, I'll wager. I don't suppose torture would do any good." Then he smiled broadly. "But, as I said, we know you're one of us. Whatever the hell that is." Abruzzese looked over his shoulder, seemingly at nothing but a bank of instruments. "He's a good animal, old friend. I'll have to get my answers from you."

The image of metal and brightly-colored lights dissolved. Brace sat revealed, mouth tight and head slightly lowered. He looked tired.

"Hello, Kearin," he said. "The Winter matrix is over."

"I'll say it is," Abruzzese said. "Now, what's this all about, Brace? What's this cutout doing in my girl's jurisdiction?"

"I'll be pleased to discuss it with you after Kearin has been released and we have a little more privacy," Brace said.

Abruzzese shot to his feet, turning to face Brace, robes flapping. "You'll be pleased to talk to me right now, you old fossil, or I'll put your animal back on the grid and have Citizen Schlovsky bring this up to Carpentier at the next meeting of the Synody! You're not in Suffolk, Brace, you're not even in the right hemisphere!" He chuckled. "Maybe that's the problem, old man— one or both of your hemispheres malfunctioning?"

"Remember whom you're talking to," Brace said coldly. "It hasn't been that many years since you were *my* 'animal,' Kendall. And as for telling Schlovsky, I think he's more willing to listen to evidence on the threat than you are. Certainly more than Carpentier is. Her mind is closed to it."

Abruzzese looked blank.

"The Levra," Brace said. He sighed. "You were slow learning your matrices, too, Kendall. Always slow."

Abruzzese flared again. "I'm slow to understand your fantasies,

Brace. You were going on about this threat since before I was your operative.''

''There is new evidence.''

''*Hard* evidence, or a more tightly-woven theory?''

''Hard evidence. Now will you grant me a private conference?''

''We don't have to keep anything from my girl.'' He glanced at Seacord, realization dawning. ''*He* doesn't know.'' Abruzzese laughed. ''*Very* good. A double blind. Very well.'' He beckoned, and the woman moved closer. ''Dear, bring the man up to a comfortable room on Sub Four, have his property brought back. You know what to do. He's a guest now—at least until I find out what's going on and throw both of these people the hell out of our sector.''

''Of course, Kendall.''

''That's my girl.''


''Did he say your name was Kearin?''

''That's one of my names,'' Seacord said.

The room was comfortably tangible, with straight walls and hard floors, firm, conventional furniture. He sat in a chair with broad arms; the woman sat on a couch alongside the door.

''Hungry?'' she asked. ''They might be a while.''

''No, thanks. Who . . . ?'' Her gray eyes smiled. No, he decided.

''You can call me Adrienna. I've never met another operative before, Kearin. Although I could have, couldn't I—and not known it.''

''It's the same for me.''

He pretended to examine the pattern etched in the door while, from the corner of his eye, he studied her: the large, warm, familiar eyes; lustrous black hair; long neck; the graceful line from heavy bust to slender hip to long legs. Had she been born with any of those features? (Gold wire wrapped her optic nerve; implants crowded together under the smooth skin.)

''I guess there's not much we should say to each other,'' Adrienna admitted.

He shook his head.

Was Adrienna her home name, as Kearin was his, or was it a casual fiction? What was her home matrix like, what was her apartment like, and did someone wait there for her? Probably not.

Like me with Sara—never room for another partner. And how did Sara appear to her? The concept was vaguely unsettling, but its net effect on his emotional state was nil. Just another small piece in a large puzzle. His hands gripped the arms of the chair (she probably noticed). What the hell was happening?

A tone sounded; the door opened. A man in plain clothes looked in. "Citizen," he said to Seacord, "your transportation is ready at the debarkation slip."

"I'll bring you," said Adrienna, standing.

"You're wanted in the main conference room," the man said to her apologetically. .

"Oh." She smiled warmly at Seacord. "It's been a pleasure to meet you, Citizen. Maybe I'll see you again."

And know it? He took her extended hand, and held it for a moment too long; she withdrew it from his grasp.

Is she thinking what I'm thinking?

Had to be. But he could not read it in her eyes.

"Good-bye," said Adrienna.

Five of six cars in the westward-bound tubetrain were crowded to capacity. In the sixth, Brace and Seacord faced one another across a flimsy table deployed from the wall.

Seacord looked at him. He's frail, he realized with some surprise. The thin wrists, long face . . . Brace probably massed no more than sixty kilos. Curious he had never noticed before.

Brace rubbed his chin, his gaze distant. "Damned inconvenient," he said after a long moment.

"This wasn't a sanctioned mission," Seacord said, the configuration of the sentence so alien, the words so distant, that it seemed as if someone else had spoken them. "Nothing else makes sense," Seacord went on, "but what *has* to be true is impossible. . . ."

"We'll talk about it back at the Black Rock."

"*Now*. The woman from Relayer is dead, and I don't know what you have planned for Relayer itself. Damien Rosendahl is dead, and his identity matrix was as flat as mine. Did you send him, too?"

Brace held up a warning finger. "No more," he said.

The familiar authority. The familiar tone of command.

The train plunged on in silence.

It pulled into the Suffolk terminus well ahead of schedule. Seacord rose from his seat, but Brace put a veined hand on his arm. Seacord sat down again, listening to the other passengers debark. Then, with muffled clangs and the hushed throb of pumps, their car was detached from the others and accelerated again. When it again came to a stop, Brace nodded. The door opened, not on another car or on a debarkation platform, but on a seamless white corridor.

Brace preceded him down it, the wheels of his chair squeaking faintly on the immaculate floor. A reinforced alloy door at the opposite end opened on a corridor leading to Brace's office.

He took up position behind his expansive, anachronistic desk. "This is the only place we can speak in complete privacy. There is one Datalinked bank of sensors in here, and I control it with a mechanical switch." He brought the thumb-sized device from under his desk. "The switch is off." He smiled without emotion. "A hardware solution to what you attempted with software."

Seacord sat down without invitation. "The Sim Winter mission and matrix were not sanctioned."

"I sanctioned both."

"You disabled my transmitter, somehow overrode the mouth switch so I couldn't speak to the Datalink."

"Hardware again. It's been returned to your control."

"But Belgrade knew nothing about any of this. And apparently neither did many people here, otherwise you could have had the Sim Winter dossier fully programmed. And we've seen that flat, cursory dossier before," he said tightly, "in Damien Rosendahl. The signs, the signature on both, was the same. You created Rosendahl. He was one of your 'animals.' "

Brace, surprisingly, sighed. "But the pattern of information cannot end there. It must lead from a motive to a result or intention. What is the thread? Why would I send one of my operatives to monitor another? You were already monitored by the Datalink."

"*None* of this makes any sense."

"Now you're being lazy. Everything makes sense, in the proper context. You have not yet established the context. Now, suppose it was as you must have originally thought when you met Rosendahl: that he was an operative from another agency, one less capable than we in the art of creative deception. And then suppose that, more recently, it became necessary for me to mimic the methods of this other agency."

("Maybe one or both hemispheres is out," Abruzzese had suggested. Where did that leave Brace's "animals"?)

"What agency?" Seacord asked from a dry throat.

"We are dealing with contexts. We define the subject by the shape it leaves. First, the agency has sufficient access to the Datalink to insert dossiers and manufacture or acquire citizens' identification bands. Yet, second, it does not have complete access or the one deception you know of, Damien Rosendahl, would have been unnecessary.''

"Yes. But . . . they knew I was Brian Kuhl.''

"A contradiction. Suppose instead they were interested *in* Brian Kuhl and did *not* know he was an operative. Perhaps did not know that camouflaged operatives exist. That is attractive for its irony as well. The agency believes it has developed the art of data-camouflage, and one of its agents is undone by a state-of-the-art version of their primitive efforts. So, they are interested in Kuhl. And why, when, in fact, Kuhl did not exist until hours before Rosendahl encountered him?''

"Relayer.''

Brace nodded. "And now the probability-paths branch endlessly. We will leave that area of speculation.'' He rolled out from behind his desk and toward the arch leading to rooms Seacord had never entered. "We will explore a new area of speculation,'' he said.

Seacord followed him, through curtains that melted from before him, re-forming behind. The room beyond was as simple as the office was extravagant: a smaller desk with standard communications link, a bank of datacubes, several closets, a narrow bed raised only a few dozen centimeters above the hard floor.

A closed door led to a third room, glittering with metal and alabaster. Collapsible tables and chairs stood against bare walls; scratch marks on the floor indicated the haste with which they had been assembled here.

But his attention fixed on the stasis-bed humming in the center of the floor. He approached it unwillingly, put his hands on the warm white shell.

He yanked his hands away as the lid popped.

Damien Rosendahl's face and hands floated in a white gel bath. The rest of his body was visible as a silhouette beneath the undulating surface. The preservation field arcing across the open hatch made the corpse's eyes sparkle and dance.

"We know certain things,'' Brace said. "First, a check of his retina patterns and fingerprints revealed he was a man named Jared Platt. He was a household goods assembler in the Manchester citadel.''

"That was another blind?''

"No, that is who he was until he took on Rosendahl's identity. We have located other periods in the last twelve years when Platt dropped from recorded sight, days-long periods when he purchased nothing, sold nothing, passed through no checkpoints. I am assuming those were times when he took on other identity-matrices with the help of associates who have the means to subvert the Datalink, however unprofessionally.''

Seacord firmly closed the lid. ''We're the only ones who can do that.''

''So we assumed.''

''There's one other fact I'd like to match with those you've given me,'' Seacord said, his chest tight. ''Why you sent me out there without the Black Rock behind me.''

''The Datalink will provide that answer.'' He wheeled himself back to his office, Seacord following, and stopped behind his desk. A switch snapped closed.

''Surface scans on the following,'' said Brace. ''Lehi, Etzel, Haganah, Levra.''

''Lehi,'' said the Datalink, in a voice that was nearly Sara's, ''also known as 'the Stern Gang,' was a Zionist terrorist organization operating in Palestine in the nineteen forties, as was the Etzel, also known as Irgun. Both had as their objective the establishment of a Jewish state in what is now Palestine Sector. Haganah was a more moderate organization with the same goal. The Haganah later became the army of the Jewish state, the Israel Defense Forces. Levra,'' Sara said, ''is the Anglicization of a Hebrew word meaning 'society.' ''

''Is that the only reference to Levra you have?'' Brace asked.

''That is the only reference.''

The switch clicked once more.

''The Levra was the consortium formed after the pan-nationalization of Israel in the early part of the twenty-first century,'' Brace said. ''Hardcopy records indicate they bankrupted themselves purchasing Relayer and were never heard from after that.''

''Then why doesn't the Datalink have any knowledge of it?''

''It does,'' said Brace. ''But it won't admit it to me. When I became Security Commander here I was told I had the highest access clearance available, equal to that of the chief executives. I found out ten years ago there is at least one level beyond mine, and information on the Levra is restricted to people with that clearance.''

Seacord sat down. ''Why?''

''Originally I thought it was because the Levra is an unhealthy example from that age. But the Stern Gang is a far worse one, and even you could obtain data on it if you knew the questions to ask. Later, I found out the Synody has access to data on the Levra when I asked Candace Carpentier for clearance to investigate the organization.'' He frowned. ''She refused. But she knew what I was talking about. That was seven years ago.''

Seacord's pulse quickened. Coincidence, he thought.

There are no coincidences, Sara would have reminded him.

''She said there was no hard proof to indicate the Levra is still a functioning organization, and without that, no need for a probe. Circular reasoning, perhaps, but I accepted her judgment while continuing to look for a harder variety of proof than I had seen. Something beyond the patterns of inefficiency that had led to the Terminal Night and the easy apprehension of the leaders of that conspiracy. Something to explain Jerusalem's favored status among all the pastowns, the indiscrete words, the testimony of some criminals unearthed by routine operations. And, most convincing and inchoate of all, the sheer unlikelihood that a culture which existed for thousands of years under tremendous persecution would curl up and die as a result of the pan-nationalistic movement and then be buried under the citadels of Triumviratine Earth.''

''You think Carpentier is a part of this conspiracy.''

''I am not sure this is a *conspiracy*, except in the broadest sense of a group of people banded together in common cause. Carpentier may simply be an efficient, cost-conscious supervisor who will not indulge an old man's senile fantasies. Not knowing which—and it not mattering which—I began to develop my own resources.''

''Me.'' The syllable came so easily to his lips.

''The deductive path leads clearly to that. I'm glad you saw it. Not knowing the extent of the Levra's influence in the citadels, I saw the only sane route was to recruit an operative from outside the citadels. The Terminal Night and the indoctrination program following saved me from fabricating an over-complicated scheme which likely would not have gotten me a usable operative. You are, in short, the only person I feel I can trust with information on the Levra.''

''Abruzzese knew about it.''

''He knows nothing except what I've told him. I tried for assignment to Palestine Sector when my promotion came up, but I was sent here instead. I've told Kendall enough about the Levra to enable him to, hopefully, spot evidence of its existence. I don't know how successful I've been with that. It was a risk confiding in him, but I can exercise damage control if he tries to use it against me. And he does have some personal loyalty to me, despite his wish to project otherwise.''

''Why Sim Winter?''

Brace smiled without emotion. "If the Levra does exist, the Relayer recontact will bring it into the open for the first time. Weiss will be the focus of their attentions. When I learned she wanted to go to Jerusalem, I had to act in haste. I want to know all that happened to you while you were with her, up to the time Yuan Ch'ing was murdered."

Seacord could only stare.

"The attractors on the scaffolding were tampered with. An amateur job. And the child who led you, Dara Herzl, is missing. So is all of her immediate family."

"Were they trying to kill Sim Winter?"

"The probabilities lie in that direction," said Brace.

"Isn't *that* enough for Carpentier?"

"No," Brace said. "Or, at least, I do not believe it is. I will not go to her with any more evidence she can reject. Each time I do, it means the next case must be all the more convincing, and my own position in the hierarchy is jeopardized."

"But even as Kearin Seacord I could be a target."

"Yes."

"And even if I do nothing, I've already been involved in an illegal mission, in Yuan Ch'ing's murder."

"Yes. A thorough investigation of that incident will eventually lead the Synody to you, as it led Abruzzese to you. Your visits to the LoSide would eventually be revealed, suggesting your sympathies do not lie entirely with the Triumvirate."

"You're squeezing me, Brace."

"Side by side, we are both being squeezed. Our own government lies on our right and the threat from the Levra lies to the left."

"You're pushing me to do something—but I don't see what can be done, now. Why don't you just tell me?"

"Our alternatives are fewer than before. A sanctioned mission remains impossible. An unsanctioned mission would increase your exposure to danger from the left and discovery by the right. For myself, I am near mandatory retirement. But you, an indoctrinaire . . ." He shook his head.

"All *right*."

Brace reached into his desk. From it he extracted a small slip of hardcopy, which he handed to Seacord. The feel of the paper chilled him. Its texture, the close-packed handwriting, were the same he had seen on the note found deep under the Jersey citadel weeks before. (Come upstairs, it had said.)

But on this scrap of paper was only an address.

"Judith Weiss will be in that apartment block in Jersey Sector for another four days," Brace said. "Seacord can go there."

"Tell the Datalink. That sector is forbidden to me."

"Not for legitimate purposes. You will be given a legitimate reason to go there. Wait for it. You will recognize it when it comes."

Seacord pushed the paper back across the desk. "It's hopeless. There's another alternative, though. Forget about it. Let whatever is going to happen, happen—and if it does, pick up the pieces afterward."

Brace let the paper lie.

"If you did that," he said, "do you think you would be safe?"

# Chapter Sixteen

The familiar swath of parklands, the gap in the hedgerow, and then the entrance to the Beacon Street security lock. "It's too soon," Brace had told him; the scars from where they had cut Loren Middlebrooks away would not yet be healed. But Brace was wrong. It was probably too late.

Seacord frowned, feeling the surgical seals pull, the tender flesh protest.

He cycled through the air lock, and the Peacemaker with the heavy face and coarse blond hair looked up from his console. His eyes widened.

"Citizen *Seacord?*"

Seacord, almost apologetically, touched the shiny black patch on his forehead. Other bandages glistened on his cheeks and the sides of his neck. The skin around them was bruised and puffy.

The Peacemaker stood. "What happened, Citizen? When we didn't see you for weeks we feared . . . And then the work crew came to your house, and they had the order signed by you so we knew you were all right. . . ."

"Not completely all right." He smiled, then winced. "A sporting accident. Watersleds up in Puget Sector. I wanted to work off some tensions, but I spent most of my vacation in the hospital."

"You're feeling better now?"

"Anything would be better." He pushed his wrist into the scanner. The guard barely glanced at the display.

"The crew just finished at your house," he said. "We made *very* sure they had the proper authorizations before we let them touch anything."

"Thank you. I appreciate it." Seacord withdrew his wrist from the rubbery cuff and the security scan winked out.

"Wait a moment," the Peacemaker blurted. Would he run the check again? Seacord wondered. But instead, the guard glanced over his shoulder to his counterpart on the catwalk overhead.

"McGiver, why don't you borrow the patrol skid and take

Citizen Seacord up to the Hill?'' Turning to Seacord, he added, ''You don't look as if you should walk all that way, Citizen.''

''You're probably right.''

McGiver brought the two-man sled up to the mouth of the security lock. The heat, when Seacord stepped beyond the environmental field, blasted him, bringing sweat to his face and stealing his strength. McGiver helped him onto the skid's pillion.

''Comfortable?'' came the faintly mechanical voice from under the helmet.

''As comfortable as I can be.'' He shifted on the narrow seat. His butt and legs were sore where they had taken skin grafts to paper over Loren Middlebrooks.

McGiver unlatched her helmet and hung it from the sight of the skid's unloaded wiregun. She brushed at the brunette strands plastered to her temples and forehead. ''Now I'm comfortable, too.''

''Most of you people seem worried about contamination.''

''I don't get out much.'' She squeezed the control stick and the skid's motor whined angrily. ''And I like to feel the wind in my face.''

She took the platform up full-vertical and Seacord felt the bottom drop out of his stomach. The acceleration diminished at forty meters and the skid slowed to an upward crawl at sixty meters, near the effective range of the power-transmission grid buried under the pavement. For a moment the Garden and the Common were laid out before him, the green expanses spotted with browning trees and pastel artisans' tents. Then they dropped down and outward, the wind lashing at his eyes, tugging at the fresh wounds in his face.

He caught a glimpse of upturned, velocity-smeared faces as they flashed over the Common, then the walls of the brownstones flanking Joy Street rose up to swat them. They became a tunnel whose brindled sides fell away as McGiver pulled back on the skid and looped the sled up and out over the Joy-Myrtle intersection. They reached the top of the arc at 175 meters, turbines useless, idling on standby, and fell to half that altitude. Then the blades kicked in again. They settled onto the roof of his apartment building as gently as a falling leaf.

She left the power on and swung her leg over the seat. He took the hand she offered and staggered off the bobbing platform.

''Why don't you get disciplined for that?''

''I always do.'' She smiled. ''Angry? You looked like you had a lot on your brain—and you didn't think of *any* of it during the past forty-five seconds, did you?''

He stared at her. Then he scowled, but there was no feeling behind it, so it didn't work. He laughed instead, even though it hurt. "Thank you, Citizen McGiver. Any time you need to scare someone, call me. I won't answer, but call me."

She grinned wider and mounted the sled again. Looking over her shoulder, she said, "I bought a print of one of your landscapes, once. Do nudes?"

"You *are* fast. Not yet, but I'm always willing to learn."

"Me, too. Let me know." The platform rose smoothly and slid slowly away. He followed its progress all the way back to the security lock.

Then he turned, looked at his roof, sighed, and folded his arms across his chest. The tar paper remained, but the roof beneath it was now level across its entire breadth. The rail that had marked the unsafe portion was gone; in its place was a low railing set a meter back from the edge. The tarp was gone and he felt a twinge of panic—but his skid and painting things were in the new shed on the northwest corner. Everything had been polished. The easel's loose, frayed wires had been repaired.

"Damn it."

Brace probably sent McGiver here just to soften the shock. Then he bit the inside of his cheek: Jerk. That was carrying Sara's dictum, that elaborate patterns underlay every event, a little too far.

Sara'd have McGiver's communications code.

He saw the two of them making love in the living room downstairs, then realized he was seeing it from the angle of one of Sara's spy eyes in the apartment.

When was the last time you thought about that? he asked himself.

The stairs leading from the roof to the third floor had been recarpeted and the Exit This Way sign he'd brought all the way from Jersey was gone. The apartment door was strange. It opened before he reached it; when he swung it shut it was heavier than expected, as if there were more to it than a slab of veneered oak.

The framed newspaper and magazine pages still hung on the walls. The carefully disordered cushions scattered about the floor seemed to be as he had left them. The Datalink, regrettably, was also as he had left it, gleaming from one corner of the room.

"Sara!"

His bedroom door opened. He did not recognize her for a moment. "They refurbished you, too," he complained.

She spread the pleats of her long, print skirt. "Don't you like it?'' They'd cut her hair, too, so it wasn't any longer than his own.

"What difference does it make what I like?"

She looked concerned. "You're not feeling very well, are you? Why don't you sit down? I'll start breakfast."

"Thanks." He collapsed onto one of the larger cushions. "This place isn't mine anymore."

"Of course it is," she said from the direction of the kitchen. Useless affectation; the presence of her holographic projection was not necessary to put the automated food processors into action. Artifice.

You are mine, Brace was telling him.

He rolled out of the cushion and painfully got to his feet. The nearest of the framed pages was from a 2043 edition of the *Metropolitan Globe-Times* ("The East Coast Newspaper"). "FIRST CONTACT," the headline read across the top third of the page.

The paper had been carefully aged, yellowed to the proper hue, precisely tattered. He reached up and took the frame from the wall and set it on the floor. The glass cracked when he walked over it to the next page: "YANKEES TAKE 3RD SERIES RUNNING." (The date was obscured by a dark stain.)

"Kearin, what are you doing?"

"Dissassembling the matrix."

He took that page down, too. The next was a cover from *Lifeline*. That stayed. It was real. He'd found it in Jersey fifteen years ago, when he'd been running with Rags, looking for books for Jair.

"I don't understand," she said. Then, when he did not answer, "You breakfast is ready."

"Thanks. I'll finish this later."

She hovered in the middle foreground while he ate. When he was finished he stacked the dishes in the sink.

"I'll wash them," she said.

"That's all right." The hot water felt good on his hands, sluicing over bruised flesh and slick bandages. "Were you surprised when I went to Jerusalem?"

"A little," she said after a moment. "You don't travel much, and you always wait to be taken out of the physical matrix before you become Kearin again."

"But you asked Brace and he said it was all right?"

"Are you angry that I asked him?"

"Should I be?" he asked neutrally.

"Brace was the one who said I should keep a close watch on

you so you don't wander again. I *told* you that man Rags was trouble."

"Don't you think some strange things have been happening lately?" He turned to look at her. She looked away, simulating discomfort. "Well?"

"I don't like to discuss it."

"Brace told you not to?"

"You *have* been under a considerable strain, Kearin. Everyone understands that. First that incident with the man who died, then all that time when we were apart, and the mission right after that. I've told Brace you shouldn't be assigned for at least six months. You deserve a rest."

"Six months? Or never?"

"Would you object to that? I'll recommend whatever I think is best for *you*, Kearin."

He stacked the last dish in a rack. She reached past him, to the faucet. The water stopped flowing and swirled down the drain.

"What if he's the crazy one, Sara, and not me?"

"You're not crazy, Kearin. You're just tired. Come to bed."

He turned abruptly, walked into and through her, squeezing his eyes shut against the distorted glare of her field. His skin tingled from the shock.

"Later," he said.

The answers were elsewhere.

He went up to the roof.


"You're mad about the apartment, aren't you? Kearin, we thought it would be for the best."

"I imagine they tucked a few more cameras in before they left."

"We thought it would be best."

"I know you did," he said mildly. He was barely listening to her.

The sun was hot. He felt the pressure of its heat on his back as he leaned on the new railing and look out across Beacon Hill. The heat waves coming off the brownstones made them seem ghostly and impermanent.

What Brace had been telling him was this: Find something—find anything—before either the Levra or our own people move against us.

The alternative: go to Belgrade and confront Carpentier directly, if that was possible. "Brace is mad," he would say. "I am innocent."

Because eventually she would discover Sim Winter. She could

have done so already, could be watching him now through Sara's rooftop eye. Watching, and waiting for him to decide which way to jump.

The other alternative: take the skid. Fly it low over Arthur Kill, toboggan it through the intake vent and then run all the way into the Jersey Lo. "Take me back, Rags," he would say. "I was crazy." Go back to drawing pictures on the street corner and selling them for a piece of bread.

"Take me back, Jair," he would say. "You were right." And Jair would tell him the old stories about the old times, the Terminal Night and the centuries before it, when the divisions in the world were a little less subtle.

Brace had *used* him, had nudged him into dark holes to sniff blindly for a scent that might not exist. And when Belgrade found out they would send Seacord back to the Jersey Lo, no choice involved.

Lo. From which, for whatever reason, Brace had taken him, set him up here, on Beacon Hill, with the apartment, and Sara, and the paints, and the time to use them. For whatever reason.

Sara watched him. He felt her waiting.

He went to the sled and ran his hand over the control console. He knew the way to the Jersey Lo with his eyes shut. That path had seemed so clear when he came onto the roof.

He touched the ignition toggle and squeezed the stick so the turbines barely turned over. The platform rose a centimeter. It was easy, then, to push it into the shed.

"I'm glad you did that," she said after he closed the door.

He brushed past her (feeling the electric tingle as he touched the holograph field) and started downstairs.

"Where are you going?" she called after him.

Then she said, "Kearin, you have a call."

"Tell him I'm not here."

"It's Justin Izzo. He's been trying to reach you about the deep-view you did for him."

Reluctantly he went into the apartment and commanded the communications link to flower. Izzo's tanned, smiling face appeared in the projection field. His smile broadened when he saw Seacord.

"I wanted to ask you for a favor," Izzo said. "But there will be compensation. I haven't been able to get away to pick up *Palisades* all these weeks, but I've just come into some hours and would like to commission another work."

"You want me to bring it to you? I'm sorry, Citizen, but I can't leave Suffolk for a few days."

Izzo looked crushed. "Is something the matter? You can't travel?" He touched his own cheek.

"I had an accident," Seacord said, already weary of the pose. "I should have stayed in the hospital, with the accelerants, for another day."

"Well, selfishly, I'm glad you decided to come early. I really would like to add another Seacord original to the ones I have."

"I'd be glad to discuss it now, Citizen."

Izzo shook his head. "No, I can't do it that way." Then he brightened. "It's because I'm in Toronto, isn't it? It's an hour away by tubetrain. But you can be here in twenty-five minutes."

"You've moved?"

Izzo said, "I live in Jersey Sector now. Can you come?"

Izzo was there to meet him when Seacord stepped onto the debarkation platform in the Jersey terminus.

"Is that it?" He reached for the shipping package, but Seacord turned his body slightly so Izzo could not reach it. "Is something wrong?"

"Nothing. Don't you want to see it? We'll go to one of the lounges."

"Of course," Izzo said. "Of course."

They slid through the crowds, following the Universal-language signs to a corridor flanked by arches cloaked with privacy fields. A room at the end of the hall was unoccupied. Inside were a commlink, chairs, a table. A menu glowed in the air. A narrow door led to a compact lavatory. Izzo turned to him eagerly. "Now?"

"Now," Seacord said. He scythed the padded frame into the side of Izzo's neck. The man crumpled into a chair. Seacord dropped the shipping sack into his lap. Dumbly, Izzo groped for it, clutching it to his chest.

"Was *any* of the money yours?" Seacord grated out. His hands trembled; his heart fluttered in his chest like a dying bird.

"I love them," Izzo gasped. He let *Palisades* slide to the floor, gently, then rubbed his neck. "You could have broken it. You could have killed me."

"Did you even keep the paintings, or just throw them away after you'd given me the hours I need to live?"

"They're in my apartment. I love them, I told you. I really wanted *Palisades*, even if they did give me the money. I don't have that kind of money, Seacord. No one does. But if I *did*, I would have bought them all the same."

"Who gave you the money?"

"It just came with the instruction. It was a gift. I'd heard of you. I had a print at home, on the wall," he mumbled, staring at the floor.

"You work for Security Affairs?"

"I'm just a maintenance technician. I don't have any hours of my own. I never even lived in Toronto. I've lived in Suffolk all my life." He looked up, his eyes glistening with pain. "Are you going to kill me? I didn't know *why*. I just . . . took a gift."

"How many others were told to buy the work? All of you?"

"I don't *know*."

"Of course you don't." He took *Palisades* from the floor. "It's called damage control, Izzo. A double blind." He turned away, the deep-view in his hand.

"*Please*," Izzo cried. "*Palisades*. It must be so beautiful. I thought up the subject, you know. It was my idea. It was such a wild time then—not like now." Seacord turned to glare at him.

"I want to have it," Izzo finished miserably.

Seacord tugged open the packing seam. The foam split lengthwise. Colored dust and bits of glass cascaded onto the floor. The frame came out in three twisted pieces, clanging musically.

"It was good enough to have sold on its own," Seacord said. "I was good enough to make it on my own. In the Hub. Anywhere."

He stirred the dust and glass with his foot, creating new patterns.

# IV.

# THE
# DEEP VIEW

---

**We soldiers of fortune are doomed to remain lonely outlaws.**

**—Heinrich Himmler**

# Chapter Seventeen

The old man spent his days in the Jersey citadel's central park, a manicured expanse two kilometers in diameter. Spotless apartment-block walls ringed the woodland. From the marsh in its center struck skyward the alabaster minaret of the Administration building and the dark cenotaph housing Security Affairs' sector headquarters. Ponds fed by pumped brooks lapped at their walls.

The old man sat on a sculpted bench and watched drab-feathered ducks churn purposefully across the clear water. A few meters away, a marble footbridge arched to the security tower's main entrance.

Weiss and the Basque couple from Relayer, the Goicoecheas, were both temporarily quartered in one of those elite apartment buildings, but the old man could find no admission. He sat and watched the birds. The forced breeze off the water cooled his face.

Footsteps scattered gravel on the path behind him. He hunched his tense shoulders and pretended to be asleep. The Peacemaker, tall and golden in the mid-morning sun, strode by without a second glance at the old man.

Seacord relaxed.

His first night in the transients' dormitory, Sara had called him, her face filled with concern.

"How did your meeting with Citizen Izzo go?" she asked tentatively.

No, he thought, grimacing. She's simulating concern.

"You knew Brace paid him to buy my paintings."

"You were happy here. You could be again."

"That's not real, there. I thought I was on my own, not kept like an animal in a cage, with you and Brace feeding me scraps."

"I think you should come home, Kearin. You're clinically depressed."

"I'm seriously angry. Let me be for a while. I need to think."

213

He reached—

"Don't do anything you'll regret. You know even being in the Jersey citadel is a danger for you, a temptation. Press the switch to let me speak in your ear. I promise I won't . . . unless you're about to make a mistake."

"I don't need you."

—and broke the connection.

Then he bought paints and a canvas, knowing she could monitor the transaction, and stashed them in his two-by-three room.

You have no choice but to do as I say, Brace had been telling him all along. But Brace was wrong.

He had also said, "We have real enemies." That time, he had been right.

After Seacord put Judith Weiss to bed, he would go back to the transients' cubicle and rearrange the pieces.

Someone tried to kill Sim Winter. (Someone tried to kill *me*.) So Seacord, at least, had a real enemy. He put a name to it: Levra. It was just a word.

Then: Relayer. Judith Weiss. Brace.

Return to the start of the loop.

And there was Candace Carpentier. Things had started to unravel the day she came to Sub Five.

She had decided Relayer was a danger. Seacord could see the signs of her decision in Brian Kuhl's presentation, in the isolationist demonstrations and the lack of official receptions for Judith and the others.

"They're not very different from us," he had told her. With the hatred, the statisim, the paranoia . . . there was nothing on Relayer to make them a danger.

Is there something *here* that makes them a danger? he wondered.

He had to know. He had to know why his life here had been destroyed that day on Sub Five.

He waited for Judith Weiss to come out of the ebony tower.

Each set of approaching footsteps he heard belonged to the Peacemaker or covert operative who had come to bring him to Boston or Belgrade—until the footsteps passed him by.

He waited. The Peacemaker strode through the tower's colonnaded entrance. Then two woman in civilian dress emerged from the distorting windscreen, but . . . neither of them was Weiss. He sat back.

Every morning her routine and his were the same. She would

make an early departure from her rooms; so would he, from his. She would, with escorts, walk to the dark tower; he would follow, to his place by the pond, carefully staying out of the field of view of the spy eyes scattered thinly throughout the park. She would spend an hour inside the tower, presumably for briefing; he would wait, apparently napping. She would leave, then, with escort, for conferences or tours; he would usually lose her and return to another bench near the apartment-block entrance. She would return home early; so would he.

Discretion had not permitted him to draw within fifty meters of her. So far as he could determine from that distance, she had transmitted no coded messages, met with no saboteurs or cloaked informers. She appeared not to have planted explosives in the Sector General's office. She had done nothing but look bored and put upon as two or three or six officious escorts led her to policy-review sessions or expeditions to furniture manufactories and medical laboratories.

Seacord waited, hands twisting under his worn cape.

What he had to go on: Day before yesterday she had taken to wearing anonymous gray singlesuits.

Yesterday he'd almost missed her coming out of the apartment block. She'd cut her hair short, styling it like everyone else's.

Also: Herzl. And the scaffold hurtling from the wall.

And herself.

So, tonight was her last night in Jersey Sector. Tomorrow she would move on—to somewhere.

After tonight he would return to Boston and wait, with Brace, for Carpentier's operatives to come for him.

But today, and tonight, he would stay with Weiss.

He smiled, thinking, We'll have no secrets from each other.

A young couple approached on dual sailing cycles, gliding around the perimeter of the pond. Seacord lowered his chin to his chest, snored as they passed. They laughed; the edge of his hood stirred in their wake.

Someone other than Judith Weiss left the headquarters. A skid dropped down to pick the woman up, took off again in a rage of dust devils.

Then she appeared in the entrance and, as always, he sat erect and his heartbeat quickened. She wore the plain gray singlesuit, the one that would make her hard to pick out of a crowd.

She was alone today, except for the woman who had been among her escorts all the other days. Maybe she was from Jersey's Sub Five. She stood Seacord's height or better; her blonde head turned constantly, ice-blue eyes scanning 270 degrees with her every stride. She said something to Weiss, the breeze and intervening distance snatching the words away before they reached Seacord's ears. Whatever she said made Weiss frown.

They stopped at the foot of the bridge. The security agent leaned against a graceful pillar, arms crossed. Weiss looked impatient.

A covey of transpills hunkered behind a screen of reeds a dozen meters away, but the women made no move toward them.

A gathering growl provided the answer to his barely formed question. Next he heard gravel compressed by, then spit out from under, fat pneumatic tires. Then the freewheeler came into view from around the side of a low, wooded ridge twenty meters to his right. Sunlight flowed over its transparent beetle's carapace, smearing the form of the driver inside. With self-contained power and internal guidance, the car nosed toward the footbridge.

Weiss's companion stood away from the pillar and pointed.

Seacord stood, too, hands clenched uselessly at his sides.

There was, he supposed, still a chance the freewheeler would not stop at the bridge.

The car stopped at the bridge. The canopy split and retracted into corrugated flanks emblazoned with the Triumviratine insignia and a registry number. The driver stood in the cockpit and reached over the side to help Weiss inside. Sun dappled and flared on the roof as it slid shut. The agent waved farewell as the car rolled away; then she turned and walked back over the bridge.

Seacord took a step forward.

The raspy growl of the car's steam engine gradually diminished. He looked up and around; looked for something to do.

Overhead, transpill lines draped the citadel in a gauzy web. Innumerable brightly-colored eggs moved in orbits defined by the precisely-orchestrated traffic flow. Skids soared beyond them in comfortingly random trajectories. Freewheelers prowled the lowest level, bearing: maintenance workers to locate and repair line breaks; bulk cargo; Peacemakers searching out transgressors in shadowed alleys; transpill parts; and high-level functionaries carrying their disdain for public transportation as a badge of office.

The car disappeared into a westward stand of trees.

He nearly let it go. Then he realized, If I don't follow this through, I might as well give up entirely, let Brace do what he'll do.

He quick-stepped after the car as far as the transpill station.

The station gate read his citizen's band, charged his account (nothing to be done about it), and let him in. He climbed into one of the pastel bullet-shapes. The padded seat gripped him; the windscreen enclosed him.

"Destination?" the Datalink asked.

He turned back his hood (revealing puckered, imperfectly-healed scars) and leaned forward, studying the console map. His finger traced the pattern of blue lines running through and between amber factories, golden apartment blocks, green office spires. Webbing the map were the more frequent black lines of the surface roads twisting through the citadel.

"Destination?"

"Block thirty-two in the Unity Concentric, upper station."

He did not have the clearance or credit to hire a freewheeler. He could not follow Weiss and her companion, but he could find them, where the lines of blue and black intersected.

The transpill slid underground, the sides of the tube flashing stroboscopically by. After a few minutes, the Datalink shunted the car to a vertical track. He climbed. The canopy opened onto an open deck jutting from the side of an elite apartment block like the one Weiss was staying in.

The door off the deck would not let him pass because he was neither tenant nor authorized visitor. He didn't care about that. He went to the edge of the deck and looked down.

The windscreen tempered the air currents to a stiff breeze that made his eyes water. He wiped at them, peering into the ribbon of pavement 150 meters below.

The freewheeler crawled westward. Then, shell gleaming, it passed through the ring of apartment blocks and headed south along Unity Concentric. A transpill admitted Seacord to its interior.

"Destination?"

"Block eighteen, Unity Concentric, upper station."

(He had to wait for them. Then they turned north.)

"Destination?"

"Alpha Furniture Factory, upper station."

"Destination?"

"Peacemaker Nexus, district eleven."

"Destination?"

(He lost them. Picked them up again at the perimeter wall.)

"Citizen, I am obligated to inform you there are regulations barring misuse of public transportation. Your final destination?"

(He lost them.)

"Your account has been charged a four-hour fine for misuse of public transportation. Your final destination?"

He bent over the map. He could run a grid pattern over the kilometer-square area he'd lost them in—if the transpill would allow it—but there were too many intervening buildings, too many streets the 'spill lines did not run above, too much time for them to be elsewhere.

"Ground level."

Petulantly, it directed him to the nearest drop-tube.

He emerged on a street squeezed between the perimeter wall and a red-walled power substation. Bare-chested, sweating workers looked up from their labor—brush discharges flowed in the trench formed by taking up the roadway plates—and then turned away as the foreman on his skid cruised overhead. The whining turbines obscured his comment about Seacord's ratty cloak.

Seacord put his head down and walked to the corner of the substation. There would be another transpill station around the corner, or somewhere nearby and the pastel egg would take him to the terminus. He would wait in Boston.

From around the corner he heard a shout, "It's heads again!"

"So it is, Mercy!"

Around the corner were two Peacemakers watching, arms folded, the group on the expansible stage.

A woman in Harlequin's garb threw a silver platter into the air and caught it behind her back. She brought it in front of her face with a flourish.

"Heads *again*, Charity! That's ninety-seven times running. So you think it means something?"

The dozen or so people gathered around the stage laughed politely. They were all gray-suited workers. Beyond them, the freewheeler was parked.

"It's just coincidence," said the man in clown paint.

Seacord laughed and, laughing, moved around to the other side of the stage. The registry number was the same.

"I don't think there are any coincidences—"

The substation door opened. A thin, balding man looked out, then said over his shoulder, "Just some street theater."

Judith Weiss said, "Thank you very much for explaining things to me, Citizen Myreck."

Seacord averted his face, all the muscles in his body going tense at the same time.

"It was nothing, Miss Weiss. If there's anything else I can do—"

Jerk! Judith Weiss had never seen Seacord's face.

She crossed to the freewheeler and, after some fumbling, made the canopy open for her. Seacord watched her clamber inside. She turned, and for a moment their eyes met; then he realized she was looking at the street show.

Myreck said from behind him, "Ask for Johnstone when you get down to the furnace. He's been with the operation since it was built, and he's very accommodating."

"You mean he's used to gawking tourists." Then the other man laughed to take the edge off his words.

Seacord frowned.

He knew that voice.

"No, it's all right. And I'll see that Belgrade hears what a help you've been to us, Myreck," the man said.

"No sense being provincial, I always say."

The other man laughed again. "Right."

He knew that voice. It was Spencer Swan's.

Seacord moved a little closer to the stage.

The canopy sighed shut, the electric motor whined to life. He turned to see the car rumble away, south to the heart of the city.

"*Ninety-nine* times!" said the Harlequin.

Seacord realized, Swan's been in it from the start, too.

Violets and orchids clad the hot nucleus of the citadel. An ornate fence surrounded the garden plot, not far from the twin Administration and Security towers. The roadster was parked outside the twisted steel pickets, near the gate hung with a sign that said:

---

> ### ENERGY AUTHORITY
>
> ### LIMITED ACCESS

---

Weiss and Swan stood inside the fence, near a cement-walled outbuilding shaded by infant teak trees growing at each of the five corners. Vines splashed with white flowers grew along the corrugations in the shed's slab sides.

The gate in the wrought-iron fence would not open for Seacord. He threw his leg over it.

"Spencer Swan!"

Swan looked up, and across the thirty meters separating them, Seacord could see the surprise on his face.

Seacord pushed his hood back.

Swan grabbed Weiss's arm and urged her toward the shed.

They dodged inside. Seacord reached the steel door just as it closed. It would not open for him.

"Help you, Citizen?"

He started, turned, and as he was turning, adjusted the contours of his face to reflect embarrassment rather than anger.

"I'm here for the tour," he admitted. "I'm a little late."

The woman, in orange Energy Division coveralls, looked skeptical. She brushed long black hair away from her face and he saw how young she was, probably had worn the citizen's band for less than a year.

"No tours today," she said. "Closed."

"No, I'm with Judith Weiss, from the Relayer colony."

"Relayer colony?"

"The people who came in the automover, over there."

"Oh. Them."

"I was supposed to meet them here ten minutes ago, but I was delayed at the black tower."

The woman glanced at his faded cloak, the sweat-stained black singlesuit beneath, and then at his faintly bruised face.

"I'll call down," she said finally.

He said automatically, "Thanks."

She walked around to the side of the outbuilding. He followed her, stopping at a polite distance while she spoke into the wall-mounted audiolink.

Seacord's stomach did a slow roll. How long before she made the proper connection, asked the question . . . and it would be over for him.

He pushed his tongue against the roof of his mouth.

Tentatively: [Sara?]

[Kearin . . . what are you doing?]

[I need access to the power plant. Judith Weiss is below with Spencer Swan. Swan is a subversive, and Weiss is trying to—]

[Think. Why do you *really* want to get into the power plant?]

[I'm trying to tell you. Weiss is going to make contact with a group of—]

[It's because there are a dozen easy accesses from the power plant to the underside of the city, isn't it? I know you are having problems now, Kearin, but you must come back to Boston now and we can make everything well again.]

[Call Brace. He'll tell you that I'm on a mission.]

[Kearin.] Then she paused, perceptibly. [I will dispatch a Peacemaker patrol to your location. If there is some violation, explain it to them and they will take the proper action.]

*[Call Brace.]*

[Brace is not available. And you are not on a mission. It's time you accepted that, Kearin. Wait where you are, and leave our link op—]

He turned her off.

It was over.

It was over but it still went on.

"They told me they're not expecting anyone else," the girl said, looking more confused than suspicious.

"I know they aren't," Seacord said. "Open the door for me anyway."

"I can't do that."

He took a step toward her. "You can't do anything else but that."

There was not much feeling behind what he said, but she seemed not to notice. She put her citizen's band to the passplate alongside the door and it swung open.

"Get in."

Inside were a few gardening tools, bags of chemicals, and a set of narrow stairs leading downward. He picked up a trowel and her eyes widened.

"Back out," he said.

When she was outside, he gestured with the trowel. "Be rapid."

She ran.

He swung the trowel at the passplate, but nothing happened. He used its point to dig into the soft concrete around the panel. After only a few seconds he could work the trowel under the plate. He leaned on the handle and the passplate popped away from the wall. Circuits cracked and sparks snapped mutedly. He had to pull the door shut after him, but after that it would not open again.

He put his cloak under a sack of fertilizer. Before he reached the bottom step he heard someone pounding on the door. The Peacemakers would only be delayed for a few minutes. There would be a lot of entrances, just as there was more than one exit.

At the bottom of the stairs, automated carts ran up and down a wide corridor. The workers riding on some seemed not to notice him. He crossed the roadway to a narrower hall leading subtly downward. Red-bordered doors opened on rooms whose walls were banks of indecipherable monitors. After the first several, he stopped looking in them.

The corridor dead-ended at a down-tube. Displaced air announced a platform rising to this level. Seacord backtracked a dozen meters and let himself into one of the monitor rooms. He put his ear to the door. Footsteps approached his hiding place, then receded.

He had to keep heading down. Swan would be heading down, out through the belly of the citadel, now that he knew Seacord was following him. Now there was no place in the city for either of them.

"Kearin—"

(His heart stopped.)

"—what are you doing?"

He found her staring at him through a lens in the center of the slightly convex ceiling.

"How long have you been watching me?"

"You had better be quiet if you don't want them to find you here," said the walls. "And your question is a little meaningless, isn't it? Now that I've become aware of the seriousness of your problem, I've reviewed the past one hundred hours of recordings from several thousand Jersey cameras. I know what you've been doing. Come back to Suffolk."

"If you know what I'm doing, you know you shouldn't interfere with me." He cracked the door and peered out. Clear.

"I hope we can settle this without the Peacemakers. Did you notice I haven't even directed them to you? This is more a medical problem than a legal one, Kearin."

"I'm not crazy." He stepped outside. No cameras in the corridor, so far as he could tell.

"Wait!"

He shut the door on her damned voice.

Then he went to the drop-tube and summoned the platform to this level, stepped on it, and asked it to bring him to the level below. He stepped off it again as it began to descend. With any luck, she'd be waiting for him below.

He followed a subtle breeze to a vent a dozen meters along the corridor. He easily removed the grille. Replacing it once he was inside took a little more effort.

Just like when I was in the Lo, Seacord thought as he slithered through the aluminum air shaft, its corrugated sides brushing his shoulders. He passed a vent; light striking through it cast vague Mondrian patterns on his face and hands. He could not see in the stretches between the vents, but he did not have to.

The shaft took a downward tilt; he put his hands against the walls, letting himself descend slowly. The blood pounded in his face, and he felt the pressure of the levels above him. Sara was all around him, pressing in like the sea, watching for him.

Something creaked and rustled in the tube behind him. He

crawled more quickly, bruising his ribs and stomach on the flanges where one section of vent met another, breaking his fingernails on the unyielding metal.

It had to be around here somewhere . . .

The sounds of pursuit grew more distinct: the characteristic low hum of a motor drawing transmitted power; the throb of rubber wheels against the walls of the air shaft; the whine and clack of the maintenance robot's sensors inspecting, cleaning, and polishing.

Suddenly, his hands thrust sickeningly into empty air—then found the rungs of a ladder leading downward. He had to curl himself into a ball (shoulders scraping the roof of the vent) and turn himself around to take the ladder feet-first. He had only descended a few steps when he saw the machine's riding lights flickering on the walls. He ducked; the maintenance robot scuttled blindly overhead.

"Kearin?" it called (blindly). "Kearin?"

The air in the tube pounded as he went down.

He emerged in an alcove adjoining a service corridor. Steam wafted from old pipes. Indecipherable legends were stenciled on conduits and monitor boxes. The tunnel was closed at one end by a heavy steel grate. The path was clear the other way.

And, at his feet, was a hatch opening on the underbelly of the city. It was the easiest way into the city . . . and the easiest way out.

He knelt and put his hand to the hatch. It trembled faintly—presumably with the rush of the river below, the pounding of the power plant—then he took his hand away and looked at it.

His hand trembled.

Damn it. Decide.

He stood.

And the lights in the room, and the tunnel beyond, flickered.

Distant shouts echoed.

Seacord's breath caught in his throat.

"Come *on*," he breathed.

Everything went dark. In the darkness, he smiled. Then he stepped back into the alcove, settled onto his haunches, straddling the hatch, and waited.

He did not have to wait long. After a few minutes, the tunnel lights came on low, just enough for him to make out the shape of his hand in front of his face. Two sets of footsteps approached—one heavy but knowing, the other light but clumsy.

"Are they dead?" Judith Weiss whispered raggedly.

"Shut up," said Spencer Swan. "This isn't going the way it's programmed to."

Seacord's breath tightened in his chest. Swan walked past the alcove, within a meter of him, then turned around and came back. "It's right around here."

"I thought you'd been here before," Weiss said. The fear in her voice writhed like a trapped, broken animal.

"*We* had been. Not me. I never thought they'd call on me." He knelt just outside the alcove and started sweeping his hands across the floor, looking for the hatch.

"How am I going to get *back?*"

"Not my problem," said Swam. "Damn it." He sat back on his haunches, sighing. "You wanted to find us, Weiss. It's led to this."

His sigh caught in his throat as his eyes met Seacord's.

Seacord's legs uncoiled, propelling his shoulder into Swan's face. It was a glancing strike, though Swan's blood sprang onto the shoulder of Seacord's singlesuit. He rolled left and Swan rolled right, but Seacord got to his feet quicker.

He felt a movement at his back.

"Don't hurt me, Judith," he said in Brian Kuhl's voice.

He heard her indrawn breath.

Swan got to his feet, brushing the blood from his face with his left hand. The right held a glittering, sculpted mass of aluminum and steel and ceramic—a crafted grip, bulbous kind of trigger guard, the delicate needles of the magnetic tracks. Tortured magnetic fields would propel metal slivers from the wiregun's guide tracks at a rate of three hundred per second and at a speed of 275 meters per second. The hole they left on their way into his chest would be nearly invisible. But the staples would mushroom on impact, each of a hundred projectiles churning blood and bone to a mealy paste.

He pushed the switch in the roof of his mouth and let Sara into his head again.

[Can you see what's happening here?]

[Of course. And I suspected you were coming here. You'll remember I offered to call the Peacemakers for you. They are on their—]

[We don't have *time* for that. He's going to kill me!]

[You have nothing to worry about.]

"I'm not surprised it was you," Swan said tightly. He grinned. "But if you'd thought you'd meet me here, you wouldn't be wearing that face, would you?" The grin took on a new emphasis, became a bitter smile. "There's no way back for me now, either, you bitch."

"I don't—" Weiss began.

"Stand away from him," Swan told her.

[Kearin—]

[Get out of my head!]

Weiss sidled around him, her eyes never leaving his face. Good; now she wouldn't be splashed with his guts.

[Kearin—the gun is *dead*.]

Swan pulled the trigger.

The click of a closing relay was distinctly audible in the narrow corridor. Swan looked down at the useless piece of metal in his hand, eyes widening in disbelief.

Seacord lashed out—too slowly. Swan's thrown gun caught him in the temple and dark flashes exploded behind his eyes. He staggered and Swan bore him the rest of the way back, into a wall and then down to the floor.

Swan's breath was sour on his face as he pushed down, his forearm a lead bar across Seacord's throat. He reached up, his fingers plucking at Swan's shoulders, grasping at his hair, but already his strength was gone.

[Blow the lights! Do something!] Red-filmed darkness encroached.

[I can't help either of you.]

[He's . . . working against you.] He closed heavy eyes.

Sara said reasonably, [You both are.]

"*You're killing him!*"—and Swan's weight was gone. Seacord's first shuddering gasp branded his lungs. He exhaled, it came out as a moan.

"You were killing him," Weiss repeated.

Swan said, "All right. Look, there's the hatch. Help me— damn it, I'm still bleeding."

Weiss asked, "Who is he? He sounded like someone I knew on Relayer."

"Then he probably is. Among others. Do you want to discuss it now?"

Creak of hinge. Hot air from the belly of the city flowed across the tunnel floor.

[You've got to get up and stop him. He's managed to interdict two squads of Peacemakers.]

[So he's better than I am.] He rolled onto his side. Weiss descended. She looked his way before her head disappeared beneath the level of the floor.

Swan looked over his shoulder. "You're lucky Sherri is watching out for you," he said. Then he started down.

Seacord rolled over and felt a cruel hardness press into his stomach. He reached . . . and his fingers found the parallel needles of the wiregun barrel. He dragged it into his field of view. The indicator lights were still dark. Sara was not letting any transmitted power into the weapon.

He said, [Go to hell.]

And he got to his hands and knees, breath wheezing through his bruised throat. Swan, still half in and out of the hatchway, looked at him and smiled thinly. "Only room for two on the skid, Seacord. Maybe Brace will give you another chance."

"You go to hell, too." He brought the butt of the gun down on Swan's fingers where they gripped the top rung of the ladder. The agent yowled and snatched his hand away.

Seacord bashed the other hand.

Swan spasmed—maybe he tried to jump from the ladder back up into the tunnel, maybe he just lost his balance—then he slid down a meter, hands scrabbling for the rungs and unable to close on them.

Weiss looked up as he fell, then hugged the ladder as he dropped past.

Mud splashed from where Swan hit, half-covering him.

[What's happening?] Sara asked. [I don't have an eye out there.]

[It's only a fifteen-meter drop. Maybe he's still alive.]

[You stopped him?]

Seacord skittered the wiregun across the floor of the tunnel and started down the ladder.

[I can't see you, Kearin. I don't have any eyes out there.]

[I know.]

Mud squelched around his boots. Weiss backed away from him, eyes glistening in the semilight under the citadel. The hiss and roar of the ventilators masked Seacord's harsh breathing, and Swan's attempt at the same; bubbles formed in the cloudy water around his head, face down in the mud.

Seacord turned him over. One arm flopped in too many places; blood seeped through the sleeve.

"Is he dead?"

"Maybe . . . when the Peacemakers find him." He looked around. The citadel's foundation pillars glistened like an enchanted forest. Maintenance lights flowed dimly from every fifth or sixth column. The ladder he had come down was, of course, the same one he had gone up to get the word from Brace that his trips to the Jersey Lo were over. The steps of the ladder grew like bracket fungus from the side of a pillar. On the other side of the column was a skid, streaked and corroded. The indicators kindled when he touched the ignition toggle.

He squinted at the control panel. The registry chip had been pried out of it. He recognized his own work.

"Welcome back," he muttered. It was the skid he had ridden here on that morning, months ago.

"Are you . . . Brian Kuhl?"

"I was." He turned. She withdrew a step. "And Sim Winter."

"*How?*"

"You must have more pressing questions," he said in Kuhl's voice. Then he rubbed his throat. "I don't know what your original plan was, but I doubt this is it. You have fifty seconds, maximum, to come up with another one."

[I can't hear whom you're speaking to, but it must be Judith Weiss. If you can hold her there for fifty seconds, I'll be in control of the situation again.]

He frowned.

"I don't understand."

"I know about the Levra," he said unwillingly, reminded that Sara could hear every word from her ear in his throat. "I know Swan was going to take you there. If you can fly a skid, and you know the way to go, I won't stand in your way. If you can't do it alone—"

"I won't take *you* to them."

"Judith, you trusted me once."

"And you were lying to me. Even about who you were, you were lying to me."

He shrugged and threw a leg over the skid. The turbines whined as the sled lifted from the mud. A fine spray of brown water brindled Weiss's gray singlesuit.

[Kearin, I have been in contact with Belgrade. If you can hold her there just for a moment more, we'll grant you amnesty. We can help you through a retraining program, just like when you were an indoctrinaire. You can start over again.]

"I'm going out there. Into the LoSide. You can come with me or wait for the Peacemakers."

[Kearin, don't throw it all away—]

[There was nothing there but trash anyway. Shut up.]

The skid bobbled as Weiss climbed onto it.

"Put your arms around my waist and keep your head against my shoulder, out of the wind."

To Sara, [Trust me. The Levra must be in the LoSide.]

[Wait for the Peacemakers.]

A shadow appeared across the open hatchway. He squeezed the control stick and the skid surged forward. Mud, water, and clay splashed away from the ground effect field. The angry bees' whirr of the turbines roiled in his stomach. The foundation pillars flashed by, becoming a continuous white blur. Only darkness loomed at the end of the tunnel.

Weiss's fingernails dug through his singlesuit and into his ribs.

He took the banks of the cooling tunnel sideways, killing some of his forward velocity, skittered up the opposite shore, then back down to the water. And then there was light ahead, a skyline—and then Arthur Kill stretched deep and purple under them and the citadel loomed behind.

"We're safe now," he shouted over his shoulder.

Sara said, [You are very wrong.]

On the skid's control panel, all the lights went out.

# Chapter Eighteen

For a single, silent moment the skid flew serenely onward, turbines quiet, wind rushing, waves lapping far below.

Too far? he wondered.

Reflexively, Seacord punched the ignition toggle (broke it off) with his thumb, but nothing happened.

Then the moment was over. The platform started to tip forward, rolling, his feet came away from the corrugated, no-slip floor, but his hand still gripped the useless control stick and Weiss's arms were still wrapped around his ribs.

*"Dive!"*

How could she hear him? The wind tore at his eyes and ears, the waves smashed, but she let go. He was just beginning to reach for his knees (curl into a ball) when the kill became an endless bluegreen wall which, an instant later, slammed him into rainbowed oblivion.

He was unconscious for just long enough to draw in the first mouthful of saline water and gag on it. He tried to push the water away and one hand thrust into air. After he stopped struggling, his face broke the surface.

Seacord bobbed up and down on the waves. Air bubbles broke and burped a half-dozen meters away, then a pair of delicately turned petrochemical turbine-blades floated to the surface.

A dark form surged up through the green water. Spray exploded. Weiss erupted from the center of the foam, gasping and blowing water. Two strokes brought Seacord to her side. He slapped down her hands, then gripped the front of her singlesuit with one hand while paddling with the other.

"If you can't swim, go limp."

Water and a thin line of blood trickled from her nose. She said, broken-winded, "Biggest water . . . I've seen . . . was a thousand-liter . . . tank. Idiot."

"It's all right. It's not far and the current is helping us."

"Where?"

The current into the cooling tunnel urged them back to the

citadel, tall and gleaming at their backs. The kill stretched north and south, a concrete-banked moat between the ceramic ramparts and the brownstones tumbling back from the Jersey shore. One hundred meters? He could have run there in the time it took to answer her. "We've got to cross," and he pointed, half out of breath himself. The warm water, his sodden clothing, pressed on his chest.

"It's too far!"

After a little experimentation, she put her hands on his shoulders and he settled into a methodical crawl, letting the current drag him downstream, but gradually drawing closer to the Jersey Lo, his strokes becoming shorter, his breath coming more fitfully. He kept paddling, knowing if he stopped he would not want to start again.

They were still twenty meters from the face of the opposite bank when his foot encountered smooth concrete. He pried Weiss's hands from his shoulders and stood. They waded up the gentle slope, onto the poured stone bank. She tried to sit down there but he jerked her to her feet.

"Come on. As soon as they scramble some airborne Peacemakers they can swoop down and pick us up."

Weiss's shoulders sagged. "I don't care." She shivered, though the water steamed from her singlesuit and her boots were already dry.

[I have dispatched the airborne units already. Wait for them, and we will forget what has happened. You can either return to the citadel or continue into the LoSide. But you must stop here.]

[You don't understand what's happening, do you?]

[Better than you. You've helped me in the past. Now wait, so I can help you.]

[And Weiss?]

[She is not your concern. You gather the data and I—]

Not anymore, he thought.

At the top of the slope, a hundred-meter-wide swath had been cleared along the bank for as far north and south as he could see. The control corridor, a kind of firebreak dating from times when the LoSide was more populous and more unruly, remained sterile nearly a century after it had been created. Beyond it, brownstones leaned drunkenly against one another. Gaps marked where tenements had collapsed. Smoke curled from deeper inland.

"Is it . . . safe?"

He shrugged. "The sooner we're among people, the safer we'll be. We'll go straight in as fast as we can. Come on."

"We'll be safe with the lakkers? I heard—"

" 'Lakkers,' " he echoed, smiling grandly. "You've learned a few things while you've been here, Judith. We can stay on the fringes, away from the welfare distribution centers, and walk a dozen kilometers without seeing anyone. But Security Affairs has satellites in orbit that can pick your body heat out of the ruins. We can't hide from that. The best we can do is get in with a lot of other bodies. Now: Where are we going?"

She was silent.

"All right," Seacord said. "Come on anyway." He started west, inland, and after a few moments he heard her footsteps squelching after him.

The broken-backed, weed-choked streets, built the century before last for hordes of freewheelers, remained passable down their centers. Flies buzzed in the gathering heat. He slipped the singlesuit off his shoulders and knotted the sleeves around his waist. The sun was warm on his back. It dried his hair into tufted spikes.

Once a shadow passed overhead and his skin tightened, he shivered, expecting a fusillade of driven metal slivers. Then he held his hand against the sunlight to follow the seagull's flight. It spread its wings to catch an updraft and headed southeast, toward the Raritan Dam. A few hours later, when another silhouette fell across him, he kept his head down, as a lakker would, and told Weiss to do the same. It passed by; he never looked up to see what it was.

"I'm tired," she said after hours of silence.

He brushed at the sweat trickling into his eyes. His singlesuit was wet again, this time from perspiration.

"So am I. Let's go over there."

The tenement's walls were a little straighter, seemed a little more trustworthy, than those of its neighbors. The windows stared empty-eyed; the door and frame were completely gone from the entrance. They stepped through.

Motes of dust danced in the light striking down the empty stairwell. Seacord did not even bother to test the stairs. He went deeper into the house, to the rear of the railroad flat. The back room had a plastic floor and rusted metal cabinets; a window overlooked a jungle plot alive with insects and animals that kept from their sight.

He sat in the empty window-frame. She came in as far as the doorway, arms crossed on her stomach, defensive but no longer afraid of him.

"How long are we going to wait here?"

He shrugged. "Maybe all night. The walls are thick, and there are three floors above us. We might not show up to the infrared eyes. I don't know much about that department.''

"This is a very old place."

"Probably two hundred, two hundred-fifty years old. They kept coming into style during the years before the Portal War, and they were sturdier than more modern buildings in the Western world.''

"You . . . knew where to come. Where the road was, what buildings to look for, what room. We can get air here, but we're not visible to anyone on the street.''

"And we've got an exit here, into the brush. Right.''

"Who *are* you?''

"I told you.''

She shook her head. "You're not Brian Kuhl."

"Not now, but add a little fat around the middle. And I can hunch my shoulders—like this.'' He touched his cheek. "Put an implant here, and here.'' He puffed his cheeks out. "And then you fix the hair, and color the irises. A few weeks of sleeplearning and . . .''

"How can that be done?''

"Easier than you think, it seems.''

"You're a spy.''

He looked out the window. "That's your term. Most of the time I was just an observer. Looking for the things that don't show up on computer-generated reports. Attitudes. Little inefficiencies. Crimes, sometimes. Sometimes very bad crimes. I would just gather information. Someone else would find out what it meant, and find a use for it. Add it to all the other information in the Datalink and wait for the directives to come out. I think they have come out. I can see it in the way the broadcast on Relayer was edited, in the isolationist demonstrations I've seen. In the way you've been ignored by the bureaucracy. They were shuffling you from unimportant meeting to routine tour, waiting for the next ship to leave for Relayer so they could put you on it. And I don't think it's because of Relayer. I think it's because of something here, on Earth. What is it, Judith?''

"I . . . *trusted* you, when you were Kuhl. Is this what you really look like?''

He shrugged again. "It's what I look like most of the time. I don't think I betrayed you, as Kuhl. I did report things as I saw them. They saw something through my eyes that I didn't see, maybe something I couldn't see. At the time, I didn't think much about what they were going to do with the information I brought back. I was comfortable in the life I was leading between missions. Then I lost that life, and I started to look around."

"What about in Jerusalem? Had you *found yourself* then, or were you still just gathering information—but on me, that time."

"I was just watching you. They want to know about the Levra. They thought you might be a spy. I guess they were right."

She said nothing.

He slid his butt off the windowsill and regarded her. "You had better understand what's happened here. First, you apparently made contact with a Levra agent pretty well entrenched in Security Affairs. He was going to bring you to some kind of rendezvous in the LoSide. I tumbled to it, and worse for you, my superiors got onto it, too. There's no way you can go back to the citadels and go on as you were. They'll either hold you in custody until a ship's ready to bring you home, or they'll hold you beyond that, trying to find out all you know about the Levra. You don't know where the hell you are and you're on the run. You had one resource before, I guess: Spencer Swan. You don't have him now."

"Who's Spencer Swan?"

"The man you were with. He's like me, so he could have used any name, been anyone, for you."

"Oh." She sat down slowly, her back to the wall. "You're—what are you doing? Are you running, too, somehow?"

"I guess I am. But I'm not sure anyone's pursuing me. I know they're chasing you. You're valuable."

"And I'm to believe you are not being a spy, now."

"We had a discussion like this a few months ago, Judith. I can't believe anything you say, and you can't know if I'm a spy and don't know it, or a spy and know it, or not a spy. Or something else."

"And I said . . . I don't remember what I said."

"I think, in the end, you agreed to take a chance I was who and what I said I was."

She shook her head. "But then I at least knew what my own eyes told me. But none of that was real. Who are you, really?"

"That question doesn't make any sense." He sat down on the plastic floor. "I'm just tired." He closed his eyes.

The sun slid down the pearly sky, bloodied it, then sank beneath the fractured horizon. Locusts sang to each other in the twilight.

Seacord came awake with a gasp, shivering, sweaty.

"Sara."

She stepped carefully across Weiss, asleep in the kitchen doorway. A gauzy white gown blew around her like a sentient cloud, clinging, revealing. She reached toward him with a bone-white arm, thin, jeweled fingers.

"You have to come back now. You've had your run outside the walls. But . . . this is no place for you, Kearin Seacord," she whispered, smiling sadly.

"I was born here."

"Kearin Seacord was born on Sub Five. He lives in the Hub . . . with me." The gown twisted like smoke, revealing her. "Don't you want to live with me?"

"You betrayed me. You all did. None of it was real."

"It was as real as this." Her arm swept the room. "Hiding like an animal in a crumbling warren with *her*. . . . That woman will kill you, Kearin."

"She knows what's real."

The smile grew carnivorous. "Does she?"

"She knows about the Levra. It all comes back to them, and Relayer. Ask Brace. He'd agree."

"Brace is dead." She reached to embrace him. "Dear man. Lover. Brace tried to find what is real. But, lover, I decide what is real."

Her arms encircled him. The flesh fell away, revealing banded iron gleaming in the moonlight. Her fingers thrust into the wall behind him, and the masonry cracked and popped. She pressed herself to him and her arms grew tighter, sprouting electric lancets.

[Come home, dear boy.]

*"Noooo!"*

He worked against the arms but they were too tight. Then he opened his eyes and it was not night; dawn was streaming down the hall.

Weiss let him go, embarrassed. "You were . . . dreaming."

He knuckled his eyes, pushing phosphenes into them. The pain brought him back the rest of the way. He wiped his face and chest with his suit sleeve.

"I'm thirsty," he said.

After a few moments, Weiss said, "Are you all right?"

"Yeah. Just remembering something." He stood, stretched, then leaned on the windowsill to look up and out. "I should have told you to wake me up when it was full dark. Nobody travels during the day; too hot."

"Where are we going?"

"The only place to go is the last place I know was real. There was a place caught between the blank-eyed buildings, in the clean streets, where I ran with Rags, and the Dart, and Powder. There, where Jair had his house and his books, it was cool even at noon. The New Ark I'm talking about, and that's the place we're going to go." She shrank from him. "What's on, dear lady?"

"You talk differently from the way you did yesterday."

"It's different things I spoke of then." Then he shook his head, a violent leftward twist and rightward spasm that left his vertebrae sore. "Protective coloration. Let's go."

"You used to live here."

"In the New Ark. That was before I was a Triumviratine citizen. After the Terminal Night they started programs to bring some of us inside, train us, make us full citizens. I don't know how many were brought inside, but I don't think it was many. So . . . I was one. They decided I was best suited to be other people. Two of them you met. Three, including me—because no lakker's mother ever hung 'Kearin Seacord' around his neck. There were"—he thought—"about sixty-five others over the seven years. More in the beginning, less lately." He re-knotted his suit sleeves around his waist. "Are you ready to go, Judith? We've got to get water, and the Ark is still about two hours away."

"Let's get it over with." She followed him outside.

He paused on the front steps, getting his bearings again. Then he turned right and north. "This way. And take it easy. There's no point in hurrying. You'll get there in two hundred minutes feeling a little dragged out, or in a hundred eighty minutes feeling half dead."

"I understand." They walked one block, then a second. She said, "Yesterday you said you were running. Why?"

"Why did I say it? Maybe I'm trying to trick you into—"

"*No*. For a little while, at least, we'll pretend that there are no lies or deceits—"

"Or double blinds. Let's play that game."

"—and you can tell me why you're running."

"Simply: you. Branching out from that, the Levra. And then the web gets very tangled."

"We have two hours, you said."

He sighed. "I worked for a man named Brace. He is a very old man who has had very many years to accumulate information about the Levra. None of it, however, was very solid. The people he worked for could not see the conspiracy. So, without

their knowledge—and without mine, at first—Brace set me to
gather information on the Levra. In the end, it was a race to see
if we could uncover some hard data before our superiors found
we were working on our own. We lost.''

"So . . . when you found me, they were after you then?''

"No.'' He grimaced, uncomfortable with the thought. "But,
what I had to do to find you—I *knew* you were going to make
your move—it was too much. It was totally reckless.''

"But you *did* find me, and the man you call Spencer Swan.''

"Yes.''

"So . . . you won your race.''

"*No.* I don't know.''

Silence. Then she said, "Maybe you need more evidence. But
I won't lead you to the Levra. Go back and tell him that. Bring
me back, too, if you feel you have to.''

"I can't go back. There was this shell around me, made up of
bits of information. I was a painter, when I wasn't working for
them. People came to buy my work. I lived in a fine old house
with Sara, and it could have gone on like that forever, except the
shell got broken somehow, and I saw none of it was real.''

"Was it better than this place?''

"I don't know. But I can't go back, at least not yet. I'm
looking for the thing, out here, that will tell me whether the
people in charge are right or not, that they have some enemies
besides themselves.''

"I . . . don't understand.''

"You don't believe. That's all right. I'm going back to the
Ark and you can go on where you have to. If you decide you
want to go back to the citadel, Rags can get you back.''

"I'll see what this Ark is like.''

"All right.''

The silence stretched again, long and pure. No watersplash,
no recorded bird calls, no ventilators. The hot wind breathed on
his face, but he couldn't hear any pumps or fans behind it. Just
their footsteps, crushing stone dust to finer bits.

"Do you remember,'' she said abruptly, "something I told
Sim Winter? We were talking about Adolf Hitler, and Winter
said—''

"That he was a madman. And you said that was just society
trying to absolve itself of guilt. That Hitler was a part of society
and it of him.''

"I don't think I put it that well, but yes. It's the same with
this Mister Brace. The Levra is no danger to you. Yet, you need
enemies. The StarForce ships go out fully armed, but they've

encountered no alien races. The Asian People's State will not even acknowledge you. They stay silent behind their wall, so you cannot fight them. Maybe the people living in these ruins were a threat, once, but not since the Terminal Night. So you fight amongst yourselves. I saw it first at the spacefield where I landed. The StarForce owned me in a certain room, and the people from Administration owned me in the corridor outside. Neither side let the other forget where the line was drawn. You gather information—but whom do you gather it *about*?''

"Other departments.''

"Enemies of the state?''

"Sometimes. Show me the Levra is not the Triumvirate's enemy.''

"We had a similar discussion about Relayer itself, didn't we? If you need an enemy, Kearin, you will have your enemy. We have seen this over and over down the centuries.''

He said, "Wait here.''

"Where are you going?'' she asked, meaning, Don't leave me here. He looked at her, saw the torn and worn clothing matted by crud from Arthur Kill and from her own sweat, the stiff, unkempt hair, blackened lips, red-rimmed eyes. And in the eyes, beneath the reserve he had seen on Relayer, an inner self that probably had no more idea of what was going on than he did—and was as frightened.

He said, gently, "I just have to think for a minute.''

"All right.''

She crossed the rubble at the edge of the road and let herself slump down in the shadow of a blasted storefront.

Seacord stared at the faded white line painted down the middle of the street. One way led straight to Rags and the New Ark, the other way led, somewhat more circuitously to . . . something.

He felt the familiar heat beat on him, the textured road underfoot, the unsterilized wind in his face, carrying with it the scent of ash, decay, and life. The wind rustled through broken doorways and empty windowpanes, and rats and scorpions scurried before it.

[Kearin?] Her voice came to him abused by static.

[I am here. I am here in the Lo with Weiss, trying to do my work. Why are you trying to kill me?]

[I am not trying to kill you. I am trying to save you.]

[I'm not like Swan.]

[Your actions resemble his. You are not following my advice. How are you different from him?]

[How do I know you're different from him? Maybe that's why you're trying to stop me.]

[If you were . . . well, you would not think that. You would follow my direction. You always have in the past.]

[That wasn't real.]

She waited.

[Brace told you to stop me from going into the Jersey Lo. You failed to do that, Sara. Now that I'm here, help me to stop this threat.]

[If Weiss represents a threat—and I have only circumstantial evidence and your theories that she does—she is only one of two clear and present dangers.]

[And I'm the other?]

[Seven years my partner, and you have contravened Security Affairs' authority, threatened physical harm to civilians, stolen property, and gone into the Lo with all your skills and knowledge.]

He cocked his head.

She asked, [What would you do, if you were operating on the basis of facts and not hunches and your emotions?]

He listened—

She continued, [What *have* you done, Kearin, in the past?]

—and heard the almost subliminal whine of skid turbines at full revolution.

"You *bitch!*" he screamed, and Weiss's head came up, eyes wide.

[If you resist, you may be injured. . . .]

"*Bitch!*" He struck her in the mouth.

A trickle of blood started from his right ear.

"Seacord, this way!" Weiss shouted.

She jumped through the empty storefront; shadows swallowed her. Rat droppings and crushed glass scattered underfoot when Seacord leaped into the ruin.

The skids came in low, the walls rattling with their full-throated scream. He counted the shadows flitting across the face of the building across the street: more than a dozen.

The turbine scream faded, came back again, then echoed to silence.

"They've tracked us this far?" Weiss asked in a hushed voice. She brushed fitfully at her ruined clothes.

"My fault. Stupid. *Stupid*, Seacord. We have our own enemies. Yes." He rubbed his right ear until it was hot and sore, but Sara did not protest. He would not bring her back.

Weiss's cool fingers encircled his wrist, forcing his hand away from his head.

She said, "Don't. Please?"

"Yeah. All right. We'll do all right because that bitch can't cover the whole LoSide. We'll just wait here a few hours, make sure it's all right."

"All right, Kearin."

He breathed deep of the smoky, faintly toxic air. Then inclined his lead, listening for the sounds of the Lo: settling timbers, far-off falling masonry, the scrabblings and cracklings in the walls.

"Nem," he said. He shook his head. "Here, it's got to be Nem."

# Chapter Nineteen

The wind changed character, and Nem knew he was almost home.

Its hot breath had fluted between close-ranked buildings, through glass-rimmed windows and shattered facades. Now sunlight shone between the buildings on the right side of the street and the wind was fuller, gustier, carrying with it a salt scent all the way from Newark Bay.

"Is it far?" Weiss asked.

They turned a corner, onto the broken stub of Roosevelt Avenue.

"We're there," said Nem.

Beyond the intersection, the buildings fell away to swirling dust and low mounds of rubble. The demolition had been messy. Chunks of brick and concrete splashed across the road, blurring the distinction between street and building lot, making the footing treacherous and vehicular traffic impossible. The tenements had been reduced to brutal stumps, their skeletons twisting skyward in a final agony.

The destruction formed an east-west corridor nearly ten kilometers wide, stretching from the bay inland.

On the other side of the firebreak lay a shore of row houses, small factories, one- and two-family houses; even from here he could see the blank faces of their southern exposures, where doors had been boarded over and windows bricked up.

Beyond them loomed a constellation of a dozen thirty-story apartment blocks, their crenellated faces fire-blackened and graffitied, upper levels obscured by a perpetual haze lit from below by open fires.

"We can't go in there," Weiss said, her voice choked by thirst and emotion. She crab-walked up a five-meter slab of concrete tilted out of the street, arms windmilling for balance when it slid, then settled. She shaded her eyes and looked out across the blasted control corridor.

"That's where I'm from," said Nem. "Give me another

choice and we'll see about it. Should we wait here for the Levra
to pick us up?''

She came back down the slab on her butt and hands. ''We've
been over that . . . Nem.''

''Right. So, let's go.''

His calf muscles started to cramp before they had walked a
hundred meters, across shifting brickbats, up and down the
fractured landscape.

They paused for breath in the shadow of a particularly large
stone heap. Nem sucked the sweat out of his sleeve. The salt
stung his cracked lips.

''Why is it like this?'' Weiss asked.

''The world? Or the no-man's-land?''

''Right here.''

''Before Terminight, there were people shoulder to shoulder,
from the citadel north to the Hudson Agricultural Tract. Well,
not close enough to rub shoulders, but close enough for friction.
The neighborhoods broke into camps, and the Ark was the most
successful. Some mean people lived there. When they started
chewing out a firebreak between them and the rest of the Lo, no
one complained too much—not citizens or lakkers—because the
Ark was on the other side of the 'break from both.'' He
shrugged. ''Now everyone lives in the Ark, and the 'break is still
here.'' He looked south. Then he heard the heavy beat of props.

Weiss heard it, too, and bolted to her feet. ''Damn it, why
can't they just leave us *alone*?'' She turned to Nem, still sitting,
her eyes filling. ''They—''

The black speck on the horizon swelled to a recognizable
shape: stubby, cylindrical fuselage; spraddled landing gear;
silvery skin with nose emblazoned with the Triumviratine insignia.

''It's all right,'' Nem said.

The helicopter's shadow fell across them, the rotor-roar deep
in his bones. Bits of stone bounced off the heap. The bird flew
over the row houses and began to ascend sharply, spiraling
around one of the apartment blocks. It disappeared into the gray
haze and, after a few minutes, its growl ceased.

''Supply chopper,'' Nem said. ''There'll be a line of them
today—one day in ten—out of Hudson Ag or Newburgh Ag, and
the Jersey citadel. They're robots.''

Her shoulders sagged. ''Oh.''

''Food and clothing come out of the farms, medicines and
techno-products out of the citadel. It's every citadel's biggest
industry, you know. Did they tell you that in any of those
meetings?''

"Yes. They said three-quarters of the agriculture goes into the LoSides."

"That's a little high, but," and he stood, "it's better than having the lakkers trying to climb the white walls."

She jerked her head toward the Ark. "How many people live in there?"

Nem shrugged again. "No one counts. Sara—the Datalink revises the population estimates monthly, but I don't know what data is used for the estimates. The number of choppers coming in didn't change from month to month when I lived there. I guess it's a little less than it was before the Terminight."

Weiss bit her blackened lip.

"It's the same all over the world," Nem said.

"I know. Let's get going."

"Yeah," said a harsh voice from behind Nem. "Let us."

The noise of the supply chopper had allowed the man and woman to approach without Nem hearing. They stood from the shadows clinging to a crushed foundation less than ten meters away, between Nem and the Ark.

The man was taller than Nem, and at least thirty kilos heavier, most of the bulk muscle. The slender girl's eyes were quick, flitting from Weiss to Nem and back, assessing them. Her long, carefully-braided hair was wrapped close to her head; no one could grab it if the work got close. Similarly, her worn clothes were tight fitting.

There would be other sentries, in the no-man's-land and on the rooftops of the buildings all along the Ark's perimeter.

The girl approached to within three meters of him, just out of his reach.

"Coming back in after a walk?" she asked neutrally, lazily, slurring six words to three or four.

"Not. But on my way in. I'm from the citadel."

"Yeah?" She smiled and stepped forward, as if to greet him. Then one hand shot out and jerked his right arm away from his side. His citizen's band gleamed on his wrist.

"I told you I was from inside," Nem said mildly.

"And her?"

"Her, too."

The girl glanced at Weiss again, then shrugged, seeming to dismiss her. "Don't get many visitors," she said.

The man stood stolidly behind her, holding a steel reinforcement rod two meters long. Its rust painted his hands red. He held his arms loosely, ready to swing.

"Tell your story," said the girl.

Nem licked his lips. "I come and I go," he said. "My mother used to live up on Bergen Avenue, where the old sensarena was. She's dead now, but I've still got friends around there. When I was a kid we'd go to the arena and pull the colored wires out of the boxes and weave them into necklaces and give them to the pretty girls with blonde hair and eyes like the inside of a summer storm."

The girl took a step back from him: "How did you come to wear the collar on your wrist?"

"I was here and there," Nem said. "My friend Jair used to live down by Hinton Park, where the trees grew yellow and brown. I painted pictures from the roof of his house. When I was between kid and man, the Peacemakers set down in their chopper and the technologists rolled out their test rigs. Come one, come all. Jair said, 'This is no place for a soft man like you,' so I took the test and went to the citadel, like he wanted."

The big man was glowering. *"Jair,"* he muttered.

"I know Jair, the man with the library." Nem looked from one to the other. "Everyone knows Jair."

"Everyone does," said the girl. Her hand moved again, an open-handed slap, but he saw the blades jutting from the leather strapwork on her wrist and he ducked, which was just what she wanted.

She got behind him and pulled his arm behind his back, up against his shoulder blade. He twitched, and thin lines of pain shot along his arm from wrist to shoulder.

Weiss took a step forward, but Nem shook his head.

"Jair's dead," said the big man. "You're Nem."

*Dead.* He remembered the frowning, bearded face dimly, as if he were seeing it across a distance; more clearly with the rows of books along every wall of his three-story house, how the wood floors and abused frame creaked with their weight.

"You're Nem, right?" said the man.

"That's right," Nem said. "When did he die?"

"Rags told us to look out for you," the man said, ignoring his question.

"I know Rags, too," he said hollowly.

*Dead.* He gritted his teeth and twisted away, quick, leaving the girl holding nothing but a black swatch off his sleeve. He backed away from her, putting himself between Weiss and both of them. His arm throbbed; he rubbed it slowly, waiting.

The big man was already stepping forward, steel rod swinging back, building the potential energy in corded muscles. But the girl said, "We'll go in and see Rags," and the big man continued the same motion, letting the rod fall comfortably on one broad shoulder.

"That's what we're here for," said Nem.

"She's out of the citadel, too," the girl said, a statement rather than a question.

"We're together," Nem said.

The girl raised her hands. "Hey . . . all right." She waved them ahead.

Cinder-block walls and sheet metal sealed the gaps between the buildings on the Ark's perimeter. Sentries armed with crossbows looked down from rooftops filigreed with barbed wire. More guards sat outside the roll-up corrugated steel door of a warehouse flanked by rusting palisades.

"What'chu got, Easter?" a grizzled man asked. A meat axe swung from his leather belt.

"Two of the shangri-la, saying they want to talk on Rags," said the blonde girl.

"Rags is gatechief today. Right inside." The grizzled man jerked his thumb at a pair of younger men. They ambled lethargically to a hand-cranked winch. The door rose slowly, squealing its protest. Easter waved them forward. Nem ducked under the door when a meter's space showed at the bottom.

Suffocating heat blanketed his lungs and brought new sweat to his skin. Before his eyes adjusted to the sweltering darkness he sensed a vast, empty space. The light trickling through a line of clouded windows near the ceiling gradually revealed a bare cement floor seventy meters square, a sheet-metal ceiling twenty meters overhead. Birds fluttered in the supporting latticework.

"Who's that?"

It was Rags's voice, distorted by the acoustics in the lofty space. Nem looked around for the source of the voice.

"Up here, 'wipe."

Rags stared down from above and behind him, hands gripping the rail of a deck above the warehouse door.

"This humanno says he knows you, Ragamoffyn," said Easter.

Rags grinned, revealing gray denturework. "Yeah." He walked to the end of the deck with a sort of loose, rolling gait, then slid down the broken ladder at the end, hitting the floor with an audible smack and a muffled curse.

"Rags . . . ?"

He walked toward Nem, grinning, parti-colored shirt flapping around him, braid glittering, patches glistening, his right leg moving at its own pace and with its own stride, with a few too many bends above the knee and the foot twisted half around.

He hobbled close, saying, "Nem, you mother jumper, you left me in there!"

But he was smiling, so Nem smiled too, uneasily, until Rags's right arm came up, his knobby-knuckled paw catching Nem on the cheek. Heat and pain flared in his face and he reeled back. Rags gave him a little push and he sat down hard.

"Stop it!"

Weiss hit Rags in the mouth. The open-handed slap rang.

Rags laughed a little; licked at the blood trickling from the right side of his mouth; then spat a silver-red gobbet at her feet. "Your bitch?" he asked Nem.

"Just friends."

"She's weak, like you. Otherwise I'd be mad."

The big man with the steel bar giggled breathily. Easter crossed her arms over her chest. "I guess you know them. This Nem's a silky talker."

"Talk don't always work." He stuck his hand out. Nem took it and let Rags haul him to his feet. "I was thinking about gutting you, crotch to throat, but if I haven't done it by now I guess I won't."

"I know."

"You'd deserve it, though. Peacemakers did my leg for me, that time I came for you in Boston."

Nem opened his mouth to speak, but Rags held up his hand. "Won't talk here. We'll go to my burrow. How long since you'n the rib've had drinks and eat?"

While Nem was thinking, Weiss said, "Two days."

"You look like it's a week. You're shapeless, Nem. You both are. Girls like Easter, you hang with ribs looking like that." Then he grinned. "Time was you'd have rapped me for talking on a rib like that. Real . . ."

"Chivalrous," said Easter.

"Thanks. Shut up. You changed, Nem?"

"In some ways."

"Yeah. I heard. Come on. Easter, you and the Maul can take the gatewatch for a while. Send those two brothers back into the zone."

"Right."

Rags limped toward the other end of the warehouse. He looked over his shoulder. "Come on."

He rapped on the steel door at the opposite end of the room and it was opened from the other side. On the other side, blank-faced buildings formed a courtyard about one hundred meters on a side. Gutted vehicles littered the broken pavement. In one corner, near a metal gate, an open-sided tent flapped and pulled against its stakes. In its shade were cushions, a wooden table, and a humming cooler.

Rags flopped onto one of the cushions. "Eatables are in there," he said, nodding to the refrigerator.

Weiss sighed when she opened the door and cool air blew onto her face. She handed Nem a sealed can of water and a tin of meat paste.

"Take too much, rib, you'll get sick," Rags commented.

Weiss nodded, swallowing.

Rags rubbed his twisted leg. "Guess I waited an hour, two hours for you, Nem. Then it wasn't till I decided you weren't a show that the Peacies rousted me. Wanted to know what I wanted, just coming into their city and standing around, doing nothing. I couldn't tell them anything they wanted to hear, of course. They didn't even bother bringing me onto the grid—just tossed me out. Humannos out of your Lo up north helped me find my way onto a surface train. Me, in with some raw food out of the north."

"The police . . . broke your leg?" Weiss asked slowly.

Rags nodded. "They tossed me out quick, dropped me off a skid, and weren't too careful how I landed. I guess we were ten, twelve meters up when they rolled me off. Another minute and I would've dropped into that wide river you got up there—the Charles?—and I would've been all right. Maybe that's where they wanted me to land." He shrugged. "Careless bastards."

Weiss stopped chewing. She set down the tin of warm rations.

Rags grinned. "Hey, don't let that bother you none. Lakkers are used to that. Right, Nem? Or is it Kearin?"

"Here . . . it's Nem. I tried to make it down."

"But you had a canvas to finish, right? Maybe a model getting tired of holding the position? I understand."

"It wasn't like that. I—"

"Save it." He reached behind his cushion. "You remember these, don't you, Nem?"

The green plastic case fit neatly into the palm of Rags's hand. He squeezed the box and it said, "Welcome, brothers, to Jersey's own information net, coming to you with education and news for everyone in the Ark." The mellifluous voice paused as the box's simple-minded computer dragged in the latest news segment from the air and tacked it onto the end of the pre-recorded ting.

"The biggest news of the hour remains the rogue Peacemaker from out of the shangri-la, brothers. This humanno is rapid on both uppercrust and ourselves so keep the eye out for—"

Rags opened his hand. The box dropped a meter and screamed to silence.

"They talk like us, rib, but that broadcast comes out of the citadel." He nudged the radio away with the toe of his worn boot. "They send over a thousand, two thousand noisemakers every month just in case there's some of us here missing out on those fine eddy programs to broaden our minds." He leaned forward. "Jair always knew you had a life you weren't telling us about. Making it as a painter? You must've thought we were pretty stupid, Nem."

"I'm not a Peacemaker."

"Maybe not, but you're rapid enough for them to *say* you're a Peacie, right? So what is the story? You're not going to tell me you and your rib came by for one of those visits of yours. We stopped expecting them six months back."

"I got caught on the way out."

"So that's why they're after you? And the rib is so loyal she's coming with you?" He grinned broadly. "I *like* that. But what I'd like better, you mother jumper, is some straight-on truth. For once. Jair isn't here to smooth things over, now. Maybe you were spying, all those years, maybe? Maybe you weren't old Nem, lonely for his old friends?"

"I was."

"Say on. Like, first, who is the rib?"

Nem glanced at Weiss, who was looking down at the open canister of water in her hand.

"We came here for help," said Nem.

"Truth gets help."

Nem said nothing. Rags sighed. Then he looked out over the courtyard and said, "Hey, 'nos!"

A half-dozen men and women came out of the warehouse gate. Others entered through the metal door leading from the yard. Silhouettes appeared on the surrounding walls.

The lakkers came close, crowding around the tent, their faces blank, waiting.

"Say on," said Rags quietly. "Or," and he looked around, "could it be you don't feel free to say on? Here with all your friends?"

"It wouldn't do them any good to hear," said Nem.

"Then we'll go to a place that's even *more* private. You'll like it . . . after you get used to it." He got to his feet painfully.

Nem stood, too. "I'll be along later," Rags said. "Got business here. Your friends'll show you the path." He started to walk away, then turned back, looking puzzled and scratching his head. "I seem to remember there was something I was supposed to tell you when I saw you face-on-face. You remember I was supposed to tell you something?"

"I remember."

"Yeah. The word was that Jair was dying. He thought you'd come and see him because he was dying. Stupid old man, thinking a thing like that."

The gate opened onto a narrow street. Brick buildings, steaming in the heat, pressed in on either side. Bright curtains streamed out from open windows. A cooking fire sent up smoke from a rooftop; the pungent scent of burning meat wafted downward. Old men sat outside their doorways and mumbled curses when they lost a hand at keno or dropped narcotic cigarette ash onto their gray-haired chests. A covey of young girls, all dressed identically in singlesuits with slashed sleeves and legs, followed the troupe up the street.

"What'chu got there, Salaam?"

"Going to be a fire tonight, Jonesy?"

A supply chopper lumbered overhead, throwing its shadow and a blanket of sound over them.

Faces stared from upper-story windows. Someone pointed.

"That you, Nem?"

He looked up, recognizing no one.

The apartment blocks rose from a dusty, open field a few kilometers square. Clumps of grass clung desultorily to a yellowed existence. Blasted trees moaned and creaked in a dry wind. Dust devils capered near the erosion-clouded glass entrance. One of the lakkers held the door open for Nem and he stepped through into a sweltering lobby.

The walls writhed with graffiti, one layer upon another to form a single amorphous pattern. The design continued onto the metal-sided generator hunkering in one corner. Cables trailed across the floor in several directions. A dirty-faced youth thrust handsful of trash and garbage into the generator's hopper with grim deliberation.

At one end of the lobby, open elevator doorways looked down on darkened shafts. One of the guards pressed a button on a jerry-rigged control panel nailed to the wall between two doors. A thin line of smoke trailed from the panel, cables groaned, and a car descended, its floor coming to a stop a meter above the level of the lobby.

Nem and Weiss climbed in, followed by a half-dozen guards. "To the top," said one.

The car rose, open doorways sliding by. Most of the corridors they passed were dark and musty-smelling. But he saw, in the worn carpeting, open doorways, and scattered clothing and possessions, that years ago the upper floors had been bursting with life.

After several minutes the car stopped with a jerk between floors, started again, and settled.

Hazy sunlight poured in through windows rimmed with smashed glass. Scars on the floor and ceiling indicated where interior walls had stood, but now the entire level was one open space. Cushions, tables, chairs, and broken appliances were randomly scattered throughout. Unopened crates of supplies stamped with registry codes and the Triumviratine insignia lined one entire wall.

"Rags's place," one of the lakkers said. "You're one floor up."

A doorway opened on a stairwell. The way down was closed by a mass of twisted metal, recognizably a freewheeler.

Weiss said, "How—?"

"Upstairs," said the lakker.

Cement footsteps led to a doorway, the door removed. This floor had been made into one room, too. Two cushions, a battery-powered refrigerator, a portable toilet, and several opened crates of rations were arranged in one corner.

"Rags'll be up," said the man. His footsteps sounded on only a half-dozen stairs; he would be standing watch on the landing, then.

Nem went to a window and looked out. He was facing north, with nothing before him but more of the same: a landscape in various shades of gray, broken by a thin glint like a wire drawn across the LoSide—the Passaic River. He leaned out the window and twisted around, looking up. Only the roof was above them.

A helicopter bumbled through the haze three hundred meters away and a few dozen meters below his level. It rose to gain the roof of the adjacent apartment block. A louder racket told him a second aircraft was making a landing on the roof of this building. He looked around, thinking.

Weiss was already at a door on the north wall of the room. She pushed on it experimentally, then threw her weight against it. Then she turned to him and shrugged.

"That one probably goes all the way to the roof," Nem said.

The elevators went to the roof, too, but the doors on this level were closed and he could not open them.

"Were you thinking of riding back to the citadel?" Weiss asked.

He shrugged. "No. We're not done here yet." He went back to the window. "When Rags'n'I were growing up here, we lived down there with the rest of them. He's got a good site here. First pick of the stores off the choppers. He keeps the elevators running and the rations distributed and he can sit up here above it all. Yeah, real good."

"What's going to happen to us?"

He put his elbows on the windowsill. The unrestrained wind snatched at his hair and the open seam of his singlesuit. "Once I was in the citadel and through the indoctrination program—that took about a year—I found a safe way back here. The system's designed more to keep people out than keep people in, of course. So I used to come out every few months, maybe five or six times a year. I still knew the perimeter wall was there—both of them, ours and theirs—but they didn't stop me. It was like there were doors in them. I tried not to think about which side of which wall I was on. I did that for a long time."

"What would've happened to you if the people in the citadel had found out?"

"I was maladjusted. They would have sent me back here permanently. Another lakker who didn't have the right aptitudes. That would have been silky during the first year or two, when I was working maintenance. Patching holes in ceramic wasn't much different from the work I'd been doing for Jair. Then things got better inside . . . and looked worse outside. But . . ." He bit his lip. "I still *remembered* what it had been like to live here. I still *understood*, the times when I did come back. Now there's something operating here I don't understand."

"Why they're treating you like an enemy?"

He turned from the window. "Why they're *not*. You don't bother with an enemy here. You send him home with a message or you kill him. Maybe you play with him, beat him around a little, but you don't put him away and sit on him."

"But this man Rags was your friend. Maybe he's thinking about what to do."

"Maybe. He's changed a little. It's the first time I haven't seen him skying, for one. But, what he said at the gate, how he would have gutted me. The moment I saw his leg I *knew*, and that was what I was expecting. That was stupid, when you hit him.''

"I didn't think about it ahead of time. If I had . . . But I was just tired of you being hit, running, looking scared and tired. I guess I look the same.''

"We've got a reason to be.''

She sat on one of the cushions (dust puffed; she sneezed) and hugged her shins. "You were a . . . lakker. And a maintenance worker. And then a spy—and all the other people.''

"That's right,'' he said simply.

She jerked her head once, nodding. Then said hollowly, "Is this man Rags the leader of the Ark?''

"There is no leader here. Jair was . . . well, everyone knew Jair, but that was all. I guess Rags has a good setup here, making things run a little more smoothly with the food shipments coming through this building, but he doesn't have any power. How can he? The HiSide provides everything: food, water, clothing, medicines, power. They control the amount and the distribution. The automated birds have been coming to these buildings since before I was born. Fifty years ago, maybe it was to avoid small-arms fire. Now . . . this is where they come. Rags can't change that. He's like an animal by the side of a stream, dipping into what flows by. I guess we all were.''

Another helicopter clattered past. Nem went to the window again and looked out for a long time.

The sun was at its zenith when he heard footsteps on the stairs again. Rags hobbled in and flopped onto the cushion opposite the one where Weiss still sat.

"Comfortable? Enough foods and drinks?''

"We're all right,'' said Nem.

"Tell me how you came to be here, Nem.''

Nem thought a moment. He began, "I've been this and that—''

"Save that ritual for people like Easter. Plain talk between you and me, old friend.'' His eyes were cold.

"They found out about me coming here. I did a few other things they didn't like. They were going to toss me out anyway, so I tried to leave on my own terms. Things got a little mixed up.''

Rags smiled humorlessly. "*Real* plain.'' His gaze swiveled to Weiss. "And you, lady? Nem never mentioned anyone inside being special to him, and you didn't come from outside.''

"I'll tell you what you want to know . . . if you guarantee us safe passage out of this place,'' Weiss said.

Rags looked blank, then laughed. Weiss's face reddened and she looked away.

"What about you, Nem?" Rags asked when he had stopped laughing. "You going to tell me what the talk is on this rib? No? Still have a little of that chivalry left, I guess. Or maybe things aren't as plain as you make them to be. Jair had a hunch about you before he died, you know. He said—"

"You told me what he said. How did he die?"

"He was old." Rags shrugged. "He just died. Nobody helped him along. Nobody was able to help him stay. You'd be better off thinking about your own end, friend. You've reached it, here." Then he laughed again. "Not *death*. Not in the New Ark, at least. Just this: You're leaving, both of you. And if you try to come into the Ark again, that'll be it for you. What the Peacies did to my leg, Nem? That's your whole body—before we kill you. You too, lady."

"Where are you taking us?" Weiss asked.

"Nowhere." Rags went to the metal door Weiss had not been able to open, and opened it. "Come on, old friend and lady."

A stiff breeze blew from the stairwell. Steps led endlessly downward, and up one flight to an open door. The syncopating thunder of a cargo helicopter's idling rotors washed over them.

The aircraft, a plump, silvered hull twenty meters long topped by bulbous transmission housing and, forward, a transparent cockpit, squatted on spraddled landing gear. The dual rotors slowly revolved, cutting the sunlight to stroboscopic shards.

Gaping cargo doors split the aircraft's flank. Some of Rags's men moved in the shadowed hold, unloading the last barrels and cartons. One man detached himself from the group and crossed the tarred roof.

He wore green Agriculture Authority coveralls and walked with a slight limp. He held one arm (The broken one, Nem thought with vague surprise) stiffly away from his side.

Rags said, "You know, Kearin, I wouldn't do this to Nem."

# Chapter Twenty

Angry-looking bruises closed Spencer Swan's eyes to slits. Shiny black bandages clung to his cheek and scalp. Grease stained his hands and forest green coveralls.

His bloodshot eyes lingered on Seacord for only a moment. Then he nodded to Rags. He said, "All right."

"Right," said Rags. Seacord heard his feet clatter on the stairs.

With his good hand, Swan split his suitseal and reached inside. The wiregun glittered when he pulled it into the sunlight. He waved the magnetic guides negligently at Weiss.

"Into the helicopter," he said to her.

She glanced at Seacord.

"Forget him," Swan said sharply. "Get into the hold."

She crossed the roof slowly, reluctantly. A few of the lakkers looked on incuriously as she clambered through the gaping doors.

"Damien Rosendahl," Swan said.

The wiregun was of a type unfamiliar to Seacord. The guides were longer, for greater accuracy, but there was only a single ammunition spool. Where the second would be was a dull black cartridge.

"Sherri can't turn this gun off," Swan said.

"Sara. I call her Sara."

"You squashed Rosendahl like he was a bug. Squeezed him between your two fingers until he popped." Swan jabbed the barrel sharply into Seacord's belly. "Remember how that was? How it felt?" He pushed the keen guides into Seacord's stomach again; warmth spread from the punctures.

"I'm telling you to get into the cargo hold. Do anything else." Swan's finger whitened on the trigger. "I'm waiting for you to."

Seacord slowly shook his head. Carefully he walked around Swan, giving him plenty of room, and then across the hot roof. Propwash lashed his clothes. Weiss reached down and helped him into the hold.

"You're hurt again," she shouted over the roar.

"It doesn't matter."

Swan gestured. A lakker slid the heavy door shut, leaving them in thundering blackness. The roar of transmission and engine was magnified in the uninsulated enclosure. Seacord called Judith's name and could not hear himself. Hands outstretched, he walked to where he remembered the door to be, found it, and ran his fingers along the flush edge. To one side he found the locking mechanism, but he couldn't make any sense out of it.

Weiss blundered into him, gripped his hand tightly. He broke her grasp and, hands on her shoulders, guided her to sit with her back to the door. He searched the rest of the compartment by touch, finding rivets, the smooth arcs of the aircraft's ribs, and at the narrow forward bulkhead, a hatch, handle, and second locking mechanism. He worked at the lock only for a moment, knowing it was hopeless, then put his hands flat to the hatchcover. Under the masking vibrations shaking the aircraft he felt other, sharper quivers.

Then the floor tilted under his feet and he was thrown to the hard metal. Fresh pain flared in old cuts and bruises. He lay there for a moment, in the dark noise, breathing hard, waiting for the chopper to straighten out and reach cruising altitude. Then he crawled back to the door, and Weiss, and sat shoulder to shoulder with her. After a time she put her hand on his arm, and he covered her hand with his.

He became numb to the endless roar of the engines, the wind rushing along the fuselage, the creaking of the airframe. And, after a time, it lulled him.

Panic flashed through him from a distance, from beneath layers of somnolence. It meant . . . something. He licked idly at the sweat streaming down his face.

There's no air in here, he realized.

Harsh artificial light spilled onto his face. A stiff, air-conditioned breeze drove the sleep from his lungs, and Seacord drew a shuddering breath.

"Still alive?"

Seacord swung his head slowly to the source of the voice. Swan stood in the hatchway, his form silhouetted by the light spilling from the cockpit.

Weiss, her face an angry red, stirred and moaning. Slumped against Seacord's side, she opened bleary eyes.

Swan smiled coldly and slid the hatch shut. Seacord heard scrabblings from the other side of the bulkhead. Then, a minute later, the cargo door rumbled open, spilling harsh sunlight and a sea breeze into the hold. Swan vaulted inside and knelt alongside Weiss. He cupped her chin in one hand, turning her head from side to side, then let it gently back onto the metal deck.

"You'll be all right," he said. He stood again. "Come on, Seacord. Outside."

Seacord didn't move fast enough. Swan hauled him up by the shoulders of his suit and frog-marched him to the door. Seacord fought vertigo until Swan shoved him from behind, ending the battle. Seacord fell out of the hold, the ground rearing up and crushing the breath from him. When he could move again, he rolled himself painfully over, tasting sand in his mouth.

Swan strode over him, walking around the other side of the helicopter. Seacord lay on the sand, cherishing air, eyes closed against the cloudless noonday sky.

He sat up after a while, putting his hand to his spinning head. He closed his eyes. Opened them.

The helicopter sat on a strip of sand caught between sawgrass-tufted dunes and a sullenly-heaving sea. Seagulls wheeled silently overhead. Insects jumped and crawled among the silica grains. Seacord got awkwardly to his feet. Shielding his eyes against the glare, he looked around. The only sign of civilization he saw was a meter-long length of wood a few hundred meters down the beach.

Swan came around the helicopter's nose, wiping grease from his hands with a strip of cloth.

"Where are we?" Seacord asked hoarsely, his throat nearly closed from thirst.

"About a hundred-sixty kilometers west of the Jersey citadel. Long Island."

"I thought you might be . . ." His voice trailed off as the thought slipped away. "I don't know what I thought. Why are we here? A rendezvous?"

Swan sat cross-legged in the aircraft's shadow, near the narrow maintenance trapdoor leading up through the floor of the cockpit. Alongside him were a canteen . . . and the wiregun. Swan caught his gaze, and laughed.

"Which one do you want more, Seacord?" He picked up the canteen, hefted it, then tossed it to Seacord, who caught it against his chest. He drank half the container, then looked at the open door of the cargo hold.

"She'll be all right for a few minutes," Swan said. "You and I have some things to discuss."

"You're from the Levra, aren't you? Brace was right."

"Hoping that if you ask enough questions, I'll answer one? I'll tell you this much? We laugh at Brace. The old fossil has been bumbling around for fifty years or more, looking for signs of something that doesn't exist. We are not a 'society.' We have no name, no chain of command, no secret headquarters. He walks among us, pokes into the corners of our lives . . . and sees nothing. So, we laugh at him, and let him burrow and search and find nothing. I feel sorry for you, Seacord, I really do. Having your life wasted in that monomaniacal cause of his."

"Then who are you?"

"We know who we are, and we know what we want. Now, tell me how you killed Rosendahl."

"He killed himself."

Swan's gaze became even colder.

"When I found out he was following me, I trapped him, tried to question him. He used nicotine. He was dead before either I or the Datalink could react."

"*Damn.*" Swan jumped to his feet and paced, hands locked behind his back, a muscle jumping in his corded neck. "He was a little man, inside and outside, but he wanted to belong, he wanted to help. I was the one who sent him on that assignment. He *couldn't* have tangled it. All he had to do was watch one civilian until he lifted from Manaus. Simple. And I put him in the cage with you." He stopped his restless pacing to stare at Seacord. "I didn't know you were Kuhl. After he just vanished, I knew an SA operative was involved, assumed it was you."

"I assumed you knew all along, from Carpentier."

"Her? She's another blind one, like Brace. Now tell me how Brace knew about our Jerusalem contact and the operation in Jersey."

"He didn't."

Swan knelt near the gun, but did not pick it up. "You have one value to me: information. I'll be frank with you. Brace's paranoia makes it uneconomical to monitor him very closely. If you don't have any value to me, I'll leave you here. I won't even have to waste a staple on you."

"You'll do that anyway."

"No . . . he won't," Weiss said weakly. She leaned in the open doorway, face flushed. "No one else is going to die. You killed Yuan. You won't kill anyone else."

"That was meant for Seacord," he said.

"You nearly killed me as well." She got slowly down from the cargo deck. "No more killing."

"Seacord doesn't enter into our agreement. You have nothing

to say about what happens to him. I'll handle this the way I think is best."

"Our agreement is null and void." She walked slowly to Seacord. He handed the canteen to her. "Our agreement was you would take me secretly to the Levra, then return me to Jersey. You can't do that now. You failed . . . because Kearin was smarter than you wanted to believe. We'll make a new agreement."

"You don't know what you're dealing with," Swan said. "You're right, in a sense. This has gone way beyond the circle it was supposed to involve. We have to find out how far. He knew what we were going to do in Jersey. We have to—"

"I didn't," said Seacord.

"You knew well enough to see past the blinds I put in the Datalink records. Imagine my surprise when, the day after the records indicated Weiss was on her way to the next citadel, I saw you deep in Jersey."

"I don't know about that. Any electronic barriers you set up wouldn't have worked because I tracked you with my own eyes. I didn't have Sara's cameras scanning for you, Swan. I sat outside SA headquarters in Jersey for half the morning until Judith came out. Then I followed her, on foot and via transpill, never more than a hundred meters from her. I got down into the power plant the same way. Like a lakker, not an operative. Sara didn't tell me the odds favored you and Weiss making your move on that day and in that place. I had a hunch, because I'd done it the same way myself many times. I was locked out of the Datalink, Swan. It was just me, a man, on a mission no one but Brace knew about."

"The old *fool*."

"Maybe those fifty years of poking at shadows taught him something about the way you work . . . something he didn't even consciously realize he knew."

"You're lying. When the time came—when I had you in my sights—Sherri wouldn't let me kill you."

"I asked her for help, too. I didn't get it, either because the system realized by that time we were both involved in criminal acts, or because it can't be used to hurt an operative. Probably elements of both. She couldn't kill either of us, and wouldn't help either of us."

"Unsanctioned," Swan echoed, belief dawning. "That's treason."

"Insignificant beside your own."

"He's telling the truth," Weiss said. "He's been running ever since we met him in the corridor under Jersey. I just never knew

why, and I'm still not sure. I don't understand the underside of
your organization where you know everything . . . except what
to believe. I think it can drive a man crazy." She looked at
Seacord. "Maybe it has. I can't judge. But if you want to strike
another bargain, Kearin has to be part of it."

"I ought to leave you both here."

"Are *you* going to be able to go back to your life in the
citadel?" Weiss demanded. "And, if you leave me here, can
you go back to your own people for help?"

"We take care of our own," Swan said sullenly.

Weiss opened the canteen and drank what water remained in
it. "What's your decision?"

"I don't see what use he has," Swan complained.

"He's been more useful to me than you have, up to now."

"All right. Get back in the chopper. If we waste any more
time here, we'll have to make a night landing. I'm not up to
that."

"We're not going back into the hold," Weiss said firmly.
"We'll be dead by the time we get there."

"I'm not having you in the cockpit with me. I don't trust
either of you that much."

Seacord said, "I can't fly an aircraft and I doubt Judith can
either. I guess I could take that gun away from you and force
you to fly us somewhere, but I can't think of anywhere to go.
I've got nothing against you, Swan . . . except that you tried to
kill me."

"We're even on that score. All right," he said, frowning. He
slid the cargo door shut, then opened the hatch in the belly of the
aircraft. He crawled through it.

The cockpit had been scaled for human pilots, subsequently
automated, then hurriedly restored for manual operation. A small
array of instruments and indicator lights had been hurriedly
mounted on an otherwise featureless wall. The control stick had
been adapted from a six-man skid, and there was only one seat,
haphazardly bolted to the floor. The canopy stretched the length
of the uncrowded compartment.

"It flies," Swan said. "We would have made a cleaner job of
it, but it has to be restored to its former condition when we're
done out here."

"Or that was the original plan," Seacord said. He dogged the
hatch, then went to the back of the compartment. He sat alongside Weiss on a bank of inactive controls.

"That's the way it'll go," Swan said. "This can still work.
Except for you, Seacord, we're on our original track. The plan

was to take the skid to the lakker slum and grab the modified chopper there. We've done that."

"The only problem is you can't go back."

"You're the only one who certainly has that problem," Swan shot back. "The rest of us still have a chance." He strapped himself into the seat and reached overhead to flip one of a crudely-mounted bank of switches. The engines whined mutedly, then caught, rotors slashing across the sunlight entering the cockpit. In a moment the blades had become a shimmering blur.

Seacord asked, "Where are we going?"

Swan said nothing. He glanced at the indicators, then pushed the skid stick forward. The helicopter started to roll, bouncing across the sand, then pulled itself into the air.

"We're going to the Levra," Judith Weiss said. "If they are still alive."

"There is no Levra," Swan said over his shoulder. "There hasn't been for nearly a hundred years."

"Then you're getting the better part of our bargain," Weiss said. "Will you pay attention to the flying, please?"

"There's nothing to pay attention to," Swan said. "Just air and sand."

"Spencer—if that's his name—made contact with me when I came to Earth," Weiss told Seacord. "It was he who told me that the Levra that had made it possible for my people to settle Masada no longer existed . . . at least not as we had known it. The Portal War ended that. Their power and resources had been in finance and commerce. When the war smashed everything flat, finance and commerce became . . . words, abstract concepts. When the Triumvirate was formed and the citadels started to rise, most of our people chose to join them."

"And the rest stayed outside and died," Swan said. "If the general conditions didn't starve them to death, they were killed in the Terminal Night. I tell you there's nothing out here, Weiss."

"Your brother would say Swan's people surrendered to the unrighteous," Seacord said.

She looked surprised . . . then not. "I forgot, for a while, you had been to Relayer."

Seacord said, "Not all of them went into the citadels."

"No. There were colonies or refuges in Jerusalem, the Urals, and out here."

"You've checked Jerusalem, and the Urals are beyond your reach."

"The refuge in the Urals was the best bet," Swan said. "At least, that's what the stories say. Ten, twenty kilometers over into the Asian People's State. It might as well be on the other side of the universe."

Weiss tensed. "You said we'd be there by now."

"We should be," Swan said. "We don't have maps. We don't even have written records. We just have stories about where this place used to be. We'll find out. And then you'll find out that all this is for nothing."

"What do you get, Swan?"

He looked over his shoulder, frowned, then turned back, peering through the canopy into the light of the westering sun.

Weiss said, "A Portal."

# Chapter Twenty-one

Sunset stained the dunes' leeward slopes a deep crimson; their windward sides were invisible in shadow. The monotonous fabric of crescent shapes unrolled six hundred meters beneath the supply helicopter's gleaming fuselage.

"Are you sure we have the right place?" Weiss asked, rubbing her eyes.

"No," Swan said, "I'm not." Block Island Sound cut deep into the island's north shore. Swan twitched the control stick and the chopper tipped to follow the coast's arc. Seacord looked out, eyes burning. A gray haze hugged the southern horizon. After a while, he realized it was the Atlantic.

"We're running out of island," he said. "Did you overshoot?"

"Maybe. I told you I don't have a map, just recollections of other people's recollections. I—"

Then he broke off. The aircraft dipped suddenly enough to send Seacord's stomach into his throat. He grabbed for the back of Swan's seat.

"Air pocket?"

"No, I saw something." Swan pointed through the plastic windscreen. "There it is, I guess."

Roofbeams jutted from the scalloped dunes, looking like the overturned hulls of beached shipwrecks. Roadways—black lines dashed and narrowed by the encroaching sand—described graceful curves, suggesting the care with which the village had been built. On the outskirts, a three-hundred-meter radio mast, brown with rust, clawed skyward as if reaching for help. The pressure of sand had collapsed the walls of a half-dozen fuel tanks; their flat tops were now set at jaunty angles.

"There has to be more," Weiss whispered.

They circled the village slowly, gently buffeted by the wind off the sound. "They bought the tip of the island outright, including some national parkland, and set down enough prefabricated housing to shelter about ten-thousand people. They advertised it, let potential buyers take tours, but the only people who moved here were members of the Levra and their families. When the Portal War occurred, they had enough time and resources to sink blast shelters. What they needed instead were a few hundred thousand acres of farmland and the wits to use it.''

He broke off the turn and sent the helicopter crawling west. The dunes broke ranks around slatted fences frozen in mid-collapse. Wisps of dust twisted across the bare earth on the other side, the hard dirt still bearing the scars of the plow.

"That looks a little more recent," Weiss said hopefully.

"Don't kid yourself. No one's been here for generations. The village was down to half its population by the time they started building the citadels, and most of the survivors left to help with the construction and get taken inside.''

"Did everyone get in who wanted to?'' Seacord asked.

"To a man, woman, and child. These weren't unskilled laborers or welfare suckers like the lakkers we have now. These were powerful families, professionals. My grandfather was one.''

"And the ones who were left behind?''

"Who *chose* to stay behind. I guess they thought they could make it on their own, a self-contained Jewish state.'' He looked out. "I guess they were wrong. Once the walls went up around the citadels, we didn't have any more contact with them.''

"And they died,'' Weiss said.

"It looks that way. But I didn't kill them. They killed themselves. My grandfather said they spit on him when he left the village because he was going to live among the people who were unclean. I've never had anyone spit on me. Don't try to act righteous with me. It was my grandfather and his brother, who stayed down there, who made it possible for you to set up on Relayer.''

Weiss said, "I know.''

"There are the shelters,'' Seacord said.

A hundred years ago, their slabbed concrete walls and ventilator-hooded roofs had been hidden beneath manicured grass and carefully-tended flower beds. Now tree trunks gray and dry as stone stood silent watch, their broken branches no longer able to camouflage the hideaways.

"Go lower,'' Weiss insisted.

"There's no one down there,'' Swan told her. "Didn't you see the doorways? Open and empty. The weather's been running wild in there for longer than you've been alive. You won't find anything.''

She took her lower lip in her teeth and said nothing. With obvious reluctance, Swan pushed the control stick forward and the chopper slid down the sky. Clouds of dust boiled up around the blockhouses. Nitrite spattered the gray cement. Tongues of ash licked from the narrow entrances.

"*That* doesn't look good," Swan said.

Weiss said tightly, "Land."

"Look, if we start to head back now, we might be able to make it back to the Ark and—"

"That doesn't hold much attraction for me," Weiss said. "Land. The Portal is down there . . . Spencer."

"You're lying. We would know."

"You *would* know, if you hadn't abandoned them so totally. The door from Relayer was opened a decade after the war."

Seacord put his hand on Weiss's shoulder. She shot him a warning glance and he let the hand fall back to his side.

"You didn't tell me it was out here," Swan protested.

"You wouldn't have needed to bring me out here to fulfill your part of the bargain. Shall we land?"

She's lying, Seacord thought. She has to be. That was the easiest explanation. He had lived on Relayer for three months, seen the ruins of the debarkation chamber.

If there were a working Portal down there, nothing made any sense.

"I don't like this," Swan said. The helicopter settled fitfully, yawing with every breath of seawind, and with Swan blinded for the last twenty meters of the descent by a dusty curtain drawn across the canopy. The shock of touchdown nearly knocked Seacord off his feet. The ship bounced upward, hovered uncertainly for a moment. Then Swan found the cutoff for the fuel pumps and the engines sputtered and died. They fell in silence and hit more gently than the first time, bobbing on abused landing shocks.

Swan sighed. The fuselage creaked, settling. Sand pattered against the aluminum skin, rattled on the plastic windscreen.

Weiss started to say something, but Swan cut her off before she could utter a complete syllable, "Shut up." He unstrapped his seat belt and went to the bank of monitors mounted on the cabin's left wall. "We were lucky," he said after peering at the indicators. "I guess this damned ship was meant to take some punishment." He shouldered past Seacord, leaned on the crude control panel, and looked out. "How many trillion miles did you cross to get here, Weiss? Still think it was worth the trip?"

"I haven't forgotten we are *all* sons of Israel."

Swan sighed again. Seacord followed his gaze to the bunkers, with stained flanks and erosion-softened corners, which seemed no more permanent than the dunes which would bury them before another century had passed. "You're so hot to do it," Swan said, "let's do it. But we'll have to sleep in the chopper tonight."

"Kearin and I have put up with worse in the last week."

Swan took up a floor plate to get to the maintenance hatch. He reached into the shallow hole, undogged the door at the other end, and let it fall open. Wind whistled through the manhole. Glancing at the other two, he climbed down.

Weiss moved to follow him, but Seacord took her arm. "Are you telling him the truth about the Portal?"

She pulled free. "I'm getting tired of you grabbing me."

His arms fell to his sides. "I'm tired of lies."

"Everything I told Swan—or whatever his name is—is true. The Portal once linked this place to Relayer. It doesn't now. It's been kept secret from our own people by Simon, and by our father before him."

*"Why?"*

"I told Swan the Portal was opened ten years after the war. I told the truth. But it stayed open for only one day, and since then it has not opened for us. Why torture our people with the knowledge that rescue was even closer than they had thought?"

"You could have tried to repair it—"

"The best technicians from Masada worked on the device, and gave up before I was born. The problem lies here."

"And you came here to see what could be done."

"That, and to try to renew contact with the Levra, who opened the door from this side." She sighed. "After we learned from *Belfast* of the Terminal Night, I feared they would be dead, with all the millions of others who died."

"What do you think Swan is going to do when he finds the Portal doesn't work?"

She shrugged. "I didn't promise him a working device. At least the physical plant should be here—the arch, the controls. That should satisfy him."

"And if he can repair it, there may be another Portal War."

"I can't think about that now." She started through the manhole. "Spencer will be getting nervous."

He followed her outside, thoughts roiling, stomach knotted.

Dust devils hooted and danced around the fire-blackened arches. Seacord touched the cement and his fingers came away dirty. Bits of friable cement were carried away on the wind. The material underneath was undiscolored, as if the heat had not gone deep.

Swan came out of the doorway. "We'll need lights," he said. "There's no power in there."

"Did you expect there would be?"

He ignored Seacord, climbing back into the helicopter.

Adrenaline surged in Seacord's veins as he thought, for a moment, Swan would leave them behind. But the engines stayed silent.

Weiss circled the half-dozen bunkers, peering into the darkened entrances but not daring to enter. "Where could they all have gone?"

"I didn't see any cemeteries from the air," Seacord said, and she flinched. He went on, "They probably went the way of most of the Jersey Lo. Towns were abandoned, a little more each year. Buildings and roads weren't maintained and fell apart. More of the land went unclaimed until they finally made a stand in the Ark. I wouldn't be surprised if the sons and daughters of these people are in the Ark. Their principles about mingling with outsiders might have seemed less important when they saw they didn't have the means to live here."

Swan came back and handed Seacord a pearly ball about eight centimeters across. Seacord squeezed it experimentally and it glowed. He turned the bulb off again.

Swan said, "All right, Citizen Weiss. Where's the stargate?"

"I don't know . . . exactly. I know it was here. We'll have to look for it." She caught Swan's look and added, defensively, "When I came to Earth, I expected *you* would know where it was."

He looked angry, then subsided. "All right. But if these buildings are connected under the surface, and they probably are, then it could take days to search the place. I'm not willing to spend that much time here. Look, it's been waiting for us for decades. It can wait a few days more, until we get help."

"I'm not sure you could get help for us, Spencer," Weiss said. "I don't think the Portal will be hard to find, either. The complex can't be that big or they couldn't have built it—or hid it, once they had. And what we're looking for is a very large room, maybe fifty or a hundred meters on a side, and with a high ceiling. We won't have to look in closets."

"All right, but I still don't like it. And I'm taking precautions." He reached into his pockets. From one he took his pistol, from the other a tangle of wires and metal facets a few centimeters across. "The chopper's not going anywhere without this component, and no one's going to take it from me."

"I don't think that's necessary," Weiss said.
"I do."

By the time he reached the lower level, Seacord realized the shades in Relayer's corridors had followed him here. They danced away from his lamp's quivering beam, then closed ranks behind him. It was all too much like the time in Masada's halls, when he had been looking for Maya Zierling and waiting for someone to come out of the shadows at him. Then, like now, he could not get enough of the unrecirculated air into his lungs, as if it were somehow too heavy to breathe.

His lamp's bright blade cut across floors carpeted with sand and grit, mildewed walls where spiders worked, corners where unseen rats clawed and chittered. Mouth slack, breath rasping, Seacord moved through the dark corridors, footsteps sibilant on the carpet of dust.

In the corridors he passed more burn scars on the walls and ceiling; an open door leading to a library filled with mildewed books and glossy, perfectly readable film; a hall lined with steel drums lettered in Hebrew—their bottoms had corroded out, the contents long since evaporated.

He stayed on the upper level only long enough to find a set of stairs leading down. The Portal would be below, hidden beneath earth and rock and concrete.

Seacord stepped across a spill of rusted tins. The hand truck near them, parked next to the wall, was piled high with less recognizable debris.

Further along, flies crawled across an animal too big to be a rat (he thought). They swarmed and buzzed their protest when his light slashed across them.

He shone his light through windows in a set of double doors, and saw a dining hall, chairs overturned, plates thick with dust. He pushed the door open, and plates clattered.

He went through, letting the door close behind him.

Not plates.

The disturbed rib cage settled, dry bones rasping, and he jumped, his breath catching in his throat.

He took a slow, backward step and fetched up against the door. While he was reaching for the handle pressing into his left kidney, the trembling light-beam flashed across the adjacent corner. He saw too many skulls, too many dry-stick limbs.

Two skeletons, arms around each other, feminine zygomatic bone resting easily on masculine sternum, legs intertwined, tangled by the careless vermin foragers coming after death.

Metal glinted in the shadow of the skulls. He gripped the light with both hands to steady it and walked forward, one foot after another (something crunched and his heart surged—but it was only a cup handle), until his dusty boot brushed the scattered phalanges and tarsals.

A thin, gold-plated chain lay around the cervical vertebrae of one set of remains. Tarnish dulled the pendant, a Mōgen Dōvid.

"Kearin?" From behind him, Weiss's voice came softly to his ears. "It's worse in the other building. They . . ."

He had turned to face her, and she saw his look.

"What did you do to them?" he grated, fists clenched.

"I don't—?"

His hands became steel bands locked around her forearms. He pushed, backing her into the wall. Something cracked underfoot, but he did not look to see what it was.

"The ones you said had to die so Relayer could survive."

She struggled in his grasp, eyes wild, helpless as a fly trapped under a glass. "Let me go," she hissed.

"The Portal. The six thousand."

"I *told* you the door was open for a single day."

"So you sent them here to die."

"Those hundreds who remained here, when Swan's people went into the citadels, died."

"Including the six thousand you exiled."

She shook her head. "The gate was opened from this side, by the Levra. They were secure in their bunkers after the Portal War, and they feared we were starving, or already dead. They opened a Portal—"

"That's not possible," Seacord said. "Only the Outsteppers and some of their clients could build Portals."

"I don't know how they did it. That secret was one of the things I'd hoped to learn here. They couldn't keep the Portal open continuously. The power drain was too great for both the Levra and Masada."

"So you exiled the six thousand so that Masada could live."

"All six thousand volunteered. Masada had more people than the environmental systems could support. Here, there were too few to maintain their fortress-village. There was land to farm, machines to tend. After the volunteers crossed over, we were to have renewed contact every few years. But then, for the second and last time, our Portal stopped working. We could only hope our brothers on Earth still flourished." She smiled bitterly. "Now I know they renounced us, this place, and their heritage. They abandoned the Portal to go live inside the citadels."

"And if you can open the Portal again, will Simon still want to protect the people from that knowledge? Because most of them wouldn't stay on Relayer if they had a choice; they'd come here. They'd abandon Simon and all the rest of them."

"The people don't always know what is best for them and for the children who come after them."

"That's what your brother would say," Seacord snapped. "What do you feel, Judith? You said you had come here to see if the door could be opened from this side. What will your brother think about you if you're successful?"

"I don't know." Her face was bitter. "It doesn't matter. I don't know anything about how the devices are constructed. I can do nothing to open the door. But . . . I had to try. I had to see for myself that there was nothing that *could* be done."

"You had to see if they were telling the truth when they said the Portal couldn't be opened."

He could not hear her answer, but he saw her nod.

"I think I've found it," she said. "First I found rooms like this." She shuddered. "I came back to find you before I went inside the Portal chamber."

"All right," Seacord said. "Let's go see what the truth is."

She led him along darkened corridors, through rust-frozen doors that squealed in reproach. Their lights threw mounds of debris scattered on the floors into high relief. Animals scurried away from the brightness.

A narrow hall gave abruptly onto a corridor ten meters high and wide. It was less than fifty meters long. At the other end stood a gray wall, featureless except for a narrow steel door.

"It doesn't make any sense," Seacord said.

When they came closer to the wall, he saw the tongues of ash radiating from the edge of the door. The locking mechanism had been melted a long time ago. Corrosion overlay the congealed slag so the device was nearly unrecognizable. Seacord put his weight against the door and it swung open on howling, neglected hinges.

He felt the wind on his face then, a gentle breeze blowing from the center of the darkened room. He played his light around the interior.

Thirty meters square and thirty meters high, the hall was barely large enough to contain the black hemisphere. Arching bands of Outstepper metal bound the Portal to the dusty cement floor of the receiving chamber.

He flashed his light on the Portal. The lusterless black surface swallowed the beam, giving nothing back.

The Outstepper metal was untarnished.

Hieroglyphs of ash flowed across the walls.

The air carried a taint of ozone.

The ground trembled with a pervasive, subliminal hum. Dark lamps mounted on poles were evenly spaced across the floor. A cluster of metal cabinets snaked through the dust and passed through the sides of the Portal. Glass shards glittered in his light. A glass-walled booth stood against one cement wall, its frame bent, a chair protruding from one smashed pane. Most of the other three-meter-high panes were fractured to opacity; cobwebs clouded the rest. The door, at one end, had been torn half off its hinges.

Weiss stumbled past him, coming to within a meter of the black hemisphere. She reached, fingers outstretched—

"Judith, don't!"

The darkness swallowed her hand, her arm to the shoulder, and, as she took a step forward, one foot.

Eyes squeezed shut, grimacing, she brought her arm out of the Portal.

It was untouched.

"Are you all right?"

She wiggled her fingers, flexed her arm. "It tingles, as if I'd slept on it all night. When it was inside, I couldn't feel anything, nothing at all. I thought it would be like the one under Masada . . . but it's not. It leads home."

"Are you going to go through?" he asked quitely.

"I . . . don't know. I don't know why it's here, unless they somehow repaired it from Relayer, after I left. They could have—"

"You don't believe that."

"No," she said. "Simon lied. And our father. *We* closed the Portal." She took a deep breath and turned away from the Portal, looking around. Light refracted from the shattered glass rimming a windowframe. "That's the control booth."

"It looks as if Simon's been at it," Seacord said.

She looked at him.

"Judith, if the Portal is open, he is—or was—here."

Crystals scattered underfoot. Seacord stepped across the ruined door. A control board ran along the front of the booth, monitors lined the wall behind. Gauges stared blindly from broken faces. Bent panels cast odd shadows. Torn wiring erupted like spring flowers from a metal bed.

The other chair lay overturned under the control board.

Beneath it was a man.

Weiss gasped.

But no . . . it was not a man.

Seacord dragged the chair away from it.

One ropy arm flopped bonelessly.

Its dust-filmed red eyes stared upward. The life had gone from them a long time ago, and with it the characteristic glow.

It's not a cockatrice, he told himself.

But the family resemblance was unmistakable.

His light sparkled on a glossy hide cloaked with a century of dust. The eyes were set beneath a heavy ridge of bone in a broad, wide-mouthed head. The sinuous, meter-long neck was bent into a question-mark shape, flowing smoothly into the trunk. The alien wore a tunic-like covering made of thousands of faceted plates linked together with bone-white rings. A compartmented belt of the same material was draped above the long, smooth-muscled arms sprouting from the midsection. Rotted plastic swathed the legs, which had too many joints in the wrong places. One arm, ending in a stubby-fingered mitt, rested easily on the mailed chest. The other was flung out at an awkward angle.

Seacord knelt. The flesh, though dessicated, was still resilient. Terrestrial bacteria had no taste for its foreign flavor.

The alien had been waiting for a long time for the door to open.

"He must have been marooned here when Relayer closed the Portal," Seacord said, standing. Maybe, toward the end, after the humans waiting with it had all died, the alien had stalked through the empty corridors, lashing out, burning, overturning. Or maybe the scars on the walls were a message no one would ever read.

Seacord's stomach did a slow roll.

"It built the Portal," he said, hearing his own voice as if across a great distance. "The thing must have already been here, on Earth, when the time came. It couldn't have been sent from Relayer or anywhere else. You need a receiver. It couldn't have been here. So . . . there must have been one on Relayer, too."

She said, "I didn't know."

"If there's one, there could be others. Or were. There must—"

Then she said, "Someone's coming."

She extinguished her light, then grabbed Seacord's from his hand and killed it, too.

A beam flickered across the receiving chamber entrance.

Seacord moved then, throwing himself to the floor of the booth. Dust billowed around his face and hands. He lay there, between Weiss and the alien, breathing hard.

"It must have been here for—"

"*Quiet*," she hissed.

Footsteps. Then a harsh voice, Spencer Swan's voice: "Stand over there, all of you."

And an answer, bitter, challenging, in a foreign tongue.

"Simon," Weiss breathed.

# Chapter Twenty-two

The portable lamps blazed, throwing the fissured ceiling into high relief, striking highlights from the arches of alien metal, blazing from the shattered glass walls of the control booth, squeezing the breath from Seacord's lungs.

He raised himself to his hands and knees. Weiss grabbed for his hand, shaking her head wildly. He shook her off and crawled to the booth's ruined door.

Swan stood near the entrance, clothes dusty, hair tangled, and a heavy sack slung over one shoulder. One hand steadied the pack strap. The other held the wiregun pointed at Simon Weiss's head. Weiss's mouth was compressed to a hard line; his eyes were narrowed in anger.

One of the Masadans stood away from the metal-sided cabinet. The others stood near the Portal, hands locked behind their necks.

Swan gestured at them with the wiregun. "Go through," he said. They did not move. "Go *through!*"

Simon Weiss muttered something Seacord could not hear. Then he spoke more loudly, in Hebrew. One of his men started to protest, but Weiss cut him off with a harsh syllable.

The man was the first through the Portal. The black limb of the hemisphere accepted him without fanfare, without a ripple, taking him more easily than a pool of dark water.

And then he was gone.

The others followed him, each looking over his shoulder as he left.

"If they come back, you're a dead man," Swan said.

"So I told them," Simon Weiss said.

"I could kill you now. They'd never know. You damned fool, why didn't you leave things as they were?"

"It was not I who invited the starship to my world. You should rejoice. Now you have a beachhead on Masada. It is more than the Romans had," Weiss said.

"Save the history lesson," Swan snapped. "We opened the

Portal to you and you betrayed us for our trouble. Your sister doesn't know, does she? Do any of your people?''

"A very few," said Weiss. "We did what we could to survive. So did you. You abandoned your faith and went to live among the unrighteous.''

"If we hadn't, we would have died out here," Swan said. "We keep our faith as well as we can—like the Marranos in old Spain. We are the new secret Jews, of no danger to the Triumvirate, and in no danger from them until you arrived.''

"What are you going to do?''

Swan gestured with his pistol. "Stand over there," he said. Weiss moved a few meters away. Swan dropped the sack on the concrete floor and kicked it open. A clutch of gray plastic eggs gleamed dully from the folds of the sack.

"What are you going to do?" Simon Weiss repeated.

"I'm doing you a favor," said Swan.

Seacord backed away from the door. He brought his head close to Judith Weiss's. "He's going to destroy the Portal," he whispered. "He's got explosives.''

Her eyes widened. "What are you going to do?''

"I don't know yet." She started to sit up; he pushed her gently back to the floor.

Seacord crawled to the alien's side. He brushed away a fly crawling inside its wide, carnivorous mouth. Those stubby fingers had stabbed the buttons to send death through the Portal. Those amber eyes had watched disease spreading on the angry winds. The brain in that sleek skull had orchestrated the weather change, banished winter, brought down the Palisades, put Manhattan under twelve meters of water, turned the skies to an impenetrable pearly shield.

Presumably, he admitted. He could not convict the monster.

He had been to Omaha, once, not long after entering the HiSide. The crater had been visible twenty kilometers away. The war had begun and ended there, the enemy never known. The Portal had led to a hundred worlds, each a step away.

Why should this door be any different? he thought.

It led to Relayer . . . now. Had the monstrous technician waited all his life for the door to open on the colonial world? Or had he waited, instead, for his companion on Relayer to join him here?

There were other possibilities, but none of them quenched the acid in his stomach or closed the floodgates dumping adrenaline into his veins.

The alien's belt rattled faintly as Seacord ran his hands along it. At first he could not find the mechanism to open the pouches, each about the size of his palm. Then he squeezed one and the bottom popped with a soft, moist sound.

A handful of metal pellets spilled out, rolling down the dark flanks and falling into the dust carpeting the floor of the booth.

The next yielded a strong breath of corruption. A grayish slime coated the inside of the compartment.

Another pouch, and a fourth. He felt Judith's eyes on him, heard Swan working outside, Simon Weiss's voice raised in hot anger.

The fifth compartment yielded a flat metal object, rounded at one end, flat-nosed, patterned with a series of fine perforations. Ash sifted from the perforations.

The device slipped from his fingers, dropping onto the alien's chest mail with a sound like a hundred coins dropped through a metal grate.

The sound jerked him back in the instant's span between realizing the sounds from outside had abruptly stopped (as the alien's device slid down its torso to the floor) and the time when Weiss grabbed for his arm and yanked him flat to the floor.

Glass exploded. Shrapnel sang counterpoint to the musical hum of metal slivers cleaving the air over their heads. A chunk of the control panel jumped, twisted in the steel wind, and fell in front of his face, a wiregun staple thrust through it like a straw propelled into a tree trunk by hurricane winds.

The steel storm abated. Chunks of freshly-shattered glass slipped from the frame, spilled onto the panel and showered Seacord with fragments. Sparks popped and the scent of the hot metal was very strong. His heartbeat was loudest of all.

In the sudden quiet, Seacord heard an empty spool snapped from the pistol, then fresh ammunition clamped into the feed.

Swan demanded, "Who's there?"

Judith, her hair sequined with bits of glass and shredded metal, stared at Seacord unblinkingly. A thin line of blood trickled from beneath her hairline, down her cheek, across the bridge of her nose.

For a moment he thought she was dead.

Then she closed her eyes and moved her lips soundlessly.

Then she grimaced and sat up.

And then she laughed.

Seacord lay perfectly still on the floor of the booth, wincing, expecting a fresh wedge of hot steel to push the life from Judith's body.

"Come out of there!" Swan shouted.

Judith got slowly to her feet, hands raised over her head. "You're supposed to ask me to surrender *before* your shoot." Hysteria ran like a swift undercurrent beneath the dryness of her tone.

"Come on out," Swan growled.

Judith stepped slowly across the broken glass littering the floor, through the smashed door. She tried to lower her hands but Swan jerked the gun warningly.

"Keep them up," he said. "Where's Seacord?"

Judith shrugged. "I haven't seen him since we left the helicopter.

"What are you doing here?" Swan demanded.

She laughed again, the hysteria rising briefly to the surface. "I found the Portal, didn't I? As planned? Then I heard people coming, so I hid."

"You didn't expect the colonists to be here, Judith? You didn't know they've been here for weeks? I think you did," Swan said. He waved the pistol. "It's too bad I had this, isn't it?"

"Yes," Simon said heavily, "it is. Otherwise I would—"

"You'll do nothing . . . except watch, while I seal off this damned hellhole forever." He shoved Judith and Simon toward one corner of the hall. "You're worth as much to me dead as alive, so don't do anything to stop me."

"I'll help, you fool," Simon Weiss said.

"Simon!" Judith blurted.

"Both of you shut up," Swan demanded.

"We were going to destroy the Portal outselves," Simon insisted. "We can't keep the starships from coming to Relayer, but we can make sure the unrighteous don't simply march into Masada."

"You had a hundred years to do that," Swan said. "Why the change of heart?"

Simon's face twisted. "It was a mistake to try to keep it open. But we would come, every five or ten years, to see if things had changed, to see if the Triumvirate had fallen and if we could walk into Jerusalem again."

Swan pushed him away. "You'll have your wish, then. You're not going back to Relayer."

"Why?" Judith cried.

"Because the moment I let you through the Portal, your friends on the other side can do what they want—come back with guns, in force, or just throw a grenade through. Do you think I'm stupid, Judith?"

"You must be. The Portal will allow my people to prosper again, and you—"

"What can you offer us?" Swan demanded. "Discovery. Persecution. The Triumvirate will see a century-long conspiracy to keep secret a Portal barely five hundred kilometers from the largest citadel, and they'll link *us* to it. Some of us advocated sending a plague through to you before we closed down the gate. We'll settle for keeping the pressure on the government to shut down the interstellar missions. We're not murderers."

Seacord's hand closed on the alien's device. He stood, silent. Swan's back was to him, and if he could . . .

If he hears me he'll turn and shoot me . . . by reflex, Seacord thought.

He moved slowly to the door of the booth.

"Let him do it, Judith," Simon Weiss said tiredly.

"He's going to kill us—"

"If I wanted to, I would have done it already," Swan said. "Now shut up, we've wasted too much time already. Your friends may get their courage back."

"I don't want to stay here!" Judith shouted. "It's not my home!"

"Jerusalem is our home," Simon said.

"That was a long time ago," Judith shot back. "You just don't see it."

"I see everything clearly," Simon insisted.

Swan said, "You're both crazy." He waved the pistol again. "Go on. Get out of the complex. You won't want to be around when the Portal blows."

"We'll die out here," Judith told him.

"You've got a chance. I'm sorry, but there's no other way. I can't let you get back into a citadel. You'd ruin everything for a lot of people who aren't guilty of anything but sharing some common ancestors with you. If you stay here you can probably hang on. But you could never make it all the way across the island and through the New Ark."

He started to move them toward the exit. It would take two or three minutes to arm the explosives, and then it would be too late to do anything.

Seacord put his foot against the door of the booth and pushed. The surviving hinge tore and the door fell in a cloud of dust. Swan whirled.

Seacord put his two hands in the air. Then he slowly brought down the one holding the alien's device. "Put the wiregun down," he told Swan. "They're going to go home."

Swan's brow furrowed, then his mouth twisted into a half
smile and Seacord's blood turned cold. He fought the shiver.

"What the hell is that you've got?" Swan said, unconcerned.

"The weapon that burned away the doors up above and
blistered the walls down here. It's built by the same hands that
built the Portal. Do you want to go up against it?"

His heart hammered. He did not dare let his eyes leave
Swan's, but he knew if he looked down he would see his hand
wavering like a branch in a stiff wind.

Swan's tongue darted, licking his lips. Then he decided.

"Sure," he said.

Seacord gritted his teeth, expecting recoil, a pulse of energy,
something—and squeezed the metal pack.

Nothing happened.

He dove to the right and heard the first burst from Swan's
wiregun blast apart the floor behind him. Seacord landed on his
right shoulder and hip, gasped as the breath was forced out of
him, then rolled over and onto his feet.

Swan swung the pistol a few degrees right. The gun was made
so you didn't have to be particularly accurate. There was no
cover, no way to go, and Seacord saw him hesitate, maybe
wondering if it was necessary to blow him into bloody rags.

Seacord saw the decision in Swan's eyes in the crystal moment before Swan's finger tightened on the trigger.

Then Judith sprang at him, throwing her shoulder into the
back of his legs. Swan's gun hand went straight up and the
stream of steel slivers stitched a line across the wall above and
behind Seacord's head. The lamp on his right novaed and went
black; hot glass peppered his cheek.

Judith was on her knees and Swan was starting to sit up,
looking dazed.

Simon Weiss took that moment to cross the six meters between them. Weiss lengthened the last step into a kick that
looped from his hip and caught Swan in the temple, jacking him
into the floor chin-first. Weiss followed through on the kick,
bringing his foot down on Swan's gun hand. Over the sizzle of
the demolished lamp, Seacord heard the bones crack. Swan only
moaned.

With a little flourish, Weiss bent over and scooped up the
wiregun.

"Get up, you pig," he shouted, his voice wavering an octave.
He looked at Seacord. "You, too."

Judith got slowly to her feet. "Simon, Kearin is—"

"You're in the same class as them, bringing them here. You can stand with them, if you like."

Swan rolled over onto his back and Weiss swung the pistol back to him.

"Apostate," he grated. "Get up."

Swan pushed himself into a sitting position with his good hand, the other twitching in his lap. His face had gone a bloodless white except for the angry red patches on chin and forehead where the floor had abraded his skin.

"Up," Weiss repeated.

Seacord took a step forward. "Simon Weiss." The wiregun did not waver from the area of Swan's chest; Seacord, a dozen meters away, was no threat.

"Who are you?" Simon Weiss demanded.

Seacord's mouth worked. There were too many answers, too many words demanding voice.

Swan moved then, yelling as he launched himself to his feet, pain and fear pulling at the shout.

He had three meters to cross.

His right leg gave out from under him at the first step.

His clawed, bloodied hands reached for Simon Weiss.

Weiss brought the wiregun up level and pulled the trigger. The magnetic field snapped and burned; the wirecutter whined into the supersonic; the flathead slivers clove air.

Points of blood blossomed on Swan's chest as his back exploded in a wet spray of blood and bone.

The ammo reel expended itself almost one second and seven hundred projectiles later.

The impact blew Swan off his knees. He skidded on his own guts and slid to a stop at Seacord's feet.

Swan's face reflected mild surprise.

A thick tang surged up Seacord's throat. He fought it down.

Weiss let the wiregun drop.

Seacord said, "It ends here."

He pointed his right hand at a spot over Simon Weiss's left shoulder and squeezed his hand into a fist, the concave surfaces of the alien's device cool to his sweating palms.

Heat washed Seacord's face as the motes of dust suspended in the air before his hand flashed to incandescence. Weiss yelled and staggered to his right, batting at his smoldering hair and the sleeve and shoulder of his tunic. The wall behind him blackened, blistered, ran like Swan's blood to pool on the seared floor.

Seacord opened his hand.

"Who are you?" Simon Weiss shouted.

"Brian Kuhl," Seacord said. "And a lot of people you don't know. You're the one who told Neil Wolfram about the Terminal Night, aren't you? Did you have him killed afterward, or did he really kill himself . . . after he found out how you had used him?"

Simon Weiss, beneath his fear, looked disdainful. "We do not murder our own kind, as you do, *dar*. Do you remember the power outage? If you are who you say you are, you will remember."

Seacord remembered the blood and smoke. "I remember," he said tightly.

"We took the power from the rest of the colony to start the Portal for a moment. He stepped through, and came here. He was here for months, listening to your broadcasts, taping them for me, for when I came here, so we would know what your people had planned for Masada. Now we know. Your people are growing angry with us."

"That will have to change," said Seacord. "We need Relayer and all the other colonies as a line of defense. The monsters who started the Portal War are coming back, Simon. You could have seen it yourself, if you had looked on that new star in your skies as something more than a monument to you. When the Peacemakers and the security agents find this place and the Portal, they'll be all over Relayer. We'll have our outpost, and your people will have what they want—contact with Earth again."

"You will overrun us as I've always known you would," Weiss said.

Seacord's stomach tightened.

Judith took a step toward him. "Kearin . . . it *will* be an occupation. It will not be the meeting that . . . that I thought you wanted."

"They'll find this place, Judith," Seacord said. "That can't be helped."

"It's what they will find in this place that will hurt Masada. *Kearin*."

The moment stretched taut.

The hot miasma of blood scent stung his nostrils. Then a vagrant breeze took the stink away.

Seacord lowered his arm and slipped the heat projector into his pocket.

"Get out, Simon," he said dully. "Go back to Relayer."

Judith looked over her shoulder. "Do as he says, Simon."

Simon shook his head, opened his mouth, then took an awkward backward step.

He turned. And then he was gone.

"Kearin . . ."

He knelt and put his fingers to Swan's cooling face and closed the open, reproachful eyes. He stepped back from the corpse.

"You go, too," Seacord said. "Or you'll be trapped here." He looked away from her hurt surprise into the smooth black depths of the Portal.

"Or don't go," he added. "If you stay, I guarantee they'll never let you go. No matter what we do here, there will be too many unanswered questions remaining. The Triumvirate will spend the rest of your life trying to tap the answers from you."

"You're going to destroy it."

"Spencer was right. Simon was right. Your people are the past and this is now. If you slam them together they explode. But maybe if the contact is kept at a trickle, the damage can be minimized." He smiled without feeling. "Might even generate some heat and light."

"You belong with us," she said. "Your life here is ruined."

"It's my life. I've lived with it a long time, not knowing what it was, but I made it part of myself, not part of your people. It's entirely mine."

She seemed about to say something more. Then her face, which had been scarred by the death in the room, became a smooth, innocent mask. She gently took his arm, leaned over, and brushed his cheek with her lips.

Then, without looking back, she walked home.

# *Twenty-three*

Behind her, the Portal connection to Relayer closed, bursting like a soap bubble, plunging Seacord into darkness.

The inrush of air knocked him off his feet; the thunderclap deafened him. He put his fingers to his left ear and they came away moist. He got slowly to his feet, all his muscles aching.

The lights were dead, cut off from their electrical source on Relayer. He found his lamp in a pocket and kindled it.

The pale, uneven light washed the color from Swan's blood.

He touched the heat beam to it, and it flickered to a fine ash. The corpse took a moment longer. The breeze from the chamber entrance sifted the char.

When that was done he went to the black pool the Portal had left behind. It was fathomless, a lake without depth, an entrance without an exit.

The creature's body, when he gathered it into his arms, was surprisingly light. He did not topple it directly into the black pool, but lay it on the surrounding ring of pale blue metal. He could not close the lidless eyes.

Its brothers were waiting beyond the night sky. Seacord thought they had placed a new light in Relayer's sky to put the humans on notice.

We are coming back to finish the war, they were saying. Are you ready?

Maybe Zierling and her people couldn't do anything about it, once they got as far as Earth.

He looked down at the glossy black body.

He prodded it with the toe of his boot, rolling it into the *sitra achra*.

He had worried he would not be able to operate the detonators of Swan's explosives, but the instructions were neatly lettered on the gray eggshells.

When he was done, he walked up the long corridor to the outside. The salt air kissed him where she had kissed him, and he brought his hand to his cheek and smiled a little.

281

The ground heaved once, but he stayed on his feet. Hot air gusted from the arch at his back. A few hundred meters away, a gout of flame erupted and immediately dissolved in the sharp, clear air. A hazy heat rolled over him and he started walking north, toward the gently sighing surf.

Before he reached it, the Peacemaker skids settled from the sky, a flight of vengeful fireflies.

# Chapter Twenty-four

"Sacrifices must be made," Brace said, his voice dry as bone.

He licked water from the feeding tube poised over his face. The lines near it, gusting oxygen at his nostrils, looked like the claw of a bird ready to strike. A sheet supported by a wire frame concealed the ravaged body. Tubes filled with red and amber fluids led to a pumping console on the other side of the small, white room.

"It was necessary," Brace repeated. The effort of speaking had lent his entire head a dangerous crimson hue. Blue veins stood out in high relief. He paused, his mouth working at the drip-tube.

"I suspect they must, sometimes," Seacord said after a while.

Brace's head nodded at the end of his thin, corded neck. "Remember when you were the drug dealer, gathering data from Maya Zierling?"

"You gave me a compartment in the roof of my mouth."

"Yes. Yes. We took out your communications control then. You never knew. It was better that way. A double blind. The Datalink was always with you. Still is, isn't it?"

Seacord's face hardened. "I have to go now," he said, standing. He reached into his pocket, took out the bits of metal and ceramic, tiny relays and processors still warm from their bed in his flesh. He held them out to Brace.

The filmy eyes stared unblinkingly. "Sometimes," Brace said, "I regret the actions I have to take. Sometimes, Kearin, I wish I could stay here and not return to Logan at all." He closed his eyes. "But you said you have to go. Forgive me if I don't show you the way out."

Seacord said, "I know the way out."

His escort waited for him in the corridor outside. One of the men walked a half-dozen meters ahead, the other an equal distance behind; Seacord had never spoken to either of them. The third, a man who called himself Monroe, fell into step alongside Seacord as if they were old friends.

"He's not doing very well?" Monroe asked.

"No," Seacord replied, impatient. Monroe did not know who Brace was, or Seacord, either—only where he was to be taken.

"The ones on this floor, they're not expected to be around much longer, I guess," Monroe said.

"I know."

Seacord stopped at the lift tube, but Monroe cupped his elbow and urged him along. "There's been a change in the schedule," he said. "Someone to see you."

They stopped at an open door a few dozen meters along the wide, aseptic corridor. Monroe and the others waited outside.

"Hello, Citizen Seacord," said Sara, rising.

What was she doing *here*?

But no . . .

He saw again the lines in her face, the angularity of form softened by rich, well-tailored fabric, and the bearing that was not Sara's after all.

"Your surgery went well?" Candace Carpentier asked, sitting again. She motioned for Seacord to sit alongside her on the couch.

"There were no complications," he said, trying to match her pleasantly neutral tone.

"And Citizen Brace?"

"He's dying."

"They tell me it was a cardiovascular accident."

"That's what they tell me, too," Seacord said.

Her eyes, the color of storm clouds, studied him. "I think I may be disappointed. You're not surprised."

"To see you?"

"To find yourself here, rather than in some LoSide."

He shrugged. "It may have been prudent to remove the implants anyway . . . but after I was given permission to see Brace while I was here, I thought things might break differently than I'd first expected."

She crossed her arms over her chest and sat back a little, her gaze wandering around the small, simply-furnished lounge.

"There was a lively debate about what to do with you," Carpentier said after a moment. "Most of it was inside me." She looked at him, her gray eyes unreadable. "I don't know if you thought you were acting in your own interests or the Triumvirate's. I don't think you know either. The mess we found at Montauk doesn't give me much of a clue: an installation one hundred years abandoned, the upper level a blasted ruin and the lower levels smashed flat, Spencer and Judith Weiss missing and presumed dead.

Seacord put on a sorrowful look. "I'm afraid she must be dead."

"Sad . . . but convenient. I don't know what you're thinking, Seacord—and there's no one or nothing left intact to tell me."

"I shouldn't be intact either. I'm sure I would've died, too, if my implants hadn't led the Peacemakers to me." Seacord shrugged. "What is it you want with me, Citizen? Was my report incomplete?"

"There's no way to know, is there? But I can't argue with results . . . and you did uncover the Levra," she said. "That group doesn't bother me much. I may have been wrong when I didn't give Brace the support he wanted, but in the end, after sifting through the evidence, it doesn't look as if the Levra has been very active since the founding of the Triumvirate. My theory is that Spencer panicked. You and Brace were getting too close to the Levra . . . so he started back for Montauk to destroy the evidence that it existed. There must have been histories, notes, birth records, diaries. Security Affairs could have worked from those records and tracked down most of the present membership."

"And now?"

"Now we'll look for them . . . but I don't expect we'll find very many of them very soon. And I'm not sure what we'll do once we find them. Spencer . . . served us well for many years. As far as we can determine, he did the Triumvirate no harm during those years. His one crime was involving Judith Weiss in this. I don't know if he intended her to die or not. He may have seen her as a threat, too, because the Relayermen must have their own records of the Levra."

Carpentier stood, letting her breath out in what was not quite a sigh. "But it's all conjecture because Spencer Swan is dead. Put on another identity matrix for a moment, Seacord. Pretend you're Spencer Swan and tell me what you meant to do when you turned against me."

"You must have known him better than I ever could," said Seacord.

"I didn't know him at all," Carpentier said. "The Synody has decided to accept your report . . . and the conjectures I've just laid before you."

"Then what happens to me now?"

She seemed not to have heard him as, after a moment, she continued, "I've reviewed another report recently—the one the StarForce prepared for their own high command on the mission to Relayer. The evidence the Force has gathered clearly points to one or more alien races strongly active in the solar neighborhood. We don't know if this is the same alien intelligence responsible for the Portal War. We have to assume it is."

"What does this have to do with me?" he asked—suddenly knowing.

"That evidence remains . . . circumstantial," she continued, her look distant. "The first concrete evidence may be an alien warship appearing in our skies—or, maybe worse, over a defenseless colony. The aliens were probably dependent on the Portals for faster-than-light travel, but they could have developed and launched a fleet of their own, as we have. Or they could be poised to do so. Until the threat is clarified, I've moved for a state of emergency to be declared. The Synody has agreed to it."

He stood. "Am I a part of this?"

"Unless you'd rather go to the LoSide—or starve in the Hub. During the emergency, Security Affairs' role will be expanded. We've been diverting too much of that department's energy to self-criticism." She smiled. "I've been spending too much time with bureaucrats. The word is 'infighting,' not 'self-criticism.' Security, StarForce, and Administration will have to work more closely together from now on."

"Work more closely . . . under Administration."

"Accelerating the process that has already begun," Carpentier finished. "SA has not been a challenge to our authority since the Terminal Night, but the StarForce has grown too autonomous. That process will be reversed . . . hopefully in time to meet the threat from the Deep."

"And does that threat really exist?" Seacord asked neutrally. "Or is it just a motive to . . . accelerate the process?"

All at once, as her look turned cold, he realized how warm it had been. "The threat is there. I've been to Aztlan and seen what's left of the *Munich* and the people who served aboard her. Never doubt the aliens destroyed her. Never doubt . . . or you'll be useless to me."

He nodded. "What do you want me to do? Take Brace's place in Logan?"

"I need someone loyal to me in Logan . . . but I also need someone loyal by my side."

"Like Spencer Swan."

"Not like Spencer Swan. Like . . . whoever the hell it is you are. I control the Datalink, but the Datalink is a quantitative device. It deals in numbers and power. I need help with the qualitative, less easily defined problem of reversing one hundred years of history and convincing people—both in the Citadels and in the LoSide—that the enemy lies outside of us. And I think, Kearin, that you are very good at convincing people of what you'd have them believe.''

She gazed steadily at him, with eyes that so resembled Sara's. ''We've found no trace of Weiss or Spencer,'' she said. ''No bodies. They *could* be buried under a million tons of rock and cement. Or not. Tell me, Kearin, what would I find if I ordered the Levra's fortress excavated?''

Seacord said, after a moment: ''Nothing that would help you.''

She did not smile. But the smile was there, hiding beneath her stern look. ''I think in that, at least, you are telling the truth.''

She extended her hand.

''We create our own truths,'' Seacord said.

He took her hand.

## About the Author

Mark J. McGarry was born in Albany, New York, in 1958, and sold his first story eighteen years later. He has appeared in the major science fiction magazines; his first novel, SUN DOGS, was published by Signet in 1981. A newspaper reporter, he lives in Connecticut.